WINTER'S DESIRE

WINTER'S DESIRE

EROTIC TALES·OF CARNAL DESIRE

·AMANDA McINTYRE·
·CHARLOTTE FEATHERSTONE·
·KRISTI ASTOR·

Spice

Recycling programs
for this product may
not exist in your area.

Spice

WINTER'S DESIRE

ISBN-13: 978-0-373-60535-4

Copyright © 2009 by Spice Books.

The publisher acknowledges the copyright holders
of the individual works as follows:

WINTER AWAKENING
Copyright © 2009 by Pamela Johnson.

MIDNIGHT WHISPERS
Copyright © 2009 by Charlotte Featherstone.

LOVER'S DAWN
Copyright © 2009 by Kristina Cook Hort.

www.Spice-Books.com

Printed in U.S.A.

Also by
AMANDA McINTYRE

THE DIARY OF COZETTE
TORTURED

Also by
CHARLOTTE FEATHERSTONE

ADDICTED

Watch for the next book of Celtic stories
BELTANE FIRES
Available April 2011

Delve into the season's
most pleasurable erotic tales of carnal desire
… and awaken winter's yearning …

WINTER AWAKENING
by Amanda McIntyre

MIDNIGHT WHISPERS
by Charlotte Featherstone

LOVER'S DAWN
by Kristi Astor

PROLOGUE

Ireland, 1014

I CAN REMEMBER STILL YOUR STRENGTH AND your gentleness. A strange combination to be sure, but a potent and intoxicating one that held me captive from our very first meeting.

You were wounded, though not desperately so. As fate would have it, I happened by the place where you'd found shelter from the road. I took you by the hand to my sacred cairn, where for days I came to you, bringing food and drink. We found our way past our barrier of words, and soon your wounds, beneath my gentle hands, were healed.

We should have been enemies, you and I. Our people battled around us, but in our sequestered cocoon, we spoke not of battles. In truth, we spoke very little in those days and nights. The only evidence of battle were the scars on your flesh, tended by my hand.

Passion knows no need for words, for in your eyes shone a common language that I, too, understood. Ours was the most sacred of tongues. Transcending time and division, we worshipped one another's bodies on this most sacred ground—

this altar to the ancient ones, where magic rules the senses and gives grace to believers. My body welcomed yours, my name a whisper upon your lips. In our hidden nest, far from the prying eyes of those who would not understand or accept our passion, we made our lovers' vow and sealed it with the communion of our bodies, satisfying a hunger of both body and soul. You left me weary, yet complete. This is how it should be between lovers—surely the gods and goddesses celebrated our union.

But as the sky turned red with the dawn of the solstice, I watched you dress, girding your exquisite manhood with the skirts of my people's enemy; your long, fair hair, once my covering, now cinched firmly with a leather strap. I reached for you, my limbs sore from our joining, my breasts aching, my lips bruised from your mouth.

But it was in the subtle shake of your head that my heart was broken. The pain of it stole away my breath as I gathered the courage to ask, "Why?" In reply, you spoke the words that stopped the sun.

"It cannot be." You slid your helmet over your head, and I saw only your eyes—pale blue eyes that will haunt me for the rest of my days.

You were correct, of course. For how can a Norse raider be the lover of a Druid priestess? How can we share what our bodies yearn for, when it is considered a sin amongst both our people? Ours was a passion indulged only in darkness, and it ended with the first shaft of daylight on the dawn of midwinter.

Morning has come. The solstice has arrived once more—how many since we parted, I cannot say. Back in our sacred cairn, I wrap my cloak around my shivering form. The crimson dawn renews the earth, sending down its warmth. For a moment, the darkness above is parted, and a light illuminates the pathway to the world outside—a world where the fire between us cannot exist.

Following that path, I step outside, raising my arms to the sun as the wind caresses the ancient stones of my people. A light frozen rain descends as I turn my face to the sky. My lashes wet from the frigid mist, I speak aloud the magic that cannot die:

"Hope reborn, come with the sun
dispel the chill of darkness
bright fire of dawn
reach to our hearts
burn bright of winter's desire.

"Enchanted stream of brilliant light
amid the crystal ground
dark traverse blending of the night
bring sweet lover's kiss
burn bright of winter's desire.

"No wanderer's curse
be he thus beckoned
a slave to passion's fire
return his head, upon my breast
burn bright of winter's desire."

Believe in—
the magic!
Amanda

WINTER AWAKENING
by
Amanda McIntyre

1

Wales, 1119

I DRANK DEEPLY OF THE WINE MY COUSIN HAD provided for the afternoon. She told me it would calm my nerves. "Princess Sabeline," I murmured daydreaming about the title I would regain after I wed. I was no longer a princess under English rule, yet I still was to the people of my father's province.

Due to the unrest within the Welsh provinces, an agreement had been made between the king of England and my father. He promised that my marriage would secure a better alliance between Wales and England. Though my father relinquished his title of prince to the English king, he retained all of his authority of his province, and was given, instead, the title of baron in exchange for the king's protection.

I took another long swallow as a man with shoulders nearly as wide as the door entered the room and offered my cousin a ravenous kiss.

My impending marriage on the winter solstice, a beloved celebration of our people, to a Marcher lord had precipitated my cousin, Margaret, to come for a visit. While here, she arranged an afternoon of "instruction" for me to learn of the intimacies between a man and woman. Two years and one week older, she had always served as my older sister. Over the years she had taught me many things, so I had accepted this suggestion.

Nonetheless, virgin that I was, I had misgivings. Margaret winked at me and handed the man, one of my father's castle guards, two long strips of sheeting. In fascination, I watched as he tied the end of each piece to the bedposts and draped them over her naked body. She wrapped each end several times around her wrists and lay back, her arms stretched wide.

Margaret's plump breasts proudly thrust upward, their twin nubs puckered already with arousal. Her lover was imposing in both height and strength. He stood at the end of the bed and looked over his shoulder at me with a wicked grin, then leisurely removed each article of clothing until he stood fully naked before us. I knew 'twas meant to tease Margaret, yet the effect was not lost on me.

He crooked his finger at me and arched his brow, summoning me to join them. I swallowed and raised my cup, declining respectfully. I had not consumed near enough drink yet to participate directly in this sensual romp, though the wine had relaxed me enough that I could observe with rapt enthusiasm.

The guard shrugged and turned his attentions to my cousin, who awaited him with a wanton grin.

He was powerfully built, with dark hair cropped close, and a day's growth of beard. His thighs were firm and corded and his buttocks, tight. From behind, he was a remarkable sight, and when he lifted his knee to the bed, what jutted from between those great thighs made my heart falter.

I redirected my gaze to the breadth of his shoulders, his powerful muscles bunching as he moved over my cousin. His hands, twice the size of Margaret's, caressed her thighs, her

breasts. Engaged as far as I could be without actively partici-
pating, I lifted the cup to my lips and missed my mouth
entirely. The pungent liquid drizzled down the front of my
kirtle. Thankfully, my cousin and the guard were preoccupied
and did not notice. I set the goblet aside, my hand trembling.

Margaret's lusty groan brought my attention back to the bed
where she writhed together with her lover.

"Will you not change your mind, Sabeline?" Margaret asked.
A gasp tore from her throat, a result of the man's lavish attention to her exposed flower, and she did not wait for my response.

Margaret yanked on the tethers, rising to meet the man in
a fierce kiss as he shoved her back on the bed and covered his
body with hers. He squeezed her breasts hard, causing
Margaret to wince and then ask for more. His mouth teased,
feasting on her flesh, as if she were a succulent peach.

They spoke so low I could not make out all of what they
said. Still, I was mesmerized as I watched their limbs entwine,
the firelight glistening off their fevered bodies. I tried to
imagine how I would measure up in Lord Benedict's bed.
What soft murmurings would I speak in his ear?

"Tell me you want me, sweet woman, and I shall make
you see the heavens," her lover growled, bringing me back
to the moment.

From beneath his powerful body, I heard Margaret's giggle.
Her knees parted wide and he wasted no time in pushing
roughly into her as her ankles locked around his waist.

He held her hips, driving fiercely into her as Margaret's
hands gripped the ties attached to her wrists. Her body
writhed as he bucked against her slick folds, pushing harder
in his determined fervor.

I was frozen, lost in the utter look of pleasure on my
cousin's face. Her perfect mouth opened in arousal, mating

briefly with his tongue in a passionate kiss. With each lunge, her sighs grew louder, melding with the deep baritone of the guard's sighs. Her sun-kissed hair, a mass of unruly curls, fanned out haphazardly across the pristine white pillows each time her head hit the bed.

"Such a fine cunt, milady," the formidable guard spoke between clenched teeth as he dominated her body.

I was so highly captivated that I could not turn away. I admit, for a fleeting moment, I wanted to leap in the middle between them.

"Are—you—watch—ing?" Margaret's words were choppy as she tried to speak against the force driving at her body. Braced against the tethered strips holding her at an upright angle, she glanced at me before her head lolled back and she emitted a loud cry with her release.

I felt the blood leave my face as I watched the guard shove his ample phallus thrice more into my cousin and then collapse upon her like a sack of potatoes. My mouth was dry despite the wine and in direct contrast to the dampness betwixt my legs. I realized that my knuckles were white from gripping the arms of my chair.

There was no intimacy given after and none required, I suspected, as the man rolled off the bed, unknotted one of my cousin's restraints and began to dress. Margaret released her bound wrist and stretched languidly on the bed, rubbing her forearms as she gazed at the man's backside.

"I shall see you are rewarded handsomely for your *efforts,*" she purred.

He grunted but flashed her a grin as he strode toward the door. "Good day, miladies," he spoke with a slight bow as if he had delivered a message, then shut the door quietly behind him.

Margaret scooted off the bed and drew her robe around

her, cinching it at the waist. She poured herself a cup of wine and sat in the chair across from me.

"Well, what say you, cousin? Were you served well by this instruction?" she asked, raising her cup to me before taking a sip.

I averted my gaze, knowing the heat of my face had nothing to do with either the blazing fire or the drink. I took a healthy swallow of my wine to give me time to recover from the rapid beating of my heart. "It appears most pleasant, cousin. Did you enjoy it?"

She chuckled. "It is a rare thing if I do not," she remarked with a wry grin.

I imagined Benedict's head between my thighs, his hands holding my hips in place as I had seen the guard do with Margaret. "Does it hurt? The intrusion?"

She cast a look to the heavens. I was certain my questions seemed naive, but I wanted to prepare myself for what was to come.

"A little the first time, but it is soon replaced with a much more delicious sensation." She tipped her head back and rested it on the back of the chair. Her smile was that of a content woman. A bit envious, I could not wait to experience such a delightful event. One concern shadowed my thoughts, however.

"Is there any truth, cousin, that a man prefers to wed a woman whose virtue is yet intact?" I asked. "I have heard that men prefer to marry a virgin." I glanced at her. "I mean no offense, of course." I appreciated my cousin's sexual freedom, I just wasn't certain I was comfortable with it personally. Still, I wanted to appease my husband-to-be in the best way possible, as the happiness of our union directly reflected on my father's good standing with the king.

"Now you wish to speak of virtuousness?" She laughed. "My poor innocent cousin. Do you not think that a man of

Lord Benedict's rank and status would prefer a woman who would meet him thrust for thrust with the passion which he surely must be accustomed to?"

She arched her blond brows over her scrutinizing gaze. Where she was of fair hair and light blue eyes, I was of Scotch-Irish lineage, dark eyed and blessed with deep mahogany tresses. Side by side, we made a stunning spectacle.

"I speak only of things I have heard. That a man prefers a woman whom he can deflower himself," I said, wanting to understand why, if a man and woman cared for each other, it should make one gnat of difference.

"No one should be so naive," she responded staring into the fire. "Not even you."

I fell silent. Though I yearned to hear in detail more about her physical pleasure, I knew I would have to wait for the experience myself.

"So, is that all there is to it, then?" I asked. "A few moments of unbridled lust and then it is over?"

She glanced at me with a demure smile before she shrugged. "Pleasure can be found in many ways, silly girl. Depending on the enthusiasm and experience of those involved, the ecstasy can last for hours."

"Hours?" The thought alone caused me to squirm. "Do you think Lord Benedict will like me?" I asked, changing the subject as I tossed a new log on the fire.

"Lord Benedict? Do not fret over such things, cousin. You will learn over time what pleases him most." She smiled. "I cannot teach you everything."

"No, of course not," I responded quietly, hiding my doubts about my ability to please any man, but most especially Lord Benedict.

I carried my concerns close. I knew that there were those

in my father's court who looked down on me. As the Baron Durwain's only living child, I was in line to inherit all of my father's land and his army as well as my mother's holdings in both Ireland and France. Given to my father when they married, his inheritance would have passed to his son. However, with the death of my brother at his birth and my mother's death shortly after, my father upheld the traditions of old and I became the benefactor of all his wealth.

Several proposals followed before the dirt was hard on my mother's grave, but it was by summons to the court of the English king, that I was to meet my future husband. I was not oblivious to the tensions in my country between the Welsh tribes and the English rule. By this alliance with a Norman Marcher lord, England would gain that much more security along its borders.

My first impression of my intended was not a favorable one, but I resolved to the belief that we had both been very young. Over these past three years, I was pleasantly surprised to see his letters had grown poignant, more heartfelt. I could not help but read them over and over and imagine the passionate and virile man who conveyed such affection. Far different than the man I met that summer at court.

"Shall I read again his last letter?" I asked as I stood to retrieve it from the pocket of my gown.

Margaret reached for a plump apricot. They were a wedding gift from the king. He would be sending in his stead his most trusted knight to serve as his witness to the marriage ceremony, as it was far too dangerous for him to leave England at this time. In accordance to Welsh tradition, my father had requested that the ceremony take place at Durwain Castle. Further, in compliance with my mother's dying wish, the ceremony was to take place on the winter solstice, her favorite time of year.

Chilled, I moved to the fur rug near the fire, sliding another warm pelt over my lap. I had taken Benedict's last letter from its secret place inside the wooden box that stored every letter he had sent, every gift of a single flower, now all dried and frail. I tugged at the ribbon I'd tied around the thick, folded parchment.

"Go on," Margaret urged impatiently as she drank her wine.

"*To my future bride,*'" I began, glancing at her with a smile on my lips. "*I count my days in service knowing my victories pale by comparison to winning your hand. It has been months since I last saw your enchanting face. I confess yours is the last face I think on as I lie on the cold ground and stare into the night sky. It is the thought of lying at your side that keeps me warm, as the days grow increasingly colder. I look forward to the time when I may gaze into your beautiful eyes that remind me of the spices of the ancient lands. I remain, your ever-faithful and dutiful servant, Lord Benedict of Hereford.*'"

I brushed my fingertips over the remnant of the wax seal left on the parchment. "What say you, cousin? Are these the words of a true heart?"

She sighed as she drew a fur over her feet and popped another apricot into her mouth.

"He is well educated, that much is evident." Her brow furrowed with her thoughts. "But a true heart, I cannot say."

"Does that not sound like a man enamored of the thought of being wed?" I asked, clutching the note to my breast.

She shrugged. "I am not sure, cousin, that any man is enamored of the ceremony as much as what comes after. Still, it is believed you can tell a great many things from a man's eyes," Margaret stated with a smirk. "I will reserve my judgment on this matter until then. Though I must confess, it is not only in the eyes that I find my interest."

"You are wicked, Margaret. I daresay if your father knew the half of what I know about you, you would be on your way to a nunnery by spring."

Her look of contentment dissipated and she eyed me with quiet determination. "Is that a threat, my dear cousin?"

"Of course not. Would I send away the only woman who can instruct me in the ways of men?"

She shrugged and poured more wine in her cup.

I drew my robes around me and stood, needing a breath of fresh air. As I lifted the window's iron latch, a violent gust of wind snatched the shutter from my hand and slammed it against the wall. A swirling mass of snow blasted through the opening.

"Let us hope you are not found frozen stiff before Lord Benedict's arrival," Margaret shouted from behind as I struggled to close the shutter.

She squeezed past me and grabbed the shutter. As we fought together to close it, Margaret hesitated, her attention focused on the ward below.

"What is it? What do you see?" I asked, squinting against the driving snow. Below in the deep shadows, two figures huddled close together, making their way toward the stables.

"Do you recognize them?"

"Yes," she replied as we watched them sneak across the once-lush grass, turned brown now with winter. "The man at least. The other is likely one of the kitchen maids."

"Is that *your* guard?" I asked with concern.

"Nay," she replied, staring into the shadows of the courtyard.

"How can you tell?" I peered into the darkness.

"Because *my* guard would not be so foolish as to be *seen* sneaking off with a kitchen maid."

We watched in silence as they disappeared into the stables. Margaret slammed the shutter and gave the latch a firm twist. Despite her words, I sensed that something about what she had seen bothered her.

2

THE STEADY, COLD RAIN TURNED THE ROAD TO muck, making it difficult to navigate the horses.

"Sweet God in heaven, my horse cannot take another step. This godforsaken dampness seeps into my bones. I am in dire need of something to warm them. How much farther is the castle, Ranulf?"

I eyed Benedict as he adjusted his sodden wool cloak around his broad shoulders. The ornate brooch, a reminder of his nobility, was now marred with mud splatters.

"I wager a half day's ride more. It will be dark soon," I responded, lifting my gaze to the pewter-gray sky above. The icy mist stung my face numb from the cold.

"It would not do to meet my new bride in such a state. We shall stop for the night and continue in the morrow, after we rest and have a warm bath."

My cloak, pounds heavier than when dry, hung from my shoulders. I could not deny that the idea was tempting. But rogue warriors, displeased with the English occupation, roamed these mountains and I wondered of the wisdom of staying in a village without benefit of the Baron Durwain's protection. Still, I suspected that Benedict was thinking less of his bride and more of his own pleasure.

I first met Lord Benedict three years ago. He was barely with facial hair, at the tender age of twenty, but possessed an eagerness the king found useful. Given my experience and maturity, nearly seventeen years older than the young Marches warrior, the king had ordered me to train him in the ways of battle and knighthood. I had gained my own title as knight not by inheritance as Benedict had, but through my reputation in tournament play, earning the king's trust and a noted spot within his court that few men contested. Of all the men I'd fought in my years, I'd never seen one who was so consumed with his own pleasure and power and gladly flaunted it. Thus far, though he had stretched my patience thin, he had not pushed me beyond the limit of my reason. My duty was not, after all, to play his nursemaid and procure his manners. It was to teach him to fight, and fight well he did. In the past three years, he had made a name for himself in the Marches and his favor with the king had grown even stronger.

"Are you not anxious to see your betrothed, Benedict?" I enjoyed watching him squirm under my scrutiny. Benedict's loyalty to his new bride was sorely lacking. His passion on the battlefield was unmatched, with the exception of mine, but his passion with women was reckless and unbridled. With his wedding day close at hand, I began to wonder if the baron's daughter, Sabeline, would be woman enough to quell his insatiable lust.

"We will send her another letter. After we dine, you will help me compose it. One of my men can deliver it yet today."

I conceded, though felt it unwise. "Very well." I was anxious to arrive at our destination, my body ached from the long ride through the mountain passages. Despite my misgivings of how Baron Durwain might respond to our delay,

I could not dispute the appeal of a bath and a hot meal. I nodded to our young squire. "Boy, go secure suitable dry quarters to keep our horses from the elements." I handed him a bag of coins and he scampered off.

I dropped from my horse and sank to my ankles in mud. It was a miserable day for travel, but that was common for this time of year.

The afternoon sky had grown darker and a heavy mist had begun to shroud the road and nearby wood. Part of a decaying old fort, Roman, if my judging of it was true, looked as though it now served as a haven for travelers and soldiers.

My boots pulled at my calves as I strode toward the warm flicker of light inside. At the entrance, I stamped my feet as I cautiously scanned the large room. A buxom woman with rose-stained cheeks and silver threaded throughout her dark hair greeted us, offering a coy smile.

"I s'pose yer lookin' for a room? We have had many lookin' to get out of the bitter wind today," she spoke over the din of the crowd. Her hungry gaze lingered on Benedict before she turned her attention to me.

"Just for the night, milady. We have two other men. Our squire will stay with our horses." I had lost her again to Benedict's charming smile. I cleared my throat and jangled a bag of coins in front of her face in an attempt to draw her focus back to me.

"I suspect you'll be needin' a meal and perchance a bath as well?" She leaned forward and offered me an intriguing view of her ample breasts. "For a little extra, milord, I might be persuaded to wash yer back." She shoved her hands beneath her breasts and shifted them high in her bodice.

"I am—" I glanced at Benedict, who stifled a grin "—accustomed to bathing alone."

She looked me over, head to toe. "Pity." She shrugged. "Come along, then."

Benedict chuckled as he jabbed my side.

The table wench squealed with delight as Benedict grabbed a substantial portion of her backside and gave it a pinch. His raucous laughter rose above the room now filled to capacity. Fortunately, most of the guests were commoners taking part in lascivious acts in the corners of the room, while others, without concern, engaged in coupling in full view of the cheering crowd.

"The letter, milord?" I reminded Benedict. I was fast becoming bored in watching his attempts to seduce every woman within arm's reach. A hot bath and a few hours of peaceful sleep was my goal. "We should get your man on his way. These roads are not safe at night."

"I am considering what to say," he retorted. "I need a muse," he yelled, searching for the red-haired table wench.

I reminded myself that I had agreed to help once again with this bloody letter. Hell, was it not by my hand that they had all been penned? This young man had not a romantic bone in his Norman body. He would no more know how to woo a woman into his bed than move a mountain. *Take* a woman, yes, and with little more than the time it took to remove her clothes, were he to consider it necessary. It was not, however, his manner with women that I was sent to help him with, though the romantic in me prayed he would change after his marriage.

Sabeline. She was the daughter of Baron Durwain of Wales. A young woman when first I met her at the king's court the summer after her brother's and mother's passing. She was a prize for any man, with grace and beauty, as well as the wealth of her inheritance.

The king had invited the baron and his daughter in good faith to discuss a possible alliance to secure the provinces near the English border. By pairing a Marcher lord with the baron's daughter, a formidable barrier would be created against the warring tribes of the north who continued to be a thorn in the king's side. Fortunately for Lord Benedict, his brazen courage and his skills on the field of battle had won him the king's favor. And so, the arrangement was made. Benedict and Sabeline were to marry three years after we had finished our crusade in securing his military presence along the border region.

Cast to the side, as women generally are in matters concerning the welfare of nations, Sabeline accepted the engagement with a quiet dignity that impressed me.

As my mind drifted away from the din of the pub, I remembered the day that the baron and his daughter arrived....

It was my duty to welcome Baron Durwain and his entourage to the king's court.

"May I present my daughter, Sabeline." The pride the baron felt for his daughter was evident in his eyes as she offered a regal curtsy to both Benedict and me. The noble lord, my charge and her intended, however, had his focus on the maid servant traveling with the baron's party. I cleared my throat and offered a congenial smile to our regal guests.

"I wish to welcome you both to England. If you will follow me, we will take you to freshen up before your audience with the king."

I waited for Benedict to respond with a special greeting of his own. When it was clear that he was preoccupied, I ushered the baron and his daughter ahead to follow the guards into the keep.

I held Benedict's arm and whispered in his ear. "This is your intended, milord. It would bode well for you in the king's eyes to make her feel welcome."

He glared at me, clearly upset that I had torn him away from his flirtations with the buxom servant woman. I offered him a sterner look in return.

"I know how I could make her feel welcome, milord." He smiled. "But I doubt you would approve."

"Do not cross me, Benedict. This alliance is very important to the future of England. You would be wise to remember that," I offered, nodding to the baron who glanced over his shoulder at us.

"I know fully the political reasons for this union, milord. You have no need to remind me," Benedict whispered.

"Then I expect you to show your attention to your intended at tonight's celebration, given in goodwill of this alliance," I responded with a quiet warning. Benedict held my gaze.

"Do not worry. I have everything well in hand." He grinned.

The king's great hall was decorated with long banquet tables laden with every culinary delight. Cheese and roasted meats, exotic fruits and sumptuous desserts had all been presented in grand scale, as only would befit the king of England.

The room was crowded with nobles and dignitaries of the court who had come to see the baron and his daughter. Unfortunately, I could not keep Benedict's wolflike gaze from flicking maiden to maiden.

"So many fine young ladies here this evening, wouldn't you agree, Sir Ranulf?" Benedict was fairly salivating as he leaned over to whisper in my ear.

I ignored his remark. "Perhaps the Lady Durwain would enjoy hearing of your travels, Benedict?" I hoped my suggestion would distract him from the allure of the woman smiling at him from across the hall.

If Sabeline had noticed Benedict's preoccupation, she chose to ignore it and instead focused her attention on me. "Are you two related, then? Cousins, perhaps?" she asked, looking up at me with wide brown eyes. They reminded me at once of the exotic brown spices I had tasted in my pilgrimage to Spain to serve orders of the church at the will of the king.

Her remark served to capture Benedict's attention, and his laughter prompted heads to turn. "By the grace of God, good woman, this tyrant is *not* of my blood!"

I smiled congenially and refused to allow Benedict's lack of propriety rankle me. I took Sabeline's delicate hand and kissed it, lingering longer than I should, enjoying the softness of her flesh. "I have no siblings, milady, but I am your most humble servant."

"Are you still using that ancient line, milord? No wonder you have not married," Benedict said with a quiet chuckle.

Sabeline's gaze remained on mine. I ignored Benedict's impetuous remark and held a cordial smile.

"And where are you from, Sir Ranulf?"

I clasped my hands at my back, gripping them tightly so they would not be tempted to smack the back of Benedict's head. "I lost my parents at a very young age, milady. I began as a squire here in court. With the exception of my travels, this has always been my home."

"Sir Ranulf, you are being far too modest. What he has not said, milady, is that he received his title from the king himself due to his superiority in tournament play. He is unmatched by anyone, anywhere to date. Is not that true, milord?" Benedict spoke, offering me a side glance. His gaze scanned the crowd, looking, I suspected, for the red-haired woman previously eyeing him like a delectable dessert.

"Is this true, Sir Ranulf?" Sabeline tipped her head as she stared at me, her eyes sparkling with her curious gaze. "I am impressed."

I glanced at the floor. "Perhaps the fair Sabeline would enjoy a dance?" I gently nudged Benedict's arm.

The Welsh beauty did not hesitate, nor did she wait for Benedict to cease ogling the other women. Instead, she curled her hand over my arm. "I would indeed."

"I meant—"

"Be my guest, Ranulf. If you will excuse me, I am parched and in need of something sweet to appease my palate," Benedict urged, nodding at me to join the dance forming.

"Bened—" I spoke, but it fell on deaf ears as he wound his way through the crowd. "My apologies. Benedict has yet much to learn about women." I bowed as she curtsied and we began our dance.

"He is young yet, and I am told, quite passionate," she replied, never taking her eyes from mine as she raised her hand to meet my palm.

"While that may be true, he should know better how to treat a beautiful woman." I held her gaze, aware of the slow thud in my heart as I looked down upon her angelic face. She was a natural beauty. Earlier, beneath the brilliant summer sun, her hair had glistened with rich mahogany hues and her eyes sparkled with wisdom and adventure.

Tonight, however, she took my breath away. Her face appeared radiant in the candlelight, and I resisted the temptation to touch the curve of her delicate neck, revealed by her upswept hair. I knew it was wrong to entertain such thoughts, yet impossibly, they pervaded my brain even so.

She lowered her eyes, her cheeks pinking to a rosy blush.

"I pray I did not offend you, milady. I meant no disrespect. I am certain that your beauty and charm will be all the passion he will ever need." It was not the truth entirely, but I was hopeful.

She glanced over her shoulder, and I followed her gaze. Much to my chagrin, her intended had one of the servants by the hand and was leading her from the room.

The imbecile.

"I shall attend to him, milady." I bowed and started after him. She gently caught my arm.

"Please, let us finish our dance. Were you to leave now, would it not cause tongues to wag all the more?" She offered me a quiet smile.

I studied her face. She spoke the truth.

"If you are quite certain. There is nothing that would give me greater pleasure." I bowed, considering that I should thank Benedict for his bad behavior.

She placed her hand on the crook of my arm as we moved into the next dance step.

"Three years is a long time to remain celibate. I suspect it may be best if he sows his seeds now, rather than after we are wed."

"You are wise beyond your years, milady."

"I am not a child, Sir Ranulf, and I would be pleased if you called me Sabeline." Her amber-colored eyes lifted to mine.

"As you wish, Sabeline." Her spirited nature was captivating and spawned a dangerous need deep inside me.

I took her hand and stepped to her side. She offered me a side glance. "You speak as if you know much about women. Are you married?"

Her bold question took me aback. I held her hand as we circled each other.

"No, I am afraid that my duties to the king prevent me from settling down and finding a wife."

"That is not to say that you would not welcome it?"

She smiled as I turned her beneath my arm and passed her on to the man next to me. I watched her carefully as we rounded our new partners, moving through the steps until at last her hand returned to mine.

I swallowed at the impact of her flesh against mine, as my imagination flared with the image of touching elsewhere her petal-soft flesh. I forced my thoughts back to our conversation.

"It is not a subject I dwell on. Some men are born to marry, while others are born for greater service." The moment the words fell from my mouth, I saw the challenge in her eyes.

"Greater service? Is it, then, your opinion that the union between a woman and a man serves so little importance?"

The music stopped and we stood toe to toe. In all my years of tournaments and courts I had not until now met a woman so outspoken. She was purposely challenging me, and however odd the circumstances, I found it remarkably arousing.

"Not at all." I lowered my voice, hoping that those around us would not hear. "The union of a man and woman is an act most sacred and cherished in all of life. What I said is that not all men are *meant* to marry."

"I see, so while you believe the union of a man and woman is a sacred act, you would agree it permissible to enjoy the benefit of the union, but forsake the commitment of marriage. For I assume, milord, a virile man such as you does not practice celibacy?"

I blinked and wondered how in the devil we got into this conversation. Concerned that others might hear and misunderstand, I steered her gently out onto the flagstone terrace. With the music still playing too loud to speak, I guided her carefully down the stone steps that led to the castle garden. At the bottom, I turned to face her and blurted a candid warning.

"Lady Sabeline, please forgive me, but I do not find these questions proper for one who is not your intended." I took a deep breath and cast a glance to the summer sky awash with stars. There. I had settled my tension. I looked at her with a congenial smile.

Her brows rose. "Then it is all well and good that we understand that my intended has his needs, and thus is purely within his rights to appease them without quarrel?"

I sighed as I paced back and forth in front of her. She had a point perhaps, but a true lady could not afford to take the same liberties as does a man. "These accepted practices are not the same for women as they are men," I stated as plainly as I could, praying that the conversation would go no further. Having to stand alone with her too long beneath a moonlit sky caused me unease. After all, it had been a long time since I had held a woman in my arms, tasted the pliant sweetness of a woman's mouth.

"Then perhaps the way it is done should be revisited, milord. For in truth, are not a woman's needs as great as a man's?"

Oh, great goddess in heaven, this was far more than I was prepared for. I started past her up the steps, hoping she took well my meaning. It was far too dangerous, this conversation about unions. "Excuse me, I must get back to the banquet hall."

"Are we finished then, milord, because you say that it is so?"

She turned to look up at me with a defiant stare. I was going to regret going back down those stairs to meet her face-to-face. "Despite your age—"

"As I stated, sir, I *am* a grown woman." She leveled me a look that should have served as a warning. "*Old* by English standards of marriage," she added dryly.

"It is well known that a lady is able to control her needs. It is by nature's design that a man cannot. It has been determined that it can even affect a man's health."

She looked at me with a startled expression, a smile tugging at the corner of her mouth. "And how is your health, Sir Ranulf?"

My gaze rested on her mouth, the same one that had tempted me from the moment we met. I realized she was teasing me. She began to laugh.

I glanced to the top of the stairs, hoping that no one heard her laughter and questioned why she and I were out here alone. Thankfully, there was no one in sight. We were quite alone and I was no more comfortable with the wicked thoughts skating at the edge of my brain.

"I do not know, Sir Ranulf," she said, "which I find more amusing. The fact that men cannot control their desires or that you truly believe that a woman should."

I had the foolish wish that she might act upon her current need—or mine. But to risk getting caught would by certainty ruin her reputation. Still, I could not help but poke back at her with a harmless challenge of my own. "Are you saying, milady, that you have no wish to control your desires?"

Her laughter waned as I stared at her. Just one kiss to rid the urge to show her the passion of a *grown* man, not one who had no idea of the prize he was being given. Somehow I found justification, shallow though it was, to appease my desire.

I took her face in my hands and brought my mouth to her lips, intent on taking a quick taste, but one was not enough, so I took another. I was lost in the sweetness of her sigh, how she trembled when I touched her. I urgently stepped away, pushing my hands through my hair to keep from touching her again.

She licked her lips as she met my confused gaze.

"My apologies," I stated. "I lost control of my emotions for a moment."

"Shall I no longer be a lady in your eyes, milord, if I were to admit my desire for you?" she whispered, brushing her finger over my lower lip.

"Sabeline, I am old enough to be—"

She rose to her toes and kissed me fully, stopping my words. Her soft hands cupped my face.

"This cannot be." I lowered my head, seeking every grain of nobleness in me. But my mind warred with my need to have her, to take her into the garden shadows and give her that which she claimed to want.

"But what of my desire?" she asked as her hand slid between us, stroking the length hardening even now beneath my breeches. Her mouth teased mine. It was then that I realized this was a game to her. I caught her hands, holding them between mine.

"You are young yet and do not fully understand the power of your desire." I swallowed hard as I stepped away from her. "Excuse me, milady." I headed back to the banquet.

"Milord, when will you be old enough to understand yours?" she called after me.

"What shall I say, Ranulf? Shall I tell her that her eyes glimmer like the mist on a morning lake?"

I pulled myself from my memories of that night and glanced across the table at Benedict. He was taking liberty of the server's generosity who kept his goblet full. She eased behind him and cradled his head between her breasts as she poured him more wine.

"There you go, milord. Is there anything else that captures your interest this evening?" the buxom server asked.

Benedict turned and grabbed the woman's breasts in both hands as he grinned up at her. "Perhaps later, my sweet flower, after my business is concluded." He kissed her pale exposed flesh with a resounding smack and turned his attention back to me.

"Can we make this quick, Ranulf? I burn with need." He drained his cup of its contents and stood.

"Perhaps you should go with something less trite, milord?" I reminded Benedict as he scanned the room and whooped aloud as he found his mark for the night.

"Perhaps I should go for something more robust, milord, to ease my suffering. Say what you will. Tell her I shall arrive at sunset tomorrow. Make it sound eloquent. As you always do."

At least he acknowledged that much.

He grabbed the table wench around the waist and planted a fevered kiss on her mouth. She dropped her pitcher and her squeal of laughter matched Benedict's as he hauled her over his shoulder.

He glanced back at me. "You should find yourself a wench to warm your bed, Ranulf. It would take the chill from your bones and perhaps even improve your countenance."

I watched him weave through the crowd and up the stairs with the woman kicking and screaming. I dropped my quill on the blank parchment and raised my cup to my lips, drinking the last dredges of my wine.

He might have a point. Perhaps appeasing my needs tonight would snuff the flame of desire that I have kept lit these last three years since that summer night in court. Only my pen has been able to convey the secret of my desire for Sabeline. Though she believes them to be Benedict's thoughts, they are mine.

And they are all I have.

The raucous chatter and drunken behavior pushed me to look for a safe haven in the room. Someplace where I could be alone with my thoughts. I had a note to write to a very special woman. In my mind, I pictured her often, wondering how the years had changed her. I did not dwell long on such thoughts as I reminded myself she was betrothed to another man. Most painful, however, was that that it was Benedict, and the image of her in his bed was too much to bear.

A group seated near one of the two blazing fireplaces left and I gathered my things, making haste to occupy the corner. Another cup of wine later, I twirled the quill still betwixt my fingers and stared into the flames.

From above came a scream of pleasure, precipitating a brief silence among the crowd, followed by laughter.

"More wine? Perhaps some food, milord? If you are in need of warmth tonight—"

I held my palm up and shook my head. "Humble thanks, but not tonight."

The server nodded as if understanding. "You dunna like women?"

Surprised by her conclusion, I made clear any misconception. "No, milady, on the contrary, I love women, and you are quite beautiful. It is only that I am called to duty."

She glanced around the room with a puzzled look on her face.

"And what duty is that, milord?" She frowned, for clearly she did not believe me.

I waved my quill in the air.

Her expression, if possible, appeared even more perplexed. "It is my solemn duty, milady, to pen a letter to a beautiful woman who is about to be wed."

Her face softened. "She is your sweetheart, then?"

"No, milady, she is not," I responded curtly, taking a healthy swallow of my wine.

"I fear I dunna understand," she replied.

I raised my brow and saluted her with my cup. "Then it seems, good woman, that you are in good company. For I am perplexed as you."

She offered me a forced smile, and with a pitying glance, left me as I had always been—alone.

3

EVERY ROOM WAS ALIVE WITH THE SCENTS OF THE solstice season. Roped pine branches curled around the railings from the keep entrance to the upper chambers. Bright red-berried mistletoe festooned the fragrant greenery and brought the gaiety of the holiday to the entire castle.

It was, as it had been for as long as I could remember, my most favorite time of year. My mother had dreamed that I would marry on the full moon of the solstice. And with the king's blessing, allowing the ceremony here at Durwain, in a small way she would be here, if only in spirit.

The members of my father's court and the servants of the castle were bustling with the impending arrival of Lord Benedict and his entourage. His military prowess and social standing, fueled by my father's praises, had already caused tongues to wag.

"How will she keep him?" I heard two women from the village whisper once as I walked through the ward. "She knows nothing of men. Poor thing."

Though I wanted to correct their ignorance by showing them the box of letters sent to me by my intended these past three years, I chose to ignore their comments as best as I could.

However, between those letters and Margaret's instructions I confess I harbored a fierce ache that I could not wait for my new groom to quell.

"Another letter, why did you not tell me?" my cousin cried as she swept into my chamber holding the paper delivered to my father quite late the night before. "Leave us," she ordered succinctly to Nuala, my maidservant.

I nodded, excusing Nuala, as I let my robe drop to the floor. I stepped quickly into my morning bath, grateful it was near the fire.

"I was going to tell you this morning, cousin. There was no need to disrupt your plans last evening. I saw how you teased the guard last night."

I leaned back in the tub and rested my neck on the cloth-covered edge, letting the warmth ease the tension in my muscles. Torrid dreams had kept me turning all night. I had changed in many ways, in both body and desire, over these past three years and I hoped that Benedict would be pleased.

"He is set to arrive at twilight," I stated, trying not to let my nervousness show. Though I had not the experience of Margaret, I wanted to portray that I was old enough to be patient.

Her skirts swirled as she sat down with a firm thump in the chair beside me. Her forehead wrinkled as she read the letter. I sank farther into the warmth of the water and waited for her to finish.

"Can you not see that he teases you, Sabeline? He is a rogue, this one," she stated with a decisive air.

She sighed and glanced at me before rising to inspect my attire for the day. I had no doubt that if she found it lacking, she would say so. I watched her for a moment, then took the sponge and slid the warm water over my arms.

"Will you allow him to deflower you before you are wed?"

Her question I had pondered several days since I had seen her and her lover. Still, I wondered at the wisdom of it. "Would not the anticipation make our wedding night that much sweeter?" I asked.

"Surely you jest, cousin? You expect sweet from a man who has spent the last few months on a horse in battle? A man who writes letters such as these must certainly burn with need by now. Surely you do not intend to make him suffer until your wedding night?"

I smiled wryly, thinking of his roving eye the last time we met. "I doubt that Lord Benedict has suffered these past years, especially from chastity."

She shrugged as she returned to the chair at my side.

"Give me the sponge," she demanded. "I shall wash your back."

I complied and leaned forward, holding on to the sides of the tub.

"I suppose it is true that a man of his caliber has needs he could not possibly contain. There is no telling how celibacy could adversely affect his health."

"Perhaps I should take advantage of his need and tease him when he arrives as he has done to me in his letters?" I smiled up at Margaret and gained her smile in return.

She dipped the sponge in the water and brushed it up my spine. "Perhaps there is hope that my instruction has helped you realize the path to a man's heart." She grinned.

"Ah, 'tis the *heart* then, that is our aim?" I replied. We laughed as she squeezed the wet sponge over my shoulders.

Warm rivulets of water trickled over my breasts, teasing my sensitive pink nubs.

Margaret scooped the sponge once more through the water and lifted my chin as she drew the sponge down the length of my neck. Her hand stopped, resting idly between my breasts.

"It is true that we women are destined to woo our men, even while we lead them to think that it is *they* who woo us."

I closed my eyes to the delicious sensation of the water heating my flesh.

"Part of a woman's seduction is knowing what gives you pleasure, Sabeline. Men believe they are the only ones with desires. Yet women have the same desires, and it is not ill conceived that we do. It is natural as it is with men. Think of it," she urged as she continued to slide the sponge over my skin. "Each time the warmth laps against your maidenhood, does it not send shivers over your skin?"

Though I knew that women, too, had desires, I had not given much thought until recently as to how to please Benedict. Now I was hungry to learn all that I could to create a happy union.

"Do not deny what gives you pleasure. Indeed, are we not made to live our lives fully?" She stroked the sponge over my breasts and her fingertip carelessly raked over one of my soft tips, causing it to pucker.

"See, even now your body responds to touch." She swirled the sponge in the water, weaving it languidly around my legs…between them.

I glanced up, seeing her soft smile, her attention focused on the sponge.

"Do you trust me, Sabeline?" she asked as she continued to glide the sponge over one knee and then the other.

"Of course," I replied, unsure if it was natural that I should sense arousal at her touch. My fingers gripped the edges of the tub as she slid the sponge between my thighs.

"Men do not know what pleases a woman, Margaret?" I swallowed, trying to stay focused on the conversation. I had grave doubts, based on my short observation of Benedict with other women, that he did not have his own book on the art of seducing women.

"Just close your eyes and think of Benedict," Margaret's voice soothed.

"Benedict," I repeated, leaning back and closing my eyes as instructed.

"Pleasure, Sabeline, is like a ripe peach. You must learn to savor its sweetness, slowly and with purpose, finding the discovery of its ready ripeness as delightful as the consummation of the fruit." Her voice became the sponge, gliding over my skin, coaxing me to relax, to explore the pleasures of my body. My knees relaxed, parting until they rested against the sides of the tub.

"If you wish to please a man such as Benedict, then you must learn to tempt him with your body. Make him want more. What else entices a man so well?"

Curiosity brought my gaze to hers. "How is it that you came to know so much about men?" I grinned.

"Lie back and do not think, only feel. Then you will know what to do when it is Benedict's hand instead of mine."

I sighed and settled in the tub, trying to relax.

"Perhaps it would help if you touched your breast," she offered.

I brought my hand to my supple breast, gliding it over my warm, slick flesh.

"Now tease your bud gently," she coaxed.

I did as she bid, taking my pert nub betwixt my thumb and

forefinger and rolling it. A smoky sensation began to form between my thighs. I shifted, relaxing my legs as I allowed the warmth to invade my woman's passage.

"As you become more experienced in these matters, Sabeline, your body will blossom. It would behoove you to understand, however, that a man like Benedict will likely have an insatiable appetite and you will need to do all you can to keep him in your bed. Even at that, I fear that you will not be enough for him."

"And what if he is unable to appease *me?*" I sighed as the sponge stroked my maidenhood. "If he takes on a lover, then am I not also within rights to take one of my own?" Dark tendrils of desire curled in my lower stomach, creating an urgent need.

"Do not be so naive, Sabeline," Margaret reprimanded softly as she continued to move the sponge over my sensitive flesh. "For women, there is never a choice, it is our duty to please our husbands, so that they want for no other."

I sensed a rapid change happening inside me, a tightening coiled deep inside. I squeezed my eyes as Margaret's voice faded into the image in my mind.

"Savor it, cousin. Think of it as your lover, his gentle touch patient. His fingertips parting your sweet petal, his tongue teasing…"

"Sweet woman…" My imaginary lover's hot breath caresses the sensitive skin of my inner thigh. "I have wanted this for so long." His mouth kisses my soft patch, teasing mercilessly as my hips rise to meet his ardent tongue. A sigh escapes my mouth.

Margaret's presence entered vaguely into my thoughts.

"That is good, Sabeline. Let the sensation carry you."

My lover rises from the water and plants warm, tender kisses on my slick flesh. He lingers on my breasts, pleasuring me in sweet torment. "Now, I need—" I beg.

"Soon," he replies. His deep chuckle resonates with dark, delicious

wickedness. He carries me to the bed, laying me back, looking down at me as if I were a sumptuous feast.

His knee presses apart my legs as he settles his hips between mine, his hands sliding upward over my torso, cupping my breasts.

His cock, firm and ready to please, brushes against my inner thigh and I close my eyes, spreading my knees wide in silent welcome. Bound by this magic, my body accepts him, tight at first then softening as he fills me completely, flesh meeting flesh. I curl my arms around his neck as his hips begin to move, his thrusts slow and deep, causing my thoughts to spin. Our hips move together in rhythm, fervently seeking mutual completion. I open my eyes and meet his smoky green-gray gaze. His face is gentle and kind, his blond hair swaying over his broad shoulders as he looks down at me and smiles.

Sir Ranulf.

I gasped, nearly falling as I stood up in the tub, blinking away the shock of my wayward thoughts. I made haste to grab my robe and cover my nakedness. My betrothed was set to arrive this very evening and the man I imagined giving my body to was not him, but his older mentor.

"What is it, Sabeline?" Margaret asked as she stared at me in shock.

I cinched the knot of my sash at my waist, my stomach quivering uncontrollably.

"It is nothing," I lied, my body still trembling with the aftershock of my daydream. "Nervousness, I suspect, at being a new bride."

"Lord Benedict of the Marches and Sir Ranulf of Dunstable, your lordship," the court page announced. Seated at my father's side, I gripped the arms of my chair. Across the length of the great hall, the massive wooden doors swung open and my breath caught in anticipation.

Both men entered the room with a determined stride. Immediately, I recognized Lord Benedict, as he removed his hat and flashed me a charming smile. He tossed part of his cape over his shoulder, revealing—for my benefit I chose to believe—his impressive build. He had filled out since we last met. My heart faltered as I took in the breadth of his shoulders and how enticing his black leather boots looked cradling his firm thighs. Margaret's words teased my mind, *"Will you let him deflower you before you wed?"* His clean-shaven face brought greater attention to his eyes, dark eyes that seemed to be able to read my mind. He glanced at me, and though he was not required to, knelt in homage to my father.

"Baron Durwain." He bowed, hat in hand.

"Welcome, Lord Benedict. You remember my daughter, Sabeline?"

As he rose, I caught his eye and a smile lifted the corner of his most tempting mouth. His eyes were piercing, glittering with challenge.

He stepped forward and held his hand out to mine, kissing the back of my hand as he knelt before me. "Not this lovely woman, surely? I remember a young girl only. Sabeline, I am entranced by your beauty." He stayed on his knee, unwilling to let go of my hand as his gaze held mine. "You have received my letters?"

I glanced at my father, my cheeks warming. "I did, milord, and I have kept each one." He appeared pleased. In stark contrast to the last time we met, his attention seemed focused entirely on me.

My eye caught Margaret's as she stood at the edge of the crowd gathered to welcome my betrothed. She gave a slight nod of approval.

Almost as an afterthought, Lord Benedict looked over his shoulder. "Baron Durwain, milady, may I present Sir Ranulf. Ranulf was at court, three summers ago, if you remember?"

He removed his hat, which before now had hidden his features. His hair, the color of harvest wheat, brushed against his collar as he bowed to my father. His captivating moss-green eyes barely grazed over me as he took my hand and offered a brief kiss. The short stubble of his light-colored beard tickled my flesh and I drew in a quiet, sharp breath as the memory of the kiss we shared that summer leaped into my mind.

"Milady," he spoke in his reverent, quiet tone.

I remembered now the intensity of his eyes, always watching, always aware.

"It is pleasant to see you again, milord. Welcome to our home."

He bowed and I stared at his dark blond hair tousled from his ride. My body responded with a quick jerk as the image of him in my daydream popped into my head. I yanked my hand from his and offered him a guarded smile. Curiosity flickered through his eyes, before he bowed once more and returned to Lord Benedict's side.

My father summoned one of his men to escort our guests to their chambers. I watched—as did every woman in court—with avid interest as both men left the room. Margaret's brows rose as she looked at me and grinned.

"At last the day your mother dreamed of approaches, daughter. Are you happy?" my father spoke, pulling me from my gawking.

Taking my father's arm, I looked up and met Ranulf's eyes as he glanced over his shoulder. He offered me a quick nod. How was it possible that his look alone created such scattered sensations in the pit of my stomach? Indeed, I was happy, but my traitorous emotions caused me to question who I was most happy to see.

4

I WAS A FOOL TO LOOK BACK. YET I HAD SEEN something, perhaps wishing it to be so, in her amber-colored eyes that compelled me to hazard a quick backward glance.

If anything, Sabeline had only grown more beautiful. No more the gangly young girl, her luscious curves would now tempt a celibate man. I would know, for I had carried the memory of that single kiss around for three years.

Her skin was soft, smelling of lavender. As I knelt at her feet, other ways to worship her on bended knee flooded my mind. I wondered if she sensed something carnal in my touch, given her strange reaction. I had to remind myself that it was not me she was to wed, but Benedict. I prayed that he appreciated his good fortune.

"Your castle is most impressive, Baron Durwain," Lord Benedict commented as he heaped his plate with more of the succulent pheasant the castle chef had prepared. No expense was spared in honor of the groom's arrival. Our meal began with a tantalizing stew, accompanied by cheeses and fresh bread, then followed with roasted venison, pheasant with apricots, and nutmeats. My cup was never without wine and minstrels entertained us with whistle, drum and fife.

"We are a humble people, milord. But we do enjoy the gifts bestowed upon us and share them freely with our good neighbors," the baron responded, raising his cup.

We joined in his salute of goodwill and drank deeply of the sweet wine.

I purposely kept my focus on the food and entertainment. In a few days, my duty here would be complete and I would return to England with news that the alliance was complete. Bearing in mind the nature of my duties made it far easier to be around Sabeline.

"And what say you, Sir Ranulf?" Sabeline leaned forward to peer around Benedict in order to speak to me. Her gown, cut low in front, left no doubt as to the woman she had become.

I swallowed the meat that seemed to be stuck in my throat as I dragged my eyes from her bodice to her face. With a quick glance at Benedict, I leaned closer, unable to hear her words for all the chatter and music.

"My apologies, Benedict. I could not hear what Lady Sabeline had to say."

Benedict flashed me a smile. "Of course. I understand that loss of hearing is one of the first hallmarks of age."

He slapped me good-naturedly on the shoulder. I wanted to knock him off the chair. "I will let you know, Benedict, when, or if, that happens."

The young lord chuckled as his eyes scanned the room. "I am suddenly overcome with fatigue and ask that I might take your leave, milady." He stood and I noted the shock on Sabeline's face.

He bowed. "Ranulf."

I nodded as I bid him good-night, not entirely upset to have an empty chair between Sabeline and myself.

"But they have not yet brought dessert. It was created in your honor," Sabeline said, staring up at him.

Benedict leaned down and touched her cheek. "Very well, then let me walk around the castle a bit. I fear riding all day has made me stiff."

I opened my mouth to speak against the idea, suspecting that the young servant girl he had been eyeing all night might be the reason he was stiff.

My mouth clamped shut as my eyes met Sabeline's troubled expression. It was as if we were reliving that night three summers ago.

My gaze followed Benedict as he wove around the tables filled with court guests. He picked up a goblet of wine from a tray carried by one of the kitchen maids. With a slight nod of his head, he raised his cup to her and left the room.

"It seems he is quite changed in some ways, milord."

Sabeline stared after Lord Benedict before she turned her attention to me. I could not say that I minded it. No doubt, the wine I had indulged in had dulled my senses, because I could think of nothing that I wanted to do more than to take her wondrous face in my hands and kiss her until neither of us could think straight.

"He has mellowed," I lied as I averted my gaze from hers.

"Tell me about you, milord. Have you since found a wife?"

"My pardon, but was this not the topic of our last conversation? Why is it that you seem utterly preoccupied with my marital status?" I snapped, the wine clearly having gone to my head.

Her eyes widened and I saw her visibly swallow. I looked away, immediately contrite and even more furious with Benedict's foolish behavior.

"My apologies, milord. Then by all means, let us speak of other things." Her lips pressed together in a thin line as she toyed with the food on her plate.

Guilt at my reaction besieged me, and it occurred to me that she, too, was likely concerned as to whether Benedict had changed over the years. I prayed to God that he would see his duty clearly, but I was not certain that if God were to meet him in the corridor in person, he would listen. Still, I thought it best that I go speak with him. "If you would excuse me." I rose and dipped my hands in the cleansing bowl.

"Oh, but of course! Let it be recorded that I was able to run off two men in less time than it takes to drink a cup of wine." She raised her goblet to her lips and tipped it back, drinking whole its contents. I watched, mesmerized by the gentle movement of her slender throat, envious of that wine.

My hands paused on the back of my chair as I questioned the wisdom of leaving. She summoned a servant to bring more wine to the table.

Torn between duty and desire, I knew that if I matched her drink for drink there was no telling where it would lead. Still, this was the feast of her groom's arrival. A woman should have her mind set at ease.

"You have not run off anyone. You heard Lord Benedict most plainly. He is stretching his legs."

"Yes, so he said." She sipped her wine but did not look at me.

"What troubles you, Sabeline?" It was unwise for appearance's sake, but I eased into the chair beside her.

"May I ask you something?" She stared straight ahead, as if lost in her thoughts.

"Of course." Three years had not changed her ease in speaking openly with me and I found the fact absurdly comforting. I studied her profile. She had a small dimple in her chin that I had not noticed before. My fingers yearned to see for myself if her cheek was as soft as it appeared, and if her lips still tasted like honey.

She shifted in her seat and faced me with a puzzled concern etched in her beautiful face. I took a sip of my wine, pretending I was listening and not thinking of that kiss three years ago.

"Have I grown, in your opinion, to be a woman at least *pleasant* to look at?"

I was grateful that I had swallowed before she posed the question, though I choked on the wine as it slid down my throat.

She patted my back, concern in her eyes. "Are you well?"

I nodded and held up my hand, taking a moment to recover as I thought how best to answer.

"Do not be alarmed. It is not your approval that I seek, merely your unbiased opinion as a man," she offered.

I recovered from the shock of her query, only to question whether it was possible I could remain unbiased. Alas, that was not an option, no matter how I tried.

"Of course, I understand. You are concerned whether Benedict sees how astoundingly beautiful you have become."

"I remember you were good at reading my mind." She smiled softly turning from my gaze.

Was it possible that, like me, she had tried to forget that night three years past?

"What say you then, milord?" she asked, worrying her lip.

I was accustomed to the volley of strategy on the battlefield, but this woman placed me in a position with a clear disadvantage.

"What, again, is the question?" I asked, scratching my head, vying for more time to formulate my response.

She leaned back in her chair and took a bite from an apricot. The juice dribbled down her chin, dipping into that dimple where I wanted to capture it with my mouth.

"There are those in this court who do not feel that I am an adequate match for Lord Benedict." She tapped her other hand on the table.

Clearly, she had a great deal weighing on her mind, but her intent was lost in translation between her mouth and my ears. "Why should you be concerned with what others think, if you pardon my asking?"

She shook her head. A short laugh accompanied her wry smile.

"Because it seems from the first day we met, Lord Benedict's interest in me is like the wind—here one moment and gone the next. How shall I know if I am woman enough to please him?"

She had noticed. Should I have expected her not to? I scanned the room and realized Benedict had not yet returned. I noted also that the serving wench was nowhere to be seen. The bloody fool.

"You assured me once that it was his youth that made him impetuous," she said, slowly turning her gaze to mine. "Has he *truly* changed? His letters are so far different than he is face-to-face."

It was an awkward position she placed me in. I wanted to peel Benedict's flesh from his sorry hide. "My good lady, I have no doubt that Benedict finds you a ravishing beauty and that his passion runs deep only for you."

"Would you swear your life on that, milord?"

Her eyes narrowed as she studied my face.

Damn, I am going to hell for this.

"I have always thought you to be a man of your word," she stated, twisting the saber of truth deeper into my gut.

My conscience caused me to look away. I sighed and prepared to leave. "If you now question your judgment of me, good lady, perhaps you should address your personal inquiries elsewhere."

"I have offended you."

"Nay, good woman, but I can no longer speak for Lord Benedict. My duty is as my king's witness to this alliance…er, marriage. Matters which concern you and Lord Benedict would be better discussed with him directly."

She said nothing, but nodded.

"Good evening, Sabeline."

"Milord," she responded quietly.

I was infuriated. As I left, I sensed her gaze upon my back. I hated to lie, but what choice was I given? My duty was not that of a romantic matchmaker, nor was it to ensure her wedded happiness with Benedict or anyone else, for that matter.

A high-pitched moan caused me to pause at Benedict's chamber door. I darted a quick glance down the corridor, pausing with my hand on the curved metal latch, sickened by what I knew I would find. Without a doubt, what I heard were the unmistakable sounds of unbridled passion. I was tempted to tear the door from its hinges. I rapped gently once, before lifting the latch and stepping inside.

My gut churned as I took in the scene before me. Benedict, on his knees in the middle of his bed, was in the throes of finishing with the kitchen maid. He glanced over his shoulder, though his hips never lost their determined rhythm. "One moment, Ranulf." He grinned as he dug his fingers into the soft flesh of the woman's hips.

I turned away, wondering what I could say to change Benedict's view of his commitment in marriage. I was beginning to understand that the man had no concept of the word when it came to women.

"Ah-h-h, mi-lord," she panted. The ropes of the bed creaked in unison with their appreciative sounds. I held my hand on the door, preparing to leave, but I hesitated, fearful of meeting Sabeline in the corridor.

Benedict let out a groan. "No—wait—Ranulf-f-f," he spoke, spacing out his words with each thrust. "Ah-h-h, there, there—it—is," he groaned.

A moment later as I faced the door, the woman hurried past me, tugging her arms in her sleeves, covering her naked torso. I held the door as she left, counted to three and faced Benedict. "What in the bloody hell are you doing?" I strode toward him, having to clench my fists to keep from strangling his careless neck.

Benedict chuckled as he drew his tunic over his head. "If at your age you need an explanation, Ranulf, then perhaps that is why you have not yet found a wife."

"You know well my meaning. There is a woman sitting out there who is your intended," I spoke in a tone low, but no less filled with stern warning.

Benedict's brows rose. "I know fully why I am here, Ranulf," he responded, apathy lacing his words.

"Then perhaps you wouldn't mind bloody well keeping your cock inside your breeches, then? Do you not understand, Lord Benedict, the dangerous game you play? What if you were to father a bastard child? Do you think that the baron would simply look the other way? If you are caught, it brings dishonor down upon us all."

He offered a short laugh.

"No one will know, and in a few days I shall bed my lovely bride as a dutiful husband should. Though based on experience, I find that nobility tends to be a bit stilted in the bedroom."

Before realizing the harm that could come from it, I had him by the neck and shoved his head against the wall. I felt the rapid beat of his pulse. "You do not deserve a woman such as Sabeline," I uttered between gritted teeth. I was seething inside that he could take such liberties against his intended.

"Be careful, Ranulf. Your king would not be happy to find how you treated his newest puppet."

My gaze narrowed on his. "What is your meaning, *boy?*"

His hands covered mine and tried to shove it away. "I am not your *boy* any longer. Do you not think that I know this alliance is for the benefit of the king and not truly of the Normans? Were it *my* choice, I would not marry a *Welsh* bride."

I tightened my grip on his neck, delighting in the gagging sound that emitted from his pompous throat. I felt him swallow hard beneath my palm. A flicker of angry concern crossed his eyes and then a slow, deliberate smile crept up his face.

"It is only one wench, Ranulf. No harm done as long as the secret is kept between old friends."

The king's intent for this marriage I could not deny. My only interest was in how he intended to treat Sabeline after they wed.

"Hold on." His gaze narrowed on mine. "You…you actually care for her." He grinned as if he had discovered a piece of gold.

I dropped my hand and stepped away. "Of course I do, Benedict. She plays an important part in this alliance. To offend her father or her would indeed serve to muddle the king's political alliance, and that is more important than either you or me."

"And is that all, my good sir? Does not the legendary knight that has served not one, but two of England's kings find the fresh, young Sabeline a tempting morsel? Perhaps, you too, hunger for just a quick taste?"

Guilt moved my hand to the blade I carried inside my tunic. "Silence, before I silence you myself," I warned.

Benedict shrugged.

"You and I agree on this. Sabeline has indeed grown into quite the beauty since that summer in court. I venture her womanly attributes are ripe for the picking and it is my good fortune to be the first to enjoy the harvest of her fruits. Most willingly, I might add."

"Enough. I am giving you fair warning, Benedict. Be at your best. Once you are wed, it is your head the king will have should you continue to play these games."

He chuckled as I opened the door. "As if your good king himself does not have his array of bedmates to choose from, eh, Ranulf? Much as I find your warning a trifle amusing, I will heed your words to the best of my ability. However, we have a few days left before my wedding. See to it that my bride comes to my bed still a virgin."

I hesitated with my hand on the door. "I shall warn you only once to be cautious of how you speak of the king." I slammed the door behind me, rattling it on its hinges. This bloody wedding could not come soon enough.

5

"IT IS AS IF I AM A SPECTER, MARGARET. HE LOOKS right through me." My breath blew out in frosty puffs as my cousin and I took an early-morning stroll in the outer ward. One of the guards followed on horseback, watching closely, his eyes intent on the woods beyond the outer wall.

"Sabeline, he is preoccupied," Margaret stated impatiently. "The man is, after all, about to be married. His carefree days of bachelorhood are slowly dwindling." She glanced at me, her blue eyes bright and her cheeks kissed by the chill.

I pondered her words. "Will that make a difference? When has marriage ever stopped a man from doing as he pleases?" I pulled my wool cape close against the harsh winter wind. Margaret glanced at me, her eyes glittering with curiosity.

"You question Benedict's loyalty?"

"I do not understand. I have tried these past few days to garner his attention and it is useless. He is *preoccupied,* of that, I am certain. It is the why that baffles me."

"Perhaps he needs enticement, cousin. Men are such vague creatures at times. We are forced on occasion to place before them our needs in a fashion that would seem most brazen." She held my arm and my gaze. "Understand that I would not suggest such measures unless I sensed that you were of a most desperate state."

I studied her face and lifted my eyes to the view of the vast, bleak valley that lay over her shoulder. Naked trees and a dank, gray sky settled like a dismal premonition over my marriage plans. Should I not at least be *happy* about my upcoming marriage? Why did I feel akin to these stark trees when I thought of it? "He is far different than the letters he sent." My eyes followed a swarm of wrens arcing in the sky above before settling in the wooded glen.

Margaret grasped my shoulders.

"We make our own happiness, Sabeline. Do not wait for happiness to find you. Go after it with a firm hand and a strong will."

My eyes rested on her serious expression. I offered her a smile. Perhaps she was correct. Perhaps I needed to be more brazen in my approach.

I pressed my hands beneath my breasts and shoved them up as my maid tied the strings of the corset tighter. The gift from Margaret most certainly did wondrous things to my form. Though not as well endowed as my cousin, I was sure to catch Benedict's eye wearing this.

With my head held high, I entered our private dining room where my family and special guests broke our fast. My intent was to find Benedict's eye and offer him a brazen smile, but it was Ranulf's heated gaze that took away my breath.

His eyes raked over me in silence, but my breasts tingled as if his very hands were exploring my body. He stood as I neared the table, his gaze resting on mine, appreciation shining in his eyes.

Benedict, previously engaged in conversation with one of

the servants, followed Ranulf's gaze and I watched as his face transformed with avid interest. He made haste to meet me and escort me to the seat beside him.

An odd flutter of apprehension caused my stomach to quiver as I took my place between Benedict and Ranulf. I was painfully aware of how the torturous corset cut into my waist. Nonetheless, my breasts jutted forth in proud display. I searched the faces at the table and caught Margaret's attention. She offered me a wide smile and raised her brow to signal her encouragement.

I chanced a small, shallow breath as I tried to relax. I doubted I would be able to eat a morsel.

"You are looking quite… *fit,* this morning," Ranulf muttered quietly, looking at his plate.

"Fit, Ranulf? Is that all you can say? Good God, she is a vision, breathtaking as the dawn," Benedict gushed openly, causing my cheeks to burn.

His eyes slipped to my bodice and I was content that my discomfort was not in vain.

"This color suits you."

Benedict took my hand and leaned over to kiss it, giving him closer proximity to my cleavage.

"You are too kind, Benedict," I returned, playing along as Margaret had instructed me. "Perhaps you might consider a walk in the gardens this afternoon? It seems we have barely had a moment to speak alone."

His brows rose as he blessed me with a charming grin. "But of course, I will place it high on my list of responsibilities. Forgive me for I have been negligent in not making more time for you." He kissed the palm of my hand and I felt my flesh heat under the wolflike hunger in his eyes. I found his rapt and sudden attention both flattering and a bit frightening.

"My pardon, sir, did it slip your mind that we were to ride north today to check on your troops?" Ranulf interjected as he stared straight ahead. He bit off a piece of bread, chewing slowly as he gave us both a side glance.

"Is this not a task you could perform as his representative, Sir Ranulf?" I stared openly at him, hoping he would see that I required his help to secure but a few moments of my intended's attention.

He continued to chew as he held my gaze for a moment, before looking past me to Benedict.

"The men, of course, will be expecting *you*. The winter has been especially hard. It would be best for morale that they hear from their captain, would you not agree?"

I heard Benedict clear his throat and turned too quickly to face him, wincing as the corset pinched my flesh. I was aware of the pleading look on my face, and I did not attempt to hide it as I awaited his response.

"A great leader is called upon to do what he must, daughter. For Sir Benedict that means his troops come before you," my father interjected, putting his final seal on the matter.

Lord Benedict offered a congenial smile of resignation.

"I shall return by nightfall, my love. And come the morrow, we shall have our walk." He glanced past me toward Ranulf. "You have my word." He touched his hand to my cheek, and a curious challenge flickered across his eyes.

"We should make haste, if you hope to return before nightfall," Ranulf spoke, pushing from the table. His heavy chair squawked loudly as it scraped across the stone. He strode down the length of the great hall without a backward glance.

"You will have to forgive my mentor's gruffness, Sabeline. He has been alone so long with only his horse and sword to offer him comfort that, I daresay, he does not understand the needs of a woman." Benedict took my hand and gave it a slight squeeze.

"I am sure you speak the truth. Still, it is a pity to see a man go through life with no one to share it with." I stared after Ranulf frustrated and curious at the same time at why he should be so ill behaved toward me. Surely he did not believe I was the same naive young girl of three years ago. Then again, perhaps Benedict's assessment of him was correct. If only to put our guest at ease, I would speak to him on the matter as soon as possible.

As soon as Benedict left the room, I hurried back to my chambers and asked my maid to help me peel off my clothes. "Hurry, I can barely breathe." I felt faint between being so constricted and eating only birdlike bites. As it was, I could scarcely sense my lower extremities.

"You made quite the impression on your betrothed, Sabeline. I am so proud of you." Margaret nodded to my maid as she eased inside my chambers. "Leave us," she ordered sternly. I found her tone as abrasive as Ranulf's at times. Perhaps Margaret should be the one to speak to him.

"Yet he left anyway," I cried as I rubbed my upper thighs to improve my blood flow.

"'Tis true, but you left Lord Benedict with a vision of your yearning. I am sure that even now he carries it with him."

"It was that infernal Ranulf," I muttered as I smacked my hands together and wondered how long it would take to regain feeling in them.

"What is your meaning, cousin?" She opened my wardrobe and began to rifle through my gowns, looking for the one I should wear for Benedict's return that evening.

"*He* was the one who insisted that Benedict ride to see his troops," I spat, free to express my frustration in the privacy of my chamber.

Margaret was silent. She pulled out a muted, gold-colored velvet gown decorated with intricate embroidery and small sparkling stones.

"Wear this. It will enhance the tone of your skin." She dropped it on the bed.

I drew on my robe and slippers and slumped in the chair by the fire. The scent of pine and cinnamon tossed on the burning logs wafted through the air, calming my senses. "I fear that it is Ranulf who plots against Benedict's true happiness, and therefore, mine." I hugged my arms.

"What reason would he have, cousin, to do such a thing?" Margaret asked.

I stared into the fire. I had told no one of that night at court, and to confess it now would not serve any good purpose. A part of me wondered if his surly behavior was due to what he could not have. "I do not know, but I mean to ask him at the earliest convenience."

Margaret placed her hands on my shoulders and gave them a friendly squeeze. "You focus on Benedict and leave Sir Ranulf to me."

I turned my face to hers. "Be careful, cousin. He is a quiet man, but very cunning."

She chuckled, patting my shoulder as she gazed into the fire. "You need not worry, cousin. He is no match for me."

I had full faith that if anyone could capture Ranulf's attention, it would be my cousin.

"Do not fret so. Remember what I told you about finding your happiness." She patted my shoulder again. "I am going to my chambers to lie down before our guests return. Perhaps a rest will do you some good, cousin. Your eyes are rimmed dark and your face pale."

I was not sleepy, but restless. I considered taking a walk to ease the tension inside me, but a midday snowfall hindered my desire to venture outside. I chose instead to wander the castle, stopping in my father's parlor to peruse his collection of books, many sent as gifts from the king of England.

As I ventured back to my chambers, I overheard the conversation of two of my father's kitchen servants. On their hands and knees with fistfuls of straw in their hands, they scrubbed the stone floor of the great hall. I remembered that one of them had spoken to Benedict during our first evening meal.

"He is impressive. Ne'er before have I seen a staff so large as his." The fair-haired woman giggled. "I pray to welcome him again to my bed."

"Not without me, surely?" The woman with coal-black hair looked up in surprise.

The fair-haired woman's expression softened as she glanced around before reaching forward and brazenly cupping the woman's breast. "It would not be as pleasureful without you." She smiled as the two shared a prolonged and passionate kiss.

I watched in fascination

"He says he will come to you again?" the dark-haired woman asked the other.

"Aye," the woman replied, lowering her voice.

I had to strain to hear their conversation.

"He says his staff is enough to satisfy the both of us." The fair-haired woman slipped her fingers beneath the edge of the other's bodice.

"You cause me to need, my love," the brunette maid whispered as she leaned forward, pressing her breast against the woman's hand.

"Tonight, my dear, you shall have all the cock you want and I shall enjoy watching your body fall apart even as I know you will bring him around for my pleasure."

A pot clattered in the room beyond and both women broke apart in haste, flashing one another secret smiles as they resumed their task.

I eased back against the wall, my head reeling with what I had been privy to. Surely they did not speak of Benedict? Nor did I believe that Sir Ranulf was the type of man to engage in such activities. Not, of course, that what he did in private mattered the least to me.

My slippers brushed against the stone floor as I hurried to Margaret's chambers. I raised my hand to knock and heard the sound of heavy breathing inside, followed by a woman's breathy sigh.

I stepped back as my eye caught a trail of muddy prints leading from the side entrance to her door. I fell helpless against the wall, frustrated that all manner of passion surrounded me, and yet I could not capture the undivided attention of one man. Perhaps it was time that I took matters into my own hands, as my cousin suggested, matching him thrust for thrust? No longer could I stand on innocence and propriety. With a man whose fire burned so bright, I needed to walk into the flames with willing determination.

A steady thump began to rattle the chamber door on its hinges.

"Harder, yes, yes-s-s…" Indeed, it was Margaret. Her appetite for passion seemed as great as Benedict's. I smiled, glad that he was far from the castle. It was most likely her guard lover again.

Margaret's scream jarred me away from the door. There was the sound of a man's growl followed by silence. I stared for a moment at the door and thought of the pleasure I had seen on my cousin's face the day she had invited me to observe them. Tonight I would wear nothing at all beneath my gown. I smiled at my wicked thoughts. With the magic of solstice to my advantage, I hoped to stir Benedict's passion for both his pleasure and mine.

6

IT HAD BEEN A LONG DAY. MY MUSCLES ACHED from the driving winter wind. A storm had surprised us, beginning late morning, and had increased in its fury as we made our way back to the castle.

Heavy snow clouds hung low in the valley and the snow hindered the ability to see much beyond a few feet. Eventually, the winds subsided but the snow continued to envelop everything in a thick blanket of white. My horse emitted a loud snort as we plodded forward and I squinted ahead, signaling the others to be cautious. From the dense snowfall emerged a rider accompanied by two men. Relief flooded me as I realized it was Benedict. Durwain could not be far.

"Welcome back, Ranulf. I trust you found my troops in good spirits?" Benedict spoke as he brought up his horse alongside mine.

"They are well. I took them your good wishes and the ale. They seemed content."

"Always content. I treat my men well, Ranulf. They appreciate what I do for them," he replied. "And what about you? Are those bones of yours stiff yet from the cold?"

"My bones are as fit as yours and I will gladly take your

challenge to prove it anytime you wish." I glanced at him, far too tired for his bantering.

Benedict laughed good-naturedly in response.

"I trust you had an enjoyable day with your betrothed?" I asked as I made pleasant conversation. In truth, I did not wish to know the details of their time alone. My guilt for insisting he ride with me when I knew fully that I could handle the task alone weighed heavily on my head as we left the castle. In a moment of regret, I insisted he go back and spend the day with her.

"My afternoon was splendid, thank you for asking. Would you care to know the details?"

I shook my head. "A gentleman keeps such matters to himself."

"And pray tell me, Ranulf, what do you think of the good lady Margaret?" he asked.

"Sabeline's cousin?"

"The fair-haired beauty, yes. Do you find her appealing?" Benedict asked.

"I have come to learn that the women in Wales are astoundingly beautiful," I remarked, wondering where this conversation was leading.

"I am glad to hear it. Does she appeal well enough to you that you would consider approaching her father to ask for her hand in marriage?"

"Why do you insist on marrying me off to any woman who crosses my path?" I asked, urging my horse to a gallop. I was anxious to arrive where it was warm and, even more, to end this dialogue.

"I ask only because, unlike me, you live by a code of honor and propriety that offers you no alternative to the pleasures of the flesh, unless bound by marriage."

"Let me ease your mind, young lord. I am no virgin. I have had my share of women, make no mistake. It is the sacredness of the marriage bed wherein you and I differ, friend."

"Ah, then it is well to have your fun while single, but once betrothed the shackles of propriety bind you to no one but to your bride."

"You speak as if honor in the marriage bed is something ancient and without merit."

"By no means, sir. If you are fortunate to have both passion and marriage, then so much the better. I have not personally experienced marriage, but I am a loyal student of passion."

My silence confirmed that I agreed.

"Has there ever been anyone special for you, Ranulf?" he asked.

I rode on, refusing to answer him.

"She must have been extraordinary," he remarked.

"She was," I stated simply, "and I prefer to leave it in the past."

"I understand."

I glanced at him as we headed over the drawbridge to the inner ward. I did not understand the meaning of these questions, but I resigned myself to the fact that he and Sabeline were to be married. Once the ceremony was over, I would be free to get on with my life.

Benedict leaned over and took hold of my reins, halting me as we passed between the great stone bastions to the keep.

"You do not believe that she will be happy with me, do you, Ranulf?"

I studied him, weighing my words carefully. "I believe that it takes more than a man's skills in bed to maintain a happy marriage."

"And you feel I lack in these other areas?" he prodded.

"It is your reputation that precedes you, Benedict."

"And does the good lady Sabeline know of this alleged reputation?" he asked, narrowing his hardened gaze on mine. I would have challenged him instantly would it not stir up greater harm. Instead, I answered him plainly.

"If you imply that I have presented you with ill will, you are mistaken. Whatever the good Sabeline thinks of you is based on other information, not mine. Know this, however, if you bring dishonor to yourself, I will not defend you."

"So much for loyalty, eh, Ranulf? Forever clinging to your weary code of honor."

I rode on in silence, knowing that if I responded to his insolent jabs, the skirmish would end with the blade. The man would never be a true knight.

"I suppose your honor is all that a man like you has. I cannot fault you for that, Ranulf," he called as I rode on ahead.

I had no cause to respond, but for the sake of my pride, I turned in my saddle and felt the harsh pull of my muscles, stiffened by the cold. "I cannot be something I am not, Benedict. Some things a man is born with, others he must acquire. While it is true that my title is not by fortune of lineage, it has been found honorable by our king. It is to him that I answer only, not you. You make your own choices and hence decide the outcome of your future."

As I anticipated, he offered a short laugh.

It was painful. With each day that passed, I was forced to watch as Sabeline tried unsuccessfully to capture Benedict's interest. I found myself growing more restless and more agitated. Yet my duty was clear. I was the king's emissary and nothing more. I had to remind myself that it was not my place to warn her of the character of the man she was about to marry. Moreover, I could not trust that my intent would be pure if I took it upon myself to do so.

"More wine, milord?"

One of the kitchen servants placed the pitcher on the table. Her eyes were clear blue, the color of a peaceful summer sky. I held out my cup to her. "I have not seen you before today," I said, enjoying the faint rush of color to her cheeks.

"I have just arrived to court, milord." She smiled as she filled my goblet. A lovely thing she was, with light brown hair and a pleasing shape. I was under the influence of too much wine, I was certain, for her smile reminded me of Sabeline's.

"Come here," I whispered, coaxing her to my side with a crook of my finger. "Do you see that man? The dark, handsome lad two seats down?"

"Lord Benedict?" she whispered, her eyes darting a look at him.

"Yes, shh now, come close, let me whisper in your ear." She bent so that my lips skimmed the soft flesh of her ear. Her skin smelled of fresh-baked bread. "Be wise of him. Do not be seduced by his charm, for he is a wolf in sheep's clothing. Do you understand my meaning?"

She turned her face slightly to mine and I found it all too tempting to satisfy my loneliness with a quick taste of her mouth. She gave me a curious look.

"I believe I do, milord," she answered, glancing at Benedict, who was absorbed in his conversation with the baron. Sabeline, seated between us, focused on her plate. I sensed the wheels of her mind turning with yet another plot to gain Benedict's attention.

"Splendid. You will heed my words, then?" I whispered to the woman.

"Yes, milord, I will do as you ask," she replied as she stepped away and lifted Sabeline's goblet to fill it.

I could not take my eyes from the woman as she moved from table to table. Now and again, she would glance up at me and smile.

"Are you well this eve, milord?"

Sabeline's voice gently nudged me from my thoughts. I had managed thus far to keep my mind and body at a comfortable distance from her, having discovered that, when too close, my body reacted with less-than-honorable intent. "Tired from the journey. Nothing more, I assure you." I did not look at her directly, but I sensed that she studied me.

"You are not much for conversation, milord, I thought perhaps that I—"

I dropped my roasted chicken to my plate and dipped my fingers in the cleansing bowl. "You are mistaken, good lady. I could not be in better spirits." I stood before she had the chance to say anything more. I did not wish to embark on the small talk of how she spent her day with Benedict or how I spent the day riding through the cold winter wind thinking only of returning to her. "If you will pardon me." I garnered the attention of the servant girl.

"Certainly, milord, I do not wish to detain you." Her reply was curt and I suspected she was frustrated with her inability to capture Benedict's attention.

The servant woman found her way back to my side, as Sabeline looked on. "Milady," I offered, choosing to let Sabeline think what she wanted. It was less complicated that way.

"You are leaving us, Ranulf?" Benedict spoke, watching me as he reached for Sabeline's hand and placed a lingering kiss on her palm.

I foolishly clamped my arm around the woman's waist. "I

bid you good evening, Baron Durwain, Benedict, Sabeline."
Once out of view in the corridor, I released the woman and
cleared my throat as I mulled over how to tell her that I did
not wish her company this evening.

I dug in my pocket and finding a coin, handed it to her.
"I ask only that you wait a short period of time before you
return to the hall. Say nothing if anyone asks what happened
betwixt you and me."

"But nothing has happened, milord, though I am willing
if you are."

She undid the top lacing of her chemise. I swallowed hard
considering whether a night of raw passionate sex would rid
my mind of these incessant thoughts of Sabeline. "I am
honored, truly, but I would not be good company tonight."
Without further discussion, I stuffed the coin in her hand,
hurried down the corridor and out into the still, dark night.

I aimlessly walked the castle grounds, glad for the bitter cold
that numbed my senses. I scolded myself for the yearning
thoughts that I had allowed to linger far too long inside of
me. Sabeline had grown into a fine woman and it was evident
by her actions that she desired Benedict, even if he was fool
enough not to appreciate it. I had to find a way to reconcile
these emotions steeped in the past. She was his, and that kiss
long ago was motivated by nothing more than the impetu-
ousness of youth. The sooner I resigned my needs for the sake
of my duty, the better for us all.

I braced my hands on the wall overlooking the barren
outer ward. Torches burned around the perimeter of the yard,
casting strange shadows on the new-fallen snow. The sky was
a vast dark blanket, sprinkled with stars. The moon shone
brightly above, not quite full, reminding me that in a few days
a wedding would be taking place.

I pounded my fist on the ledge, sending a spray of snow into the frigid air. I did not look forward to the day when I would bear witness to this event.

Unable to sleep, I tossed my tunic on, slipped into my breeches and headed toward the baron's parlor, hoping his books would settle my mind enough to sleep.

"Milord, it is late."

I lifted the torch I had taken from the wall outside my chamber door. Coming toward me was Sabeline's cousin, Margaret. She offered me a bright smile as she tucked a loose blond curl behind her ear.

"I see you were unable to sleep, as well." Her gaze dropped to my unlaced open shirt. "But what good fortune, for I wanted a moment to speak with you."

"Of course, milady, how may I be of service?"

"You are truly a most noble man, Sir Ranulf." Her eyes danced with keen interest. "Ready, it seems, to tend to the needs of others."

I wondered at her motive for this late-night meeting. "Indeed, milady, what needs have you that I may address?"

She was a lovely woman, though, in my opinion, not possessing the charms of her younger cousin. It was clear that she was familiar in the art of seduction and in my present state I found her brazen behavior tempting, if not too convenient.

She backed against the wall and smiled demurely as she tucked her hands behind her back. My gaze dropped to the creamy white swells of exposed flesh in her low-cut gown.

Prompted by loneliness and drink, I leaned over her, brushing her breasts as I tucked the torch into its iron sconce. I rested my hand above her head and offered her a challenging gaze.

She smiled and laid her warm palm against my chest, then slowly trailed her fingers down to the top of my breeches.

"Tell me, are you betrothed, as well?" I whispered. In my drunken state, Sabeline's face swam before my eyes.

"Nay, milord, but I am no innocent when it comes to the needs of a man." Her hand slipped lower and she began to stroke my staff through the cloth.

"I can see you possess fascinating skills, milady." I closed my eyes to the pure pleasure of a woman's hand on me.

"I have no doubt that *your* skills are as splendid, milord."

I looked down at her through hooded lids. True it was that I could satisfy the whims of this wicked little enchantress as well as my own. *Sweet Sabeline.* I opened my eyes, and the image of Sabeline dissipated as Margaret's face materialized in front of me. I dropped my hand and stepped away from her caress.

"Sir Ranulf? Margaret?" Sabeline suddenly emerged from the dimly lit hallway, her gaze darting from one of us to the other. Though I had no cause to feel guilt at the surprised look on her face, I nonetheless turned away and took a deep breath before facing her.

"My pardon, milord. I did not mean to interrupt." She lifted the hem of her skirts and turned to leave. The mere thought of her returning to Benedict caused me to blurt aloud "Wait, milady. Was there a matter which you needed to discuss?"

She slowed her step and looked over her shoulder. The glow of the torchlight sparkled in her gaze.

"I would only keep you a moment, if I might, milord. In private, if possible?" Her eyes darted to where Margaret waited in the shadows. "That is, if I am not interfering with my cousin's plans."

"Sir Ranulf and I were finished. Perhaps, though, we can

continue later?" Margaret smiled at me and patted Sabeline's shoulder as she disappeared down the corridor, her skirts swooshing along the stone floor. The sound faded in the distance, and Sabeline and I were left standing alone.

I swallowed hard and tried to clear my head of the lust-filled thoughts dancing in my brain.

"Perhaps we should step into the parlor, as it is a bit more private?" she offered, gesturing toward the door.

"As you wish, milady," I responded. "After you." I waited as she hurried by me. Mesmerized, I summoned every bit of nobility to surface as I took in the gentle sway of her hips. Her dark tresses hung loose, cascading over her shoulders, held back at the temples by two carved ivory combs.

I was grateful that she could not read my thoughts. How I wanted to pluck out those combs and run my fingers through her hair. How I wanted to find her tempting mouth and possess it entirely. How I wanted to loosen the laces at her back and allow my hand to slip beneath the fabric and cover her warm, pliant breast…

She turned without warning to face me and, lost in my thoughts, I ran into her. I grabbed her by the shoulders to prevent her from toppling backward and stepped away in haste. "My apologies." I took another step back, distancing myself.

"You may leave." Her eyes flashed with authority.

I offered her a frown. "I do not understand."

Her gaze locked over my shoulder to a servant who had just brought in a load of wood for the fire. The young man left in haste, closing the door gently behind him. She walked over and latched the door.

"I want no one to overhear us, milord," she stated as she returned to me.

I scanned the room, searching for a spot where I could

distance myself and be attentive at the same time. There was not much in the room. A writing desk, a chair and a wall of shelves filled with a few books, gifts and tokens I presumed were from the baron's travels abroad.

I leaned my hip on the table and glanced down at the thick pallet of sheepskin furs spread before the blazing fire. My thoughts immediately drifted to easing Sabeline to that rug and having my way with her.

I licked my lips and found my fingers tightly gripping the edge of the desk. I was glad that I wore my jerkin over my cambric shirt as it covered the arousal of her cousin's teasing.

"What is it that I may do for you, milady?" I cleared my throat and shifted so that the fur rug was out of my field of vision. I watched her pace in front of me, lost in her thoughts and completely unaware of how I mentally undressed her, one piece of clothing at a time.

"Sir Ranulf?"

I blinked, brought back to the present by her voice. "My apologies, my mind is elsewhere."

"*That* is precisely what I wish to speak with you about."

Finding it perhaps more wise to sit than stand, I sat down and folded my hands atop the desk, glancing up at her as she continued to pace. "Please continue. I fear I do not understand."

"It is you, Sir Ranulf," she said, her gaze darting to mine. "You refuse to speak to me—nay, to acknowledge me at all. Lately, you run off after every meal."

Were it Benedict seated in this chair, I would better understand these reprimands. "Milady, permit me to point out that it is not *my* attention which you seek?"

She gave me a shocked look. "Are you daft? This is entirely about appearances, milord."

I raised my brows to challenge her statement. "Of course it is," I muttered.

"I am finding it difficult to explain." She chewed the tip of her thumbnail, lost in her thoughts.

"Forgive me, milady. I would like to help ease whatever troubles you, but how does this involve me?" I shrugged.

"Do you not see how your behavior affects me?" She slapped her hands on the table and pushed her face close to mine.

"*My behavior?* Nay, milady, I do not." I drank in the curve of her cheek, the slight bow of her kissable mouth. Unable to help myself, my gaze traveled to the view offered as she leaned toward me. What sweet warmth I ventured lay in the valley between those breasts…damn.

"For this very reason, sir." She searched my eyes. "I have noticed how you look at me. How you watch when you think no one else notices."

"I am truly sorry if I have caused you discomfort." I narrowed my gaze on hers.

"Were it me alone that noticed, it would not cause me discomfort, though I must confess I do not know whether your looks stem from pleasure or disdain."

My eyes met hers. "Would it matter?" It was dangerous, I knew, to press her on such matters but the alcohol had loosened my tongue.

She straightened as if I had struck her. Fear and desire warred in her eyes. Did I truly want her to answer? I held my breath.

"This was a mistake, milord. My apologies for taking leave of your privacy."

She turned to exit the room. I reached out and grabbed her hand, knocking the chair over as I stood. "I need to understand why you sought me out tonight." I did not let her go as I came around the table to face her.

She started to speak, but stopped each time, as she did everything she could to avoid looking at me.

I took her chin between my fingers, holding her gaze firm on mine. It was wrong of me to insist she remember, too, the power of that kiss all those years ago. She was older now, her future clear, her purpose to be the wife of another man. Every reason I could think of to walk away lay before me, yet I could not remove my hand.

She looked up at me then, her soft amber-colored eyes filled with desire. I wanted to finish what we had begun those many years ago. I had to know that the torment was not all mine.

"That night three years ago, milord...I did not mean for it to happen," she whispered. Her gaze lowered to my mouth.

"Any more than you mean for this to happen, Sabeline. Let the blame fall on my head, but I cannot walk away this time." I lowered my face to hers. I did not want to think on the reasons I should stop, or to think about the risk I was taking. She could never be mine, not the way I wanted. Even now, I could not be sure that I was not a substitute for her failed attempts with Benedict. Still, for one night, to quench the fire she ignited long ago, I would be her substitute.

Her fingers tentatively touched my lips and, had a sword been at my throat, I could not have stopped myself. I captured her mouth to appease the hunger that lay buried in my soul.

A small whimper emitted from her throat as I slanted my mouth over hers. She was as sweet as I remembered, pliant and giving with fierce passion, a preview of how she would be in my bed.

I plucked the combs from her hair, driving my fingers into the silken strands. I sensed the pulse of her heart beneath my palm as I cupped her delicate neck and held her face to mine.

Fervently pressing for more, our mouths mated and my hands found the lacings at the back of her gown. I freed the knots and her gown loosened, slipping with ease over her slender, pale shoulders.

I met her eyes and waited for her to reveal how far we would venture into this dark and dangerous moment. With her gaze locked to mine, she lowered the gown farther, exposing the gentle swells of her creamy flesh. My breath caught as I traced my fingers down her throat, over the delicate flesh that lay between her breasts.

I held my hands around her waist as I bent to lavish one peaked, rosy tip and then the other. Desperate to feel her soft flesh against the hard planes of my body, I unbuckled my jerkin and dropped it to the floor. Her hands joined with mine to draw my cambric shirt over my head.

In all of my life, I had never been so aroused than by the look of appreciation and desire in her eyes.

Her palm came to rest on my chest, and I closed my eyes at the savage desire welling inside me. I clenched and un-clenched my fists at my sides, allowing her exploration— withstanding the tenderness of her kiss upon my skin, the warmth of her face nuzzling the curve of my neck, until I could no longer keep my hands off her.

I cupped her face, bringing her lips to mine as I drank deeply of this forbidden wine that consumed all reason. Receiving no protest, I drew her down, turning her beneath me on the soft fur rug warmed by the fire. Driven by passion long denied, I took my fill of kisses that would have to carry me through the lonely years ahead.

"Milord," she whispered, pressing her breast into my palm, fiercely holding my face to hers, devouring any noble intent left inside me. Her hips lifted to mine, seeking connection, completion. Our hands tugged together at her skirts as she intermittently captured my mouth, satisfying her need for another kiss.

My heart pounded against my ribs as a need greater than I feared I could control built inside me. I teased her breasts, drawing her pink pearls between my lips, lavishing them with my tongue as my hand found the heaven of her naked thigh. I wanted her as I had never wanted anyone.

"Beautiful Sabeline," I murmured, brushing the pads of my fingers over her velvety mottle and finding her silken glove seeping with arousal. She held my face in a thorough kiss as my fingers slipped inside, stroking, coaxing her arousal, making her want only for me.

Her sighs soft, she turned her head to allow access to the warm curve of her alabaster neck. Her skin glistened, brought to a fever from the passion and the fire, and I breathed in its sweet, musky scent, searing it into my memory.

Though my cock was more than ready to find the warm, sweet spot of her core, I fought the need to quell a niggling doubt in my mind. "Milady," I spoke, kissing her softly. I inserted my fingers deeper inside her warmth. She arched with a soft moan of pleasure. Her muscles contracted around my fingers, her hips bucking gently with her release. I held my breath, nearly coming undone. My body on fire, I held her face so I would see the truth in her eyes when I asked her what I must. She looked up at me, but in her eyes was not the rapture of desire, but sorrow and guilt.

"Milady, be certain of what you want, for I swear to you in a moment you will be unable to stop me." I waited with a parched throat for her answer.

Unshed tears welled in her eyes as she reached to caress my cheek.

I closed my eyes, pain stabbing my chest. Flogging myself in silence, I struggled to my knees.

"I—I am sorry, forgive me, Ranulf. I cannot place you at such risk. My father expects me to marry Benedict. It is by his decree, and neither you nor I can change that."

I sat up and rested my arms over my knees, my teeth grinding against the thought of taking her anyway, just to appease the burning she had started inside me. I shoved my hands in frustration through my hair. I knew in my heart that she was right.

In an attempt to relieve the pain, I rubbed my hand over my chest, still sensing her mouth upon my flesh. I could still taste her skin on my tongue. A lump formed in my throat and I squeezed my eyes shut, resigning myself to the inevitable truth. *Damn Benedict. Damn the baron. Damn alliances.*

She was not mine, nor could she ever be mine.

"Well, *I* do not apologize." I offered a short laugh, laced liberally with cynicism and pain. "I do not regret what has happened here tonight. I regret only that we are not able to finish this."

She placed her hand on my shoulder and my body came alert. "Do not touch me, Sabeline, I beg you. I am no nobleman at present. In a heartbeat, I could deflower you and you would enjoy it most assuredly."

She moved her hand away and I heard behind me the rustle of her clothing as she struggled to make herself presentable.

"You must give me your word that you will not speak of this."

My mouth tingled yet from the passion of her kisses. God forgive me, I wanted to taste them again. Pain greater than the thrust of a sword dug deep into my chest. My jaw clenched in frustration. I shook my head at the injustice of it all. "Surely you cannot mean to marry him? Not now." I glanced over my shoulder, watching as her sumptuous breasts disappeared from my view.

She adjusted her bodice, covering her shoulders.

"It is not in our hands, Ranulf. What is done is done. We cannot risk all that my father has worked for, all that your king has worked for, to enjoy a few moments of passion."

Was that all it was to her, a few moments of passion? I wanted to roar my indignation in response. How could she think that what transpired between us was nothing more than shallow passion, no better than that which Benedict was a slave to? My chest rose and fell with agitation as I stared at her. What teasing game did she play with me?

"Can you lace my gown?" She scooted on her knees and faced away from me, lifting her dark hair. With her gown undone, revealing the soft curve of her spine, I could not help but think what it would be like to be her husband, helping her each night with such requests.

I leaned down and placed a kiss on the back of her neck. My hands came around her, capturing her breasts in my palms, caressing them more roughly than I should. "Do not tell me that this means so little. That the thought of my hands on you doesn't make you desire the union of our bodies more than life itself."

She dropped her cheek against mine as I kneaded her breasts. My lustful urge to push her to her knees and satisfy my craving grew stronger.

"It cannot be, no matter how much either of us desires it," she spoke in a dreamy whisper.

"Then you do not deny it?" I kissed her temple as I pressed her breasts together, memorizing the scent of her hair.

"I do not deny it," she said, barely perceptibly, and turned her face to mine.

Her lips parted as she waited for me to take her. It's what she wanted, I reasoned, my heart pounding fiercely against my ribs. I wanted to scream for the noble part of me to step forward, the part of me that reminded me the king had not appointed me as her husband.

I leaned my forehead against hers. "Nor do I." I swallowed, as my hands drifted to her back and I clumsily tightened the lacings on her gown. I reached for her as she rose, but she did not look back as she grasped the latch on the door.

"Why did you seek me out?" I asked one last time.

She hesitated with her hand on the latch.

"To ask how I might find a way to please your friend, milord."

I could not hold in my laugh and let it dissipate into a weak cough.

"It is not my intent to hurt you, Ranulf. But it is my duty to marry Benedict." She turned to face me. "You are the one that taught me that duty is more important than selfish desire."

She closed the door with a quiet click that echoed in the hollowness of my soul.

Damn duty to hell.

7

MY MIND REELED WITH CONFUSION, MY FACE burned with guilt. How could I have allowed it to happen? I wanted to discuss with him his relationship with Benedict, to see if there was something more that I could do to gain his attention. But the dark look in his eye caused me to address another matter altogether that had pressed at me from the moment he glanced back to smile at me on the day of his arrival.

My head was dizzy, my body vibrating still from the passion of his touch. I hurried from the parlor and nearly ran into Margaret and Benedict as they exited the great hall together.

"My dear cousin, how goes it with you? We worried when we could not find you."

I was grateful she did not give away where I had been. Margaret placed her arm around my shoulders.

"You look as though you have seen a spirit, my dear," Benedict interjected, taking my hand in his.

"I was taking a walk and heard a wolf. I—I guess it must have frightened me," I lied.

"Out without your cloak?" Benedict asked in surprise. "You should take better care of yourself than that. May I remind you that our wedding is but a few days from now?"

I gave a shallow curtsy, unable to look him in the eye. "Yes, milord, it was foolish of me. If you do not mind, I would like to return to my chambers."

"I will come with you, cousin. To be certain you do not take a chill."

"Be well, my beloved," Benedict spoke as he leaned in to kiss my forehead. "Your hands are yet warm. That is odd for being outside. Perhaps you have taken a fever?"

I snatched my hand from his and hurried around him, keeping my eyes to the floor. "I will go to bed at once, milord."

He grabbed my arm, his gaze softening with his grip as I glanced up at him.

"Indeed, that is where I would have you be," he said.

The very idea only conjured images of Ranulf in my bed. "Pardon, milord, but I am not feeling well." Behind me I could hear the swish of Margaret's gown, but neither of us spoke until we were secure in my private chambers.

"You must tell me what happened, Sabeline," Margaret stated, closing the door behind us. "Where is Nuala?"

"She had to tend to her cousin, ill with fever," I replied, watching the flames of the fire in the hearth. But I saw only the image of Ranulf's half-naked body next to mine. Tears welled in my eyes, for what I had done and for what could never be.

"Sabeline?"

She came to my side and touched my arm, startling me back to the present. I stared at her, not knowing where to begin.

"Here, let us get you out of this gown and into your bed-clothes." She turned me so that she could untie my lacings and if she noticed they were not secured in the manner in which she had done earlier, she made no mention of it.

"How was your discussion with Sir Ranulf?" she asked quietly as she tugged the gown down my body.

"Thank you for not telling Lord Benedict that I did not go for a walk." I drew my gown over my hips and the chill on my skin reminded me of Ranulf's gentle touch.

"Yet you have not answered my question, cousin?" she reminded me, as she folded my gown over a chair.

"I wanted to speak to Sir Ranulf to see what Lord Benedict's interests are. So that perhaps I might use them to gain his attention."

"Clever girl. And was he helpful?"

I worried my lip, wondering whether I should tell Margaret what happened. "I fear he was not as helpful as I had hoped."

"'Tis a pity. I find Sir Ranulf a most intriguing man. Quite a catch for a woman who can see past his age," she replied as she poured each of us a small cup of wine.

"He is most adequate, for any woman," I replied in haste as I accepted the wine. She held it from my grasp for a moment, studying me.

"You speak as if you know this from experience. Is there something more you wish to share with me, cousin?"

"No, of course not. It is only that I find Sir Ranulf, as you say, a most interesting man. But I daresay he may never marry." I took a sip of my drink and lowered myself into the chair in front of the fire.

"Here, let me ready your hair for bed." She picked up my hairbrush and stroked my hair, smoothing each section with her hand.

"I must gain his attention, Margaret," I spoke as I stared into the fire.

"Lord Benedict's?" she offered quietly as she brushed.

"Of course. Much hangs in the balance if he does not find me to be a suitable wife."

"I believe that Benedict has made his intentions clear, Sabeline. Look how he showed his care for you this eve."

"I sense that he is being kind, Margaret. But a marriage cannot be sustained on kindness alone."

"Those are things which can be addressed after marriage, Sabeline," she responded.

"I have heard rumors," I confided in her.

"Rumors? What kind of rumors?"

"There is more that goes on behind these closed doors than you think." The wine and the fire caused my tongue to loosen. "Did you know that two of my father's female servants find each other attractive?"

"Finding a person of the same sex attractive is not strange." She chuckled.

"I saw them kissing!"

"Really? In the open?" she asked.

"There in the great hall, while they were cleaning. And they spoke of meeting with a third person for sexual favors… a man."

"And so you assume that this man is Benedict?" She continued to brush my hair, seemingly unaffected by the information I shared with her.

"Who else? Surely not Sir Ranulf," I replied. Still, hadn't the possibility crossed my mind when I heard them speaking of their midnight tryst?

Margaret sighed as she ran the brush through my straight hair, then began loosely braiding my locks.

"I do not know what more I can teach you, Sabeline. You know well Benedict's thirst for passion."

I stared into the flames as my mind landed upon a most scandalous idea. "I will go to him," I blurted. I would show him firsthand the passion inside me.

"Benedict?" Margaret's hands paused, holding my hair in their grasp.

"Of course to Benedict." I shifted and turned my face to meet her eyes. "I will steal into his chambers and seduce him. He will see firsthand the passion that awaits his marriage bed and ever after want for no other."

Margaret yanked my braid as she completed her task.

"Do you think that wise, cousin?"

"Margaret, what choice do I have? If I do not do this, I will continue to be a ghost to him and a fool to everyone else."

She studied me carefully.

"Very well, you must then prepare yourself to go to him. Here, drink some more wine."

"Should I require it?"

"It might…help. Your first time can bring a small measure of pain if you are unduly tense."

I held my cup and Margaret poured, taking no more for herself, I noted.

"You intend to go through with this plan, then?"

I took a deep swallow, letting the sweet liquid warm my thoughts. As much as I wanted to please Benedict, my body yet remembered Ranulf's touch and the yearning I sensed when in his arms. I finished my wine and held out my cup for more.

My cousin glanced at me as she poured me another half cup.

"Do not go unless you are certain, Sabeline. If you make clear the intent to give your body to a man, nature will take its rightful course. And few men are able to stop themselves once the process is begun."

I opened my mouth to refute her claim but brought the cup to my lips instead and took a large swallow.

"Slowly, cousin, you do not want to take leave of your senses," Margaret cautioned.

Too late, I tipped my head back and drained the contents. A slow warmth began in the pit of my stomach and radiated through my body, creating in me a delicious sense of freedom.

"I no longer wish to be a virgin," I spoke loudly, grabbing Margaret's hand to twirl her in a circle. "I want to taste the sweet fruit of desire."

I halted and took a step back as the room spun before me. My gaze narrowed on my cousin. "And whose passion will *you* partake of this night, dear cousin?"

She looked at me as though I had slapped her. "I do not know your meaning—I believe the wine speaks."

"Perhaps." I wagged my finger at her with a grin. "But, 'tis true that you have been secretly seeing someone, and I think I know who it is."

"You do?"

"Of course. Did you not think anyone would notice the mud prints leading to your chambers?"

She stared at me, her expression not portraying the gaiety that I felt at my teasing.

"The guard, of course. Have you forgotten so quickly?"

Her expression softened and she relaxed with a smile.

"Of course, the guard. Yes, in fact, I nearly forgot." She raised her cup and took a healthy sip. "It was not what I had hoped, either."

Her blithe response gave way to the cold reality of my plan. Was it wise? What if the whole affair turned out to be a horrid experience? "Am I doing what you would do if you were in my place?"

Margaret looked toward the fire and appeared deep in thought.

"Yes, cousin, I think you are. Go now, the night wanes."

I kissed her cheek, tied my robe tight and opened the door.

I peered up and down the dark corridor, dimly lit by torches placed every few feet. I summoned my courage, knowing I had quite a walk to Benedict's chambers located above the great hall.

"Milady, what are you doing out at this late hour?"

My heart faltered as my maid, Nuala, rushed from the shadowed hallway. "Ah, Nuala, your cousin is better, then?" I tried not to allow my nervousness to show. She would not be pleased with my current plan.

She nodded, but her eyes were curious.

"Milady, I must offer that it is unwise for a woman to walk the castle alone in the middle of the night."

"Do not fret so, Nuala. I have not far to go. I must ask that you return to your rest and ask no more questions of me. We will talk come the morrow."

"Milady, as your maid, I am your keeper and so must caution you of the wisdom—"

"Then so you have performed your duty exceedingly well." I patted her hand. "Now go take your rest. I will be well."

She stared at me as she contemplated whether to heed my words or belabor the point further. With a deep sigh of resignation, she kept her ground as I continued down the corridor. When I looked over my shoulder a moment later, she was gone.

My footsteps echoed as I passed through the silent foyer that led to the circular stairs. I kept my palm against the stone wall as only a single torch provided light for my ascension.

My fingers brushed the tattered hem of the massive tapestry that hung above the stairs. Woven into the dense fabric was my maternal grandfather's tribal crest of Ireland. With this marriage, the lands it depicted would become property of the Lord Benedict and, hence, of England as well. Its colors faded, it was still a symbol of my father's allegiance and respect for my mother. Theirs had been an arranged union, also, but a happy one and their example was what I hoped for with Lord Benedict.

A mouse scurried across the floor at my feet, and I covered my mouth to stifle a scream. My heart thudded against my chest as I approached Benedict's chamber door. I hesitated, my hand resting on the latch. With a deep breath, I summoned all my courage and eased open the door.

The room had begun to cool and the stone floor was frigid through my thin slippers. The fiery remains of the embers in the hearth bathed the room in an eerie glow. From where I stood, I could see the end of Benedict's bed, a fine piece my father had had constructed especially in honor of our wedding. The heavy drapes, hung from iron rails, blocked out the cold as well as the light.

As I tiptoed to the bedside, I prayed that he did not sleep as many warriors did, with a blade at his side. I drew back the drape, adjusting my eyes to the darkness and saw that he slept with his back toward me.

A loud snore stopped my heart and my body went stiff with the fear of what I was about to do. In the dim shadows, my breath hung in frosty puffs as I hastened to drop my robe and gown to the floor. Stepping from my slippers, I peeled back the corner of the quilt and slipped effortlessly beneath, edging close to Benedict for warmth.

Trembling, I leaned forward to place a chaste kiss on his cheek, his eyelid, and finally his mouth. With a quiet murmur, his hand snaked around my waist and he drew me into his embrace. His mouth found mine, soft and warm, hesitant at first. His kisses fueled my desire, quelling all concerns of my previous tryst with Ranulf.

He was gentle, his hands moving over me, caressing my breast, sliding down the small of my back, drawing my thigh over his as his fingers traced the valley to my waiting maiden-hood. His hardening cock teased my opening even as his fingers slipped between my petals, stroking until I grew soft, seeping with need.

Lost in his kisses, I gave over to him entirely, wanting him to possess my body and make it his own. In all that I knew of Benedict, I had not anticipated such thorough loving, such gentleness with his passion. In our cocoon of darkness, he lavished me with the attention I craved. He was everything I desired. I gave in to his musings, taking delight in what he was able to command from my body. Passion consumed me with each touch, each stroke. I grew bold, curling my fingers around his thick cock, impressed by its powerful length, anxious to know what pleasure it would give.

His mouth moved hungrily over mine, my desire to please matching his. He tasted of wine, and I surrendered to the ex-pertise of his hands, sliding languidly over the insides of my thighs, his thumb brushing teasingly between my thighs. Dark tendrils of smoke curled inside me, clouding my reason as need took control of my body and my mind. He nudged my knees apart and I offered myself willingly, the need for becoming one with him so strong I would not have known how to stop.

Fully clothed, Benedict was a most impressive man, but without the hindrance of his clothing, my hands were given fully to caress his sinewy arms and shoulders. The sensation of his hard muscles flexing against my tender flesh took me deep into a euphoric bliss.

With another kiss, he nestled himself between my thighs as he pushed his rigid staff slowly into me, stretching my virgin sheath. A stab of pain brought a gasp from my lips and he hesitated as I pressed my knees against his ribs and bit my lip against the sting. Insistent to see through my plan to seduce him, I held his face and kissed him hard until my body grew pliant. He rocked gently against me until my body accepted the slick, heavenly friction of him.

His sigh turned to a quiet groan as he shifted and pressed deeper still.

Liquid heat coursed through my veins as I lifted my legs to welcome him. I wanted desperately to possess him and sensed his body was determined to do the same. In the black-velvet darkness, I found with him the rhythm of life, of passion, my hips tilting to meet each fervent drive of his cock.

"Sweet goddess," his hot breath whispered near my ear. My mind spun, abandoning itself to this carnal magic. My fingers gripped the corded muscle of his arms, hot and damp with his aroused fever. I sensed him above me, his breathing labored, insistent with each determined thrust.

My body coiled tight, I held the sensation as long as I could while I teetered on the brink of joy until my body at last broke free. Tumbling with each magical wave, I surrendered, pressing my thighs against his ribs as my glove tightened around him. I heard the sound of his breath catch and twice more he pushed deep, spilling his hot seed inside me.

Only then did I consider the possibility of a child. Yet would that not be all the better to give him an heir? I gripped the muscled flesh of his hips, holding him deep inside me as residual ripples of pleasure cascaded over me.

He leaned down, offering a slow, lingering kiss before he rolled over and drew me against his chest. I lay awake, sensing the change to my body, realizing that I was no longer a virgin. Wetness trickled betwixt my legs and I used the sheets to dab myself clean, wondering if I should reveal myself to him now instead of at dawn. A few moments later, I heard his steady breathing and realized he was asleep.

Certain the fates had left the truth for daybreak, I snuggled my back against his chest, content within the security of his strong arms, and fell into a deep sleep.

I dreamed of my dark lover, his face obscured, but his familiar hands dominating my every other sense. He seemed to know what gave me pleasure, how to bring me to a dizzying need, and when to let the desire ebb before building my body to desperation once more. I dreamed of the days to come, of how complete our life would be with both passion and purpose. In spite of the uncaring, unseeing man I had thought him to be, Benedict had proven otherwise with his tender loving.

I was nudged from my ethereal dreams with the delightful sensation of Benedict's hands upon my breasts, gently caressing as his mouth planted soft kisses on the flesh of my shoulder. I turned to speak, but his hand touched my chin, gently pushing my face away from him as he lifted my hair and focused his kisses along the curve of my neck.

His palm slid down my thigh and instinctively I lifted my leg, allowing his fingers to stroke me deeply until I could barely breathe. Wrapping his arms around me, he lifted my leg over his thigh. He was hard and ready as he entered my ready quiver from behind, introducing me to yet another new pleasure as I held my leg aloft. One hand cradled my breast as the other stroked my mons, fostering a dizzying need within me. My body jerked with each delicious, fervent drive, pushing my body to a shattering climax. With a quiet groan, his mouth gently bit my shoulder and he emptied himself deep inside me. His phallus spent and still nestled betwixt my legs, he wrapped his arms around me and, satiated, we both drifted off to sleep.

8

MY COCK AWAKENED, AS DID I, TO THE WARMTH of a woman's body snuggled against mine. Too much wine the night before gave me pause to wonder whether the slumbering woman next to me might be the good lady Margaret come to finish what she had begun in the hall. I raised up on my elbow and rubbed the sleep from my eyes. The drizzle of early dawn seeped through a crack in the curtains and there, cradled in the crook of my arm, was the serene and very satisfied face of Sabeline.

The crumpled bedsheets, the stains of her virgin blood and her unclothed state put quickly into perspective what had transpired. Yet I had no regret for one stolen moment as I stared down at her, mesmerized by her beauty and by the emotions that stirred within me. The sheets pooled at her waist left exposed the soft, round breasts that my mouth had a few hours before taken pleasure in teasing. I could not help but be curious as to her change of heart, until a cold realization came over me.

Benedict had come to my chambers last night and we drank far too much, exchanging stories of shared battles. He'd fallen asleep on my bed and, seeking an empty bed, I'd barely made it to his chambers…

Nausea roiled in the pit of my stomach as I watched her sleep.

She stretched and I fisted my hand to keep from touching her. She was even more beautiful in the sobering light of day. I grew hard, knowing how her body responded to mine. Unable to keep from tasting her lips once more, I leaned down and placed a soft kiss on her mouth.

Warm and pliant, her mouth responded to mine, and her arms came around my neck. If this was a temporal moment, let it be the one I carried with me for the remainder of my days.

"Mmm, that is nice to awaken to, milord," she whispered, her eyes still closed.

Encouraged by her enjoyment, I savored the last dredges of this mysterious moment, lifting my face from hers. She slowly opened her eyes.

Satisfaction shone in her eyes just before they grew wide with fear. She sat up and drew the bed linens around her nakedness.

"Why are you here?" She searched the bed as if she might find Benedict lurking amid the sheets.

"Milady, let me say this before all else. I do not regret one moment of what has happened between us." I reached up to brush away the hair hiding her face.

"Where is Benedict?" she asked again.

Though I had expected her response, my heart squeezed painfully. I dropped my hand, wanting more than anything to draw her into my arms and make her forget Benedict.

"We were drinking and he fell asleep in my chambers. I came to his, but I swear to you I had no idea this would happen."

"Yet you made no effort to stop it?" she asked, her gaze landing on the red stain on the sheets.

"I was overcome with drink, milady. I responded only as any man would when seduced by a beautiful woman in the middle of the night."

She did not spring from the bed as I had fully expected she would. Yet I dared take that as a good sign. "I do not regret one moment, Sabeline," I spoke, hoping to quell the concern in her eyes. "I pray that I did not hurt you."

Her eyes skirted over my torso. The mere sight of her in my bed and the way she looked at me caused me to grow hard. I was glad to have the bedsheets wrapped around my thighs.

She worried her lower lip as her eyes met mine. "You were most generous and gentle, Ranulf. As loving as I could hope for, it being my first time."

She started from the bed and I stopped her.

"But you thought it was Benedict who worshipped you through the night?"

She nodded. "It is true, I cannot lie."

I closed my eyes. "Then the dawn brings you disappointment, and for that I am deeply sorry."

She did not look up.

"No, Ranulf, God help me, I may be many things, but I am not disappointed."

I opened my eyes and searched her face to be sure I understood what she was saying. I took a moment before I spoke, the anticipation causing my body to heat. Still, I needed to be certain. "Were this night to happen again, would you wish it was with Benedict?"

Her beautiful eyes rose to mine.

"It is no longer the night, but the dawn. What shall happen now?"

Perhaps desperation spawned my words, perhaps the hope that desire alone could change the outcome of our lives. "Sabeline, were it in my power I would awaken each day to capture the sweetness of watching you sleep, to kiss that most tempting mouth and feel your body stir beneath mine," I said, leaning toward her, my heart praying that she would not turn away.

There was no protest.

A soft whimpering sound escaped her throat as her mouth melted with mine. I dared to touch her face, her cheek velvet against my callused hand. I do not possess the charms of noblemen, nor am I one to tease, or to be teased. But as with all else I have attained in my life, once I set my sight on my goal, I do not waver until I attain it.

But she was more than that. She was inexplicably a part of me and now I could not just let her go—at least, not without a fight.

I eased her back to the pillows. There was, this time, the understanding of the choices we made, of the risk that we took.

Her gentle hands moved over me, exploring my flesh. I cradled her breasts, satisfying my need, drawing her pearled tips gently through my teeth, taking pleasure in her sighs.

She surrendered to my touch and the result was more intoxicating than any wine, drugging my senses, quelling whatever concerns had come before.

I held her gaze as I covered her body and eased into her swollen glove. Her legs came around my waist as she raised her arms above her head in abandon. I fought the urge to drive madly into her, resting instead inside her as I stole a lifetime of kisses from her.

If our joining was a sin that would damn my soul forever to a fiery hell, I was prepared to go there for her. "I want you to know whose body you claim, Sabeline. For even as you do, know that you have already claimed my heart, no matter what it may cost."

I held her close as I rolled to my back, my staff impaling her deeply as she straddled my thighs. Her gasp of surprise turned quickly to one of satisfaction as her hips settled over my rigid cock. I rested my palms on her thighs, giving her time to find what pleased her about the position. The sight of her body perched atop mine, her eyes closed and her lips parted would remain forever etched in my brain.

She pressed her palms to my chest and leaned down to kiss me. In that instant, she had no idea of the thoughts I had of spending an entire lifetime at her side. She awakened yearnings in me that I had not known existed—yearnings of family, home and children.

"It is your pleasure I wish to see." I cupped each breast, suckling the rigid nubs as her fingers laced through my hair. Seated on my lap with her warm thighs wrapped around my middle I kissed her swollen mouth as she began to rock her hips back and forth.

"Ranulf," she whispered, her eyes glazed with arousal.

She held tightly to my shoulders, our gazes locked. More than fleeting passion passed between us as my body approached ecstasy.

I gripped her waist, our bodies moving in heated rhythm. I kissed her as if it would be my last. "I want you to know the depth of my feelings for you." I struggled to speak as my body grew tighter.

"M-milord," she whispered, her voice cracking with emotion.

"If it were my decision, I would be the one you marry and not Benedict."

"Ranulf." She held my face as tears streamed down her cheeks. With her next breath, she thrust her chin upward and cried out, succumbing to her release.

I lay back and pushed deep as her sweet glove milked me. "Do not regret one moment of this, my love. Tell me that you do not. Let that be enough for me to carry to the end of my days."

She wove her fingers through mine and turned her angelic face to mine. Her words came in short breaths, "If my life… ended today…I would have no regrets."

My body shook with the ferocity of my climax, knowing it would be the last time our bodies would join as one. As I offered one last thrust, the sound of footsteps registered in the back of my brain.

Sabeline collapsed on my chest and I wrapped the sheets around us, expecting that Benedict's servant was about to get an eyeful.

The drapes were torn aside, sending in a rush of light as Sabeline sprang from astride my hips and covered herself with the rumpled bedsheets.

Benedict stared down at us with an amused but puzzled look clouding his face.

"The noble Sir Ranulf and my bride? Now, this is a surprising turn of events. Not to find Sabeline in your bed, of course, but that you had it in you to serve a woman."

"There is a simple explanation, Benedict. Do not blame Sabeline for I forced her submission." I swung my legs over the edge of the bed, grabbed my breeches, and pulled them on in haste as I scanned the floor for Sabeline's clothing.

I found her robe and gown and lay them on the bed, standing as a screen between her and Benedict as she dressed behind me.

"Is that quite necessary? I have been privy to naked women," Benedict said as he rounded the bed and perched on the edge of the writing desk. "Just not my intended…yet."

For a man destined to wed this woman in but a few hours, he seemed far too at ease in finding her in my bed. "There is no reason that this should change anything, milord." It tore at my gut to say the words, but I had to on Sabeline's behalf. "We both want what is best for Sabeline."

"And for England," he reminded me pointedly.

"Yes," I conceded, "and for England."

He folded his arms.

"Yet, Ranulf, all this time, I had no idea that you conspired to your own goals." He narrowed his gaze on mine.

"This was not planned, Benedict," Sabeline said as she came to my side. She took a deep breath and twisted her long mane of mahogany-colored hair over her shoulder. "It is not Sir Ranulf's doing. The choice was mine. I came of my own free will with my aim to seduce *you*," she said quietly, looking at Benedict. "I wanted you to find me as alluring as the others in this court that you have bedded."

Benedict slapped his hand over his heart in mock sincerity. I wanted to wipe that smile from his face, but I needed to hear what Sabeline had to say before I went any further.

"How very noble. You flatter me, milady, with your efforts to garner my attention." He stood and walked up to her, tracing his hand softly over her face as he glanced at me. "But you could have simply asked your cousin."

Her surprised gaze shot to his. "Margaret?" she asked.

"Oh, indeed, a delightful distraction," he responded blithely. "You see, it is Ranulf here who is to receive credit for our first meeting. He ordered me back to the castle to spend the day with you." He shrugged. "But I found your cousin instead, most receptive to a poor stranger coming in from the cold."

Sabeline's expression grew pale. Her hand shot up and Benedict caught her wrist midair.

I gripped Benedict's arm. His brow rose and a smile played on his lips. "I would consider, Ranulf, the pleasure of your company in our bed, once we are wed, if you were to agree, of course. Variety stimulates me." Benedict offered a short laugh.

"I would share no woman with you, Benedict. Least of all, Sabeline. What will it take to keep your mouth silent?"

He clasped his hands behind his back and eyed us both. Now, Sabeline would see the true character of this man.

"As I see it, there are a number of options open to discussion here," he stated.

Benedict knew that the move was his in this game of chess and we were now his pawns. I waited for what diabolical plan he would put forth, knowing it would likely have no benefit to Sabeline or to me. "You stand to lose more if you do not go through with this wedding," I offered.

"I am aware that what you say is true." He shrugged. "Let us be fair. There is only one reason I complied with the king's desire for this alliance. My apologies, milady, but you alone were never the prize. A happy benefit, perhaps, given enough of my sexual tutoring, but that is all."

I lunged at him but stopped short when he drew his short sword and pointed it at my throat.

"I suggest you think, Ranulf."

I straightened and took a step back. We both knew he spoke the truth.

"You will leave. You have broken the bonds of our trust and I will leave it in your hands how you explain your absence to your English king when he asks how went the ceremony."

"You cannot punish him without also punishing me," Sabeline spoke.

Benedict's predatory gaze went to her. "As for you, your silence will be required or I will be forced to reveal this affair to your father at court. Talk of betrayal and sin travels quickly through kingdoms, milady. You would not wish to be the ruin of your father's house and reputation, would you?"

"If I do as you say, you must promise that you will care for her, Benedict."

His dark, emotionless eyes turned to mine. "I owe you nothing. In fact, you are fortunate I have not run you through as would be my right at finding you in bed with my betrothed."

"You do not truly care about her, Benedict," I countered.

"Forever the strategist. That is your strength, Ranulf." He grinned. "Very well, it is true. With Sabeline the heir to her father's kingdom and wealth, his armies, his lands, automatically become mine once we are wed."

"And in alliance with the king, Benedict, they would become England's," I said, the realization of his goal beginning to crystallize in my mind.

"True, but only if I command it. With my army and those of the good baron, I would join those rebels who do not wish to be under English tyranny. We would convert their loyalties, one way or another."

"My father would never agree to such a plan," Sabeline interjected, anger rising in her voice as she bolted toward him, pummeling his body with her fists.

I took advantage of the distraction, moving quickly to overtake him, but he turned her as a shield, one hand clamped around her waist as he held the knife to her throat with the other.

"My dear woman, I have no concern that your father will be alive to dispute my plan," he responded quietly.

"You will not get away with this," I warned.

"I already have. If you do not comply, I have several witnesses who will attest to seeing the two of you together on more than one occasion."

"That is a lie!" Sabeline elbowed his stomach.

"It is your word against many, my beloved." His gaze turned to mine. "My guards wait to escort you to the edge of the kingdom, Ranulf. We wouldn't want you to get lost."

9

BETRAYED. NAUSEA ROILED IN MY STOMACH, YET I could only pretend, as instructed, to behave as if all was well.

"You look pale, cousin. Is it your monthly?"

Margaret sidled up beside me. I held up my skirts as I hurried with Nuala to my chambers. "I have no more to say to you, Margaret. And I no longer consider you of my blood." She kept pace with my stride.

"For reason, I venture, that I was bedded by your intended?" she scoffed. "Would you have preferred it be Sir Ranulf? Did you think I was blind to how he looked at you and how you ran to him at every turn?"

I halted in my steps. "How dare you—"

She laughed. "You have no right to pronounce judgment on me."

I did not care what my maid heard. If she valued her job, she would turn a deaf ear.

"You aided him," I spat, ready to strangle her scrawny neck.

"I only bedded him, dear cousin. What he did from that point was of his own design."

I held my hand to my mouth, preventing the bile rising in my throat from coming forth. It was not that I cared anymore whom Benedict had been with in the short time he had been here, but to threaten my father's life was a deed lower than a snake's belly. Then there was Sir Ranulf, riding away this morning flanked by heavily armed guards. I had to find a way to expose Benedict and make things right.

"I will not listen to your half truths, Margaret. My concerns do not include for whom you spread your legs. But heed well that with Lord Benedict, you skirt the very edges of hell, so watch well your soul."

I swept after Nuala into my chambers and slammed the door behind me.

My trusted maid kneeled at the hearth, stoking the embers, adding small pieces of wood until bright flames snapped and licked at the stone. She silently went about her task, but I sensed she had something to say.

"What is it, Nuala?" I asked. Frantically, I searched my mind for a way to resolve the mess I had made. My father's life and Ranulf's lay in the balance.

"I can see you are concerned, milady," she offered, wiping her hands on her kirtle.

Her dark eyes met mine and for a moment, I wanted to tell her everything, expose my sin and ask for a miracle. However, I realized at that moment that it would not have mattered. What happened between Ranulf and me was a welcome excuse. Benedict was all along making his plans. Now he had justification to dispose of Ranulf.

She took a deep breath, looking at the door as she spoke.

"There is someone who might be able to help you, milady."

Her fingers worried mine. I sensed her nervousness. "Who is it?"

"It is the crone who lives at the edge of the village. They say she practices the magic of the old ways."

"You do not mean the Druid priestess?" I dropped her grasp. "I do not partake of the dark arts."

"I understand, milady. Forgive me."

I turned my back to her, staring at my bed, still in its perfect state since yester morn. I thought of Ranulf's hands upon me. Even now, I tasted him on my tongue. "Wait, how do you think she can help me?"

Nuala hurried back to me, tugging from her pocket a tattered sampler. "If you take this to her, she will explain."

I held the piece of unbleached linen in my hand, surveying the words in Gaelic embroidered in intricate detail. "What is this?" I asked, staring at her.

"It was given to me long ago, by your mother. She trusted me for its safekeeping. She said that one day you might have need of its power. I have carried it with me always."

"And what has this to do with the old crone?"

"She is the only one who knows how to release its power. You will need her guidance, Lady Sabeline, if you wish to use it now."

"Where does she live?" I pulled on a warm gown, stockings and shoes and then folded the sampler, stuffing it into the pocket of my dress.

"I will take you to her."

I hesitated at the consequences if Benedict were to discover my absence. Still, he had given me no choice. I grabbed my cloak. "Meet me near the east wall of the ward and speak to no one of what you are about to do."

"Aye, milady." She nodded.

Moments later, we hurried through the market crowd in the keep's outer ward and sneaked over the drawbridge into the small village beyond the castle. Left mostly for soldiers and travelers, it was not a safe place to tarry too long. A late-morning mist hovered over the road, shrouding the rooftops of the village huts. Tendrils of frosty white smoke curled high into the blue-gray winter sky as Nuala tugged me in haste toward the outskirts of the village.

Dodging the errant remarks of a passing soldier, we veered off the main road to a path where the wood grew dense. I questioned the wisdom of this venture as the dim shadows enveloped us. The air was saturated with the dark stench of rotting wood and wet moss. We had to step over the gnarled branches barring the narrow path.

After several moments, the trees departed and at the end yawned a clearing. In its midst sat a primitive, thatch-roofed house. I knew my father's views about the old ways. He would not be pleased that I was venturing to see the old woman.

"Some say she cast spells on those who can not pay her," Nuala whispered. "Take this."

She stuffed a coin in my hand.

"I canna go any farther, milady." Nuala hesitated at the edge of the wood.

"Thank you. Go back to the castle and tell no one you have seen me," I said, and continued through the golden waist-high grass toward the house.

Nuala hesitated before calling after me, "Are you certain I should not wait here for you?"

Through the heavy ground cover, I noticed an odd collection of tall moss-covered stones jutting from the ground in the form of a circle. I wondered if this was where the Druids practiced their ancient magic.

I shook my head and looked over my shoulder at my maid. "I will return soon."

She nodded and walked back through the wood, disappearing into the thickening mist. Taking a deep breath, I forged

on, over the tangled brush scratching at my legs. A thin plume
of ebony smoke curled from a hole in the crude roof. My gaze
dropped from the smoke to the decaying old fence surrounding the yard. Several posts were missing and other sections lay
on the ground, left to rot and join the soil. Two small black
goats, a donkey and a few chickens scattered as I pushed open
the gate fashioned of willow and twine. A cold shiver snaked
up my spine.

The front door stood ajar and from inside a three-legged
dog appeared, its tail wagging in friendly greeting.

"I 'av been awaiting your arrival, Sabeline."

An ancient woman teetered through the open door with
little more dexterity than the crippled dog. To ask how she
knew of my coming was unnecessary.

"'Tis the magic of solstice that brings ye, daughter."

I could not move. My limbs seemed frozen in place, from
fear or cold, I could not say. I sensed a power drawing me
toward the door, though my feet had not moved. Determined to state my purpose, I found my voice. "I am in desperate need of your help." I kept my distance, ready to bolt
should the need arise.

"Are you afeard of me, daughter?" she asked.

I swallowed. "I have come to seek help for one unjustly
accused." I straightened my shoulders, bolstering my courage,
and held the old woman's gaze.

The crone nodded, her silvery strands of wiry hair lifting
haphazardly in the bitter winter wind. Her garish yellow smile
was marked by black gaps.

"It takes a great deal of courage to seek the powers of the
earth and sky. Make certain, child, that your desire is pure and
true. For once begun, the fates control what is to be. Come
now, join me for tea."

I glanced up at the darkening sky, ripe for snow. The old ways had diminished over the years and now, only small isolated groups of Druid believers lived to carry on the ancient teachings. Whether or not I believed in the dark magic, perhaps I might learn something that would absolve Ranulf and save my father from Benedict's terrible plan.

I entered the one-room hut and was set back on my heels by the suffocating scent of boiling vegetation mixed with a rancid odor I could not identify. I scanned the interior, noting the odd array of small animal pelts and dried herbs strung high in the rafters overhead. The dirt floor had been swept recently and a small wooden table with two chairs sat in front of the fireplace. The rest of the room stretched into dark corners that I could not see clearly and decided it was best I couldn't.

"Tell me what you seek, daughter."

The old woman shuffled to the fireplace and poked the embers beneath the iron cauldron. "It is in regard to a man," I replied, curiosity causing me to peer into her cauldron. Her gaze snapped to mine, the wrinkled flesh of her elderly face a contrast to the youthful flash in her gaze. My eyes drifted to the black pot.

"What did ye think ta see, child?" She let out a raggedy laugh.

I took a step toward the door.

Her gaze softened. "'Tis a widower's clothing I am washing, nothing more. My herb and flower water takes the stain of animal blood from the cloth. A little rosemary and anise root gets rid of the foul smell." She wagged a crooked finger at me as she stirred the contents with a stout wooden stick.

"Come close, child. You are cold, see fer yerself what's in the cauldron," she soothed.

I stepped forward and the intense heat of the fire warmed

my face, the light bouncing off the surface of the water, making it quiver as if it were alive.

I hesitantly drew the sampler from my pocket and handed it to her.

She smiled as she held the cloth lovingly in her hands.

"I was told that you might be able to tell me its meaning and if it might help me. It was my mother's," I added as an afterthought.

She nodded. "I know, my child," she stated quietly. "The words sewn into this fabric hold a very powerful magic."

I peered into the black water, seeing it stuffed with clothes, just as she'd said.

"Deep is the magic of solstice," she murmured. "It is buried far beneath the earth, awaiting the warmth of the new sun to bring new life."

As I stared into the glittering black water, its surface rippled and images appeared to begin to form. I blinked, certain I was seeing things.

"There is legend of two lovers torn apart, their passion, forbidden, could not be extinguished."

Her voice faded into the recesses of my consciousness.

Swirling in the water, I saw a man and a woman, their bodies as one, lost in their pleasure. I was entranced, uncertain whether the image was real, or simply my imagination. I could not speak for the feeling of divine ecstasy rising inside of me. I turned to ask the old woman what it meant but found myself in a cave, watching the couple.

As his hands skimmed over her flesh, I felt their roughness. Though I could not discern the couple's faces, my body grew tight as she turned on her hands and knees and he drove into her from behind. His long wheat-colored hair hid his face as he leaned over the woman, gently kissing the back of her neck.

His hands, strong like a warrior's, his wrists wrapped in leather gauntlets, held the woman's hips firm. She bowed her head, her breasts dangling like ripe pears as her body accepted him again and again. My gaze traveled over the great strength of the man's thighs, the sinewy muscle of his buttocks bunching with each determined thrust. I drew in a sharp breath. My body sensed the woman's every pleasure as if it was me.

"Pure is the seed of truth. No darkness can imprison it forever. Neither sword nor death, nor decree, not even time can tear it asunder."

The old woman's voice filtered through the swirling haze of my mind. My breath caught and my body shuddered as the man pushed hard against the woman and cried out with his release. I could barely breathe as she turned and stared at me. My gaze darted to the man now spent, tucking her in his arms, drawing her to his lap as he whispered to her. His eyes met mine and there was no doubt of their familiarity. *Ranulf.*

I stumbled as I turned away and hit the table in the crone's one-room hut. Unable to catch my breath, I collapsed in a chair.

The old woman eased her frail body into the chair across from me and folded her shaking hands.

"Tell me, daughter, what did ye see?"

I buried my face in my hands. "It is not right what I have done."

She reached across the table and her cold, wrinkled hand took mine.

"Because ye loved that which ye thought was forbidden?"

"Because I allowed my lust to destroy a man's life," I pleaded. "And so, too, my own."

"Surely, for the depth of yer grief, ye care much for this man?" she said.

Was it possible that I did not know my own heart? That

what I thought was only passion was something more? If it was so, then I might as well be dead, for I would never again have the only man who had awakened me. "I am betrothed to another." I turned my guilt-ridden gaze to hers.

"And this man, this forbidden lover, does he return yer love?"

My heart squeezed. "He says he has no regrets. But what does it matter if he feels more for me or not? He has been banished, and I must wed another. That is the way of things and I have no choice."

"Nay, daughter, there is always a choice." She patted my hand. "Ye must listen and do as I say if ye wish to turn the dark tides that would threaten yer happiness. Dunna leave out a single part, for it is a single thread, stretched through time. All of nature is connected and all of nature's strength ye will need to claim what ye desire."

"But what if my desire is nothing more than mere carnal desire?" I asked as I fished in my pocket for the coin Nuala had given me. "How can I be certain my desire is true?"

"There are no answers I can give ye, daughter. Ye must find them fer yerself."

I pushed up from the table. I was no better off than before I came, for I had no way of understanding this magic. I placed the coin on the table and started to leave. The crone grabbed my hand. She had great strength for an old woman. She studied my face with glittering dark eyes.

"What would ye sacrifice for yer deepest desire?"

I saw no escape from my fate, and, therefore, no loss attached should I speak my truth. "If I could, I would make things right. Had I the chance to speak to him, I would reveal the truth in my heart."

"If what ye say is true, daughter, then listen and heed my words well. Ye must return to your earth goddess as ye once came. Ye came into this world with no stain, no covering, an innocent to the darkness that mars the soul. She wants ye to come to her, as ye once did and speak to her these words issued from a pure and contrite heart." She handed the sampler back to me. Though the words were embroidered in ancient Gaelic, I could now read them clearly.

"These are the words that ye must speak at the hour between day and night. The Mother Goddess will know whether they issue from a pure heart. But know this, that there will be those who will attempt to thwart yer happiness. Ye must have great courage. Dunna fear, no matter what happens."

The castle seemed empty without Ranulf. I hurried directly to my chambers, considering how I could warn my father of Benedict's deceit.

Nuala was waiting, wringing her hands when I entered.

"Oh, milady." She hugged me. "It does my heart good to see you. How was your visit? Did the old crone offer you any comfort?" She went about laying out my clothes for the evening meal.

I was too tired and confused to explain, and I knew I could not face Benedict yet. "Nuala, please give my father word that I shall be in my chambers this evening as I need to rest."

"Aye, milady," she said with a curtsy.

I held the embroidered piece of cloth in my hand and wondered what I was to do if the chant did not work.

"Milady. I heard today that Sir Ranulf was called away."

I glanced up at her. "I know, and it is my doing, Nuala. I have committed a terrible sin, and I fear that I may not be able to make it right."

She was silent a moment and spoke quietly as she moved to my side. "I am not one to partake in rumors, milady, but

I heard something with my own ears that I am pressed to reveal to someone."

"Speak quickly, Nuala. Tell me what you know," I insisted.

"'Twas the afternoon before today, I heard two people whispering." Her cheeks blushed crimson. "I heard the words of passion, milady. They did not know that I stood just beyond the door of the alcove they hid within."

"And why would their conversation be of importance to me?"

"I believe one was Lord Benedict, milady."

"Go on," I urged, my interest growing.

"He spoke to her as a lover would, and she asked if he still planned to marry you."

"Did you know the woman's voice?"

She shook her head. "Nay, milady."

I nodded. It could have been anyone, from Margaret to one of the kitchen servants. However, to be so bold as to ask Benedict about the marriage she would have to be someone who was interested in more than just a quick romp.

"Speak to no one of what you've heard. It is for the safety of us all. Go now, and keep watch over my cousin. Do not let her near Benedict."

She nodded. "Ay, milady."

After Nuala left, I paced the floor, pondering what more I could do to help my father and Ranulf. My thoughts were confused, my emotions worse. Exhausted, I fell into a deep sleep.

The sound of insistent rattling awakened me. Groggy and cold, I stumbled from my bed and fumbled in the dark for the window latch. A bitter winter wind caught my hair and sent it flying in a tangled mass about my head. The sight of the pale moon near full and rising high in the midnight sky made me remember the old woman's words.

Washed in silvery moonlight and covered with snow, the deserted ward below and the village beyond lay in crystal blue-white radiance. An owl hooted from the rooftop of the stable below.

I kept my gaze on the moon, praying the clouds would not swallow its brilliance. Quickly, I slipped out of my robe and gown, letting them pool at my feet. My flesh grew numb with the cool night air, causing me to hug my arms. Fighting the chatter of my teeth, I held the cloth in my hand and raised it high as I stretched my other hand toward the midnight moon.

"Hope reborn, come with the sun
dispel the chill of darkness
bright fire of dawn
reach to our hearts
burn bright of winter's desire."

I drew my arms again to my body, holding myself against the bitter air, summoning the courage to continue.

"Enchanted stream of brilliant light
amid the crystal ground
dark traverse blending of the night
bring sweet lover's kiss
burn bright of winter's desire."

My body warmed as thoughts of Ranulf flooded my mind. Our first meeting, his palm against mine in our dance, the gleam of mischief in his eye, the smile of a man who knows much, yet has no need to boast. My skin tingled at the thought of his beard chafing my sensitive flesh. For a moment, I sensed his presence, the scent of his skin chilled with the winter, a male musky scent of leather, earth and wind. His hands upon me, his body molded to mine, drawing me close as he had our last morning together. Indeed, our first morning together, I thought, pushing away the fear that it might be the last. I continued with the Gaelic recitation, the words wrapping themselves around me, entering me, becoming one with my soul.

"No wanderer's curse
be he thus beckoned
a slave to passion's fire
return his head upon my breast
burn bright of winter's desire."

I closed my eyes and reached heavenward, my body drawn to the power of the stars and the moon sky. My skin shimmered from the dew of the snow blowing over me.

A moment later, the clouds obscured the light, and blackness as thick as pitch settled over the earth. I hurried back to my warm bed. Naked beneath the quilts, I turned my face to the open window, hoping for a celestial sign that my heart was deemed pure enough to return Ranulf to me.

I awoke the next morning to the sun streaming through the window. A drift of powdery snow blanketed my robe and gown, still lying where I had left them. I made haste to dress, not waiting for Nuala, and made my way to the private dining hall where I knew I would find my father, and I hoped Ranulf.

"I trust you are well rested, daughter," my father greeted me.

I kissed his cheek and glanced around the room. We were alone except for the servants.

"Today is a very special day for us all." He ushered me to sit at his side.

Guilt riddled my thoughts. I had to tell my father the truth and pray that he would find it in his heart to forgive my indiscretion. I grabbed his hand and leaned in close, hoping that no one would hear me. "I must speak to you in private, Father."

He patted my hand as he offered me a gentle smile.

"I understand more than you realize, my daughter. It is the day of your wedding. Of course you would have questions. I only wish your mother were—"

"No, Father, it isn't that," I interrupted.

"Surely you are not having second thoughts about me?" A low-timbred voice issued from behind us. Standing just to the left of my chair stood Benedict, looking handsome and polished. A wolf in sheep's clothing, as my mother would have said.

"Ah, good morrow, Lord Benedict. Come sit here beside me and tell me how I might quell my daughter's nerves."

Benedict smiled as he leaned between my father and me and took my hand in his. He brought it to his lips, despite my hesitation.

"You have no need for concern, milady. I am a most patient and gentle man. By the morrow's dawn, you will have forgotten all of your concerns."

I pulled my hand from his grasp, averting from his penetrating stare.

"However, it saddens me to have to be the bearer of bad news on such a joyous day as this," he remarked, bracing his arm leisurely on the back of my chair.

Both my father and I turned to give him our full attention.

"What news do you bring, milord?" my father asked, concern sobering his expression.

An icy dread formed in the pit of my stomach.

"I fear it is disturbing news about Sir Ranulf. Renegade warriors from the north attacked him and my guards as they were on their way to deliver my solstice greeting to my troops. My guards bring news that Ranulf fought bravely, but was overtaken and received a wound from which he did not recover. There was nothing more that could be done."

His eyes glittered with deceit as he spoke of Ranulf's demise. The enjoyment he took in conveying the terrible news was evident.

"With your permission, milord, I have ordered his body brought back here for proper burial. As you know, he was without home or lands."

My father nodded. "Of course."

I wanted to claw Benedict's eyes out.

He had maneuvered events to his advantage, knowing that if I challenged him he would carry through on his threat to harm my father.

My stomach roiled. How could I now explain to my father about Benedict's deceit without hope of Ranulf's word to confirm it?

Still, I was certain that if Ranulf was dead, that Benedict had a direct hand in it. Somehow, I had to find a way to prove his guilt and protect my father.

"I am light-headed, Father. Forgive me, but I must rest." Benedict held my chair as I rose.

"Shall I escort you to your chambers, milady?" Benedict offered with a slight bow.

Nuala, who had been waiting nearby, rushed to my side and took my arm.

"I shall see to her, milord."

I grabbed her hand and squeezed it, grateful for her presence.

"Rest well, my dear. I do hope you feel better. My happiness depends on yours," Benedict called after me.

My legs barely carried me as Nuala helped me to the safety of my chambers. *Ranulf, dead? Was it possible?* "The old woman said that the Earth Mother would hear the desires of my heart," I said aloud, challenging this ancient magic that had betrayed me.

"Milady, drink this. It will calm you."

Nuala handed me a cup and, without thought, I tossed it down my throat. My eyes watered as I swallowed the bitter liquid. "What is this?"

"It is a special drink, milady. Something the cook is tinkering with."

I handed her the empty cup and wiped my hand across my mouth. My chest felt on fire as I tried to speak. "I want a horse made ready. I have to go to the village. I must speak to the old crone."

"Is that wise, mi—"

"Now!" I demanded. I had to find out why the chant did not work. Was it due to the blackness of my heart? What manner of deceitful magic had the old woman lured me into? I could not—would not—marry Benedict, even if it meant my father's disgrace.

The crone looked at me, the folds of skin crinkling near her eyes as she narrowed her gaze. "Ye must be patient, Sabeline. Magic takes its own time. The goddess waits to see if your belief will falter."

I stared at the old woman. Had she not heard a word I had said? "Ranulf is *dead*. They are bringing his body even now to the castle for burial. I did exactly as you instructed. This is the day I had hoped would be one of joy and instead it is the furthest thing from it." I pressed my face into my hands, tormented by thoughts that somehow this horrible magic had played a part in Ranulf's death.

"Child, even though we canna see everything before us, does not mean that life and hope dunna exist."

★ ★ ★

Uncomforted by the old woman's words, I returned to the castle despondent, prepared to incur my father's wrath in refusing to go through with the marriage to Benedict. As I entered the village, I noted a cart covered with furs. My gaze drifted to where a man's arm dangled from beneath the furs, and my heart twisted.

"May I see the body?" I asked, pausing a moment by the cart. Benedict's guards had made haste in returning Ranulf's body to the castle.

The burly guard shook his head. "Nay, milady. Lord Benedict's orders are to let no one touch the body."

He waved me on and to protest was unwise. I wrapped my cloak about my arms, glancing back at the cart, I sensed no magic, only my dismal future void of love.

Inside the castle, preparations had begun for my twilight wedding. Great cords of evergreen draped the windows and doorways. The chandeliers were being fitted with new candles of white, and draped with greenery and berries. Bright polished red apples and oranges peeked from the boughs and brought a heady scent of freshness to the pine.

The sights and smells of the season rekindled memories of my childhood. I longed to go back to those days. My mother's tablecloth donned the head table, her wedding cloth of ivory and dusty blue adorned with ornate beadwork and embroidery. It was her wish that I use it on my wedding day. I could not picture myself in her wedding dress made of the same colors and rich detail. My eyes welled at the thought.

A low chuckle from a room in the corridor caught my attention. I crept toward it, listening intently as I moved past several rooms. I stopped at my father's parlor, shutting my eyes to the vision of Ranulf and I in the same room. From behind the door came the sounds of fervent passion.

If I was forced to marry Lord Benedict, I would no longer tolerate my own cousin's impropriety. Determined to make my position clear, I eased open the door, certain I would catch her with Benedict. I discovered Benedict, but thankfully, not with my cousin.

Seated in front of the fire, his knees spread, Benedict held a goblet in one hand, while a woman, her face obscured by the angle of his body, knelt before him.

Benedict's low moan was all the proof I needed of his indiscretion. Stunned by his ludicrous behavior, I stared in disbelief, listening to the sounds of his impending release. He grabbed the woman's hair and yanked her up to meet his face in a violent kiss as his cream drizzled over the woman's ample breasts.

At that moment, the kitchen maid opened her eyes and her horrified expression met mine. She scrambled to retrieve her clothes. Benedict merely glanced over his shoulder as he casually tucked his spent phallus back into his breeches.

"Sabeline, I am pleased you had the sense to observe. Now and again, I prefer to relieve the tensions of the day in this manner. I am a prisoner of my pleasure. I admit that I require variety. Do not be concerned if you are not prepared—it will come easier with time and practice."

The woman lowered her eyes and skirted past me.

I clenched my fists at my sides. "I will not marry you," I ground through clenched teeth.

"Because of her? Or because I am a man of great physical needs?" He swallowed his drink, dropped the cup on the table and proceeded to arrange his clothes. "I think you will find my insatiable desire will benefit you as well, if you allow yourself the freedom to enjoy it."

"I am not your judge, Benedict, when it comes to your

carnal needs. But I know you had more to do with Ranulf's death than you confess."

He offered a shrug and grinned.

"Your deceit will be found out. I will see to it. And I swear to you, if you harm my father, I will go to the king myself and reveal your plans."

He sauntered toward me with a lazy smile. His eyes were filled with hate. He tried to touch my cheek, but I turned my head. He grabbed my chin and forced his gaze to mine.

"Unless you wish to plan a funeral mass for your father, I suggest you hold your tongue, like the dutiful wife I hope you will be."

He smirked as his fingers traced my lips.

"Besides, there are much better uses for that sharp tongue."

Before I could escape, he pushed me back to the wall and brought his mouth down on mine, forcing his tongue between my lips in a brutal, sickening kiss.

I shoved him away and when he stumbled, I took the opportunity to run from the room.

"Until tonight, my love," he called out.

His mocking laughter chased me down the hall. I ran outside, sliding along the snowy path to the garden where I emptied my stomach. A swarm of black wrens, startled from their rest, swirled high in the late-day sky, a dark omen on this Solstice Day.

The flames of the traditional solstice bonfire reached high into the darkening winter sky. A thousand stars began to dot the heavens as the frost moon peered down over the castle bastion like a great dragon's eye.

The cold was no deterrent for the happy villagers, having just received my father's gifts of bread and coins. They danced around the fire, some daring to cross where they had spread the embers flat, while others tossed in tokens to the Mother Goddess, making their desires known to her. As in the ancient tradition, musicians played their crude instruments, to drive the dark night of winter away.

I stood next to my father, dressed in my mother's pale blue wedding gown. The intricate beading shimmered in the glow of the fire. On my head, I wore a crown of twigs, holly berries and evergreen, fashioned by Nuala to look like the one my mother had worn. I looked through the flames, seeing the blur of faces, none of whom I recognized but all there to witness the marriage they hoped would provide them with a better future. An icy chill swept over my shoulders and my body shivered in response.

I glanced at my father and he smiled, patting my hand, unaware of the sorrow I felt. My groom had yet to appear so that we could begin the procession to the castle chapel where the vicar awaited to perform the sacred ceremony.

Across the castle yard, I heard the muted thunder of horses. Seven dark figures emerged from the mist of the outer ward, shadowed by the night, frozen puffs of breath snorting from their black horses.

The jovial chatter of the crowd subsided and the musicians ceased their playing. All eyes were turned on the lead figure as he drew his horse to a stop and his guards, still mounted, positioned themselves around the perimeter of the crowd. I squeezed my father's hand.

Benedict dismounted his steed and pushed his way through the crowd. He wore a green velvet surcoat that drew attention to the breadth of his shoulders. He wore his cape with one side draped over his shoulder, to reveal the polished sword hung at his hip. His gait was determined and sure.

His steady gaze held mine as he strode toward us. Many of

the guests stared in awe at his entrance and forgot to bow as he passed by. He had them in the palm of his hand with his noble air, just as he had my father. However, I knew his true character and vowed to find a way to reveal his treachery.

He stopped and knelt before my father.

"Welcome, my son. Arise, and meet your bride," my father spoke.

"My lord," he said and flashed me his radiant smile.

"You are a vision, milady Sabeline. I am a most fortunate man."

A cheer went up from the crowd as he knelt and kissed my hand. The musicians began again their music, stirring the villagers to dance and hold their candles high to begin the procession.

An explosion of light burst from the bonfire, causing the fire to rise ever higher into the sky. Cautious whispers tittered through the crowd as the revelers backed away. In the midst of the flame, the image of two lovers appeared. Their features at first obscured by the bright light, I recognized them immediately as the couple I'd seen in the old woman's cauldron. The rippling image of the couple began to clarify and as it did, my cheeks grew warm with the realization that it was Ranulf and me.

My father turned to me, his face drawn in anger. The shame of my secret affair was now disclosed to the entire kingdom. Why was the old crone allowing this to happen? Benedict now had the right to refuse to marry me, and worse, he could have me stoned to death for my infidelity. I could only stare into the flames, unable to speak.

"Daughter, have you anything to say in your defense?" my father asked, his voice revealing his disappointment.

I could deny it, calling it a form of trickery, or I could admit the truth and join Ranulf in the hereafter. I glanced at Benedict, his sinister gaze awaiting my word. I looked at my father. "It is true. I had one night of passion with a man I thought was my intended. But that one night filled me with more passion and love than I could possibly have in a lifetime with this man."

Low murmurs sounded from the crowd and my father held up his hand to silence them. I held Benedict's hard gaze.

"Baron, though it pains me to say it, by authority of the king and by the tradition of your people, I stand as a betrayed groom and accuse your daughter of infidelity, punishable by stoning."

The crowd's attention, and too my father's, turned to me. My eyes welled as I searched the crowd, hoping that the old woman would come forth and make things right.

To my relief, I spotted the old woman as she stepped from the crowd and approached the bonfire, her eyes glistening in the fire's glow. I held my breath, unsure of what would happen next. The old crone lifted her gnarled hands to the sky.

"Hope reborn, come with the sun
dispel the chill of darkness
bright fire of dawn
reach to our hearts
burn bright of winter's desire."

The image in the fire shifted, becoming Ranulf alone, standing straight and tall in his warrior's garb, his breastplate reflecting the flames. The onlookers gasped quietly and shielded their eyes.

"What trickery is this?" my father bellowed.

I stared at the image, unmoving and yet so lifelike. My curious gaze met the old woman's toothless grin.

"No trickery, milord," the woman spoke. "'Tis the truth

of the new moon. Its light comes to dispel the darkness of deception."

"This woman is a witch," Benedict called out to the crowd as he grabbed my arm and drew me against his side.

"She bears no ill will." I raised my voice to the crowd. "Her wisdom in this village is well known."

"You will speak when I tell you, wench, and only then," Benedict growled, shoving his face to mine and yanking hard on my arm.

He turned from the crowd, dragging me with him. He stopped in his tracks, and I was brought up short.

"What is this?" Fear was etched in Benedict's voice. "You are but a figment of magic, nothing more."

I looked around his shoulder and could not believe my eyes.

Ranulf's fist met Benedict's face, causing him to spiral backward, releasing me as he fell on his backside.

No ghost could perform such an act. My heart began to pound with hope.

"Guards!" both my father and Benedict shouted, and we were immediately surrounded by a circle of drawn swords.

"Greater deception than infidelity marks this night, Baron Durwain," Ranulf began. "I was sent away, blackmailed by this man, who accuses your daughter of infidelity. Lord Benedict's plan to have me killed was thwarted when this old woman found me left for dead in the woods. It was her care that nursed me back to health and here I am, living proof of this man's treachery. If there is guilt to be slung, then I pledge my undying allegiance to you, Baron, and to my king. But I cannot deny the depth of love I have for your daughter. And it is that love for which I was sent away, that and my knowledge of Benedict's plan to assassinate you once this marriage was established."

"You have no proof of such lies. I have no way of knowing how you returned from the dead, but you will now suffer the consequence of your infidelity." Benedict scrambled to his feet.

"I am a witness to the threat you made upon my father and me," I spoke, taking my father's hand. "I beg your forgiveness, milord. But I have never loved this man, not as I do Lord Ranulf. And I wanted to tell you of his plan, but he threatened to kill you if I did. With Ranulf gone, I had no other witnesses."

"Ah, but you always did, cousin." Margaret stepped from the crowd and came to my side. "Benedict revealed to me his plan in my chambers."

"She lies!" Benedict started for his sword. Ranulf stepped forward and stopped him.

"Do you deny telling my father and me of Ranulf's death?" I asked as Ranulf took the sword from Benedict's belt. My father's guards proceeded to disarm Benedict's men. My body trembled, desiring to step into Ranulf's embrace.

"This is true, Lord Benedict, you spoke those very words this morning." My father nodded to one of his guards. "Lock him away until he can be questioned. The king will need to be apprised."

I hugged my father's neck.

"You have placed me in a predicament, Sabeline," he spoke softly against my hair. "I had an alliance with the king."

The old crone appeared at my side, tugging on my arm.

I looked at Ranulf, unsure of what the future would bring, but overjoyed that he was alive. The woman grabbed my hand and Ranulf's, drawing them together. She placed her other hand on my stomach.

"As was foretold in the days of old, return him to my breast, burn bright with winter's desire." She held her fingers to the heavens, pointing to the full moon. "This is the seed of your people, your inheritance. Born of a man of virtue and blessed by winter's desire."

She looked then at my father. "Your line lives through this union, milord. It is fate. The ancients have willed it, *so mote it be.*"

My father looked from the old woman to me. "Is this your desire, my daughter?"

"Milord." Ranulf knelt before my father. "The king had promised me a castle and land, just to the south, over the border region. We would not be far from Sabeline's home and I would see that the king accepts this alliance in his name. Under the circumstances, Benedict's plan will no doubt be viewed as treason. With your permission, I ask in the name of the king, for your daughter's hand in marriage and swear my oath that I will care for her to the day I die."

The old woman clapped her hands and smiled as she glanced up at my father.

"Rise, my son," my father spoke softly and then turned to address the crowd. "Let us proceed then with the wedding celebration," he called aloud. He took the old crone's arm, escorting her to the castle entrance.

I looked up at the moon, Ranulf's hand firmly in mine as we followed and silently thanked the Mother Goddess, believing again in the magic of the season.

In the months that followed, I spent my nights free to enjoy my handsome husband in our new home. My belly had begun to show the first evidence of the child I carried…Ranulf's child.

"You spoil me with such attention, milord." I sighed, turning my head to offer him my neck. His chuckle sent a ripple of anticipation over my flesh.

"Then I shall spoil you rotten." He grinned. planting kisses between my swollen breasts as he left a reverent kiss on my small protruding belly. "You are sure it is safe?" He glanced up at me, concern flickering in his eyes.

"The nurse said to be cautious, but it is early yet." I smoothed my hand over his dark blond hair, silently thanking the ancients for returning him to me.

I abandoned myself to his tongue, able, as always, to perform such magic between my thighs. His beard brushed my sensitive flesh until my body grew tight with need.

He drew me to his lap and I took him deep inside. As I looked into his gentle eyes, so filled with love, I could hear the old woman's chant echoing in my mind.

"Bring sweet lover's kiss…"

The fierce winter wind shook the shutters and our sighs blended with its haunting moan. I gripped Ranulf's shoulders, shoulders that would carry the decisions of a kingdom, as well as his child, one day. The thought of it made me cry out his name as we gave way to a shattering, mutual release.

My husband drew me into his embrace and lay his head against my breast.

"Return his head upon my breast." The Druid woman's voice tickled my memory. I hugged Ranulf close, opening my eyes to glance at the sampler, now framed and hanging above the fireplace in our castle chamber. For our children, and the sons and daughters after them, the promise of these words, summoned by the ancients, would always remain.

"So mote it be."

★ ★ ★ ★ ★

MIDNIGHT WHISPERS
by
Charlotte Featherstone

1

THE CRACKLING OF WOOD IN THE HEARTH AND the glowing embers that lay scattered on the warm bricks beckoned her, drawing her into their mysterious depths. In the flickering flames she saw figures melding and disappearing, then flaring to life once again. The smell of cinnamon, cardamom and pine needles boiling in the black iron pot over the fire delicately scented the air, soothing her, bringing her back to a time when life seemed less complicated, her path sure and straight, and set.

The rhythmic motion of her fingers kneading the bread on the floured wooden table lulled her further, until she was hypnotized by the twin flames that leaped up from the blackening log. They twined and tangled then parted. Two separate entities, born of the same desire.

A daydream, she told herself as she mindlessly kneaded the soft dough. A dream. Nothing more. A heart's deepest desire; a woman's most secret yearning.

In the blue flicker she saw him. Her David. His smile warm, his eyes so blue and clear. He sat atop his white horse wearing his red regimentals, reminding her of a modern-day knight. He was waving to her, just as he had that day, the last time she had seen him.

"I'll come back to you, my love. I swear it."

His voice seemed to call out to her from the flames, and shaking her head, she dislodged the image of her dead husband. Flipping the dough over, she dusted the mound with more flour while blowing away an errant strand of hair from her sweating brow as she continued to knead and think. Thoughts she should not entertain. Thoughts, that of late, would not be quieted, but instead had steadfastly grown until they occupied almost every waking and sleeping minute of her lonely existence.

Thoughts that could never be, no matter how much she wished it could be different.

It was warm in the cottage, despite the open window above the porcelain sink. The late-December wind that blew in through the lace curtains should have cooled her, but Sinead felt so very warm, cocooned in the small cottage that sat at the edge of the village and a heavily wooded forest.

The sun was setting, streaking in dark pinks and purples across the sky, the vivid colors disappearing behind the tops of the naked tree branches. Snow fell gently, like cotton fluff, from the heavy gray clouds to cover the earth in a blanket of white—as soft and beckoning as the finest goose down.

Sinead glanced away from the falling snow, and a flash of gold caught her eye as she picked up the dough and set it into a bowl to rise. *Her wedding band*. Her fingers dusted white with flour, she held her hand up, studying the simple gold ring in the light cast by the fire. It was a reminder of a past, the mark of a new life that had never had a chance to grow, the visual of a commitment and love that defied even the grave.

A haunting reminder. A source of guilt. Always the shame returned when she saw the gold band David had slipped onto her finger when he had spoken his vows to her. Vows that were never intended to be broken. Vows she had clutched steadfastly to her heart. Yet the words *with my body, I thee worship* had taken on new meaning whenever she heard them in her thoughts.

After dunking her hands in warm water, Sinead wiped them on her apron and turned to the little brick oven where a loaf of bread, golden brown and steaming hot, was waiting to be pulled out with the long-handled paddle.

"Let me get that."

The deep, resonant drawl skated along her skin, and she glanced once more at the band on her finger, fighting the ripple of awakening that coursed through her body.

She did not turn to greet him. She did not want to see him, did not want to feel his hand brush against hers as he took the paddle from her. She did not want to smell him, the scent of clean male sweat and freshly laundered cambric. She did not want to know the sensation of his broad chest engulfing her back; his hands, beautiful and strong snaking around her middle. She did not want to see that sinful mouth and imagine the kind of pleasure it could bring her.

She had thought too many times of those things, dreamed of them too many times. In her mind she had tasted his mouth, his tongue against hers. She knew what she would taste—*man*. She knew how his hands would feel on her naked body—strong, weathered, *masculine*.

With her back to him, she composed herself, willing her body under control, her mind from envisioning him overtop her, dominating her with his strength and a muscled body she knew would sexually master hers.

She had dreamed of that body, tall and thick and so warm. She had fantasized about succumbing to him, allowing him to have her. She craved his strength, his masculinity. She yearned to be a woman with him—*his* woman, in every sense of the word.

He was the opposite of David, yet no less intriguing. Perhaps, if she were being honest with herself, *he* was the most captivating and arousing man she had ever met. And every moment spent in his company was a lesson in torture, for she could not allow herself to discover the pleasures of his body loving hers.

The wood that he had just cut fell with a thud to the stone floor. The noise was followed by the tread of his boots across the small space between the hearth and the kitchen. Their fingers touched, brushing skin against skin. His so cold and roughened by the elements; hers warm, soft, slipping supplely between his like his body would slip inside hers, then out, only to slide deep within once again with a powerful thrust that would at once inflame, yet soothe.

Her core clenched in memory, her body trembling with the need to feel passion once again. She hungered for it, this physical intimacy with another human being. The warmth of being touched, held, whispered to. The heavy feel of a man on top of her, her hair wrapped around his hand, her chin tilted to receive the thrust of his tongue as he filled her with his phallus.

She had not been touched by a man in three years. *So long…*

Sweat trickled down her neck, sneaking beneath the ribbed bodice of her serviceable work gown until she felt it settle between her breasts. He would know her thoughts. He always knew. He would hear her labored breathing, recognize the flush in her cheeks, see her nipples hardened beneath her worn corset and thin cotton gown.

He would read her wicked thoughts, the vision of the two of them naked, mating like animals. He would know because he watched her. He always watched her with those black, mysterious eyes that were fathomless in their depths.

Finally, Sinead allowed her held breath to escape when he did not let his touch linger as he usually did. In the past, even the barest brush of their skin had been cause for him to stop and look at her. Sometimes he would reach out to touch her cheek, but always he would check himself, drawing his hand away and replacing it at his side. Sometimes, she was relieved when he stopped himself. Other times she was left aching, her body crying out for the simple touch of a man's hand against her skin.

Kieran's touch. It had been this way for months now, her wanting Kieran—needing him—as more than a protector and helper.

Ignoring her suffering, he slipped the paddle beneath the round loaf, pulling the fresh-baked bread from the oven onto a wooden platter before replacing the paddle beside the brick hearth.

"Thank you," she said, busying herself with a coarse brush and a little dish of melted butter. "Will you not take it home for your dinner tonight?"

There was a pause, where only his breath, ragged and fevered, could be heard. *Won't you invite me to stay?* She heard his silent question, but did not look up from the golden butter that trickled over the top of the freshly baked loaf.

"I made some stew that would go well with it. 'Tis cold today, and you've worked all day long outside. It's the least I could do in payment for all your hard work."

Swallowing hard, she evaded his gaze, which she knew would be narrowed at her. He did not want her charity. He would not take a pence from her, even though he had repaired the neglected cottage and seen to the winter preparations. Her root cellar was full of potatoes and turnips, carrots and onions.

The larder full of flour, butter and eggs. The woodshed was stocked with thick dry logs that would see her warm the winter through.

He had seen to her home, her safety, her comfort. But she dared not pay him with anything other than a full belly and conversation.

As she suspected, he said nothing as he walked past her and started stacking the logs in a pile beside the hearth. On the glowing embers, he tossed two thick logs and stirred the coals, the dry wood catching, the flames crackling, licking their way up the chimney.

From beneath her lashes, Sinead watched him, bent on his haunches, his muscular back rolling beneath the thin long-sleeved cambric shirt. His black hair, long and untamed, grazed his broad shoulders as they moved fluidly with his movements.

Kieran Thompson was as wild and black as the meaning behind his Gaelic name. Dark and quiet. Mysterious and dangerous. He was the first man since David who made her burn. The *only* man who had awakened the darker sexual needs inside her.

With David she had been a curious virgin, an inexperienced but eager lover. With Kieran, she would be a woman, not afraid to ask for what she wanted, nor afraid to take when offered. She would not blush at the sharing of her body with another, but indulge in the passion and pleasure to be found.

And there would be passion, and much pleasure, with Kieran, of that she was certain.

Except, to take what he offered would be a betrayal to David. To the vows she had said with such fervor. And yet, she knew her David was not coming back to her.

Needing to free her mind, Sinead reached around her waist and untied her apron, then laid it on the worn worktable.

Crossing the small kitchen, she stood before the window that faced the forest. The trees were heavy with snow, the sun now below the horizon, casting gray and black shadows over the earth. The windowpanes were ice covered, streaked with fernlike lines of frosted snowflakes. Reaching out, she traced the path of one line, only to have a dark hand placed overtop hers. Slowly, Kieran's forefinger traced her fingers, one by one, then slipped down to her hand, where he traced the delicate blue veins beneath her pale skin.

For several long seconds, she closed her eyes, savoring the gentle, erotic play of his hand on hers. His finger was callused, rough, yet masculine and strong. She thought of those hands touching her more intimately, and she whimpered when she felt his finger slip to her wrist where he drew tiny circles over her bounding pulse.

Greedily, she accepted his touch, absorbed it, clutching the memory for safekeeping where she could relive this moment night after night.

"You grow more lovely day after day. You intoxicate me until I cannot think of anything other than you."

"Please don't—"

"I see it in your eyes. You want this. You've wanted it to happen since that first day I came to the cottage."

She shook her head, denying the truth.

"*I've* wanted it, Sinead, your body, your warmth. I've dreamed of having you, dominating you, making you mine."

"Do you know what they say about me in the village?" she asked, her voice sounding breathless.

His head dropped down beside hers. She heard him inhale deeply of her hair, then felt his chin brush her unbound hair. "Aye, I know what they call you. *Witch*. You enticed your husband, the second son of a noble family, with little more than a wicked spell and the promise of your luscious body. You made him give up everything for you, his family, his fortune, his friends, in order to have you as his wife." Lips, warm and strong caressed the column of her throat in the softest of invitations. "Black widow," he continued, "for they believe that after lying with you, you cast another spell to kill him. They say it was not the battle in the Crimea that saw to your husband's demise, but the spell of your body and your cursed love. They say you draw unsuspecting men into your sensual web where you seduce them, break them...*fuck* them," he whispered darkly.

She shivered. He was coarse, yet her body responded as never before. Between her thighs she was wet, with just the sound of his voice whispered huskily in her ear. What if he were to touch her? What havoc he would cause inside her body, her soul.

"They say that while in the glimmer of ecstasy you enchant these men, you take their lives—the cost of sampling your abundant charms and sensual mystery."

"And are you not worried that you may turn out to be my next prey?"

"I do not believe in idle village gossip, nor the hurtful words of women who are filled with jealousy and intent on ruining the reputation of a good woman. And if it were indeed, true, that you are a merciless black widow who can cast spells and enchantments, I would risk it, just for a chance to share one night inside your body."

"You would give up your life, to...to—"

"Take you?" he asked. "What other kind of death could a man wish for, Sinead, than to die between the thighs of the woman he has waited for so patiently? Do you want that, Sinead?" he asked in a dark whisper that caressed her neck. "Me between your thighs fucking you?"

Rubbing her finger along the worn wedding band, she strove to put out of her mind the image of Kieran taking her hard. "I cannot. You must know why."

"How much longer will you deny yourself the pleasure you crave?" His breath was moist against her ear, the words warming her blood like the finest wine. "How much longer will you go on wanting, yearning? Outside, the world goes on around you, yet you continue to live inside this cottage, dying a little bit more day after day, letting the idiot talk of villagers keep you prisoner inside this house—inside this body made for loving and passion. This body made for me."

"No!" Shaking her head, she tried to pull her hand away from his, but he held her tighter, entwining his fingers with hers, clutching her tight as he pressed his chest firmly into her back.

"How long, Sinead? How long since you've felt the touch of a man? How many times have you thought of my hands on you, caressing you? How many times have you touched yourself, dreaming it was me?"

"You mustn't say such things."

"Why? Because it makes your cunt weep?"

"*Kieran!*" she cried, grasping his wrist as he palmed her sex through her skirts. She moaned as he cupped her, and instead of halting his fingers, she shoved his hand farther between her thighs so that his large palm was covering her mons.

"How many times, Sinead, have you looked at my mouth and wondered what it would feel like moving over your quim? How many times have you thought of my tongue flicking over your clitoris, wondering how it would feel, wondering if I could pleasure you like no other lover you've ever had." His hand reached deeper between her thighs and despite the layers of her skirt and petticoats she felt him knead her sex. "Do you wonder at nights when you are alone in your bed with your fingers filling your empty quim, if I could take you places you never thought to go, or make you do things you've never thought of, heard of…or seen? Have you ever dreamed of just letting go?"

She could not admit to anything, could not indulge in this attraction to Kieran. She was a widow who had loved her husband, but that was not the only thing holding her back from accepting what Kieran so blatantly offered. It was Kieran himself. His position, as the officer of her husband; his age, seven years her junior. It was the dangerous sensuality lurking so close to his surface that frightened her. Not frightened her in the sense that he would hurt her or force her, but rather, the sense that he might be able to bring forth the secret desires she carefully kept buried within her.

On so many levels he was wrong for her. Yet, on many others, he was so right.

"I wonder," he whispered as his lips nuzzled the shell of her ear, "how many times we have sat politely across from each other at the table in this very cottage, eating dinner, while mentally undressing the other and dreaming of fucking on that table. Just this morning, Sinead, I thought of laying you down, lifting your skirts and tasting your cunt."

Her legs weakened and she reflexively softened against him. David had never spoken in such a way.

"Why do you deny yourself?" he asked, rubbing his hand overtop her skirt, pressing the heel of his hand into her mons, kneading her in a slow but commanding rhythm, so that she could do nothing but respond with a sigh, and the trembling of her fingers against his wrist, which no longer knew what to do—hold him there or shove him away.

"He is not coming back, Sinead. He is dead. But you are not. You're still very much alive."

"Don't…don't speak that way—"

He didn't let her finish, but turned her around and brought her hard up against the wall, cupping her face and holding her for his kiss. He did not wait for her acceptance, but took what he wanted.

Sinead stiffened as he plunged his tongue between her lips. Shock, memory, the softening of assent. With a flick of her tongue against his, the kiss turned carnal and hard—desperate. She was clinging to his shoulders, digging her nails into his back. His hands were in her hair, tugging pins free, then they were gliding down her throat, his thumbs stroking the cords in her neck as his mouth moved greedily over hers, his tongue plunging deeper, demanding that she give him everything she fought to hold back.

Never had she felt more sensual and beautiful—womanly— than at this moment, pressed up against the wall, pinned by Kieran's body as his hands awakened her dormant body.

So long…it had been so long since she'd been touched, and she was starved for it. Yet it had never felt this way. This raw. This savage.

His hands were everywhere, traversing her body with skill and familiarity, making her pant and press into him, searching for more. He answered her, shoving his hips into her belly where she felt the hard outline of his sex through the rough woolen trousers he wore. She groaned into his mouth, clutching him tighter, allowing her nails to score down his broad back.

Tearing his mouth from hers, he reached for her bodice, pulling the string until the ruched cotton gaped open, exposing her worn corset. He tore at it, ripping it in half so that her breasts spilled out into his hands, and his face was immediately buried between them, his tongue licking a hot trail to her nipple where he flicked the sensitive tip, making her cry out.

"Kieran, God, yes," she cried, grasping handfuls of his onyx-colored hair, as he suckled her nipple hard between his lips. Cupping both her breasts, he lifted them to his lips, hungrily taking her into his mouth. With her head resting against the wall, she watched him, his tongue laving her, his white teeth gently tugging at her nipples, making them turgid, until they yearned for rougher play. Knowing what she wanted, he took a nipple and bit teasingly, sending her womb aching. Her hand flew to her belly.

"Are you wet?" he asked, releasing her breasts. His eyes were black, the pupils indistinguishable, the depths fathomless. "Sinead? Are you wet for me?"

Immobile, she could do nothing but hold his gaze as his hands worked beneath her skirt and petticoats, raising them until she could feel his fingers on her thighs, gliding up her serviceable stockings, to her garters where her sex was wet and ready—for his hands and mouth and the large phallus she felt pushing insistently into her belly.

When his hand finally cupped her through the slit in her drawers, she gasped and reached out for the curtain, holding tight when her legs threatened to abandon her. She waited for his touch while he watched her as he toyed with her— teasing her. She was trembling, nearly begging, but he saved a measure of humility by stroking her, parting her sex with one controlling stroke.

His touch was like the heat from the fire on cold fingers. It stung yet felt so wonderful. She arched up, inviting him further and he grinned, slipping his finger between her folds, teasingly stroking her in circles around her sex.

"Is this where you want me?" He filled her, not with one finger, but two, in a swift, possessive thrust. The invasion of him in her body, the way he did not gingerly test her with one finger made her quim wetter, arousing her until all she could hear was the heavy drum of blood in her ears. When he felt the wetness flow between his fingers, he gave her one more of his callused fingers and she gasped, clutching wildly at the curtain.

Sinead turned to see her hand, white knuckled, gripping the linen drapery, the gold band glinting in the firelight—a reminder, a symbol, a mockery of what she was doing.

"Don't," she whispered, shoving him away. When he looked up at her, she turned from him, trying to gather her corset to cover her breasts. Her back was to him, and she heard him, breathing in harsh, short pants as if he had been running.

His hands wrapped around her shoulders, and his lips found her ear. "He is dead, Sinead. There is no question about that. The only question that remains is, when will *you* begin living once again?"

2

DAVID PEMBROOKE'S FACE SWAM BEHIND KIERAN'S closed lids. The last person he wished to see was his old lieutenant, the husband of the woman he had loved for so long. How could he dream of Pembrooke when the scent of his wife's sex lingered on his fingers? When his body was coiled so tightly from unspent lust?

Groaning, Kieran rolled onto his stomach, burying his face in the pillow, trying to smother the memories flooding his mind. Those days were better left dead and buried. Sometimes he was haunted by the sound of the guns, sometimes the wails of dying men. Sometimes, like tonight, it was the day that fate had finally come to visit him.

He drifted off like that, his face covered in the crisp white cotton pillow slip; only, when he entered the realm of sleep he was no longer in his cottage, but someplace else. *Hell.* He did not want to go back there, but the dream called him forth, and unable to escape, he followed where the vision led…

Burying his face deep into the coarse woolen collar of his coat, Kieran fought the bone-racking chill that had settled deep in his marrow. Like the crisp, white frost on the ground, the cold blanketed him, penetrating flesh and bone, slowing his blood. Teeth chattering uncontrollably, he locked his jaw, conserving every bit of energy he possessed for the task he knew lay ahead of him.

But it was cold. *So cold*.

His boots were sodden, soaked with melted snow and caked with mud. He could no longer feel his toes. A blessing that, since he'd developed the painful condition of trench foot days before. Better to be numb by frostbite than to feel the flesh slowly being eaten away from his toes and heels.

Next would be trench mouth, and God help him, dysentery. Or worse, cholera. With winter approaching, the cold would halt the spread of disease through the encampment. But then, the cold brought with it its own set of evils.

He did not relish the idea of freezing to death in this dark and muddy hole he'd been forced to live in.

The wind picked up, howling over their heads, the hilled earth at least protecting them from the biting wind—a small favor from heaven. But only a small reprieve, for it had begun to snow again. It wasn't the light dusting of flurries of a week ago, but the heavy stuff of winter in Balaklava.

Body trembling, belly growling, he sought to find a place within himself that the elements could not reach. He was dying. He knew that. Slowly. Painfully. He and the others would not survive the winter if clothing and rations did not make their way to them. But the much-needed supplies would never reach them if they did not dispose of the Cossack army that was lying in wait for them across the field.

Fingers numb, Kieran snaked them deeper into the frayed, muddy cuffs of his overcoat. No longer able to hold his gun, he put it between his legs, letting his head rest against the barrel, wondering if it would not be better to pull the trigger and be done with it.

He had slept this way more nights than he could recall. In the beginning he had kept track of the days and nights with a scratch on the wooden gun shaft. He no longer continued to count, for the days all blended into a number that seemed infinite.

The metal barrel was cold against his dirty brow, and his hair was hanging in icy clumps against his forehead and neck. Yet despite the discomfort, exhaustion won out, and he allowed his eyelids to drop, letting his guard down only enough to doze. *Sleep.*

He wanted to sleep in a warm, soft bed, his belly full, a roaring fire in the hearth, a woman in his arms, her body warming his. Instead, he was in a waterlogged trench in the midst of the Crimean War, freezing and starving, surrounded by corpses in various states of decomposition.

Nothing went to waste in war. Not even dead bodies. With the coming of winter, everything would be frozen, and so too would the bodies, which would be used to provide shelter from the blind artillery fire that came at them nightly. Like the shields of the knights of old, the bodies were their defense, blocking enemy bullets that rained down on them like the arrows of hundreds of archers.

They had all pledged their bodies to one another to use in any way that might aid their cause. And while there was acceptance for what was needed, the horror as they banked the sides of the trenches with the bodies of their comrades so that they would absorb the Russian gunfire still sickened each and every one of them.

That, more than anything, disturbed Kieran. To see the bodies of his fallen comrades—his brothers in the trenches— lined up like sandbags.

Christ, they needed supplies, and soon. He had always been of strong mind and body, yet even he was wavering in the belief that they might be saved.

Three feet away from him, he heard the call of death, the familiar rattle of breaths through fluid-filled lungs. Hastings would be going home tonight. His leg wound had festered, the poison spreading to his blood. His body raged with fever and his mind raved with madness. The army surgeon had given up on him, refusing to use their limited medical supplies on a patient who would only succumb. They each had taken turns staying with him, holding their fellow soldier throughout the night, praying that his end would come swiftly. But it had not come quick enough, in Kieran's opinion.

Death hovered over them like an ominous cloud, and Kieran found himself wondering more and more when it would come to claim him.

"O'Leary," someone whispered. "You're a good Catholic, give Hastings his rites, man. He's going."

There was a shuffling of bodies, the murmured litany of prayers, followed by the haunting rattle of Hastings's last breath.

With Hastings gone, there was more dead among them than living.

"It'll be dark soon," said the youngest among them as he looked up at the twilight sky that was marked with a full, silver moon that hung heavily in the sky.

" 'Tis the winter solstice," Kieran replied, thinking back to his Celtic upbringing and his favorite childhood story. "The priestess will protect us, just as she saved her soldier all those centuries ago. Tonight she watches over us, guarding us well."

"Aye, she will," the young man named Drummond replied. "I've been thinking of home, and the solstice gathering in my village in Dunkirk. There will be feasting and drinking, and bonfires high enough to light the sky for miles around. And lasses. The most bonnie lasses you've ever laid eyes on—with dancing eyes and mouths cherry red from the cold, that they'll let you warm up with yours. Bonnie lasses," he whispered brokenly.

"Next solstice you will be there, Drummond, with *two* lasses," Kieran teased.

"I don't know." Kieran could hear the trembling, the terror in the seventeen-year-old's voice. "They'll be firing at us soon. The gunshots always start once the moon reaches above that bank of trees."

Kieran reached for the boy and put his arm around his neck. "Stay by my side and do as I say. If the priestess canna keep you alive tonight, then I will."

Drummond nodded and looked away, but not before Kieran saw the shimmer in his eyes. The boy was right, 'twas twilight, and soon he and his commanding officer would leave the trench to lay the copper wire for the desperately needed landline. The telegraph was their only means of winning ground in the stalemate they had been in with the Cossacks for weeks.

Correspondence was desperately needed to alert the advancing cavalry that the area had not yet been secured. If the Hussars were to arrive before the area had been cleared of the enemy, it would be disastrous.

"Goddamn British army," Macintosh muttered. "Send us out here in the dead of winter with nothing more than a thin coat. Fucking rations are frozen—even the goddamn rats have frozen in the mud. I might have thought of eating one of the blessed things if we had a fire to cook it on."

"Aye," someone answered him. "And when we leave this godforsaken place, I'm going to kill as many Cossacks as I can

and strip them bare. At least the czar has seen to properly out-
fitting *his* army. And then, when I have draped myself in furs
and blankets, I'll take their vodka and fill me belly full of it."

"Anyone got a light?" came a disembodied voice.

"No light," came the lieutenant's deep voice. "Damn
Cossacks are out. Can you not hear them?"

"Aye, I hear the bastards," Macintosh muttered, "laughing
and singing, drinking their vodka. At least their bodies are
warm, and their stomachs are full of fire from drink."

"Quit your bellyaching, Macintosh," the lieutenant commanded. "The supply wagon will be here within a few days."

"We'll be frozen before then."

"You'll be dead from my bullet if you don't watch it."

Macintosh shut his mouth. Lieutenant Pembrooke was not
a man to be argued with. Funny, since Kieran, upon first
meeting his senior officer, had thought the fair-haired second
son of an aristocrat too young and too prissy to lead a
company of unruly ragtag soldiers from the wilds of Ireland,
Scotland and northern England. With Celtic superstitions
and hard-hewn minds and bodies like their warrior ancestors,
the last thing he and the others had wanted was a foppish, ef-
feminate Englishman running the show.

Yet David Pembrooke had held his own against them, earning
their admiration, and, more important, their loyalty. There was
nothing Kieran would not do for his lieutenant—nothing.

Lieutenant Pembrooke was the furthest thing from effemi-
nate, or foppish. Kieran had seen that firsthand when the lieutenant had led a charge against the Russians, cutting them
down with his sword as if they were nothing more than wheat
chaff.

"You've got about an hour before the firing starts, spend
it as you will, men," Pembrooke commanded.

"Think any of those Gypsy whores the Cossacks drag with them from camp to camp would be inclined to come to our trench?" Macintosh asked with a wicked lilt in his Scottish accent.

Pembrooke laughed and shifted against the snow-covered side of the trench. "Save your energy, my friend, for the battle ahead. The spoils of war will soon be awarded. Use your hand if need be, but do not count on the Gypsies this night."

"I canna feel my damn hand," Macintosh grumbled, "or I would."

"O'Halloran, sing us a tune," the lieutenant commanded of the Irishman with the deep baritone voice.

"It's the solstice, sir. I would sing something to celebrate it and appease the priestess who will watch over us this night."

"I am aware it is the solstice. My wife, she always liked to celebrate it. It was her favorite time of year," Pembrooke murmured. A distant sound to his voice muffled his words. "She told me the story of this priestess you speak of. *Sinead*." He whispered his wife's name as he tilted his face to the sky and closed his eyes. The sound was full of longing and reverence, and Kieran pressed his eyes shut, shutting out the heartache he heard in his officer's voice. Hearing that love, that longing, killed him.

"I can still see her sitting by the fire, her hair draped over her shoulder, a smile on her lips. The sort each woman has when she tells a story of star-crossed lovers, a smile that is at once sad, yet wistful." Pembrooke shook his head, as if trying to dispel the memory. "I wonder what she is doing now? At this very moment in time. I can see her walking to the standing stones that lie amongst an oak grove at the edge of the village, the snow gently falling around her as the light from the bonfires shines radiantly on her red hair. Perhaps," he murmured, "we are both looking up into the night sky and seeing the exact same star. Perhaps she is remembering sharing the story of her Druid priestess, wondering if I remember it. Perhaps she is beckoning her priestess now to watch over us."

"To Mrs. Pembrooke, then," O'Halloran said. "May the priestess hear her prayers." Quietly, the Irishman began the first bars of a traditional Irish winter tune, "The Wexford Carol," and Kieran settled against the snow-covered mud wall of the trench to await the night's work.

Reaching into his jacket pocket, Kieran withdrew his last cheroot and lit it with his cold, fumbling fingers. When the end glowed red, he inhaled a long draw of it, then reached into the breast pocket of his uniform jacket and retrieved the wrinkled and faded picture of the woman who kept him alive in this hell.

She had become his sole reason for living. Her face. Her letters. The dreams of her. The fantasies of them together. Even now he thought of warming himself in her inviting body—stealing her heat, her heart—for himself.

The woman looked out at him, her skin pale and pure. His filthy, blackened fingers traced over her porcelain skin that reminded him how dirty he was to feel this way, to think these thoughts—to crave the sexual urges of his body.

If you were mine...

Mentally, he composed a love letter to her while he held the glowing end of his smoke to the picture, lighting the woman's face as he stared at her, his thumb continually tracing the outline of her stunningly beautiful face in a fruitless search for a physical connection with her.

My darling, I look at this picture of you every day, wishing somehow that you might magically appear before me. I have every line, every curve of your beautiful face memorized. The tilt of your head, the shape of your mouth.

I dream of the way your lips will part beneath mine, the taste of you. The reception of your warm embrace when I at last arrive back home, on English soil, tired and broken. I dream of that night, that homecoming.

If only he could write to her of such things. If only she were his. There would be no homecoming for him, no love from her arms, for she belonged to someone else. Someone worthier than him, a gruff soldier who had never known what it was like to touch the softness of a woman such as her. He knew physical lust, but never passion. Yet he ached for it, the beauty of a shared joining of bodies in love.

He dreamed of what it would be like to feel himself slide inside her core. To feel her hands traversing his shoulders and back, the feel of her nails digging into his backside as he drove into her *relentlessly*.

He heard the sound of her cries, felt her release as he held her within his arms. He would make it good for her, would take her to new heights, show her the pleasures he could give.

If only you were mine, I could show you everything...

The light from his spent cheroot flickered, dying, casting dark shadows over her face, rendering her expression melancholy and sad as her image wavered and began to fade into darkness.

Don't leave me...

Desperately he tilted the picture up closer to the end of the cheroot, savoring the light until it sputtered and smoked, finally dying away.

Bereft, he clutched the picture in his palm and closed his eyes, bringing to life the image of her in his mind. She was lying on a bed, naked, her red hair splayed out on the pillow, her fingers in her sex, which was wet and glistening, slick with desire. In his mind, he saw her reading his letter, relishing his most secret thoughts, thoughts he could never speak aloud, in a letter he could never send. Only in his wild imaginings could he pretend that they corresponded, for his letters to her were always only ever in his mind, never to be shared with the woman he desired. With her own hand, she brought herself to climax, and he watched her, mesmerized by the arch of her back, the way her mouth parted, the sound of his name whispered in her throaty moan.

"Kieran…"

It was at these moments, when the urge to live was all but consuming. It was her…her picture, the thoughts of her that gave him purpose. The thought of coming home to her, broken in mind and spirit. The dream of having her heal him with her body and passion, as only a woman could. It could never be, yet he refused to think of that, lest his desire to continue abandon him.

Until that day, he must love her from afar. Must ravish her in the privacy of his mind. Except, those private fantasies no longer satiated him as they once did, but left him aching, restless.

"'Tis time, Thompson," Pembrooke murmured beside him. "This will be our last chance to reach the telegraph wagon and send the message to the Hussars. Have you the copper wire ready?"

"I have, sir," he said, shoving the picture in his coat pocket.

"What have you got there?" Pembrooke asked.

"Nothing, sir."

"Have you got yourself a sweetheart back home?"

"No, sir."

A heavy hand came upon his shoulder. "A blessing, that. For one cannot help but think of what-if when one has left a woman alone."

"You speak of your wife, sir?" he asked, his voice thick.

"I have had a letter from her. She has been moved from my

family's home to a small cottage in the village. I know of the cottage. It is not suitable for livestock, let alone my wife. But my mother, you see, could not wait to evict my wife from the family estate. She never warmed to the thought of me marrying her and now that I am away, she seeks to make life miserable for my wife. It's retribution, you see, for me marrying a woman of low birth and no fortune."

"From her letters to us, sir, Mrs. Pembrooke seems the sort of woman any man's mother would wish for him to marry. She is very eloquent in her writings, and her concern for our welfare, of which she writes so often, is testament to her worth. I do not think many commanding officers' wives write their soldiers. Money and a name mean very little when there is no substance to go along with it."

"My wife is the kindest of souls. I do not deserve her, but I could not bear to let her go to another. Even though I knew I was leaving for war, I still married her—I wanted her that much."

Kieran swallowed hard and rose unsteadily to his feet. Pembrooke was already making his way to the rough-hewn stairs that would lead them out of the seven-foot trench. As he followed his officer, Kieran could not help thinking of the woman whose picture he kept so close to his heart.

He got down on his belly and snaked his way over the snow-laden field, carefully unrolling the copper wire that led to the wagon with the magnetic telegraph. As he did so, the image of the woman's smiling face flashed in his mind, soon replaced by a strange vision of a woman in a cloak, her hands raised, as if in warning.

"Shh," he suddenly hissed. Pembrooke, who was on his belly just in front of Kieran, stopped and looked back over his shoulder.

"What is it?"

"I heard something."

"What? Cossacks?"

"No, a flap of some kind."

"A bird, most likely. Let's move onward and get this done quickly."

Reluctantly, Kieran agreed. Something was not right. His instincts heightened, Kieran continued to unroll the wire as he listened and watched. It was unusually quiet here, in the space between the two opposing camps, in the land that belonged to neither them nor their enemies. No-man's-land. A place that was desolate and burned from bullets and fire.

"A moment, sir," he whispered. "I'm out of wire."

Reaching into his pocket, Kieran retrieved the metal grippers needed to fuse Pembrooke's wire with his. His hands, still poorly functioning in the freezing temperatures, fumbled, and he looked back over his shoulder to see if the handle of the tool was caught on the torn bit of wool on his pocket. It was then that he saw the flashing of white. He thought perhaps he had imagined it, but then he saw it again. A short flash, followed by a second longer flash. *Dot. Dash.*

Oh, fuck!

"It's a trap," he hissed, reaching for Pembrooke's ankle, pulling him back.

"Good God, Thompson, what the devil—"

"*It's an ambush!* The fucking Russians are here, they've surrounded the trench and they're using Morse code to signal their reinforcements."

"What—"

The first barrage of bullets rained down over their heads. Reaching beside him for his gun, Kieran shot blindly into the night, shooting anything and everything.

"Retreat!" Pembrooke roared. But it was too late. The

other soldiers heard the firing and were crawling out of the trench, returning the gunfire in a blind fury, dropping like rag dolls as the Russian snipers fired at them from their vantage on the hill above no-man's-land. Red flashes volleyed back and forth across the field as Kieran tried to make his way back to the trench. He was nearly there when he heard the blood-curdling roar.

He turned just in time to see Pembrooke fall to his knees, clutching his gut. Not thinking, Kieran ran the short distance to his commanding officer and hauled him up over his shoulder, carrying him back to the trench amidst the torrent of enemy fire.

Pembrooke was bleeding. Kieran could feel the warmth of blood on his neck, trickling down the collar of his thin coat. He heard it in the gurgling that rasped against his shoulder.

"A light!" he called, jumping down into the trench, landing on his knees with Pembrooke on his back. "Get the field surgeon," he roared breathlessly as he slid Pembrooke to the wet, packed mud of the trench floor.

"Get out of this trench," Pembrooke choked on a mouthful of frothing blood. "For God's sake, man, the Russians will burn you alive in it. That's an order, Thompson."

"I'm not leaving you," Kieran snapped, ripping open Pembrooke's overcoat and officer's jacket. The gold braid was thick and cold, stiff in his groping fingers. Finally, giving up, he reached for his gun and used the bayonet to cut through the braid. When he parted the jacket, Pembrooke's vitals spilled out in a gush of blood and tissue.

"Jesus Christ!" What the hell was he to do with this?

Suddenly a light was thrust in front of him. He looked up to see the army surgeon holding a lantern in the darkness. He gazed at Pembrooke's face, and then at the wound.

"Better find the ordinary. There's nothing to be done here."

"You *will* fix him," Kieran ordered the old doctor. "Or you will feel this bayonet in your gullet."

"Thompson," Pembrooke murmured, his voice gurgling with blood and the sounds of death. "It's no good."

Kieran leaned over his officer and put his ear to the man's mouth, trying to hear, when the picture fluttered out of his pocket and landed on Pembrooke's chest.

He gazed at it and smiled. "I thought I had lost it," he said, reaching for the picture. "Here, come closer with that light," Pembrooke commanded the surgeon.

"She is so lovely," Pembrooke gasped as he focused on the image of the woman. "It pains me that I will never see her again."

"Do not speak such things," Kieran demanded.

"You think her beautiful, don't you, Thompson?"

Kieran shrank away, only to feel a surprisingly strong hand manacle his wrist. "Do you dream of my wife?"

Kieran could not look his dying officer in the eye.

"You will go to her and tell her of my fate. You will tell her my last thoughts were of her, and her smile. *You,* Thompson, will be the one to go to her. It is my last wish."

Kieran shook his head, tried to free himself, but Pembrooke held on with the last of his strength.

"Did you think I didn't know? I have always known— *always,*" Pembrooke said. "I used to sit and watch you, looking at her picture by the light, touching her face. I doubted a man could love a woman more than I loved Sinead. But when I saw you look at her…I…I knew I was wrong. There is another who could love her—perhaps even more—"

"Forgive—"

"No," Pembrooke said, his blue gaze dull with pain and approaching death. "Protect her. Provide for her. *Love her.*

And tell her that one day, I will return to her. You…you have my blessing."

Kieran looked down at the picture, now covered in blood. Pembrooke's blood. Pembrooke's wife.

He had been in love with Sinead Pembrooke from the moment he had read her letter to her husband and seen her picture. With every letter she had written to them, her husband's soldiers, he had fallen deeper and deeper into a secret love affair with his commanding officer's wife.

For two long years he had loved from afar, had longed in secret. Had wanted, and dreamed, and fantasized about another man's wife.

She had never known him. Had never heard the name Kieran Thompson. Could never imagine that there was another man in the world who loved her, who wanted her with such fierce passion—a fierceness that he was certain surpassed even that of her husband.

The crow of the cock awakened Kieran with a start and he sat up with a jolt and stifled scream, sweating, despite the frost in the air. Daylight was just breaking over the horizon, and he fought to return from the darkness of memories. He was not in a trench in the Crimea. He was not dead, but alive.

Sinead.

He thought of her, of last evening in the cottage when he had felt her skin beneath his palms and her breasts in his mouth. She had come alive beneath his hands. He'd seen the glimpse of her hidden desire—desire for him. Her passion was deep, waiting to be unlocked, and he had wanted her, had wanted to take her against the wall, bending her to his will, giving her his body while exorcising the last remnants of her husband's possession.

She had been his in that moment. Not David Pembrooke's.

The smell of her sex was still upon his fingers and he inhaled her scent, savoring it, urging on his hunger 'til it was not just a gnawing need, but something he could barely control. Licking his finger, he tried to taste her, but the scent was fading, and so, too, was her taste. It tormented him, knowing he had been so close, that he could have gone to his knees and buried his mouth in her quim, a quim that had been wet and heavy and aching to be filled. She would have clutched his hair in her hands, holding him to her sex as he worked her with his tongue, spreading her lips so that he could leave no inch of her uncovered. She would have cried out, would have panted his name, and he would have taken her right there, against the wall, thrusting into her with unchecked emotion. And she would have begged him not to stop until she screamed as she came.

He had been so close, yet she had stopped him. Why?

Making his way to the window, he shrugged into his shirt as he gazed across the path that led to Sinead's small, ram-shackle cottage. Through his frosted window he saw the figure of someone dressed head to toe in black, shoveling her garden path. It was a man—there was no mistaking the height, the broad back. Every fighting instinct he had came to a head, and he reached for his trousers, jamming his foot into the leg while he kept his gaze on the stranger, then stilled as the man turned to face him. The stranger stared at him for several long seconds. There was something about those blue eyes that felt so familiar. Yet the face was all wrong—harder, older. And the hair was not fair and golden, but light brown, and long.

Blinking away the vision, Kieran opened his eyes again and found himself staring at nothing but white, and a garden pathway that was full of snow. There was neither man nor shovel to be seen.

A dream? A vision? A reminder of what might come?

It was the dawn before December twenty-first. The winter solstice. The moment when darkness and light were equally balanced, if only for a minute of time. But that minute, Kieran knew, could be life altering.

His life had been forever changed since first seeing Sinead's picture flutter to the ground from a letter. He knew it. Had accepted it. Why couldn't she see that they were destined to be together?

What fate, Kieran wondered as he looked up into the slate-colored sky, could be implored upon to make it all happen?

3

THE WALK TO THE VILLAGE WAS ALWAYS SOMETHING
to be dreaded. Sinead loathed the looks, the whispers behind
raised hands, the venomous glances of women when men
turned their heads to watch her progression through the tiny
village. The men thought her easy prey, a fallen woman who
indulged her sexual nature. The women thought her a seductress who would steal their husbands and sons from beneath
their very noses.

Sinead knew the slanderous accusations of the townsfolk,
knew she was considered a witch. For there had been that unfortunate incident in her past when the vicar's son had sought
her attentions. It would have been a profitable match for
someone of her lowly station, yet she had despised the young
man and his pawing hands. Everyone knew of her distaste and
her refusal of his suit, despite the obvious advantage in
marrying someone so far above her. Yet still he pursued her,
cornering her in the woods, pulling at her bodice as if she
owed him her body because he was above her. When he had
been discovered facedown in the river that ran alongside the
village, everyone had believed that she had driven him to his
death. Most had speculated that she had seduced him, had

taken him to her bed and corrupted him with her body before killing him in the river.

She had not, of course. She wielded no special power, no magic. Yet from the day of the grisly discovery of the vicar's son, she had been held up to the scrutiny of the people who entertained the idea that she performed black magic, that she cast spells on men, young and old, so that they might desire her. The dark powers had been the answer to everything. For how else could she have caught the eye and hand of the second son from the richest family in the county if not by some forbidden magic?

Sinead had first seen David when he appeared at her father's blacksmith shop. From the moment their gazes collided, the current in the air became charged, enchanted, and for the first time Sinead had felt true desire. The other men in the village who had tried to press her into a kiss or a stolen embrace had never made her blood quicken the way it did at that first glimpse of David standing before the forge, waiting for her father to repair the iron harness from his carriage.

As she had continued with her business, she had been aware of David's intent perusal. She was used to men looking at her, desiring her. But they never wanted more than a tumble. No one wanted to know Sinead as a person.

"You're as pretty as a picture," David had once told her, "with a body made to give great pleasure to a man. You should be proud, not shamed by such a thing."

Yet her face and voluptuous figure had been nothing but the bane of her existence. Had she been plain and fat, she would not have to live as she did, alone, with the village gossipers always repeating stories about her.

Bells tinkled as she stepped into the only textile shop in the village. The small store was crowded with people purchasing warm woolens for the long winter ahead. Heads turned in her direction and she braced herself for the murmurs she knew she would hear.

"There she is," someone hissed. "Brazen woman."

"Aye, and wearing a scarlet cloak, too. 'Tis fitting, for it is the color of harlots."

Keeping her head down, Sinead ignored the insults. She had heard all the accusations before—she was a wicked enchantress of men, even though she had only ever had one lover. *David.*

"Mr. Thompson had better have a care if he does not wish to follow in her husband's footsteps. Blinded by lust, he is. The witch has cast her spell."

The slurs no longer stung as they once had. She no longer felt the compulsion to correct their assumptions, or defend her honor. She knew what she was, and a seductress of men was not it.

Sinead, like everyone else, had been shocked by David's relentless pursuit of her. He had lingered at her father's smithy long after the harness had been repaired. He had gone to the solstice festival, watching her through the standing stones. He had swept her up in his arms and danced with her, even stolen a kiss at the end of the night. The next morning he had been there, at her father's door, requesting her company on a walk.

For Sinead and David it had all been so simple. Fate had brought them together. For the superstitious villagers and David's aristocratic family, some darker force was at play, for how could a man from as noble a family as David's desire a blacksmith's daughter for more than a dalliance?

Yet David had loved her. And she had loved him. It all seemed a lifetime ago when he had courted her and married her. It seemed only a dream, the memory of their wedding night, when David had taken her to his bedchamber in the Pembrookes' country home and loved her most passionately until dawn.

"I see Thompson at her cottage every day, letting himself in, coming and going as he pleases," one of the gossipers whispered with feverish delight. "She has already ensnared him with that body of hers. It is only a matter of time before he winds up dead like the Pembrookes' poor son. You mark my words, she will have him, then she will move on to the next man unfortunate enough to be taken in by her cunning wiles."

Hating how they spoke of Kieran, Sinead walked away, toward the stockings and garters—the purpose of her trip into the village. As she always did whenever she came to the shop, she looked longingly at the beautiful silk stockings that were much too expensive and impractical for someone like her. Still, she had always longed for a pair. The closest she had ever gotten was a pair of plain white cotton stockings that she had worn on her wedding day. Perhaps, if David had lived he would have come home from the Crimea to spoil her. As it was, their courtship had been brief, and their marriage even shorter. There had been little time for such frivolity. She had been packing her husband up to go to war—silk stockings and the finer things in her life had ceased to attract her. Instead of buying her things, David had lavished her with attention and kisses. It had been enough, more than enough for Sinead.

Running her gloved hand over the delicate crème silk, Sinead marveled at the overt sensuality of the pink satin bows. Even the gold embroidery at the top of the stockings was romantic and elegant. The garters, too, were scandalously sensual with pink ribbons and tiny seed pearls threaded through the gold thread. How decadent and luxurious to wear something like this, so lovely and feminine.

"Imagine the wicked deeds and goings-on in that cottage," someone muttered as they watched Sinead fondle the expensive and seductive stockings. "Wonder what spells she uses to keep him so enthralled with her."

Kieran had never been anything but kind to her, seeing to her safety and comfort when no other could, or would. Her father was dead, and David's mother had tossed her out of their home after David had been dispatched to the Crimea.

She had been all alone since David left, alone to fend for herself the best way she could. Alone with only her thoughts and memories—and fears. Alone to bear the brunt of gossip about her marriage, and the slander against her.

They could say what they wanted about her and David, but they had no right to discuss Kieran in such a way. He was a good man, a man whose kindness did not deserve such harsh scrutiny by the village gossipers who lived for nothing but spreading tittle-tattle about her.

No, they did not know Kieran the way she knew him.

Kieran, she thought, allowing herself to remember last evening when she had felt his hands on her thighs, his fingers in her sheath. The strength in them, the calluses that were rough against her tender flesh. Such power, virility, yet unbearable softness, too. There had been passion in his touch, a dark, desperate need that she had feared—and desired.

He had not come around that morning as was his usual custom. She had breakfast waiting for him on her worn table, oatmeal and cinnamon. A part of her had known he would not return; the other part had longed that he would.

Perhaps he had grown tired, or worse, resolved to her inability to give herself to him. She was not an innocent girl. She knew what Kieran wanted. After last night, she finally admitted to herself how much she wanted it, too. Yet, she could not see past the betrayal to David. Her mind would not release his memory.

It had been a year since she had first seen Kieran, standing on the threshold of her door, dressed in his best uniform, his hat beneath his arm as he looked down upon her with his dark, unreadable eyes.

She had known that David was gone. She had felt him leave her, months before. Yet the words needed to be said, and Kieran, she knew, had been sent to say them.

"I am sorry to have to tell you, Mrs. Pembrooke, that your husband, my lieutenant, gave his life on the battlefield of the Crimea. He died with honor, and the admiration and loyalty of his men."

She had not crumpled. Not then. She had asked Kieran in for tea, and he had accepted, sitting by the fire. She had busied herself with making tea and arranging the few biscuits she had on a plate. They had spent the afternoon discussing her husband, his bravery, Kieran's respect for his superior officer. And only when Kieran left had Sinead allowed herself to weep with unbridled emotion.

Despite feeling the loss of David, she had still held out hope that she had been wrong. Perhaps he had only been wounded. Perhaps she had not felt it at all, the strange feeling of emptiness where David had once resided. Yet, she *had* felt that piece of David that she had clutched steadfastly to her breast leave her. For hours she wept. She had not seen him in two years, yet still the knowledge that he was never coming home to her ravaged her heart and soul.

He was dead. She was officially all alone in the world with no one else who thought of her, who cared for her or what would happen to her. There was no further use for the dreams of his homecoming, for thoughts of the family they would have when he returned. They were all lost the moment David had left the world.

Had it not been for Kieran and his compassion, his company, she would have given up in those months after learning of David's death. Kieran had been her touchstone, her talisman. He had kept her alive, at least physically.

But Kieran's company in the past months had ceased to bring her comfort, bringing something else instead. Desire. She craved him, the sight of him working in her small garden, cutting wood, repairing the fence and the leaking roof. She watched him, his large, well-muscled body working, sweating. Her own body had responded to the sight of him and his sweat-drenched skin in the summer sunshine. She wanted that salty wetness covering her naked skin, wanted to lick it off his shoulders as he was filling her. Raw and elemental, that was Kieran, and Sinead wanted him no other way.

Over the following months, she had thought less and less of David, and more about Kieran. Her dreams were filled with him. In the dark, with her head on her pillow, Sinead thought not of David's head next to hers, but Keiran's.

Kieran…everything came back to him. His onyx-colored eyes. His hands, the ones she had dreamed of touching her, the ones she now knew intimately against her flesh. Last night had been but a forbidden, haunting tease. She craved more. She wanted to feel the hardness he had brushed up against her, thrusting inside her. She wanted the barely controlled passion she sensed bubbling just beneath his skin.

David had been soft and easy in his embrace. It had been romantic and pleasurable. But with Kieran, it would be rough, untamed. He would be forceful where David had been considerate. With Kieran, he would take her like a woman, not a fragile china doll.

She had grown over the years, and while she longed for David, she wanted to discover the kind of pleasure Kieran could show her.

"May I be of assistance?"

Sinead looked up from the French stockings and into the wrinkled, disapproving face of the surly shopkeeper, Mrs. Peabody.

"I am looking for woolen stockings," she replied, reluctantly moving from the pretty pile of silk to the more practical woolen hose that would keep her warm beneath her thin skirts and the stiff leather of her half boots.

She had only enough money for one pair of new hose. Woolen hose. Not silk. Such was the life of a widow living on her husband's army pension. There was little enough for food when the bills were paid, let alone frivolous items like pretty stockings.

"That pair will do very well, thank you," she said, pointing to the gray wool. Gray did not stain, nor turn color after repeated washings. Gray was sensible, and above all, Sinead needed to be practical. This would be the only pair of hose she could afford to buy this winter. She should not even be buying them, but she had mended hers so often that it hurt to walk on the seams that had been sewn and resewn so many times that she had lost count.

Passing Mrs. Peabody her coins, Sinead accepted the hose and dropped them into her basket. She did not tarry, not with the gossipers milling about the store, watching her, whispering about her, nor did she take one last look at the crème stockings that had captivated her.

Rushing out the door, the bells tinkling behind her, Sinead ran headlong into a tall, firm body.

"My apologies."

"Kieran," she gasped as he put his arms around her, steadying her. "I did not see you."

Had he seen her through the store window? Had he watched her while she had been lost in thought, woolgathering about David, about him?

"Shall I escort you back home?"

"I...I..." She glanced around the busy street. Everyone was out running errands before the solstice festival began that night. No one appeared to be watching them, yet still she felt as though all eyes were upon her—them.

"I understand," he said, backing away from her. "You care what people will think if you are seen with me."

"Kieran, please. You don't understand—"

She stopped when she saw him reach beneath his great coat to the pocket beneath. He pulled something out, but kept it clutched in his hand.

"This is no passing fancy on my part, Sinead. Nor is it coincidence that I have made my home in the same village as you. It was not a coincidence that it was me who came to tell you the news of your husband."

People rushed by them, jostling them in their haste. Yet Kieran ignored them and reached for her hand, putting whatever he was holding in her palm, then folded her fingers around it.

"We were in a trench when your husband opened your letter, and this fell out between the folds. It landed on the toe of my boot and the sight of you smiling stole my breath. I could not keep my eyes off your picture as your husband held it in his hand. That night, I took it from his pocket while he slept. I only wanted to see you once more. But I could not give it back. I had to have it—had to have *you*—even though I knew it was wrong. I had to have a piece of you for myself."

Sinead opened her palm, and saw the image of herself in

the photograph she had sent to David. It was wrinkled and tattered, and something rust colored smeared the corner of it. Blood perhaps. But whose?

"I dreamed of you every night, Sinead. I still do. I wondered what it would be like to come home to you, to make you mine. I dreamed of having you, of you wanting me."

He backed away, and Sinead did not know what to say. What to do. "David knew of my desire for you, Sinead. I tried to hide it, shamed that I was coveting my commanding officer's wife, but he had known for a long time that what I felt for you was not a passing fancy. With his dying breath, he told me to come to you. To love you as best as I could. He gave us permission to be together, Sinead. To be happy with one another. I'm here because more than anything I want you in my life. I want a future with you. I've made my desires known. I've laid my soul bare. It is up to you now. It is up to you to tell me what *you* want. What you desire."

She watched him walk away, disappearing down the bustling street amidst the gently falling snow.

She knew what she wanted, yet she could not reach out and take it. David held her still, despite the fact he was physically gone. She had not said goodbye. He had not released her from her vows, her bond.

Walking against the stream of people, she was lost in thought and the fear that she very well might lose Kieran. When she looked up, she was far away from the crowds, the stone circle at the end of the village looming before her in quiet solitude.

Already tables were being set up for the festival. Heavy bows of hawthorn, mistletoe and holly were being strung up in the village green. Behind the green were the ancient Celtic standing stones that were weathered and porous. They stood at varying heights, an imposing circle of ancient mystery. Sinead knew from spending each solstice morning amidst the stones that the sun, when it rose, would shine in the middle of the circle, casting brilliant shadows. When she had been a little girl, she used to twirl in the sunbeams and wish that she would one day be a princess. In a way, that wish had come true, because her love affair with David had been like something from a fairy tale.

Tonight the villagers would celebrate the priestess, whom, it was said, the stones were erected for. It was a shrine of sorts, and the villagers would pay tribute to her as she watched over them before heralding the solstice.

The evening would be a time of mysticism and magic, of passion and frivolity. The dawn would usher in the perfect balance of light and dark, if only for a moment of time, and the world would sit quietly in peaceful harmony.

Sinead realized how much she longed for those things, peace, harmony, magic and passion. She wondered if those things would ever be hers.

The snow began falling harder, and Sinead tipped her face to the sky and felt the flakes tickle her cheeks and nose. It was time to go home, yet she felt held to this spot—watching the preparations from afar, a wistfulness heavy in her breath—that this solstice might bring something special and momentous to her solitary life.

Amongst the stones, she saw a figure. At first she wondered if it was an illusion created by the snow. But then it moved, and a child with curling blond hair, dressed in a tattered white gown and threadbare cloak, stepped out of the whirling snow.

The child stood before Sinead and looked up at her with blue eyes, eyes that were much too intuitive to be in a face of one so young. She could be no more than six years. Sinead noticed that the child's feet were bare.

"Your feet!" she cried, dropping to her knees and taking a small foot between her palms, rubbing the blanched flesh. "They're nearly frozen."

The child said nothing, just watched her, and Sinead felt for the misery of the poor creature.

"Where are your parents, child?" she asked as she dug through her basket for something to cover the girl's feet. When the girl did not respond, Sinead did the only thing she could. She removed her new hose from the basket and pulled them up over the child's foot.

When both her feet were covered, and the wool pulled up high on her legs, Sinead looked up to see the girl's eyes had grown a warmer shade of blue—the color of a summer sky.

"It is meant for you," the child said in a soft voice. In the hand that she held out to her, Sinead saw a tattered square cloth. Curious, she took it and noticed that something was embroidered in the fabric.

"'Tis the chant of the priestess, who many centuries ago loved and lost her true love."

"A chant?" Sinead asked quizzically as her gloved fingertip rolled over the embroidered threads.

"A love spell," the child said. "A spell so powerful that it reaches beyond this realm and into the Summerland where those who have left us walk freely. Light and dark," the child said, her voice stronger, older, wiser. "Death and rebirth. These are the gifts I give to you on this winter's night."

"But—" Sinead looked up from the old tattered fabric, the loose strings blowing in the crisp breeze as she held it in her palm. The girl seemed to fade against the stones and the swirl of snow. Her voice, as low and haunting as the wind, chanted...

"No wanderer's curse
be he thus beckoned
a slave to passion's fire
return his head, upon my breast
burn bright of winter's desire."

Sinead let the words sink in as if they had been created solely for her. Kieran, was he this wanderer? There was no denying that he had made her a slave to his passion. And David? She wanted one more night with him, to say her goodbyes, to see him one last time. To touch him, caress him, to whisper in his ear all the things she should have but never did. Yet she ached for Kieran, to have him, without remorse and guilt.

Return to my breast. She looked up at the slate-gray sky, summoning David. Yes, she did yearn for his return.

And Kieran? He was her heart's desire on this night, the eve of the solstice. She was a slave to the fire she saw in Kieran's eyes, and the passion that burned in his body. *He* was her winter's desire.

4

HOLDING THE WARM MUG IN HER HANDS, SINEAD
sipped at the wassail as she scanned the crowd of revelers. All
the villagers were here—youngest to oldest—celebrating the
solstice and offering up gifts to the ancient gods and goddesses
so that the bleak winter months would be neither unduly
harsh nor long.

Everyone was making merry, laughing and drinking, calling
out cheers for good health and a warm home. There was
country dancing to the fiddle and the singing of old, seasonal
songs. Cheeks were crimson with the slap of the cold breeze,
and eyes were bright with the merriment of the festivities.

Walking around the enormous bonfire that was in the
middle of the village green, Sinead, jostled by the revelers,
watched from the periphery, never really part of the celebration. Despite this, she had come to the place where the
ancient stones had stood for centuries, watching over the tiny
northern village. There was magic in those stones. She
believed it, and not just because of her Celtic roots, but
because she felt it. Especially this evening. A thrilling enchant-
ment hung thick in the atmosphere, cloaking her.

Scanning the laughing faces, she did not see the one she

longed for. Kieran was not present amongst the merry gentlemen who danced and tried to steal kisses from blushing
maidens. She felt empty knowing he was not there. A part of
her had believed he would be, and that part of her had been
convinced that she'd give herself to him this night—this night
of magic and passion.

"The Mummers!" a young lad cried as he ran into the circle
of dancers. "They are making their procession into the village."

"I wonder what they shall be acting out this year?" a young
maid with rosy cheeks and sparkling blues eyes asked excitedly.

"Who cares, as long as Squire Bolton's son is leading them,"
answered her friend. The two began to giggle. Sinead found
herself smiling. She had once been like them, young and
carefree, with little more to worry about than handsome
squires, or village boys. It had been aeons since she'd had a
true friend to share a laugh with, or to tell secrets to.

The Mummers' voices were carried on the darkness as
they chanted their ancient song in Gaelic. Sinead could only
recall a few words in her ancestors' native tongue. Her grandmother had tried to keep their culture alive after Sinead's
mother had died when she was three, but soon her grandmother had followed her mother, and Sinead had been left
with her father, who had loved her, but who had been too
busy to see to traditions.

"Bandia, Sianaitheoir, Beannaithe leannan."

"Goddess, Savior, Sacred Lover," the Mummers were
singing of the priestess.

Sinead took a long sip of her drink, letting the mulled spirit
warm her belly as she waited to see the troupe of actors who
were integral to the solstice gathering. The revelers' voices
grew louder until the costumed Mummers, their identities
concealed by masks, burst into the clearing, dancing and

singing. The crowd quieted, stepping back to give the actors wide berth. Nothing could be heard but the roaring of the giant bonfire and the distant hoot of an owl as the actors found their places in the center of the green before the crackling flames.

Their leader stepped forward, holding his torch high as he walked in a small circle, addressing the gathered villagers.

"You see behind me the form of our priestess, bent over her enemy, caring for him, loving him despite the barrier of class, religion, tongue."

Waving the torch aside, he revealed the image of a cloaked woman bent over a man. Beside her, pots lay scattered, as well as trenchers. Her hands were moving over his body, healing him as she murmured words he could not understand, for the priestess was an ancient Druid, and the wounded soldier her enemy from across the sea. As the actress worked on the man who lay on the cold ground, the other Mummers broke into song, a quiet chant meant to relay the seriousness of the soldier's injuries.

Sinead did not pay much attention to the play that was being enacted, but focused instead on the narrator of the piece. The way he moved, the sound of his voice, it was all so familiar. Mesmerized by him, she followed his movements through the crowd as he told the sad story of the star-crossed lovers and the priestess whom they honored yearly.

"Despite his wounds, the two became lovers. Fierce was their loving, but with the dawn, the awakening of their divergent paths becomes all too clear. For it is the solstice, and their lives are never meant to be entwined."

Suddenly the woman playing the priestess stood up, her arms raised to the heavens, and began to recite the ancient poem.

"No wanderer's curse…"

Sinead froze as she heard the words that were embroidered

on the small square of fabric the child had given her. Her gaze strayed once more to the narrator, who pressed forward, his silhouette illuminated by the enormous flames of the bonfire. Slowly he lowered his black-and-gold mask, revealing his face.

The mug fell from Sinead's hand; warm wassail splashed onto the hem of her skirt as she stared in mute horror—hope. The eyes...the hair...

She reached out her hand, her fingers trembling. *David?*

He tried to step forward but couldn't. Nor could she move, to touch the face she remembered so well.

"Soon, my love," he said, donning his mask once more. "I will come to you. *Soon.*"

He was pulled back by the other Mummers, and the eager villagers seemed to swallow him up, concealing him from her. Sinead ran, pushing through the crowd, trying to find him, looking fruitlessly for the golden hair and blue eyes that sparkled from behind the mask. Turning, looking, she found herself moving in circles, until she came to rest on the other side of the fire, closest to the stones. And to Kieran, who watched her through the flickering flames.

Their gazes locked. Her body warmed, heating with longing. What did he think? Did he know what she wanted?

Waiting. Hungering... The whispered words seemed to burn in Sinead's belly, filling her with a warmth that curled low in her womb.

Do you want me, Sinead?

She heard Kieran's voice whisper the words. Closing her eyes, she savored the sensation of a fluttering touch against her skin, but it was impossible for it to be Kieran's touch because he was still leaning against the stone on the other side of the fire. He could not have touched her, yet she felt it again, heard his voice once more.

Come to me…

She wanted to go, wanted to obey that deep beckoning voice, but she could not command her body to walk. Their gazes stayed locked, their yearning so evident despite the enormous fire that separated them. Around them, gaiety and song, drink and food was indulged. Yet for them, there was nothing else but each other, longing from what seemed like a divide that could never be bridged.

The words of the poem were whispered in her mind, like a distant echo. It was Kieran's voice she heard in her thoughts. His voice murmuring to her so softly.

With his spirit, he reached for her, drawing her ever closer to him as surely as if he had reached for her with his large, callused hands.

She felt his presence, a current of cold air that hovered in the atmosphere like a patch of wispy fog, before it found its way over to her, wrapping itself around her.

You know I can give you everything you want. Everything you need.

Yes, her mind seemed to cry with a fevered plea. She was restless for more of the sensation that licked its way up her body—it was only the night wind, yet she could have sworn it felt like Kieran's hands touching her. Sinead's breath caught and held as the cool sensation changed, grew warm as it swept over her mons. Over and over it caressed her until she no longer felt chilled, but warm…so very warm.

Rising up, the warmth stroked her belly before it lingered over her breasts, which felt painfully confined behind her corset and tight bodice. Struggling for air, she began to breathe faster, felt her breasts rising and falling as the sensation all but engulfed her.

Feel me. Want me.

I do, she whispered as her hand came up to rest against the swell of her bosom beneath her cloak. The warmth covered her breasts like the breath of a lover. It moved to the deep valley of her décolletage, and then up to her throat where the vein in her neck throbbed.

The rhythm of her blood sang in her ears until it was all she could hear; the rushing of blood in her veins, the feel of warmth stroking the vein as if someone was breathing against her. Her lips parted as she tilted her head farther, desiring to feel more. And then she did—a mouth—warm and soft. A strong, wet tongue that repeatedly stroked the vein, priming it as if preparing to suckle the bulging length beneath the tender flesh of her throat.

The stroke of the tongue, the pressure of the lips increased as her hunger deepened. Wetness pooled within her as she tugged her bodice, silently begging for the caress to descend to her breast and her nipple, which was beaded into a hard little bud, and which throbbed mercilessly against her corset.

Fully given up to the power that was luring her, Sinead did not hear the festivities going on around her, nor did she see the villagers. She was consumed now. Consumed by the lure of sexual pleasure that Kieran's dark eyes promised her from beyond the fire where he stood watching her. She was at the mercy of the fever that raged in her blood, the crazed thoughts of being touched by Kieran when it was naught but a shaft of air that had rustled her skirts. Yet it felt so much more powerful than that, it felt real.

Tell me what you want, and I will it give it to you.

In a daze, Sinead walked amongst the crowd, meandering through the dancing couples and the children who were playing and laughing. She walked to where Kieran stood, his hand outstretched to her.

She took it, allowing him to lead her into the darkness of

the stone circle where the light from the fire could not reach, and where the altar had been decorated with oak branches and holly in honor of the priestess and the solstice that would arrive with the dawn.

Sinead knew this sacred place would be where she would lie with Kieran. She would lie on this altar and give herself to him, offering him everything she had.

As she suspected, he led her to the altar. Removing his coat, he placed it on the cold stone, then helped her to lie upon their makeshift bed. Above them the moon glowed. Surrounding them were the tall pagan stones. The frivolity of the festivities was but a distant rumble. In this enchanted grove it was only them.

Without a word, Kieran came down on top of her, his hands braced on either side of her face, supported by his thick, strong arms. His head slowly lowered to hers, his gaze holding hers steady. Suddenly his hands clasped hers and held them high above her head until her back arched beneath him, her breasts rising up to meet his chest.

"You're mine now."

"I come to you freely, Kieran."

"Do you?"

"Yes."

"With no reservations? With no one between us?"

"There is only you."

He kissed her. Sinead had no idea if he had intended it to be soft and drugging, for she rose to meet his lips and captured his in hunger—*starvation*. With a fierce growl, he consumed her with his mouth, his tongue stroking hers as his hand roughly parted her cape. Flinging the corner over her shoulder, he exposed her bodice. He cupped her hard in his palm, groaning into her mouth as he squeezed her breast. Answering him, she wrapped her legs around his waist and kissed him so hard she was deprived of breath as their tongues tangled and licked.

"Kieran," she said on a breathless plea as his lips skated over her skin, his tongue drawing tiny circles on her throat. She cried in pleasure as the cool winter air mingled with his hot breath. He clawed at her bodice, tearing it so as to expose her breast. Cupping her, he lifted her breast to his mouth and she arched up off their stone bed, needing to feel him suckling her deep in his warm mouth.

At last. He suckled her, ravenously, and she cried out, clutching at his hair, her hips rising and falling in a desperation she had never felt. It was hard and violent—desperate—the way they clung to each other, the way his hands roamed her body and his mouth suckled her deeply until her womb clenched and she thought she would never feel the hard length of him sliding into her.

His hand snaked beneath the hem of her skirts, which had ridden up her calves when she had wrapped her legs around him. He still held both her hands in one of his and she clutched onto his fingers, never wanting to let him go.

Rocking against her she felt his cock, hard, long, beautiful, straining against his coarse trousers.

"Do you want this? Me inside you? Fucking you?" he rasped as he pushed into her. Her sex was swollen, slick. She was ready for him. Past ready. She nodded, gripping his firm buttocks with her thighs.

"Then come to me."

He loosened his trousers, and Sinead felt the hot velvet of his heavy cock between her thighs. With one hard thrust he was embedded deep within her.

The shock of something intimately filling her body after

so long made her cry out and arch, taking him deeper. He drove into her again, riding against her, the entire length of his body rubbing her with each one of his thrusts, commanding her to accept his cock—*him*.

She had never been taken this way, with such purpose and intent. With possession. Her body responded as never before, blooming in a way she had never known it could. She felt sensual, womanly, as she accepted him, as her body begged him for more.

Their gazes were locked, their hands entwined above her head. He watched her as he took her, thrusting deeper and deeper.

"I knew you would be this beautiful beneath me," he said, his gaze raking over her face. "I knew you would take me like this—just as I am. Rough. Coarse."

She said nothing, but let her body answer him when she allowed her hips to meet his, and together they writhed like a wave on the stone. Her moans were loud and unbridled, feeding him, making him thrust harder. His strokes were relentless, never ending. Feeling her body begin to tense and coil with impending climax, Sinead allowed herself to grow lax, to just feel the power of Kieran's cock deep within her, sliding and retreating, only to fill her again. Her head lolled to the side, and she looked through the stones and beyond to the fire that continued to burn. There, beyond the flames was the narrator from before, his Mummer's mask concealing his face. Then he removed it. From between the flickering flames, she saw the image of her husband once more.

David…

He watched her—them, making love on the stone altar like heathen animals, and she felt wicked, wanton and so very feminine that she smiled and beckoned him with her eyes.

His own eyes flickered, dancing with desire, answering her call to join them. He stepped forward, but the flames reared up, preventing him from coming closer.

Soon, she heard his voice in her head. *Soon I will join you.*

As Kieran filled her over and over, their hands clinging to one another, she watched the man studying them, watching the way they moved, the way Kieran took her. The way she responded to Kieran's touch, the feel of his body commanding hers and it aroused her. To have both men…

Kieran found her breast and curled his tongue around her nipple. With one final thrust, he poured his seed deep within her. The image of David faded, leaving her and Kieran alone amongst the sacred stones.

"Sinead," Kieran murmured, his voice trembling, as was the hand with which he cupped her face. "Stay with me."

"Yes," she whispered against the top of his head, his silky hair tickling her throat as the wind caressed them. *My Heart's Desire.*

5

BENEATH THE COVER OF DARKNESS, KIERAN WHISKED
Sinead past the revelers, careful not to attract unwanted attention. He did not give a damn what the villagers said about
him, but he did not wish to have Sinead bear the brunt of
their biting tongues and cruel accusations. What was between
them, whatever they would discover this night was between
them only. Whatever the villagers said about Sinead, Kieran
knew the truth. She was not a witch, but a seductress. He was
as smitten now as he had been when he first saw her portrait.
She ruled his heart and soul, and after those moments on the
stone altar, she ruled his body as well.

Through the snow, they hurried, their hands clasped tightly
as they weaved through the throng until they cleared the
green. His mind was racing, his gait brisk, forcing Sinead to
run behind him.

Had he pleased her? Shocked her? He had not been soft
and lulling. He'd taken. Christ, he'd ripped her bodice and
had her for the first time on a stone altar like some kind of
pagan god devouring a human sacrifice. Yet even if he had
wanted to, he wouldn't have had the patience to take his time
seducing her with luring kisses and gentle caresses.

It had been immensely satisfying, taking her like that. The dangerous edge of his sexual hunger, a hunger that had grown to almost unbearable heights these past months, was at last somewhat at bay.

But had he truly satisfied her? The all-too-familiar taste of fear coated his mouth. He wanted her pleasured, loved. He wanted to replace the memories of David with memories of him. He wanted her to need him again, to desire the feel of him loving her body.

Tonight, he promised, he would. When Sinead awoke in his arms in the morning, she would be completely ravished and satisfied, and he would know that he had loved her as she deserved.

As they stepped through the garden gate, he heard Sinead gasp. He followed her gaze and saw on the door latch a black-and-gold mask. She reached for it, rubbing her fingers along the black velvet before finally searching his gaze.

"'Tis a Mummer's mask."

He took it from her and studied the gold braiding, the same sort of braiding that was found on an officer's uniform jacket. He thought back to that morning, to the vision of the man shoveling Sinead's walk. His next words were what he truly believed would happen. "It's a sign that you will be visited tonight by someone from the Otherworld."

She smiled and gazed up at him with eyes that had haunted his dreams for so long. "I rather hoped I was going to be visited by someone from *this* world—you."

Perhaps he should have smiled, but he was frozen with fear, knowing that Pembrooke had found a way to slip between the veil of the living and the dead. He feared that coming, the thought that Sinead might prefer her husband to him.

"Kieran?" she whispered, her eyes suddenly worried. "You're regretting—"

"Nothing. I regret nothing that we have done," he rasped, overcome by an emotion he had never felt, but that steadily seemed to consume him. At last he had confirmation that his longing was not just one-sided. So many nights he had lain alone in his bed, wondering if this desire he had for Sinead would ever be returned. So many times he had thought to end his torture by leaving the tiny village—and Sinead—far behind. But then the idea of never seeing her again was more painful than the idea of unrequited pining. But tonight he had the confirmation that she wanted him as a whole man, not just a handyman to help her about her worn cottage.

Opening the door, Kieran pulled her across the threshold, then, pressing her against the wall, he captured her mouth hard with his. She moaned, a sexy low growl, and he tilted her face up, kissing her harder, stealing her breath until she was clutching at his hair, and kissing him back with just as much hunger.

He tried to remember himself, but she would not hear of him pulling away. She clung to him like ivy and pulled at his coat, shoving it down his arms as she brushed her mons against the tent of his trousers. In a frantic rush, he shed his jacket and allowed her to pull his shirttails from his trousers. The first touch of her fingertips on his back made him arch and hiss as if he'd been burned. He had waited so long for this—to feel her soft, delicate fingers on his body.

"I want you naked against my skin," he said, his voice rough as he sought her lips once more and pulled the cloak from her shoulders. *Fuck,* he wanted that, her naked against him, her bottom in his palms as he thrust up inside her. But not yet. Her pleasure came first. He had prepared for this evening. He would seduce her. Show her every erotic pleasure he knew. But not like this. It had to be beautiful, soft, like her nights spent with Pembrooke. Pembrooke would not have taken her like this.

As loath as he was to admit it, Kieran knew he was battling the ghost of his commanding officer. Never given to jealousy before, he felt it now. How was he to compare to a man of noble blood? A man who had been rich and well-educated and cultured?

Kieran still felt the need to prove to Sinead that he could be every bit as good a lover to her as her husband had been. He could be soft, despite his harsh upbringing. He could be the type of romantic that women dreamed of. Even though he was nothing but a soldier and a farmer, he knew he could take care of Sinead and be the sort of man she needed. He was no blue blood like Pembrooke, but something told him that his simple upbringing would not turn Sinead away from him. She had not married Pembrooke because of his lineage, nor even for the depth of his purse. He wouldn't believe that Sinead was that shallow. He knew she was different from other women and wouldn't shun him because he was not a son of a noble, or independently wealthy. Sinead wanted something more out of a man, a friend, a lover, a companion to share the ups and downs of life. The trappings of his life would not matter to her, only his ability to love and please her.

He *could* be the sort of man she needed to replace David. In time, she might not even notice his rough, callused hands. In time, she might even learn to like the feel of his chafed fingers touching her silky skin.

Breaking off their frenzied kiss, he whispered, "Soon." Kissing her neck, her earlobe, then the delicate wings of her brows, he slowed his breathing, gathering his passion under control so that he could give her the sort of lovemaking she deserved. "We have all night to explore. Come," he said, reaching for her hand.

"No," she cried, reaching for him, clutching his arms as if she was holding on to a lifeline. "I want you *now!*"

Brushing his thumbs along her cheeks, he tilted her face up to meet his gaze. "When next I have you, it will be in a bed as is proper—"

"I don't want proper and controlled." She pulled him toward her and kissed him, her tongue trailing hot and wet along the seam of his lips. "I want what I see in your eyes— hunger. I want your hands on me, to feel them covering every inch of my body."

"Sinead—"

"You will take me as you did in your thoughts, when you looked at my picture, and you desired me for your own. Show me, Kieran, what it is like to be hungered for. Show me," she pleaded, "what you thought of doing to me all those lonely nights when you were in the trench, thinking of me, and I was across the ocean, wishing to feel the touch of a man caressing my body."

He had never heard Sinead speak like this. It fanned the flames of his patience, arousing him until he could think of nothing but pressing up against her like an eager youth, ready to come.

"Please," she whispered again, while she reached for the button of his trousers. "I…need to know, to experience this with you."

"Just me?" he couldn't help asking. He heard anxiety lace his words and he looked away, ashamed. But she touched his face and brushed away the fear he had of her not wanting him, of him not being what she needed in her life.

"You have been the only man for me—for so long now— that I can think of no other. You can give me something that I've never had. Unbridled passion."

"Do you ache for it?" he asked in a husky whisper as he ran his hands along her hips and started to pull at her woolen skirt and the layers of heavy petticoats beneath.

"Yes," she whispered.

"Do you want to be taken hard? To be full of me?"

She bit her lip as she ran her fingers through his hair. With a nod, she acquiesced.

"Close your eyes then, Sinead, and imagine me fucking you."

"I have. I *am,*" she panted, trying to kiss him, but he angled his head so that he could nibble on her jaw and the tender flesh of her throat. He wanted to hear her admit her need.

"What is it you ask for?"

"You. Inside me. Fucking me," she whispered breathlessly.

Beneath her skirts, his hand rested on muslin. He groaned as his fingers found the front of her drawers and he discovered, as he flattened his palm against her mound, that she had already dampened them. "Already you weep for it again."

"Yes," she said on a frantic rush of breath. "I am starved for your touch, for the feel of you against my body." She tipped her head against the plaster wall and looked at him with bone-melting honesty. "I have lain awake all these nights thinking of you. I have dreamed of pleasuring you. Dreamed of doing things with you that we…that David and I have never done. I want to experience the things you want, that you desire. I want to be the woman you fantasized I was."

"Then you shall have it. Throughout this night you will know all of my deepest, darkest desires."

Nearly mindless now, Kieran pressed his cock into her belly, captured her lips between his and began thrusting his tongue in and out of her mouth in an imitation of what was to come. When she shoved her hips against him, Kieran tore his mouth from hers and bit gently at her neck with the tips of his teeth.

He ran his mouth down her throat to suck at the swells of her breasts. Her fingernails, biting into his scalp, fueled his lust, the pleasure and pain mixed until he was blind with need.

With shaking hands he tore at the ramshackle fastening of her bodice, thrusting it aside, revealing her thin shift. His palms roamed over her full breasts and belly, and he watched her chest rise and fall in his hands, deliberately making her burn.

Roughly he shoved aside the straps of her chemise, revealing ivory breasts with nipples that were dusky pink and erect, begging for a flick of his tongue. He had imagined this, this homecoming. Her welcoming him into her body without reservation.

Their gazes met, and he skimmed his thumbs over her nipples, making her shudder against him. He had always imagined lifting her skirts and shoving himself into her in a possessive thrust. Now, he admitted, he had the desire to see her completely naked, pressed against the wall, open to him. He wanted to watch his cock sinking deeply into her. He wanted to brand her as his, and he needed to see it, her taking him into her body, his cock glistening with her arousal.

With a few deft movements, he unfastened the buttons of her gown and pulled at the strings of her petticoats. Then he waited.

"I am yours," she said as she stepped out of her skirts and the mountain of white petticoats. She stood before him in only her shift, and stockings, which were gray and worn. She deserved silk and ribbons. She deserved more than he could ever give her. In material things, he could never compete with Pembrooke. But no one could give her as much passion as he could. No one would ever love her as much as he did.

Pleasure was his gift to her.

Mine…the word reverberated in his head as he studied her standing before him. A possessive feeling stole over him and he grasped her hard, kissing her, sliding his tongue between her lips, demanding that she give herself to him. When she was gasping, he went to his knees. She pushed him down as well, her fingers digging into his shoulders. Her breath caught as he lingered over the apex of her thighs, still shielded by her chemise. He blew hot air over her, and she stirred, rubbing her muslin-covered sex against his cheek.

Soon, she would know the pleasure of his mouth on her quim.

He went lower, and a groan of frustrated disappointment escaped her lips. Ignoring her, and her hands in his hair that made every attempt to lure him back to her sex, he slid the worn wool down her lush thigh, past her knee to her ankle. He kissed the delicate bones and traced the blue veins of her foot, savoring the softness of her skin on his roughened fingers. He repeated the action on the other leg, drawing out the minutes, the seduction. Then he looked up, and pulled the chemise down over her hips until it pooled at her feet. She was completely naked before him, and he was stunned by the lust that snaked like a drug through his blood.

Mine…

Raising her thigh, he draped it over his shoulder, exposing her glistening quim. He spread her folds, and kissed her. Slowly he brushed his lips over her sex, savoring the heat and wetness against his mouth. The earthy, musky scent of their previous passion coalesced in a heady, erotic perfume that aroused him.

In the quiet of the room, he heard her breathing, shallow with anticipation. He felt her trembling fingers in his hair urging him closer. He wanted to taste her, to love her this way, but the first time he pleasured her with his mouth, he wanted her lying down, spread open to him, his shoulders buried between her thighs. And he wanted to watch her, see the play of emotions, the pleasure, the expression of climax that crossed her face as she came in his mouth.

"Kieran?"

"Later, love, when I can give you endless pleasure. When I can take my time and bring you there, slowly."

He rose to his feet, but as he did so, he pressed against her, allowing their bodies to touch. They both flinched at the warm and visceral contact.

Pressing his cock into her belly, he rubbed its engorged length against the soft rise, letting the wool of his trousers abrade her supple flesh until her gasp of surprise turned to an erotic moan.

Cupping her breast, he lowered his mouth to her nipple and lazily sucked as she watched his tongue move over her.

She whimpered and writhed against him, her head arched back, her full, red lips parted. He thought about how much he wanted her mouth on him, sucking him.

"I want your fingers inside me," she demanded.

He obliged her. Embedding his fingers deep, he stroked her until she was clawing at his shoulders begging him to join her. Only then, when she was wild with passion, did he step out of his trousers and position himself so he could take her in an act of primal possession. But she stopped him, and instead reached for his cock.

"I want to feel you, Kieran," she purred, her eyes glazed with passion. "I want you in my hand, all hot, hard man."

Groaning, he shoved himself into her hand. She ran her fingertips up and down his length and it felt so good to at last feel her hand pumping him. He touched her in tandem and she matched his rhythm, knowing just by his breathing how he wanted her to touch him. He was so bloody close to spending in her palm, but he could not stop until he felt her shudder against him. Concentrating instead on the wetness engulfing his hand, he stroked her quim. She cried out on a gasping breath as he lightly passed his finger over her clitoris. With his thumb he found the speed, the angle that made her cry out, and he worked her harder, and when she began to tremble and shake and arch her back, he gave her more, until she shattered in his arms and cried out his name and begged him, the word *please* a keening plea from deep in her chest.

He thrust his cock deep inside. She was tight, so bloody tight, despite the fact she had taken him not more than half an hour before. He penetrated her in one long stab and she groaned, a beautiful wanton sound, so beautiful that he had to hear it again, so he pulled out and entered her swiftly, feeling the rush of wetness engulf him as he lodged himself farther inside her.

Without giving her more time, he reached for her hand, bringing it above her head and against the wall as he drove inside her. Harder and harder, he thrust. Higher and higher she moved up against the wall as his cock stabbed her deeper.

"Yes," she cried, clutching his hand as he thrust his hips upward, taking her in a primal rhythm that would have her knowing she now belonged solely to him.

Outside the frosted window, David looked through the glass, into the warm sitting room and the couple beside the hearth. They were naked, writhing together against the wall. Sinead's red hair spilling around her shoulders as her feet rubbed against Kieran Thompson's buttocks. He could not hear their sounds of pleasure through the glass, but he knew there would be sounds and husky pants and erotic words whispered between them.

Sinead's mouth opened with every hard thrust, her eyes closed in bliss, her pale body glowing in the firelight. Thompson's mouth was buried between Sinead's breasts, his hands entwined with hers as he took her against the wall.

Together they rocked, fucking as if this were the last time they would ever see each other. It was primal, possessive and arousing. He had never seen Sinead this undone, this passionate. He wanted a taste of her like this.

Reaching for the latch, his hand went through the cold metal. With a frustrated groan, he returned his gaze to the couple. It was not yet time for him, but when it was, he would go to her. Would take her just like that. But would she look at him like that? Would she desire from him what she so clearly desired from Thompson?

When he saw Thompson reach for her waist and lift her, sliding her farther up the wall so that her breasts were level with his mouth, he knew he had done the right thing in sending him to her. Thompson would love her with a fierce possession. He would care for her, protect her. There was so much he wanted to say. So much he wanted to do, yet his time had run out. The past could not be changed. The future was set, and clearly, Sinead's future lay with Kieran, the man she was baring her soul and body to.

He had this one night, and one night only. He would not spend it feeling jealous of Thompson. He would spend it sharing in their passion and partaking of their pleasure, for one last time.

Kieran had pulled back, pistoning his hips, watching as he took Sinead. Sinead was scratching his back and covering Thompson's shoulders in little bites. Thompson reached for her wrist and shackled it above her head, then slammed into her, making Sinead cry out. As she came, Kieran held her, his body wrapping tightly around her trembling form.

Unable to watch anymore, David looked up at the heavens. The moon had slowly moved in the sky. Soon it would be midnight. December twenty-first. The solstice.

And then he would go to her, and he would share in their pleasure, and it would sustain him until the time she would return to him.

6

SINEAD SANK INTO THE WARM WATER, LETTING her head rest against the lip of the wooden tub. The water was warm, just the perfect temperature for a long, leisurely soak.

"What are you doing?" she called out to Kieran.

"I was stoking the fire in the bedroom," he announced from the doorway behind her. Startled, she turned to find him watching her. He was wearing his woolen trousers and naught else. In the shadowed candlelight, his chest glistened golden warm. It was a most spectacular sight, his smooth, sculpted, masculine chest. She took in his shoulders, which still wore red marks from her fingertips; his thick arms that had held her up against the wall; his beautiful, strong fingers that had given her such blinding pleasure. He was a woman's fantasy come to life. And he was looking at her like she was the only woman in the world to him.

"Is the water still warm?"

"Mmm," she murmured, sinking deeper into the depths. "It is. It was most thoughtful of you to draw me a bath."

"Perhaps I had ulterior motives?"

She smiled. "Will you not join me? 'Tis a bit small, but I don't mind."

Kneeling before the tub, Kieran brushed a damp strand of hair behind her ear. "I wish to bathe you, Sinead."

Her eyes flew open in shock. No man, not even David, had ever done such a thing for her. He must have misinterpreted her surprise, for his already dark eyes blackened further and he looked down at his hands.

"Is it wrong to wish to take care of you?" His fingers flexed, before curling into fists. "I know my hands are big... rough..."

Sinead placed her wet hand over his. "You have beautiful hands and the way they touch my body is beyond words. I would have them no other way, Kieran. I was merely surprised, that is all. No one has ever done such a thing for me."

When he looked up, there was heat in his gaze. "Then I am honored to be the first."

He reached behind himself and handed her a square of red velvet and motioned for her to unfold the cloth.

"What is this?" She peeled the cloth away to reveal a cake of soap. Not just any soap, but the finely milled perfumed kind.

"Do you like it?"

Inhaling the spiciness that was mixed with an exotic floral scent, Sinead closed her eyes and indulged her senses. She had never been able to afford such luxury.

"This must have cost a fortune—"

"Shh," he murmured, covering her lips with his finger. "No cost is too high for your pleasure."

"You could not have found something like this at the apothecary."

"I didn't. I've had it for a long time now, since the Crimea. I was afraid it would no longer smell as good as it once had, but the Turk I bought it from swore to me that it was filled with oils that would stand the test of time."

His fingertips lightly traced her collarbone, then fluttered over her shoulder. Their gazes met, and Sinead kissed his knuckles reverently.

"You bought this for me?"

"I was thinking about you one afternoon, as we were marching to the place of our next battle. We were in Turkey, and a vendor from a bazaar came up to us trying to sell us his wares. He had soaps and perfumes and trinkets of every kind. It made me wonder how you would smell fresh from a bath. How your skin would taste, aroused and perfumed. I smelled everything he had to offer, but it was this scent, with its myrrh and Moroccan rose, that made me think of you. Somehow I just knew it would suit you. Spice, with a delicate hint of floral. I had no money, of course, so I traded him my pocketknife for this cask of soap. I kept it in my bag all the time. Sometimes, when it was dark and the others were heavily asleep, I would pull the soap from my bag and smell it, imagining me bathing you. Kissing you. Drying you off and dipping my tongue between your thighs. I—" he swallowed "—I never dared hope that it might one day happen."

Inside, she melted. In that moment of vulnerability, she knew that what she was feeling was beyond the desire for his body. It was love.

"I don't know what to say, other than I am speechless at your kindness."

"Say you will let me bathe you, touch you."

"Only if you will do so in the tub, so I can touch you as well."

Kieran stood, undid his trousers and stepped into the wooden tub. He was fully aroused, and Sinead could feel his erection pressing into her back as he lowered himself behind her. He brought her back against his chest, then reached for the soap in her hand and dipped it into the water. She found his wrist beneath the rippling waves and wrapped her fingers around it.

"Sparingly," she whispered, "for I want to make such a beautiful gift last."

Instead of using the cotton cloth to make a lather, he soaped his hands and brought his palms to her shoulders, kneading them, then he slid his hands down her arms, all the way to her fingers that rested on the edge of the tub. He kissed her between latherings, and Sinead lay back, enjoying the indulgence of him touching her with such reverence, with hands that were rough and callused, yet caressed with such gentleness.

"You are more beautiful and lovely than all my dreams combined."

"You are making me feel like a princess, Kieran, when I am nothing more than the daughter of a blacksmith."

"To me you are. You are so much more to me than you can ever imagine, Sinead. Even though you were married, I thought of you as mine. Even though I respected Pembrooke and was loyal to him, I could not bear to think of you as his. Every letter you wrote to him, I read, stealing them from his bag as he slept, reading them in the dark while the others around me slept. I imagined that you were writing those words to me. And then, I would close my eyes and write my own letters to you. I should probably feel shame in admitting that to you, to sink so low as to take your letters from him, but I cannot feel shame in something that made me want to live."

"Even though I was happy with David, I would have liked to have known that you were thinking of me."

"My thoughts were never far from you, Sinead. Always, you were with me. He knew, you know. David knew of my feelings for you."

Stiffening, Sinead could not help but startle at such a confession. "Wh–what did he say?"

"As he lay dying in my arms, he told me that he would one day come back to you. He also told me that he released you to me. That is why I am here, Sinead. To make a life with you. To love and protect you. I know…" She heard him swallow, felt his heart beat hard beneath his chest. "I know I am not the man your husband was. But, I promise you, I can be that man. I will never be rich, but I will never stray. Never hurt you. I can provide for you, can make a home for you. I…" His body trembled against hers. "I can love you like no man has ever loved you before, Sinead."

Closing her eyes, she let his vow seep over her. David was gone. Her love for him was still there, but it had changed. There was a reverence in that part of her heart that David still held. But the burning passion, the love that was exploding now was not for David, but Kieran. She wanted a life, not an existence. She wanted Kieran, not cold, lonely nights spent in her bed wishing the dawn would arrive so she could see him once again.

David was gone. Each day that passed drew her closer to her own death. She no longer wanted to waste those days in mourning someone that could never return to her. She was not betraying David, or their marriage vows. She had been true and faithful in her love.

What did it matter that Kieran was younger than her? What did she care for the gossip that would be bandied about? There was a never-ending supply of gossip about her, regardless of whether she took up with a younger man or not.

Kieran was right, she was wasting away inside this cottage, clinging to a past because she was afraid of the future.

Tracing her fingers along the cords of Kieran's forearm, she closed her eyes and let the words she had suppressed for so long filter through her mind. *I could love you, as well, as no woman ever has.*

He did not press her for her thoughts. Instead, he continued to brush his hands along her body, washing her. He palmed her breasts, stroking and circling her nipples with his fingertips until they hardened into little points.

"You spoke of desiring me while in the Crimea."

"I did. I desire you more than any man has ever desired a woman."

A rush of satisfaction flooded her blood and she wanted more. To learn his secrets, to hear of his desires. "In your dreams did you make love to me?"

"Yes. Many times, and in many different ways."

"Did I…did I pleasure you as well, in your dreams?" She turned in the tub, kneeling before him. His hands caught her heavy breasts and he began kneading them.

"Yes."

Her sex moistened, arousal hitting her once again as she looked at Kieran's hard body. She wanted to explore that body, to take his pleasure in her hands, to wipe all memories and caresses of other women from his mind and body. "What did you think of me doing to you?"

"Things that would shock you."

"Like what?" she asked as she ran her fingers over his belly and the ridges of muscles that quivered. Incredulously, she thought she saw a hint of pink tinge his cheeks.

"'Tis private, a man's fantasies."

"We are private," she encouraged.

"Sinead—"

"I could love you so well, too, Kieran," she finally admitted. "I *want* to love you, as you desire."

"I desire only you, Sinead, in any way that you will allow."

Rising from the tub, she reached for his hand. "I will allow anything, Kieran. *Anything.*"

Standing before the hearth, Sinead watched as Kieran gently dried her body with a towel he had left to warm by the fire. The fire he had built was roaring, crackling with heat. He had moved the worn settee to the end of the bed, opposite the hearth, and helped her to sit when she was dried.

She was naked, and he trailed his hand between her breasts, down her midriff and over the rise of her belly until he reached her sex, which he brushed with the heel of his palm.

"Close your eyes," he murmured, kissing the shell of her ear. She did as he asked, and let her head rest against the back of the settee. There was a rustling of paper, which was followed by the warmth of his hand on her foot. Her eyes flew open and she watched as he pulled out the silk stockings she had admired so much that afternoon.

"Kieran!" she gasped, "you shouldn't—"

"Yes, I should. You, of anyone, deserve them, Sinead."

"They're too expensive."

"Do you like them?"

"I *adore* them!"

"Then the cost is no matter. Besides, I bought them because I wanted to put them on you. I wanted to see your legs in them while we made love. A fantasy, you see," he said with a wicked grin as he looked up at her. The silk slid up her calf then thigh. Kieran brushed his mouth along her leg as he dressed her in the scandalously seductive French stockings.

"A fantasy?" she asked on a shaking breath.

"Aye, a vivid one. One of my favorites, in fact."

When the stockings were on, he pulled her forward, so that

her bottom was perched on the edge of the settee. His palms were running up her thigh, and his mouth was busy working up her leg, rising higher and higher to the inside of her thigh. With his tongue he traced the pink satin edging. The sight of his tongue on her skin made Sinead's body ignite with heat. When he looked up at her, and placed her legs over his shoulders, she shuddered, growing languid with desire. She was completely exposed to his gaze. But she knew from the look in his eyes that he liked what he saw spread before him. And she liked how beautiful and feminine she felt wearing nothing but the stockings, and the body that Kieran seemed to appreciate so much.

"This is what I thought of, Sinead, all those lonely nights in the trench, in the dark," he murmured as he lowered his head between her legs. "I dreamed of tasting your cunt, just like this."

The first swipe of his tongue parted her folds. He held her open with his thumb and slowly swirled his tongue along her sex. It was too slow, but the pleasure was breath-stealing, the way he took his time tasting her, loving her. He was in no hurry to complete her, and Sinead did something she had never done before, she rested her head back against the settee and allowed herself just to feel, to care only for her pleasure. From her position, she could watch him loving her like this, and she did—the way his black hair, shining in the firelight, fell over his shoulder and onto her knee. The way his shoulders rolled and his muscles flinched as she stroked her fingertips over them.

She had never watched David make love to her body. It had been dark in their room. He had pleasured her, but not in this way, not this slow and unhurried, not as though he would never stop.

Restless, she writhed against him, but he would not be persuaded to increase his pace, despite the knot of tension that was coiling within her.

"Kieran," she pleaded, but he reached for her fingers that were curled in his hair and brought them to her breasts.

"There is no rush, my love."

"You tease me."

"No, Sinead. I'm worshipping you as I have always wanted. Don't you like it?"

"Too much," she gasped.

"Touch your breasts."

It was the darkness of his voice that made her open her eyes. He was watching her, and she did as he asked, cupping her breasts, pleasuring herself as he continued to stroke her with his skillful tongue.

Then, closing her eyes, she lost herself to the pleasure of Kieran's mouth. Time seemed to stop. Her mind blurred. Her body seemed to float and hover, and then her eyelashes fluttered and slowly lifted, revealing an image that was blurry.

David.

Was it really him she saw in the doorway of her bedroom? His hair was a touch darker, longer. His eyes were the same, but he looked older, more worldly than he had that morning she had last seen him.

Pushing away from the doorjamb, David walked to the settee until he stood behind her. Dropping to his knees, he brushed her hair back from her forehead and kissed her throat.

Kieran was still between her thighs, bringing her higher and higher, yet even as she felt Kieran's mouth, she felt David's tongue snake along her neck to her ear.

"Will you love us both tonight, Sinead?" David asked.

Kieran smiled and pushed away to stand before her. He

helped her up and ran his hands up her thighs, rubbing his fingers against the new stockings he had bought for her.

"Kieran?" she asked, reaching for him as he pulled away. Already she felt bereft of him.

"You will have me," he whispered in her ear. "You will have us both tonight. Light and dark."

7

DAVID HADN'T KNOWN HOW HE WOULD COME TO her, only that he must. A year after his death, he had wandered the earth, hovering in the place between heaven and hell. He had prayed for this moment, this last chance to be with the love of his life.

It did not hurt him to see her with Kieran, nor to watch what he had never done to her. To know she would be well loved and pleasured was enough. To see her happiness, to see the obvious love she held for Kieran filled him with peace. He was not leaving her alone, afraid. She was not unhappy.

After tonight, she would let him go and together, but separately, they would start down the path to a future that would not include each other.

"You have grown more beautiful, Sinead." She closed her eyes and pressed her cheek into his cupped hand. "Your body even more luscious than before. So soft. So warm."

"I am dreaming."

"Do you not feel my touch?" he asked, then brushed his lips against her mouth. "Do you not feel my kiss?"

"I do, but how…Kieran…"

"A woman's fantasy," David murmured as he ran his fingers down her neck. Her skin was just as soft and supple, her curves more generous, her body more womanly.

"But…but you are not…alive."

"I am for this night. For one last night together."

She looked over her shoulder, fear shining in her eyes. Kieran. She was afraid of losing him. Afraid of having him turn from her. But she didn't understand, didn't realize that she was in control of this night. What would happen between them—all of them—was in her power, her control.

"You can have me," David said in a fierce whisper. "I'm yours, and you, Sinead, are mine. For tonight. For only tonight, let there be no regrets, no pain, no tears."

"David?" Sinead said his name aloud, unable to believe that it was truly him.

"What does your heart tell you, Sinead?" he asked as he trailed his hand between the valley of her breasts. "Who does your body think it's with? Does it not recall my touch?"

Her body recalled David's touch, the memory coming to life like the spark from a match.

"Sinead," she heard Kieran's dark, velvety voice whisper in her ear, interrupting her thoughts. She felt the fluttering of his fingertips caressing the side of her cheek, her neck, the contours of her breasts before they traveled over her hips, only to roam over her bottom as they cupped and kneaded.

Shock lanced through her like a bolt of lightning. It was utterly scandalous, but true. It was Kieran touching her from behind, and from the front it was David.

But how could that be? It must be her wicked, wanton imagination. Her repressed sexual fantasies making her think such immoral things. She could not believe this was truly happening, despite the fact that it felt more real than anything she had ever experienced in her life.

"I am here, Sinead," Kieran whispered as his long fingers encased her breast. She reached up to cover his hand, anchoring him to her. "He has come back for this one night. Let us share you. Let us make love to you."

Real or fantasy, it was too provocative. This was her one chance to have both men, to experience the pleasure to be found in two men who were so different from each other.

Kieran continued to pluck at her nipples, and David watched as she squeezed her breasts together, kneading them. Arching and writhing, she moved against both men. Then David's hands were touching her breasts, too, following Kieran's path. One's touch was soft, the other's rougher, more commanding.

When Kieran offered her breasts up to David, David lowered his mouth to her nipples. Sinead gave in to the magic, the fantasy of spending the night between both men.

"Let us do this for you," Kieran entreated in a voice that she could not refuse. "Imagine the delight of him suckling you while you feel my hands covering your body. Imagine what it will be like to have both of us loving you at once."

"So very, very wicked to desire such a thing," she said as she watched David's tongue work her nipple. Kieran squeezed her breast then, filling David's mouth. Hungrily, he sucked as Kieran continued to squeeze, feeding David more of her flesh.

David lay back on the ground, taking her with him. Straddling his thighs, she tore at the buttons of his shirt. The slash of rippled flesh over his belly made her cringe. This is how he had died. Carefully she traced the wound, and he closed his eyes and moaned.

"God, your hands…your touch…I forgot how good it felt."

Kieran came up behind her then, and she felt the weight

of him, the heat of his skin burning her back, her bottom. He was kissing the line of her spine as his fingers spread the folds of her sex. She groaned and writhed as he pressed into her, his erection pushing into the soft globe of her bottom.

She felt David rubbing her arms as she kissed the uneven skin of his belly, felt his palms travel over her thighs and then his fingers pulling at the pink satin band of her stockings. The movement was halted by a dark warning.

"Leave them."

She looked down and saw Kieran's hand shackling David's wrist. She felt the tension in Kieran's body, heard his hard breathing in her ear, and she went liquid between them. Kieran's possessiveness called to her. She liked it.

Conceding to Kieran, David removed his hand and captured her breast in his palm.

"Mine," Keiran growled against her throat, reminding her of his claim.

She clutched at his fingers, which traced the flesh of her thigh above her stockings, letting him know she was his. The tension in him loosened, and he returned to kissing her.

"David…" Sinead lowered her breasts so that only the tips of her nipples grazed his chest. "You have come back to me," she murmured, then kissed his shoulder. Meeting his gaze, she brushed her breasts against him. With their gazes locked, she licked his lips with a flick of her tongue. Then she did it again, but this time she swirled her nipples against the crisp hair on his chest.

The feeling of being encompassed by both men was strange, yet heady. She was warm, front and back, her body overly sensitized as two pairs of hands worked her from every angle. No part of her was left untouched, unkissed.

David cupped the back of her head and lowered her mouth

to his. Boldly, her tongue crept out, but he tricked her and met her tongue with the tip of his. Slowly, erotically, their tongues touched.

"I want to see your tongue like that on my cock," Kieran whispered as he pressed into her.

She wanted that, too. She had never done that, David had never asked, never pressed. But she knew Kieran would not ask. He would take. And she would allow it.

"Kiss me, Sinead." Fisting his fingers in her hair, David brought her forward, crushing his mouth against hers. It was a carnal kiss and he devoured her with unrestrained passion. Breaking off the kiss, he lifted her up and brought her breasts to his mouth. Hungrily, he took from her, and she pleasured in the sensation of him suckling her—starving for her.

She reached between their bodies and opened the flap of his trousers. He was hard, ready, silken. Then she felt Kieran's fingers pressing into her folds, entering her. She was wet, wanton now with Kieran playing with her sex and David sucking her breasts. She looked up and saw the image of the three of them in the dressing mirror. Kieran caught her expression in the reflection and lowered his head, kissing the globe of her bottom, then tasting her with his tongue.

Closing her eyes, she savored his mouth, the lash of his tongue, the feel of David's teeth gently tugging on her nipple. She felt the weight of David's erection in her hand and she stroked him, burning higher as she heard him groan. His fingers set about stroking her calves, working their magic up past her knees to the inner facings of her thighs.

Kieran moved away, leaving her empty. She reached for him, and he clasped her wrist, letting her know he was there.

"I want to watch you with him," Kieran murmured. "I want to see your pleasure, and then I will watch you with me."

David took control, and she squirmed when he sank his hand between her thighs. Then he reached for her hips and lifted her to his mouth. Stabbing pleasure snaked through her body. Hissing, Sinead arched her back and felt Kieran behind her, his hands palming her breasts. Wrapping her arms around Kieran's neck, she allowed herself to be taken by both men as she studied David's golden head moving languorously between her legs.

Watching as David slowly made love to her with his lips and tongue, listening to his sighs of pleasure, catapulted her closer and closer to orgasm.

"So beautiful," she whispered, watching his mouth move along her. He looked up at her and smiled slowly, his eyes dancing in the glow of the firelight that had dimmed.

Kieran continued to play with her nipples, stroking and pulling in time to David's slashing tongue. She fell apart, shaking, her fingers clinging to Kieran as David held her still. In a boneless heap, she fell forward onto David's chest.

Turning her onto her back, David slid up the length of Sinead's body, his chest slick with perspiration, the evidence of his arousal rubbing against her belly. His finger reached out and stroked her parted lips, brushing back and forth in an erotic rhythm.

"Take me in your hand and stroke me. Show me how you want me." When she placed him into her palm he moaned a deep, guttural "yes" and began to pump himself into her hand. "God, yes," he groaned when she swirled her fingertip atop the swollen tip of him. David's hand fisted in her hair, his breath coming in short pants as he watched her work him with her hand.

She looked over and saw Kieran, he was touching himself,

watching her with David. With a smile, she motioned for him to come to her. He did, sliding beside her, kissing her lazily as she continued to pleasure David.

"I want you," she whispered to Kieran, and he instinctively knew how she wanted him. Leaning back on his elbow, Kieran stroked himself and Sinead leaned over, taking the thick width of him into her mouth. His deep guttural groan was so powerful that Sinead let go of David and moved forward, crawling over Kieran, taking all of him in her mouth. He fisted his hands in her hair as he watched her sucking him, licking him as she played with the sack between his legs.

"Swallow me, Sinead," he commanded as he filled her mouth. She took him in, drinking him down as she felt the fluttering touch of David's fingers on her side.

David reached for her and positioned her so that she sat astride him and his erection was pulsing against her swollen folds.

"I want to see all of you," David groaned as he ran his hands all over her body. "I want all of this before me as you ride me."

David let his gaze roam liberally along her body. He took his time studying her, watching as the moonlight kissed her flesh. His gaze flickered up to the gentle slope of her shoulder, to the curve of her neck, and beyond, to where a mirror rested against the wall opposite the lounge.

Reaching out, he trailed his fingers along the indentation of her waist and up and over her hip, all the while watching in the mirror as his hand roamed along her alabaster flesh.

Gooseflesh sprung to life beneath his fingers and he felt Sinead sway into him, the movement mirrored in the glass. His hand at last found her bottom and he squeezed it. He tipped his head to the side so he could see his finger disappearing into the curls that were already damp for him.

"Turn around, sweeting."

Gripping her about the waist, he helped her turn so that she was facing the mirror, her thighs draped over each of his legs. He fitted her hands around her breasts, making certain her pink nipples peeked out between her fingers. He positioned her so that she could slide her sex along his erection. He was aching to take her, but he wanted to take things slowly, to savor the moment. For this would be his last night with her.

Sinead watched in the mirror as David's hands roamed her body. She sat frozen atop him, mesmerized. Then Kieran was before her, touching her, his hands moving along her, taking the opposite path of David's, sensitizing her skin until she writhed, not knowing whether she was trying to get away or take more.

Sinead closed her eyes and savored the sensation of Kieran's mouth moving along her throat, suckling her neck at the same time David's fingers brushed between her legs.

"Your eyes, sweeting, I want to see them." When she opened them and found David's gaze in the mirror, he grinned, then ran his finger down her swollen sex, parting her. Kieran's fingers fisted in her hair as he stroked his tongue up the column of her throat.

Her eyes went wide when David raised her up from his lap and took his erection in his hand, thrusting slowly into her, telling her to sink down onto him.

Slowly she slid down, feeling full as David pushed up into her. She rode him, her hips undulating on his cock as Kieran suckled her breasts. Their hands were everywhere on her body, and every nerve she possessed was sensitized and alive.

She was nearly there, at that heavenly precipice, when David pulled out.

"No!" she cried.

"I want to see your face as I make love to you," David groaned. "I need it, to see you like that once again." He turned her so that he supported her back with his knees. She arched then, the action thrusting her breasts toward him.

David murmured as his eyes closed in pleasure. "God, the slide is so easy. All I can think of is how pleasurable it is not holding back for fear of hurting you. We can fuck now, can't we, Sinead?"

Sinead looked down into David's face and saw how his eyes had taken on a darker edge as he thrust deep and hard into her.

Resting her back against David's knees, Sinead ground her hips onto him, matching his rhythm. "Come for me," David commanded as he looked up at her with lust-filled eyes. "I want to feel your cunt milking me."

While David pleasured, Kieran nuzzled and licked her neck, his tongue alternating with the gentle brush of his fingertip along the bulging vein. His free hand skated down her belly to the crest of her sex where he circled her clitoris with his index finger.

She fell apart then. "Oh, my God," Sinead whispered before falling on top of David.

"Sinead," David whispered, brushing back her hair and kissing her brow. "I love you. Always."

8

KIERAN PICKED SINEAD UP FROM THE FLOOR AND carried her to the bed. She was sated and sleepy, like a well-fed cat lying by the fire. She had been wild with him, wanton. He had absorbed every part of her into his body. When she had taken him into her mouth he had nearly screamed, when she had swallowed him he knew he'd never get enough of her.

Allowing her to be with Pembrooke had nearly ruined him. In the days before he had loved Sinead it hadn't bothered him to share a woman, but to see her with Pembrooke, to hear her pleasure, crushed him. And yet, he'd put aside his jealousy and his own fear, knowing it was what Sinead needed, and knowing it was the sole purpose for Pembrooke's return. He had endured it, seeing Pembrooke fucking her, but he had felt savage, like an animal whose mate had been stolen. Now all he wanted to do was get his scent on her, to mark her as his, and his alone.

Brushing her hair away from her brow, he watched her sleep, tracing the way the moonlight mingled with the fading glow of the fire over her breasts. His cock was hard. He wanted to take her again, to awaken her like this. But he had already had her too many times that night.

He kissed her once more, then gathered her in his arms and contented himself with holding her. She snuggled into him, pressing her lush body up against his. With a smile, he let his head drop next to hers on the pillow, thinking about how he had despaired of never having her like this.

"I think she might have always been your destiny."

Through sleepy, blurry eyes, Kieran lifted his head and searched the shadows in the room. From the darkest corner, a figure appeared. Kieran blinked, wiping away the sleep.

Pembrooke.

Instinctively, Kieran brought Sinead closer to his body, protecting her from what…a ghost?

Pembrooke smiled, his gaze dropping to Sinead who slept soundly in Kieran's arms.

"You love her so well, and she loves you. You will love her always, just as much as you do now?" Pembrooke asked, kneeling by the side of the bed.

Swallowing hard, Kieran replied, "I will."

"It was not easy for you to allow me in tonight, I saw that in your eyes."

"You gave me a chance to have her—I owed you the opportunity to say goodbye."

"You have not even questioned how I have come back, how it is possible for me to be here with you."

"There are things in life and death that we are not meant to understand. I accept that. I also understand that when the heart has unfinished business, it cannot rest in peace."

"This heart is satisfied now. It has felt love once more and can rest easy. You deserve her," Pembrooke murmured as he touched the shape of Sinead's face. "Treat her well, Thompson."

Pembrooke kissed her, then pulled away. "She has released me this night. She is yours now."

"Wait!"

But he was gone, a shadow amongst shadows.

Sinead awoke to the feel of Kieran's callused fingers skimming along her hip. She exhaled deeply, sexually replete and satisfied by the lusty lovemaking they had shared. She thought of all the arousing things he had shown her, the things she wanted to do again. She thought of David and the coming together of both men to pleasure her. Kieran, commanding and strong, encouraging her to let go of her fears. David had been soft, reverent, accepting of her feelings for Kieran, while sharing her one last time.

She half wondered if it hadn't all been a wicked dream, but the sensitivity of her nipples and the soreness between her thighs told her that last night had been real.

Cocooned beneath the bedcovers, Sinead was becoming aroused by Kieran's persuasive hand. His hot, naked chest pressed into her back, and his heavy thigh was draped over her legs. Through flickering lashes she saw slate-gray streaks of light peering through from the heavens. It was not yet dawn, not yet the solstice. But waking up next to a man like Kieran, and having his hands roam over her body as though he worshipped her, was all Sinead needed. There was peace here in this bed. Harmony. There was love here.

Without a word, he flipped her to her stomach and mounted her, covering her back with his chest. His arms came around her and he hugged her close to his body, which was taut with sexual tension.

"Accept me."

It was not a question or a plea, but a command. Raising her hips off the bed, Sinead silently answered him, and he thrust into her. She took him all, meeting him, accepting him.

There were no words, just the sounds of their bodies mating while outside the world slept. To Sinead, she felt as though they were the only two people on earth. Just her and Kieran, and he was making love to her, giving her body such pleasure. Her heart soared and she clutched at his fists and brought her mouth to his knuckles as he changed his pace from lazy and slow to harder and faster, threatening to make her fall into a blinding orgasm.

"Sinead," he whispered, dropping his head against hers. *"Mo muirnin."*

My beloved…

Her tears trickled onto his hand as she clutched him harder, fearing that she might come fully awake and realize that he, too, was gone.

"I am here, Sinead, can you not feel me?"

She could, but she wanted more, a contact with him that she would feel the day through. That would sustain her, like breath.

He knew what she needed. He would always know.

Lifting her hips, he brought her to her knees and curled his large form around hers until there was no inch left of her body that was not touched by Kieran's.

Slowing his pace, he built her up in a slow rise. He stroked her breasts and rolled her nipples. He whispered love words in her ears and kissed her shoulder. He let her feel the trembling that rippled through his body, and when he stroked her clitoris and fed her his cock, she let herself go, knowing that Kieran was indeed with her. She felt him everywhere, but most of all, she felt him in her soul. It was beautiful and right. And the tears that fell from her eyes were not tears of pain, but of utter joy and fulfillment.

★ ★ ★

"You have made a wanton of me," she said on a laugh as she traced Kieran's lips with her fingertip.

"No, I merely allowed it to come out. It was there all along." He kissed her finger and gathered her close to his chest. Together they watched the sky slowly lighten and the snow fall silently to the ground.

She hardly knew what to say next, whether to mention David or not.

"We need to go to the stones, *mo muirnin,* for there is something that must be done."

Nodding, she slipped from his arms and the sheet dropped to her waist, baring her breasts. Kieran stilled her and traced her tender nipple and areola with the pad of his thumb.

"I will never grow tired of looking at you, Sinead. I…can hardly believe…" He swallowed and looked away. "Are you mine, Sinead?"

Cupping his cheeks in her hands, she forced him to look at her. "I am yours, Kieran, as you are mine."

"I've always belonged to you, Sinead. I always will."

The stones could wait, she thought as she bared herself to him and straddled his lap. It was her turn to show him the ways a woman could love a man.

He moaned, a shaky sound from deep within, and slowly came to rest against the pillows. *"Yes."*

It was all he could say as she proceeded to make love to him.

EPILOGUE

THEY STOOD TOGETHER AND WATCHED THE BRIGHT orange disc rise above the clouds and the snow-laden trees of the woods that lay to the east of the standing stones.

"It's such a beautiful sight, is it not?" she asked.

Kieran reached for her gloved hand and squeezed it. "I never thought I'd be here with you, watching the sun rise. I feel as though I'm in a dream, and when I wake up I will be back in that muddy trench alone."

"No." Resting her head on his shoulder, Sinead looked up at him. "Neither of us is alone anymore."

The sunshine filtered through the stones, illuminating his face. The darkness was still there in his eyes, but there was vulnerability, too—a softness that had not been there before last night. He looked down at her, tweaked her nose and laughed as the first snowflake landed on her cheek.

"Shall we?"

Sinead reached for the wooden box that Kieran had carved. It was engraved with the Celtic tree of life, a symbol for everlasting life and prosperity. In it, they had placed the cloth the little girl had given her, and between the stones, she tucked the box and gave thanks to the priestess for the wonderful gift she had bestowed upon her.

When she stood, it was to have Kieran bring her to his chest and hold her tight. "Look beyond the stones, *muirnin*."

She did, and saw the image of David standing there, looking back at them. His face was glowing as if he was at peace. Kieran held her tighter, so close in fact that she could feel the heavy beating of his heart beneath his coat.

"What do you see?" she asked Kieran, wondering if he saw David, as well.

"Do you not see him? That magnificent stag just beyond the stone—and look, a doe has come out of the woods. Can't you see them?" Kieran asked with a laugh.

"I see them," Sinead whispered as she watched the girl who had given her the cloth emerge from the snow and take David's hand in hers.

"'Til we meet again," she whispered to David. He nodded, hearing her, and then looked down at the child and allowed her to lead him off into the sunrise until they disappeared.

"What are you thinking?" Kieran asked as he tipped her chin up and brushed aside a tear that slipped down her cheek.

"I am thinking that the world is, indeed, in perfect balance. Light and darkness, death and rebirth. It is because of you, Kieran, that I have been reborn."

"Come, let us go back to bed and hide away from the world in your little cottage. And when you open your eyes, there I will be, looking down at you, loving you. And when I come home to you, there you will be waiting with arms ready for me."

There was love and peace and pleasure, so much pleasure. Amongst midnight whispers on the winter solstice both of them had been reborn.

★ ★ ★ ★ ★

LOVER'S DAWN
by
Kristi Astor

1

"HERE," AISLING SAID, SHOVING A STACK OF PAPERS onto Jack's lap as she perched on the sofa's rolled arm beside him.

Pushing his wire-rimmed spectacles up the bridge of his nose, he pulled out a page at random and began to read aloud.

"His lips, warm and moist, traveled from the swell of her creamy, rose-tipped breasts down to her stomach. Onward they moved to her navel and then below, tracing slow, wet circles upon her goosefleshed skin. Her back arched off the settee in wicked anticipation, her entire body quivering with need. At last she felt the tip of his tongue part her slick, wet folds, teasing the nub of sensitive flesh 'til she cried out in pleasure..."

"Good God, Aisling! This is positively scandalous! We'll make a fortune with this one."

Aisling arched one brow as she reached for her cigarette case. "Do you really think so? It's not a bit over the top, is it?"

"Of course it is. That's what makes it bloody brilliant." Jack's cheeks reddened. "I'll read the rest later."

"Of course." Aisling fiddled with the jeweled case, deciding that she didn't really want a cigarette, after all.

Jack removed his spectacles and laid them down atop the manuscript. "I don't even want to know where you get your inspiration, Ash," he said, shaking his head. "Honestly, if Mother knew—"

"It's called 'using one's imagination,' dear brother. You should try it sometime. And Mother is never going to know. Unless you tell her, of course."

Jack looked positively outraged. "And why would I do that? Devil take it, Aisling, you're my cash cow."

"I should probably box your ears for such a sexist remark as that." She rolled her eyes heavenward as she stood, smoothing her hands down the front of her skirts. "Anyway, the usual plan. You'll take it to the *Boudoir* when you're in London this week, collect the fee and deposit half into my account." She sighed loudly, trailing her fingertips over the couch's plush, plum-colored upholstery. "Honestly, I don't know why I give you half. They're *my* stories, after all."

"Yes, but without me, you'd have nothing." Her brother rose, unfolding his impossibly long legs and striding over to his desk where he deposited the manuscript with a *thunk*. "It's not as if you could peddle your stories yourself—they wouldn't let you past the front door of the *Boudoir*'s office. Anyway, just promise me that it *is* your imagination fueling these stories, and nothing more. I'd hate to be forced to defend your honor. You know what a terrible shot I am," he said with a grin.

"Of course it is," Aisling murmured. She wasn't a virgin, not that she'd ever admit that to Jack. But her one sexual experience had been lackluster at best—rushed and hurried, with no attempt made at pleasuring *her* at all. Aisling grimaced, remembering Thomas Esterbrooke's wet, sloppy kisses; his damp palms and unimpressive member as he'd writhed and grunted atop her. She couldn't help but shudder at the memory.

No, her stories were nothing like that. Instead, they were full of passion and longing, of expert lovemaking and deeply felt emotions—all things twenty-three-year-old Aisling Wainscott had never once experienced in her life.

God, but she was bored. Sick of Dorset, sick of Bedlington and everyone who lived there. Sometimes Aisling thought she'd go mad with boredom, if not for her pen and the escape her imagination provided.

"I suppose I should get back to the books," Jack said, a tinge of regret in his voice. "Don't forget that I've invited guests to join us tonight for dinner."

"Oh?"

"Yes, some friends of mine are in the area, visiting family. Roger and Edmund Dalton, you remember them? We went up to Eton together."

"Vaguely," Aisling said with a shrug.

"I thought we'd play cards later," he continued, "so I've invited Will Cooper—you know, to even out the numbers. He's in Bedlington for a fortnight, spending Christmas with his mum."

Aisling couldn't help but groan. "Not Will Cooper!"

Jack's blond brows drew together. "What do you have against Will, the poor chap? It's not his fault that his mother is a washerwoman. Besides, everyone knows his father was a gentleman."

"Yes, but *which* gentleman?" She shook her head. "Anyway, something about the way Will looks at me makes me uncomfortable."

"But you haven't seen him in years, not since he went up to Cambridge."

"It was all well and good to be friends with him when we were children, but now? Educated or not, he's still, well…not exactly our sort, is he?"

"Why, you little hypocrite," Jack accused, though he smiled delightedly. "Who would have thought that you, of all people, would be such a snob? All for the voting rights of women, even common women, yet you think the son of a washerwoman isn't 'our sort.'"

Aisling scowled at her brother. "He watches me when he thinks I'm not looking, and he's far too full of himself, besides."

"It's true, then," Jack crowed. "You *are* a snob."

"Do shut up." She headed for the door. One hand on the brass handle, she turned back toward her brother. "Better a snob than a pompous ass like you."

"You shouldn't swear, Ash. It isn't at all becoming."

"Oh, go fuck yourself," she called out, tossing her hair over her shoulder as she let herself out.

She could hear him sputtering in indignation as the door swung shut. As she headed toward the stairs, she passed a long, gilt-framed mirror and winked at her reflection in smug satisfaction. It was far too easy to one-up her brother.

Minutes later, she'd retrieved her gloves and coat and hurried through the foyer, past the enormous Christmas tree that was decorated with red bows and colorful blown glass, its small electric lights just waiting to be lit. Mother loved Christmastime and left no hall undecked, no mantel undecorated.

But for Aisling, Christmas simply marked another year's passing, each one no different from the one before it. There'd been no Eton for Aisling, no years at university like Jack had enjoyed. Just season after season, year after year here in Dorset, with only brief jaunts to London to relieve the monotony. Brief because Father had Mrs. Gaylord in London, of course, and how he hated his wife and family intruding on his time with his mistress.

Aisling let herself out the back door and skimmed down the stairs, buttoning up her coat. It had grown colder, and her breath made puffs of smoke in the wintry air as she hurried away from the house, toward the graveled path that led toward the now-frozen swimming pond and beyond.

I'll never be like Mother, she silently vowed. Someday, Aisling would be free. Exactly what that meant, she wasn't certain. Just that she wouldn't necessarily be dependent on a man, particularly one who didn't put her needs equal to his own; who would leave his wife and children rotting away in the country while he lived it up in town.

Shaking her head in frustration, she picked up her pace, veering off the path and through the copse of trees, toward the circle of standing stones in the distance. It was her favorite spot, just beyond the eastern border of Wainscott House's property, in a shady little clearing. In the summer months, she would sit with her back against the largest of the stones and write. The almost mystical atmosphere seemed to fuel her creativity, and she'd written some of her best work there. She liked to think of the stone circle as hers—her own private retreat, her refuge.

But now, as Aisling stepped out of the trees' shadows and into the clearing, she saw a lone figure in a cloak standing there, watching her approach. The hood's folds obscured the intruder's face, concealing the features, yet Aisling felt sure that the figure was a woman's. Dark, unbound hair escaped the stranger's hood, dancing on the breeze that caused the heavy woolen folds of Aisling's coat to flap noisily against her limbs. Icy snow began to swirl about, stinging Aisling's face.

At once the sun began to dip beneath the horizon, casting

an eerie red glow on the tallest stone. In the blink of an eye, the bloodred light moved across the stones like a serpent, undulating around the circle once before melting away on the snow-dusted ground, leaving nothing but a grayish-lavender twilight behind.

It's the winter solstice, Aisling realized with a start, a shiver working its way down her spine.

Her eyes scanned the circle—once, twice, searching for the strange, cloaked woman. Nothing. "Miss?" she called out, then tried again, louder this time. "Miss? Hello?"

The woman was gone. Vanished, in what had been no more than a heartbeat's time. Aisling dashed into the center of the circle, noticing that the wind had grown quiet—in fact, everything was quiet now, as silent as a tomb. Snow continued to fall softly, silently, making the ground at Aisling's feet look as if a carpet of glittering crystals covered it.

A queer feeling rushed over her, raising gooseflesh on her skin. It seemed as if the stones themselves were holding their breath, watching, waiting...

And then she saw it, there atop the tallest of the stones. Something that wasn't there before—something that didn't belong. A box. Aisling's feet seemed to move involuntarily, taking her closer. Before she knew it, the box was in her hands and she was staring down at it, her heart thumping noisily against her ribs.

Swallowing hard, she ran her fingertips over the lid, brushing away the dusting of snow to reveal an unfamiliar symbol—Celtic, perhaps—etched into the wood. She took a deep, fortifying breath, allowing the cold air to fill her lungs as she summoned the courage to lift the lid and see what lay inside.

A bone-and-leather fastening held it closed, and it took a bit of work to undo it, especially with fingers that trembled as hers did. She had to remove one glove, exposing her fingers to the chilled air. At last she accomplished the task and slowly raised the lid, holding her breath in anticipation.

Don't be so dramatic, she chastised herself as she peered inside. *It's only a box, for God's sake, with nothing inside but a folded slip of paper.* She almost laughed aloud at her own ridiculousness as she set the box on the ground by her feet and unfolded the page. On what appeared to be a very old piece of parchment were lines of neat, precise script, looking much like a poem. She read aloud,

> *"Hope reborn, come with the sun*
> *dispel the chill of darkness*
> *bright fire of dawn*
> *reach to our hearts*
> *burn bright of winter's desire.*
>
> *"Enchanted stream of brilliant light*
> *amid the crystal ground*
> *dark traverse blending of the night*
> *bring sweet lover's kiss*
> *burn bright of winter's desire.*
>
> *"No wanderer's curse*
> *be he thus beckoned*
> *a slave to passion's fire*
> *return his head, upon my breast*
> *burn bright of winter's desire."*

Aisling hadn't realized she'd read it aloud until the last word echoed off the stones, reverberating to where she stood. Such beautiful words! *Winter's desire.* But whatever did it mean?

And then her heart swelled with it—her *own* winter's desire, a wish held so close to her heart that she'd never before acknowledged its existence.

I wish for someone to awaken my cold, frozen heart, to make me feel things I've never felt before—longing and desire, passion and love, hurt and hate, all at once. I wish for a man who appreciates words as I do, an educated man—an artist, perhaps—whose hands are strong and rough and callused. A man who will worship me, yet treat me as an equal.

A painful lump formed in her throat as she realized exactly what she'd wished for—the impossible. A man who did not exist. What a fool she was, hoping for things she could never have, feelings she'd never experience. All these years she'd convinced herself she was satisfied with her choices, trapped as she was between her own ideals and society's dictates. But now she'd allowed doubts to creep into her consciousness, upsetting her entire sense of self, and all because of a silly poem.

Stuff and nonsense, she told herself as she briskly refolded the slip of paper and shoved it back inside the box, then refastened the lid. Tucking the box beneath her arm, she headed toward Wainscott House without a backward glance, refusing to let herself think about what had just happened there in the circle of stones.

Instead, she concentrated on getting home before darkness fell.

2

FOR PERHAPS THE TENTH TIME IN SO MANY
minutes, Aisling furtively glanced at the man seated across the
table from her, and then dropped her gaze as quickly as she'd
raised it. Heat flooded her cheeks, no doubt staining them
red as she twisted the napkin in her lap. Whatever was the
matter with her?

It's just Will Cooper, she told herself angrily. And yet it
wasn't Will; at least, not the Will she remembered. No, the
Will Cooper she remembered was slight, not much taller than
she was. His face was pale, rather unremarkable, his eyes a
shade she could not recall.

This Will was tall—not quite six feet, she'd guess, but close
to it. His shoulders were broad, his skin browned, his eyes a
startling shade of blue. She watched as he lifted his glass to
his lips, her gaze inexplicably drawn to his hand, a hand that
appeared strong, callused and entirely masculine. Just imagining those hands on her body made her tremble, made her
clench her thighs together.

"So, Mr. Cooper," she heard her mother ask, "when must
you return to Cambridge?"

"Just after the new year, ma'am," he answered.

Cambridge? What was he doing at Cambridge? By her own calculation, he should have left university long ago. He was a year her senior—the same age as Jack.

Jack turned toward the elder Dalton brother—Edmund, perhaps?—who was seated to his right. "Cooper here has a position at the Botanic Garden at Cambridge," he clarified.

"Of course, a botanist." Aisling hadn't realized she'd spoken the words aloud 'til all eyes turned toward her. "I…that is to say, you *did* study botany at university, didn't you?"

Will's eyes met hers. "Indeed. I was lucky to find a post there once I finished my studies. Have you seen the Botanic Garden's new glasshouse?"

Aisling shook her head, feeling slightly breathless. "No, I…I don't believe I've been to Cambridge in quite some time."

"Well, we must rectify that at once, mustn't we? Jack, surely you can spare the time to accompany Aisling and Mrs. Wainscott up to Cambridge. The winter gardens are spectacular."

Jack grunted noncommittally as he took a sip of sweet, mulled wine.

Mother folded her napkin and set it on the table beside her plate of uneaten sweets. "So, Mr. Cooper, what exactly is it that you do there at the garden?" she asked.

"I mostly catalog the species. Draw them, label them." He shrugged, an easy smile on his lips. "Though I don't mind getting my hands dirty now and then, either."

"Why, that sounds like fascinating work," Mother replied. "Your mother is so proud, you know. It's lovely to hear her speak of you. I saw her just yesterday, when I picked up some mending." She then turned her attention back to the Dalton brothers. "So, Mr. Dalton—Roger, is it? Do you spend all your time in London, or have you taken a property in the country, too?"

As the topic of conversation shifted, Aisling continued to stare across the width of the table, wondering how Will had grown so handsome without her noticing it. Perhaps it was the lines around his eyes that crinkled when he smiled that made his face so intriguing. Or was it the hint of a beard that shadowed his face, making his jaw appear so strong, so defined?

She shook her head, hoping to clear it, hoping to distract herself from such troubling thoughts so that she could concentrate on their other guests, instead.

As the dinner conversation buzzed on around him, Will continued to watch Aisling, wondering, as he always did, just what was going on in her mind. It was a sharp mind; of that he was certain. But beyond that, she was mostly a mystery to him. They'd been playmates as children—friends, even. But as they'd grown older, she'd become cold, distant. An ice queen, if ever there was one. The last time he'd seen her, she'd mostly ignored him.

And yet, inexplicably, she was not ignoring him tonight. In fact, he'd felt her eyes on him since the moment they'd sat down to dinner. Aisling had breezed in, smelling of violets, wearing a wispy, pale rose-colored gown that fluttered behind her like gossamer wings. She'd kissed her mother on the cheek while apologizing for her tardiness, and then taken her seat at the long table, directly across from him.

It was only when she'd raised her goblet to her lips that she'd seemed to notice his presence. She'd looked startled, almost astonished, and he could not credit why. Surely, Jack had told her he was joining them tonight. Hell, even if Jack hadn't, his appearance there at the Wainscotts' dining table was a common-enough occurrence. Yet Aisling's apparent discomfiture hadn't lessened throughout the interminable meal—five full courses in all.

In the years he'd known her, he'd never seen her so discomposed. It was disconcerting, and yet somehow arousing if his cockstand was any indication. It would prove embarrassing as hell if he couldn't rein it in before they finished with dessert.

"I say, Cooper, you've not listened to a word I've said, have you?" Jack asked, shaking his head.

"I'm sorry?" he asked distractedly. Aisling had taken a bite of pastry and a dollop of chocolate cream remained on the plump center of her lower lip. His pulse began to race as her tongue darted out, licking it away. Good God, that mouth of hers…a perfect, pink bow, just begging to be kissed. And that tongue…just imagining how she could use it, how—

"Bloody hell, Cooper, snap out of it." Jack tossed his napkin to his lap. "If you'll pardon my language, Mother."

"Might I remind you that there's another lady present besides Mother," Aisling said sweetly. "Honestly, Jack, have you no manners at all?"

Mrs. Wainscott arched a brow in censure, though the woman could not entirely conceal her smile. "Indeed," she murmured.

"Indeed?" Jack sputtered. "Why, Aisling curses more than I do, the hoyden."

"Fascinating," the elder Dalton said with a leer that made Will's skin crawl. "A gently bred lady who curses?"

Aisling just shrugged. "I only do it to get under my dear brother's skin. He's just ill-tempered because my curses are far more original than his own. I'd be happy to demonstrate—"

"You most certainly will not," Mrs. Wainscott interjected, shaking her head. "Honestly, it's as if I've raised a pair of apes."

The younger Dalton grinned, looking much like an ape himself. "I beg to differ, ma'am. Your daughter is quite the original. A breath of fresh air, if I might venture to say so."

Which meant he wanted to fuck her, Will realized, balling his hands into fists.

Jack looked entirely nonplussed. "Suffice it to say that my sister has no equal."

"I'll take that as a compliment, thank you very much." Smiling brightly, Aisling rose from her seat and moved to stand behind Mrs. Wainscott. "I think I'll leave you gentlemen to your after-dinner smoke. Mother?"

The woman nodded. "Of course, dear."

"Sure you won't join us, Miss Wainscott?" one of the Daltons called out, sounding slightly drunk.

"Quite," came Aisling's reply. Her skirt's lace-trimmed hem had caught on a chair's leg, exposing a good four inches of her stocking-clad ankle. And what a well-turned ankle it was, Will realized with a start. Delicate. Gently curved.

Slowly he slid his admiring gaze up her body, to her face, and he could have sworn he saw her shiver in response, as if she'd physically felt his appraisal. Their eyes met, her hazel ones blinking rapidly, her blond brows knitted in what looked like confusion.

With a silent curse of frustration, he pushed aside his napkin and rose. For the briefest of moments he considered offering to escort her out, but decided it best to ignore whatever impulse was tempting him to do so. After all, no good would come of it.

For what felt like an hour but was likely only a fraction of a minute, they both stood, watching one another in silence.

And then, just like that, the spell was broken. She shook her head, reaching a hand to her temple, her fingers trembling.

"Aisling? Dear?" Mrs. Wainscott reached for her daughter's arm.

Aisling threaded her arm through Mrs. Wainscott's. "If you'll excuse us," she said with a nod. Moving in perfect unison, the pair made their way out.

Will held his breath, mentally willing Aisling to turn around, to glance back just once before departing. Why, he could not say. But when she did just that, glancing back over one finely shaped shoulder, his breath caught in his throat and he stood there gaping like a stupid ox. *She's beautiful,* he realized. How had he never before noticed it? He'd always thought her looks to be rather ordinary, her features too sharp, perhaps. But now…now he realized just how extraordinary her hazel eyes were, how her wheat-colored hair was threaded with pale gold strands that sparkled under the electric lights. The urge to follow her out was overwhelming, and he literally had to grip the back of the chair to keep himself from doing exactly that.

Jack tossed his cigarette case to the table. "Good God, Cooper, you look like the devil. Whatever's the matter with you?"

"I'm not entirely sure," he answered, slumping back in his seat. Exhaling slowly, he raked a hand through his hair. "Perhaps I'm taking a fever." *Or a complete leave of my senses.* What the hell had come over him?

"Well, you can't go now, old boy. You'll leave us one hand short, and then what'll we do?" Jack frowned, tapping the end of one cigarette against his palm. "Though I suppose I could ask Mother to join us. God knows she loves to play. Go on, then, if you must."

"I think I will." He stood, nodding toward the two Dalton brothers. "If you'll excuse me, gentlemen. It was a pleasure."

"Yes, likewise," they muttered in unison.

"Wait, Cooper," Jack called out. "Before you leave, I've got that novel in my office you insisted I read. Take it home with you, if you like. I vow, I couldn't get through the damn thing. You really like that rubbish?"

"Very much," he bit out.

"Well, to each his own, I say. Anyway, it's on my desk somewhere. Dig around and I'm sure you'll find it." He dismissed him with a wave toward the door.

"What about your sister? Won't she play?" one of the Daltons asked as Will made his hasty retreat, not awaiting Jack's reply.

Not if I find her first.

He entered Jack's study and headed for the desk, his mind awhirl in thought. He had to see her again. Tonight. But how? She'd likely retired to her own room, and it wasn't as if he could just saunter up to the family's private quarters and knock on doors 'til he found her.

He grunted in frustration; Jack's desk was a mess, books piled high on the blotter, papers scattered everywhere. Where was the frigging book? He needed to find it, and fast.

In his haste, he knocked a stack of papers to the floor. He bent down to pick them up, cursing as he did so. They were handwritten, numbered pages, and scattered all out of order, damn it. He reached for a page, his brows knitting in surprise as a word written in flowing script swam into focus.

Cock.

What the hell was this? Overwhelmed with curiosity, he squinted, attempting to make out the words in the dim light.

"On your knees," he commanded, and she obeyed, sinking to the floor, her fingers wrapped around his thick, corded cock. Her shell-pink tongue darted out, skating across the sensitive tip, lapping up the drop of moisture that seeped out. "Touch yourself," came his next command, his voice hoarse now. "Finger your sweet cunny while you lick me. Pleasure yourself while you pleasure me."

Good God! It was some sort of erotica. Handwritten, which was all the more puzzling. What the devil was this doing on Jack's desk, right out in the open, for anyone to find? And more important, who had written it? He would almost swear that the writing looked like...like a woman's hand.

"What are you doing with my manuscript?" came a voice from beside him, startling him so badly that he dropped what papers he'd already retrieved back to the floor at his feet.

Aisling. Looking both fierce and terrified all at once.

"Your *what?*" he asked, his voice rising as her words began to register in his muddled brain.

Her heart thumping madly against her ribs, Aisling snatched the pages from Will's hands. How could Jack have been so careless?

"Stupid fool," she muttered, "leaving them lying around like this. I swear I'm going to throttle him."

She hurried to the door and pushed it closed, turning the key in the lock before striding purposefully back toward the desk where Will stood as still as a statue, looking as if he'd just received a terrible shock.

"You...you wrote this?" he sputtered.

"No, of course not," she lied. "How much did you read?"

He shook his head. "Only a few lines. But...but you *did* write it, didn't you? You called it *your* manuscript."

"Well, what if I did?" she snapped, stooping down to retrieve the rest. "You needn't look so shocked." Good heavens, what now? What if he told her mother? If word got out, she'd be ruined. Her mind cast about frantically, searching for a solution, searching for something she could say to protect her secret—to protect *herself*.

"Here, let me help you," Will said, stooping down beside her.

"I'll thank you not to make more of a mess than you already have, you clumsy oaf," she snapped, then instantly regretted it. It wasn't Will she was furious with, it was Jack. Stupid, stupid Jack.

"Hand me those and I'll attempt to put them back in order," Will offered, mercifully ignoring her insult. Their eyes met, and he smiled—a warm, reassuring smile. Something passed unspoken between them, and Aisling nodded in reply, relief flooding her veins.

She stood with a sigh, pressing a messy sheaf into his hands. "Thank you. Truly, I'm going to kill my brother. He's so damnably careless. What if Mother had found it instead of you? Or one of the housemaids? I must have your promise—"

"You have my word, Aisling." His gaze traveled back to the stack of papers in his hands, and he began to flip through them, putting them back in order. "But devil take it, there are so many pages here. What were you planning to do with it?"

"Jack sells them in London—my stories. Have you heard of the publication the *Boudoir*?"

"Of course," he said with a shrug. "What red-blooded male hasn't?"

Aisling couldn't help but smile at his candor. "They've published five of my stories so far. Serialized them. They fetch a fair price, too."

"Surely not under your own name—"

"Bloody hell, of course not. Here, give me that." She snatched the stack of pages from his hands and hugged them protectively to her breast. "They wouldn't even consider them if they knew they were written by a woman. I use a pen name."

"But, good God, how do you even know—" He stopped short. "Never mind. It's not my business."

She realized at once the direction his thoughts had taken. "Are you asking me if I'm a virgin, Will Cooper? I should order you out of my house for such impertinence." She tossed the stack of papers on Jack's desk.

"I apologize," was all he said in reply. Shoving his hands into his pockets, he continued to watch her with that same curious stare—the one that, in the past, had made her so uncomfortable.

Only now…now it made her pulse leap, made her skin warm, made gooseflesh rise on her skin. There was something so open, so honest, so entirely lacking of artifice in his countenance. Her chest rose and fell several times as she stared back, finding herself lost in his heated gaze, wanting to tell him the truth—wanting *someone* to know the real Aisling Wainscott.

"I'm not a virgin," she said at last, tipping her chin in the air defiantly. "What do you say to that?"

"I say that you are perhaps the most perplexing woman I've ever known," he said simply. "And also the most fascinating."

Aisling shook her head, her breath coming far too fast. "I suppose I've been called worse."

He ran a hand through his hair, further mussing the deep brown waves that fell carelessly over his forehead. "It was meant to be a compliment. I've more, if you'd like to hear them."

All rational thought flew out of her mind. She wanted him; there was no point in denying it. Her brother and his friends were in the parlor, playing cards. Mother had joined them. It would be hours before they quit their game, before anyone came looking for her.

She took two steps toward him, wanting more than anything to give in to this unfamiliar longing, this newfound hunger running through her, drawing her toward this man like nothing had ever drawn her before.

"Kiss me, Will Cooper," she said, before she had a chance to reconsider.

3

WILL WASTED NO TIME IN COMPLYING. IN THREE strides he had her in his arms, his mouth crushing hers. Aisling's hands slid up Will's back to his neck, her fingers tangling in his hair as she drew him closer, her breasts pressed flat against his coat.

With a low moan of satisfaction, she opened her mouth against his. His tongue, warm and alive, skated along her lower lip, sending a ripple of shivers down her spine. He tasted of wine, smelled of soap, a hint of tobacco. Heat coiled in her belly, radiating down toward her thighs, dampening them with need.

"I shouldn't," Will murmured, his mouth retreating from hers.

"Nor I," Aisling answered, but her lips sought his once more, her hands now clasping the lapels of his coat, dragging his mouth back to her hungry one.

She gasped as he lifted her off her feet, carrying her back toward the desk, his mouth never once leaving hers as he deposited her onto the desk's smooth edge, knocking piles of books and papers to the floor in the process.

Their hands were seemingly everywhere at once—frantic

hands, unbuttoning his coat, tugging at her bodice's neckline, pulling his shirttails from the band of his trousers. A button fell to the carpet, but Aisling couldn't say whose it was, or where it had come from.

She struggled to keep her balance on the edge of the desk while attempting to raise her skirts, to free her limbs so that she could spread her knees, allowing him to press himself between her thighs.

As if Will sensed her intention, he lifted her, scooping up her skirts and gathering them about her waist as he set her back down on the hard, cool surface with nothing between her bottom and the desk's surface but her thin cotton drawers.

Tugging on his shirttails, Aisling drew him back toward her 'til she felt the firm pressure of his erection pressed against her drawers, teasing the sensitive nub of flesh between her slick, wet folds.

Her entire body trembling with desire, she looked over Will's shoulder and eyed the closed door, knowing that, at any moment, someone could try to open it. That thought alone should have deterred her, should have forced her to flee. Instead, her pulse quickened, her heart thumping against her ribs in rhythm to Will's, their breath mingling.

Quickly, her mind screamed, urging her on. Without another thought, Aisling reached for his trousers' fastenings, her fingers clumsy as she hurried to free his cock. In seconds she held him in her bare hand, running the pads of her fingertips over the velvety-smooth surface. Wrapping her fingers around the shaft, she stroked the length of him, up and down, marveling at the contradictory sensations—smooth yet hard, soft yet corded. As she continued to explore every inch of him, she felt him grow harder, heard his breath come faster, saw his eyes growing heavy lidded.

With a low groan, he reached for her delicate, lace-trimmed drawers, very nearly tearing them as he roughly shoved them down. Aisling wriggled her hips, pushing them lower, past her knees, 'til they dropped to the floor beside her slippers.

"Now," she whispered, unable to stand the ache, the need, that grew and intensified with every breath she took. "Hurry."

Will met her gaze and nodded, his pale, piercing eyes never straying from her face as the tip of his cock prodded her entrance. In one sharp motion, he buried his entire length inside her.

Aisling gasped with pleasure, wrapping her legs around his waist. Slowly, sensuously, he withdrew, then thrust back inside her, his eyes still holding hers captive, his hands on both sides of her face. His thumbs stroked her cheeks as they found a rhythm, their bodies moving in perfect unison.

His movements were slow, determined, almost willful. She bit her lip, trying not to cry out, trying not to beg him to go faster, harder. Aisling felt herself grow wetter, slicker with each thrust, her hips bucking to meet his, her need growing more and more persistent, more tightly coiled by the second.

And then with one last thrust, she found the release she sought. Her quim tightened, pulsing against his deeply buried cock just as she felt his hot seed pump into her. For a moment her mind emptied of everything but the exquisite sensation, the oblivion she felt as wave after wave of sweet pleasure washed over her.

Neither spoke for a full minute as they fought to catch their breath. Aisling buried her face in his neck, breathing in his scent as her racing heart finally slowed its frenetic pace. At last, she sat upright, taking two deep, calming breaths.

"You're bleeding," Will said, reaching up to brush her lower lip with the pad of his thumb. Aisling glanced down, surprised to see the crimson-red smudge there, marring his skin.

She shook her head, hoping to clear it. "I bit my lip." It hurt now, a vague, throbbing pain.

He bent toward her, his lips finding hers, his tongue gently sweeping across the tender spot. "There," he said, his voice soft. "Is that better?"

She could only nod in reply.

He smiled then, a slow, lazy smile that made her heart accelerate again.

"What have we done?" she asked, shivering as his cock slipped from inside her, leaving her damp, cold—empty.

He reached down to pull up his trousers, fastening them with precise, confident motions. "Do you regret it? Here," he said, plucking her drawers from the carpet at his feet.

Aisling slid off the edge of the desk, her legs unsteady and weak as her feet found the ground. She took her drawers and wadded them into a ball, still considering his question.

Did she regret it? This…this wonderful feeling she now felt in her heart, the way her blood raced through her veins, warming her skin?

It had been lovely. Wondrous and entirely pleasurable. Nothing like her ill-considered coupling with Esterbrooke— nothing at all. That had been about satisfying her curiosity, nothing more. This had been about satisfying *her*. And it had. Entirely.

"No," she said decisively. "I don't regret it. Not a bit. Do you?"

He shook his head. "I've never wanted anything more in my life. I cannot explain it, but from the moment I saw you tonight, I could think of nothing else."

"I…I felt the same," Aisling agreed with a nod. "From the

moment I sat down and saw you there. It's like…like I was seeing you with entirely new eyes."

"Almost like a spell, isn't it?" Will said with a chuckle.

And then it hit her, like a dousing of cold water. The poem! *Her winter's desire.* She'd read the poem, there in the circle of stones, and made that ridiculous wish. And now…now…

But that's nonsense. There's no such thing as spells, she told herself.

"When can I see you again?"

Drawn from her musings, Aisling looked up at Will, surprised by the earnest expression she saw on his face. "See me again? But how? I mean, what will we tell everyone?"

"We needn't tell anyone anything. Jack said he's leaving for London tomorrow. There must be some way—"

"Of course! Tomorrow my mother has an appointment at the draper's in the village. She always pays a call on Mrs. Brandon afterward, and usually ends up staying for tea. She'll be gone by half past eleven, I'd say, and won't return 'til sundown."

"Yes, but the servants," he said, straightening his necktie. "It's not as if I can simply waltz in and—"

"Of course not. Damnation!" Aisling shook her head. "What I wouldn't give to have the freedoms a man has."

"There must be somewhere here on the grounds, somewhere we can—"

"The old gatekeeper's lodge," she interrupted. "It's not the finest of places, but it's furnished, and there's a small stove for heat. We keep it clean and the linens fresh for guests' servants, just in case. Anyway, it's empty now."

"Are you sure?" Will asked, reaching for her hand and clasping it tightly in his. She felt the calluses that marked his hands as working hands—and yet, strangely enough, she didn't care, didn't care that Will's mother was a washerwoman, that no one knew exactly who his father was. All those things were suddenly inconsequential.

She nodded. "Yes, I'm sure. At noon, then? I'll bring us a picnic lunch, if you'll bring a scuttle of coal."

"Very well. Noon, then. I'm already counting down the minutes."

"Who knew you were such a romantic?" she said with a laugh.

"I could say the same of you."

"Oh, I'm not a romantic. Not in the least." At least, she never had been before.

"We'll see about that," he said, sounding like the cocky, self-assured Will she remembered.

"See if you can melt the ice queen, is that it, then?" she teased.

His face reddened like a schoolboy's. "How did you—"

"Oh, I won't hold it against you," she teased. Jack had told her, of course. "But you should go. Truly, before we're caught."

He nodded, running his fingers through his hair. "Do I look at least moderately presentable?"

Aisling grinned. "No, you look as if you've just had quite the tumble."

"Well, they're much more likely to assume it was one of your maids I was tumbling than you."

"I suppose I can take comfort in that. Now go." She tipped her head toward the door.

He nodded, then leaned in to press his lips to hers once more. "'Til tomorrow," he whispered against her mouth.

"Tomorrow, then," she murmured.

An hour later, Aisling sat at her typewriter, her handwritten manuscript beside it on the desk. She preferred to write in longhand, but the story had to be typed for submission and Jack was leaving for London in the morn. She took a deep breath, willing herself to concentrate, but her focus was drawn instead to the strange wooden box with the Celtic symbol sitting on her desk beside the typewriter.

Warily, she reached for the box and removed the folded slip of parchment and smoothed it straight, her hands trembling ever so slightly as she did so. Wherever had it come from? And how did it find its way to the circle of standing stones?

She read the poem once more, silently this time, her lips moving as her eyes skimmed the words. What exactly had she wished for when she'd read it aloud, there in the circle? She forced herself to remember her exact thoughts, to examine them thoroughly.

A man who would make her feel things she'd never before felt. Like she had just now, with Will. *An educated man, an artist, perhaps*—and wasn't Will both? A botanist, with a university education. He cataloged plant species, drew them, he'd said. *Rough, callused hands*—just like the hands that had held her face captive while Will had made love to her in her brother's study. *A man who would worship her, yet treat her as his equal.* Would he? Only time would tell. Whatever fire had been stoked between them today would not be doused so easily.

But the poem…her wish. She shook her head. It was a co-incidence, she told herself as she folded the age-worn page and placed it back inside the box. It had to be a coincidence. There was no other reasonable explanation, and Aisling was nothing if not a woman of reason.

She could have sworn she felt a tear slip from the corner of one eye, which was nonsense, of course. Aisling never cried. *Never.* And yet, when she reached up to brush her cheek with the back of one hand, she found it strangely wet.

With a small groan of frustration, she set the wooden box on the floor at her feet, out of her sight. She turned up the lamp and settled back against her chair's plump cushion, wondering if, perhaps, she was on the verge of a crying jag. She'd always thought she might enjoy one. Still, no matter how hard she'd tried in the past, she'd never been able to summon even a single tear.

Perhaps it was the solstice, working some strange magic on her mind. Or perhaps she was just exhausted. Either way, everything felt somehow different, as if she'd stepped into someone else's skin and was now seeing the world through their eyes instead of her own. And yet, oddly enough, it was a pleasurable sensation.

Indeed, she could not deny the frisson of excitement that shot through her veins when she thought about meeting Will tomorrow at the gatekeeper's cottage. Will Cooper, of all people!

She shook her head, willing herself to focus on her manuscript, instead—it had to be typed, and tonight, if she wanted another neat little sum deposited into her account by the week's end. Nodding to herself, she began to type, quickly losing herself in the story. Every kiss, every touch she described became Will's, every wicked sensation her own.

4

WILL CHECKED THE TIME ONCE MORE, THEN dropped his heavy watch back into his pocket. Five minutes 'til twelve. He paused, setting down the scuttle of coal as he looked toward the gatekeeper's cottage up ahead. He did not want to appear too eager—or too nonchalant. In fact, he wasn't quite sure how to proceed where Aisling was concerned. He had no experience with women like her, after all.

But then again, Aisling was a thing unto herself, in no way representative of women of her class. The gently bred ladies of his limited acquaintance were not nearly as outspoken, as confident or independent minded as Aisling was. They neither cursed nor smoked nor secretly published erotic stories, as far as he knew.

And while he had no firsthand experience in such matters, he could only assume that well-bred, unmarried ladies did not generally go around fucking their brother's childhood chum while said brother played cards with his guests a few doors down.

He had no idea what to expect from her today—or, for that matter, what she expected from him. He'd come prepared, with a packet of French letters in his pocket. He was leaving nothing to chance this time. Last night he'd been caught up in the moment, careless. But today…today would be different.

Feeling restless, he checked his watch once more. Only two minutes had passed, but he could wait no longer. He picked up the coal and made his way across the bare winterscape to the cottage door. It was unlocked, and several minutes later he had doffed his overcoat and lit the stove, which now belched out sooty heat in the room's far corner. Smiling in satisfaction, he rose, dusting off his hands. As he did so, he heard the door creak open behind him, followed by the faint whistle of the wind, and then the door slammed shut with a bang.

"You're here," she said, sounding surprised.

He turned to find her there by the door, wrapped up in a heavy, woolen cloak, a basket clutched in front of her. Her cheeks were pink, her eyes bright and full of mischief.

"You look like Red Riding Hood," he said with a smile. "Only in black, of course."

"I certainly hope you aren't the Big Bad Wolf," she replied, setting the basket down by her feet and pulling back her cloak's hood.

"Did you know," he began, taking two tentative steps toward her, "that Red Riding Hood has been seen as a parable of sexual awakening?"

"Really? Quite fitting, then, that you made the comparison, all things considered."

"Are you trying to shock me, Miss Wainscott?" he teased, feeling immediately at ease in her presence.

She reached up to untie the cloak's fastenings at her throat. "Perhaps. It *is* what I'm best at. Shocking people, I mean. At least my mother would say so."

"Well, I suppose I'm of a hardier constitution, because it will take more than that to shock me. Much more."

"Well, we've got all day, haven't we?" she asked with a shrug.

All day. Will let that phrase sink in, thinking just what could be accomplished in a single afternoon. First, he would undress her. Slowly, sensuously, revealing her form inch by tantalizing inch. This time he could afford to pay attention to her breasts, to taste her, to savor her. He could picture her now, sprawled naked on the narrow bed there across from the stove, her legs spread while he feasted—

"I see you've got the stove lit," she said, effectively ending his lustful imaginings. She turned in a slow circle, surveying the room they stood in. "It's not so bad, is it? It's clean, and there are blankets in the cupboard." She pointed to a door opposite the stove.

"It's cozy," Will answered with a nod. "I'm glad you came."

She arched one delicate brow. "Why wouldn't I?"

He shook his head. "I don't know. I suppose I figured that once you'd given it more thought, you might reconsider. After all, we've never been what you might call friends, have we? At least, not since we were children."

Aisling smiled as she shrugged out of the cloak, revealing a simple bottle-green skirt and white blouse underneath, a black kidskin belt around her waist. "You always looked at me queerly," she said, hanging her cloak on a hook by the door.

"I was always trying to figure you out," he said, stroking his chin.

She peeled off her gloves and laid them on a spindly wooden chair. "And did you?"

"Not in the least. You're quite the enigma, you know."

"I've brought a luncheon basket," she said, deftly changing the subject. "Are you hungry?"

"A bit. How was your walk over? Pleasant, I hope."

"Quite so. I'm fond of outdoor exercise. I try and take a daily turn about the grounds, regardless of the weather."

"Very good. Would you like to sit?" He gestured toward the wooden trestle table beside the stove.

"Thank you, I would." She bent to retrieve the basket.

"No, let me," Will said, hurrying to take it from her.

"Goodness, Will, how long must this go on? This polite chitchat, I mean. We've known each other in the most intimate fashion, and yet here we are, acting like complete strangers. I suppose next we'll discuss the weather."

"I can't help but feel that I didn't quite court you before...well, before I took advantage of—"

"You didn't take advantage of me, Will Cooper," she snapped. "I'm perfectly capable of making my own decisions where men are concerned, and I wouldn't have let you into my drawers if I hadn't wanted you there. I told you I wasn't a virgin, and I can only assume that neither were you."

He nodded. "You assume correctly."

"Then what harm is there in two consenting, experienced adults taking pleasure in one another?"

Good God, just how experienced *was* she? For a moment, he wondered if he was simply a pawn in some game she played with men. "Is that all it was to you, Aisling? Because I must confess that I'm finding myself conflicted about it. I'm not certain I feel comfortable considering you nothing but an easy fuck." He wanted to shock *her* this time, but her indifferent expression proved him unsuccessful. "It was more than that, and you know it. But I'd like to get to know you better, before I ravish you again. If you don't mind, that is."

He could have sworn he saw a tear there, fluttering on her lashes, but she quickly blinked it away.

"Do you like ham?" she asked, changing the subject once

more as she headed toward the table. "I've also brought bread and cheese, some fruit, and a bottle of wine. I had no idea what you might like."

He followed her, setting the basket down in the table's center. "It all sounds delicious. Are you warm enough? I can make the stove hotter, if you'd like."

"I'm perfectly warm, thank you. Here—" she removed the cloth from atop the basket, and pulled out two delicate, china plates followed by cut-glass wine goblets "—I had to lure poor Cook out of the kitchen before I packed the basket. I hope I didn't forget anything. Here's a corkscrew."

Will took it and saw to uncorking the wine, a fine bottle of French merlot, then poured a generous amount into each glass as Aisling set out the food on a thick damask cloth.

"Now," she said, taking a knife and slicing the rind off a wedge of cheese. "What would you like to know about me before you can ravish me with a clear conscience?"

"Well, if you insist on putting it that way." Will shook his head, trying not to look as eager as he felt. "Hmm, let's see. Do you read much?"

"Of course," she answered with a shrug. "Do you?"

"Incessantly," he said with a smile, reaching for the long loaf of crusty bread and breaking it in two. "Though it would appear your brother does not approve of my tastes. I lent him a copy of Forster's newest, and he actually had the nerve to call it rubbish."

"Jack wouldn't know fine literature if it whacked him in the head. Anyway, he's not one for novels." Aisling handed him a chunk of cheese. "I'm surprised he even made the effort."

Will frowned. "Truly, I don't think he made much of an effort at all, the lazy bastard. If you'll pardon my language."

"Oh, don't worry, I've called him much worse." Aisling

took a sip of wine, her eyes meeting his over the rim of her glass. She set the goblet back down with a mischievous smile.

All Will could think about was taking her in his arms, touching her, kissing her. Instead, he remained seated across from her, doing everything in his power to resist his urges, to tamp down the need that seemed to grow and blossom with every moment spent in her company.

"Anything else you'd like to know?" she asked, drawing him from his thoughts. Her thickly lashed hazel eyes were positively glowing now, her cheeks growing pink from the heat of the stove and perhaps the wine. How long could he last, sitting there without touching her, without feeling her smooth, warm skin against his?

Not long, he realized. Despising his own weakness, he reached across the table and took one of her slim hands in his, rubbing slow circles on her palm with the pad of his thumb. Almost as if such an intimacy was foreign to her, she glanced down at their joined hands with wide eyes, her lashes fluttering like butterfly wings.

"Surprise me," he said softly. "What would you like me to know about you?"

For a moment, Aisling couldn't speak as she considered his question. She swallowed hard, her mouth dry and parched despite the wine. "I…I'm not right. My heart, I mean. My feelings," she clarified, knowing she wasn't making a bit of sense. "I don't…don't feel things like other women do."

She expected him to laugh at her, to make a joke of her confession. Instead, the warmth, the understanding there in Will's eyes nearly took her breath away. "How can you be sure what other women feel, Aisling?" he asked, his voice so very gentle, so caring.

It all spilled out in a rush. "Because I know. I listen, I read. Passion and hate and love…all those emotions mean nothing to me. I read about them in books, I even write about them in my own stories. But it's…it's all a sham. I've no firsthand knowledge of any of it."

He spoke slowly, cautiously, as if he was carefully considering each word. "Perhaps it's only that you've never really had the opportunity to live yet. At least, not your own life. You've been stuck up here in Bedlington all this time, living the life your parents have chosen for you. You're Sir Reginald Wainscott's daughter, Jack Wainscott's sister, Lady Wainscott's daughter. Perhaps once you've had the chance to live your life—Aisling's life—things will feel differently."

She shook her head, suddenly overwhelmed with despair. "Don't you see? I haven't a choice. Until I marry and become someone's wife, I'll just remain my parents' daughter. That's all I can ever be, nothing more than that. Just someone's possession."

"Why not? You defy convention in so many ways as it is."

Closing her eyes, she inhaled sharply. "In small ways, that's all. None of it changes anything. This…this feeling between you and me, whatever it is, it's the first thing I've done that feels as if it's truly mine, my own decision." She opened her eyes, focusing on their still-joined hands, refusing to meet his gaze, fearing what she might see there.

"What about your writing? No one knows but Jack, you said. It's your own, isn't it? Something you do for you and you alone."

"And for the money," she murmured.

"What will you do with the money?"

"I've no idea. I always tell myself that the money will someday buy my freedom, but I haven't thought much beyond that."

"Well, then, that's a start, isn't it?"

"Do you know about Mrs. Gaylord?" she blurted out, then immediately wished she could take back the words.

"You mean your father's—" he cleared his throat loudly "—I meant to say, Charles Gaylord's widow? The London socialite?"

Aisling rolled her eyes. "Go on and say it—my father's mistress. Everyone in London knows—you must know, as well."

"I spend very little time in London." He was hedging, she realized.

"Take my word for it, then. Everyone knows."

"And what if they do? Your father is by no means the only man in England to take a mistress. Besides, isn't it almost fashionable with your set to do so?" He took no pains to disguise the disgust in his voice.

"I suppose so, though most men are discreet. It's more common in marriages of convenience, but my mother... well, she loves him. Desperately. I hear her crying at night, you know. He takes no pains to hide his relationship from society, but if my mother were to even mention it, she would be considered vulgar. She would be the outcast, not him. It's so unfair."

He reached across the table and took her chin between his forefinger and thumb, tipping her gaze up to meet his. "And this is why you've remained unmarried, isn't it?"

She shook her head, surprised once more to find her eyes strangely damp. Whatever was the matter with her? "No. Yes, perhaps. Oh, I don't know!" she cried, snatching back her hand.

"Perhaps it's just that you've never met the right sort of man—the sort who would treat you as his partner and not as some possession," he said, hitting so close to the truth that Aisling's breath caught in her throat.

My winter's desire.

She took a deep, fortifying breath, willing her racing heart to slow. "I think you've been reading too much of Forster's work."

He laughed then, a soft, gentle laugh. "Perhaps. To think, all those years I had no idea what lay under that tough exterior of yours. I'm not sure you knew, either."

Aisling eyed him sharply. "Are you calling me weak? The weaker sex, is that it?"

"There's nothing weak about you, Aisling. Here, would you like some more bread? More wine, perhaps?"

She shook her head. "I'm not very hungry, after all."

He rose, nodding. "Nor I. Aisling, I…damn it, I don't know what to say. Part of me wants to do the gentlemanly thing and walk out of here today without further complicating your life. But the other part, well, suffice it to say that that one inch of bare skin above your collar is just about enough to send me over the edge."

Aisling stood, entirely sure of what she wanted. With fingers that remained mercifully steady, she started unbuttoning the row of tiny buttons that began at her throat.

Will watched her, unmoving, his hands clenched into fists by his sides. She could see the rise and fall of his chest, could see the heat there in his pale, piercing eyes. A muscle in his jaw flexed perceptibly.

"Stop," he called out, and her fingers froze. "Wait. I don't want you to do this just to prove your independence."

"That's not why I'm doing it," Aisling said, shaking her head.

"Then why?" he asked, raking a hand through his hair.

As she considered the question, Aisling's gaze traveled from the top of Will's head, where his mussed brown hair fell in soft waves that brushed the back of his collar, down to his brown coat and striped vest, to his matching brown trousers and scuffed shoes. As she watched, he reached up to straighten his necktie—or to loosen it, perhaps.

She was keenly aware of his situation, far too aware. He was Celia Cooper's son—Celia, with her reddened cheeks and even redder hands, her simple good looks faded with the strain of hard work, of hard living, of disappointment. Somehow she had purchased her own modest cottage in the village, years ago, but still she took in washing and sewing, or hired herself out when needed. No one could keep linens as crisp and white as Mrs. Cooper, rumor had it.

No man had given Will his name, and no one but Celia Cooper knew exactly who had sired him, though there were plenty of rumors. Still, he'd managed to secure a gentleman's education, a respectable position at a prestigious university. Though his hands were as rough as his mother's, his speech was polished and refined. And what's more, her own brother trusted him, respected him, treated him as his equal.

And yet all of that would make no difference if anyone were to find out what she and Will had done last night in Jack's office, or what they were about to do now, here in the cottage. Everyone would be shocked—horrified, even. Was that why she wanted it so badly? Was it simply yet another form of rebellion? Or was it something else? Something more organic? She took a deep breath, willing her mind to speak the truth.

Suddenly she was sure of her answer, entirely so—more sure of it than anything else in her life. As to the consequences, well…she would not think of that now. She couldn't.

"It's you, Will. *You*. That's why I'm doing it. I cannot say why, cannot explain it, not really. Perhaps in my heart I've always known it, always felt it. And then yesterday…" She trailed off, shaking her head.

"You should know that I feel the same, Aisling. Precisely

the same. Most men would take any woman who offered herself willingly, and I cannot pretend to be any different from them. But in this case…it's different. You're different. I hope I've made that clear."

Aisling just nodded.

Will smiled, then hurriedly set about pulling closed the cottage's worn drapes. "Now," he said once he'd finished the task and turned back toward her. "Feel free to continue what you were doing before I so stupidly interrupted you."

Aisling couldn't help but laugh. "You mean…undressing myself?"

"Yes, precisely that." He gestured toward the buttons at her throat, now half-undone.

"And you'll…what? Simply watch?" she teased, feeling suddenly bold.

"I thought I might. Simply watch, that is. Unless you'd prefer that I join you."

"I think I'd prefer your full attention, if you don't mind." She reached up and found the remaining buttons on her blouse, her fingers positively flying over them.

"Trust me, I don't mind in the least. You've no idea how little sleep I got last night, trying to imagine you naked. As satisfactory as I found our encounter in Jack's study, I was cheated of seeing what lay beneath that dress of yours. I won't deny myself that pleasure today."

Aisling felt her cheeks warm, felt her pulse leap as Will's gaze swept over her. The raw lust in his admiring gaze made her breath hitch, made her fingers work faster 'til her blouse fell fully open. She made quick work of her belt, then reached around to unfasten her skirt and untie her petticoat, dropping them both to the floor. In seconds she stood in nothing but her remaining underthings—her combinations, corset and stockings—her slippers discarded by the puddled folds of her clothing.

"More?" she asked, though she knew full well the answer.

"Definitely more," he answered, closing the distance between them. He reached out to trail his fingers down her arm, drawing gooseflesh in their wake. His breath was warm against her neck, coming as fast as hers now.

"Then you must do the rest. Go on, Will. Undress me," she whispered, feeling much like a character in one of her naughty stories.

"Oh, I shall take great pleasure in doing exactly that," he answered, reaching around her to find her pale pink corset's lacings and tug hard at them.

Aisling held her breath in anticipation, near desperate to feel his hands against her bare skin.

5

IT ONLY TOOK TWO TUGS ON AISLING'S CORSET lacings to loosen them, and a moment later the garment slipped to the floor with a decidedly loud *thump*. Next came some unidentifiable undergarment, a one-piece combination of vest and knickers, ending just above her knees. Damn the layers—he'd never get her naked at this rate.

She tipped her chin in the air, meeting his gaze as he hooked his thumbs beneath the shoulder straps and eased the garment down, inch by inch, first revealing the gentle, creamy white swell of her breasts, followed by dusty-pink nipples that pebbled when the fabric slipped over them. With a groan, he bent to lick one rosy tip, his cock now straining against the flap of his trousers.

She swayed against him, a small moan escaping her lips as he took her entire nipple into his mouth, suckling her now, increasing the pressure as his hands cupped her breasts—firm, round breasts, and surprisingly full. She smelled so sweet, like sugared violets, and tasted even better.

Fearing he might spend himself then and there, he pulled away, continuing to push down the troublesome undergarment—past her waist, her hips, until her dark curls, already damp with need, were exposed. Lower still he tugged the fabric, resisting the urge to bury his face in her curls 'til he had her fully naked.

At last the garment dropped to the floor, leaving nothing but her stockings to dispense with. Easy, he thought, untying her silk garters and tossing them aside. His fingers brushed her thigh, smooth as the finest silk, as he reached for one stocking's top. Taking his time, he knelt and pressed his lips to her skin as the stocking bared it, his mouth following the trail down past her knee, to her ankle. With the grace of a dancer, she lifted one foot, her toes pointed toward the ground, and allowed him to slip off the stocking.

One more to go and she'd be entirely bare, he realized, blood thrumming hotly through his veins. The anticipation, the need…it was like nothing he'd ever experienced before, making his breath come fast, his heart thumping noisily against his ribs. *Slowly,* he commanded himself, wanting to savor every moment.

This time he allowed himself more time to discover her soft thighs, to part them gently as his mouth explored the skin just above her stocking's top. As he rolled it down and slipped it off her foot, his fingers moved higher, to her cunt, searching for the little knot of flesh hidden in her curls.

He knew he'd found it when he heard her gasp, her entire body going rigid beneath his hands. At once his mouth replaced his fingers. The tip of his tongue danced across the hard bud, teasing it until she cried out, clutching fistfuls of his hair.

"Do you like that?" he asked, looking up to see her bite her lower lip, her head thrown back.

"Oh, yes. Yes!" she answered breathlessly. "But you must stop, you must…I mean, not yet. I want you naked, too. Now," she added, tugging him to his feet.

"Very well." He stood, ready to oblige her. He couldn't help but stare at her, transfixed, as he undid his necktie—marveling at her figure, at her posture as she stood there, entirely bared to him. She displayed no maidenly shyness whatsoever, made no effort to cover herself as she watched him unbutton his coat, then his waistcoat, and shrug out of both.

Indeed, she simply watched him as if fascinated, desire heating her eyes as she followed his every movement.

He slipped his braces off his shoulders before unbuttoning his linen and tossing it to the ground in a rumpled heap beside his coat. Moving quickly now, he unfastened his trousers and pushed them down along with his stockings, then stood in nothing save his own drawers, his cock a hard bulge in the flannel. He saw her gaze travel downward, her eyes widening. *Invitation enough.* With no further hesitation, he pushed down his drawers and stepped from them. For a moment, they both stood silently, admiring one another.

"God, you're beautiful," she said at last.

"I was just thinking the same thing. Of you, I meant," he added. "I've never in my life seen anything so lovely. Come here," he commanded, and she readily obeyed, striding proudly into his embrace. Their bodies met—hot, eager, a melding of limbs.

"Your hair," he murmured against her ear. He was suddenly desperate to see it down, unbound.

"Mmm," was all she responded before pulling away and reaching up toward the elaborate arrangement piled high on her crown. One by one, she removed the pins and dropped them carelessly to the floor. First one wheat-colored lock fell across her shoulder, its shiny end curling across one pale ivory breast, and then another, 'til at last her entire face was framed in a pale, wavy mass that fell down her back in glossy ripples.

Will could only stare speechless at the sight. How long had it been since he'd seen her with her hair down? Many, many years, he realized. They'd been children. But now...now she was every inch a grown woman, and never would he have imagined the practical, always-sensible Aisling with such glorious hair.

In one sweep of his arm, he lifted her off her feet and carried her across the cottage's small room to the narrow iron bed in the far corner.

Aisling propped herself up on one elbow, watching him with a mischievous smile. "The bed, Will? But that's so very predictable, so pedestrian, isn't it?"

He shrugged. "Perhaps, but I won't be rushed today, not like last night. You might want to get comfortable," he teased, plumping the pillow behind her. "This might very well take all day."

"As if you could last that long," she challenged, eyes dancing.

He took a step toward the edge of the bed, his cock heavy with need. "Can't I?"

"Let me see," she answered, rising to her hands and knees before him. Before he had a chance to react, she had taken his entire length in her mouth, her tongue stroking the under-side of his shaft. His entire body shuddered as he stared down at her in utter surprise.

Slowly, sensuously, she rocked back, releasing him inch by inch until nothing but the head of his cock remained between her lips, her tongue dancing over the sensitive tip. Over and over again, she stroked him with her mouth, taking him more deeply each time. She cupped his bollocks in one hand, squeezing gently, making it impossible for him to pull away.

At last she released him, sitting back on her heels and looking up at him sweetly, all innocence now. "All day, you say? Are you so sure of that?"

"Never mind," he said, nearly throwing himself to the bed beside her and pulling her atop him. "I must have been mistaken."

Aisling sucked in her breath as she climbed atop him, straddling him. Oh, how she wanted to tease him, to make him nearly weep with desperation as she tormented him with her mouth. She had no idea it would be so lovely to pleasure him like that, to taste him and tease him. She'd felt him grow harder, longer with each stroke of her tongue, and a part of her wanted to wield that power more, to see it to its completion. After all, she'd written about it so many times as it seemed something that men particularly enjoyed, if the stories in the *Boudoir* were to be believed.

But she couldn't wait, couldn't restrain herself as she sought to fit her quim over his cock instead. She felt the heat of him, the throbbing hardness as he parted her and then filled her entirely. She was already wet, slippery with need as her body found a rhythm, her hips raising and lowering with a quickening pace.

Will grasped the iron bedstead behind him as he strained against her, lifting his head to capture her mouth with his, kissing her roughly and ruthlessly as she rode him—harder, faster, the creaky old bedsprings protesting loudly beneath them.

And then he broke the kiss, falling upon the pillow. His head tipped back, the cords of his neck standing out hard and taut. "Oh, God, Aisling…now…I can't stop—" A deep groan made the rest of his words unintelligible, but Aisling no longer cared. Their bodies had grown slick, their bodies slapping noisily against one another.

Already she felt her womb begin to clench, her insides quivering, her thighs trembling. Pinpoints of light exploded behind her eyelids as she lowered herself, taking in every inch of him, allowing him to fill her, to stretch her as he spent himself deep, deep inside her.

Their cries of pleasure mingled, hers breathy and high, his low and guttural as they both arched into one another one last time. At last spent, Aisling fell across him, her lips just inches from his throat as she caught her breath. He smelled so clean, slightly salty and all male—a heady scent, she realized. Nothing at all like Esterbrooke, who'd smelled faintly of onions and smoke when she'd so stupidly allowed him to take her virginity.

"So much for all day," Will said at last, running his fingers through her hair and making her shiver. "And so much for the French letters. *Damn.*"

French letters? *Of course.* She hadn't even thought to reassure him, though she had been keenly aware of the timing herself. "Don't worry," she said, pressing a kiss against the spot where his pulse leaped below his ear. "My monthly courses came only last week. It should be safe enough right now."

She felt his lips against her hair. "And here I'd planned to take my time. It's all your fault, you know."

"Next time, perhaps," she murmured sleepily, suddenly wishing more than anything for a short nap, there in his arms.

"Will there be a next time, Aisling? Truly, how long can this go on?"

She sat up, looking down at him. His brow was furrowed, his jaw tight as he rubbed one temple. He seemed almost... angry, but Aisling could not fathom why. "As long as we want it, Will," she said, shaking her head in confusion.

"If you say so, then."

"What do you mean, if I say so?" she snapped. "I don't understand you, Will Cooper!"

"I don't quite understand it, myself." He ran the pad of his fingertip across her lips. "It's just that I find myself greedy, wanting more, not wanting to let you go. And yet I know that this cannot go on forever."

Aisling felt a lump form in her throat. Why did he have to keep bringing up the end, when they'd only just begun? She didn't want to think of the end, not yet. Yet there was no denying it—time was not their friend. Christmas would come and go, and Will's holiday would end. He'd go back to Cambridge, to his life there, leaving her—

"Do you remember that time when we were children, when I pushed you into the swimming pond?" he asked, drawing slow, lazy circles on her skin with his fingertips. "You were fully clothed, wearing a frilly white frock with pink ribbons. I can still remember the look of fury on your face when you climbed out, dripping wet."

"I can still remember the black eye I gave you not a minute later," she said, smiling in smug satisfaction.

"Jack put me up to it, did you know that? Offered to pay me, even, but I refused his coin."

"Why, that bastard!" she said, shaking her head, knowing it sounded exactly like something her brother would do. "I had to toss that dress in the rubbish bin, you know. It was entirely ruined, and Nurse was furious with me."

"Well, have you any idea what kind of hell I got for having my eye blackened by a girl?" He chuckled softly. "Jack told everyone, as if he was *proud* of you or something, and I never heard the end of it."

"I'll never understand that brother of mine," she said, shaking her head. Jack had always been her greatest tormentor, and yet her dearest friend. Perhaps it was because they were so close in age—only thirteen months separated their births. Irish twins, their grandmother liked to call them.

Will reached for her hand, threading his fingers through hers. "Say you'll see me again tomorrow."

"Tomorrow? Yes, yes, of course." But how?

"My mum's house," he said, as if he'd read her mind. "She'll be out tomorrow, in the afternoon, helping Mrs. Brandon prepare for guests. She told me I'd have to get my own tea. Can't you come up with an excuse to spend the day in Bedlington?"

"I might as well be a child, needing permission to go anywhere or do anything on my own." She sighed loudly. "But I can promise that I'll try. Will that do?"

"I suppose it will have to," he answered, his voice tight. "Do you need to return home now?"

"No," she said, snuggling back against his chest and pulling a rough, woolen blanket over them both. "I've got hours 'til Mother returns. What about you?"

"I'm not expected until teatime. If my mum shows up then, that is. Did you know she's stepping out with Mr. Beeton these days?"

Aisling nodded. "I'd heard that from Mother. She gets all the local gossip, you know. Anyway, good for your mum. Mr. Beeton is a decent man. I think he will treat her well."

"I hope so. I hate leaving her all alone in Bedlington. I've tried to get her to come up to Cambridge, but she refuses. She's so damn proud of that shabby little cottage. I just don't understand it."

"Because it's hers. I…I almost envy her that. Her own home, her own livelihood, difficult as it might be," she added.

"She could get on well enough with what I send her each month," he said, sounding defensive. "But she refuses to give up her work, hiring herself out like she does. It's almost as if she *wants* to demean herself."

Aisling could hear the frustration in his voice, could feel his body tense beside hers. "You're being much too hard on her, Will. She's proud of the work she does, and rightly so. It can't have been easy for her, all these years, raising you all alone amidst the whispers, the innuendo."

"How can you touch me, knowing I'm someone's bastard?" he said, his voice catching. "Someone's by-blow, nothing but a castoff? You, of all people? The daughter of a baronet, for fuck's sake."

The pain, the self-loathing she heard in his voice tore at her heart. A tear gathered in the corner of Aisling's eye, and she wiped it away quickly, before it fell, giving her away. "I don't care about that, Will. Perhaps I did…before. Perhaps I thought myself better than you, superior in some way, simply because of my birth. But now that I know…now that—" she swallowed hard, willing the tears to remain at bay, damn it "—I'm ashamed for feeling as I did before. Jack called me a snob, and he was right. I was a terrible snob, and I'll never forgive myself."

"There's nothing to forgive, Aisling. But you have no idea what it was like, growing up as I did, never quite fitting in anywhere. The working-class boys picked on me for my education, and my schoolmates picked on me for my working-class background. I was damned either way."

Aisling nodded, having heard such tales from Jack through the years. "I can't even imagine. But then, I've never felt as if I fit into *my* world quite right, either. I never could do what they asked of me—smile prettily, hold my tongue, act as if I hadn't the brains God gave a goat. I let a gentleman take my virtue, and then do you know what I did when he offered marriage? I laughed. The very idea of being married to him, of feeling his damp, slippery hands all over me every night…" She trailed off, her stomach pitching uncomfortably. "I couldn't do it. I knew my secret was safe. After all, it wouldn't reflect well on his masculine pride if everyone knew I'd refused him after giving him a tumble, would it?"

"Most definitely not," Will agreed.

"Anyway," she said, waving one hand in dismissal, "enough about that." Propping herself up on one elbow, she gazed down at him admiringly. Though the mischievous glint in his eyes was the same, everything else about him was so very different from the boy she remembered. Gone were the bony shoulders and skinny chest, replaced now with a well-sculpted torso with a dusting of dark hair that narrowed into a fine line, bisecting his taut, rippled abdomen.

"By the looks of you, I'd say you've broken your own fair share of hearts," she said, feeling strangely possessive now.

He shrugged, drawing her closer as he did so. "Perhaps," he answered noncommittally, then immediately changed the subject. "Tell me about your stories. Whatever made you start writing them?"

"I found a copy of the *Boudoir* in Jack's office a couple years ago, and, being the wicked girl I am, read it from cover to cover that very night. Suddenly I had this idea that I could do that, write stories like those. I wrote the first one in a matter of days, and showed it to Jack. Once he got over the initial shock, he agreed to take it to London. I suppose I have some talent, because the *Boudoir* snapped it right up and asked for more."

"You've no idea how impressed I am. And these things you write about, are they fantasies of yours?"

"A lady never tells," she answered coyly.

"You must let me read some, then. The curiosity is near enough killing me, especially after the tease of reading that one little bit in Jack's study."

She snuggled against him, rubbing her nose against his neck. "Would you like that? Reading my stories?"

"You've no idea," he said, cupping her bottom.

"Very well." Aisling sat up and looked longingly at the discarded food on the table, her stomach grumbling. "Is there any way you could bring the basket of food over here? And the wine, perhaps? I took it from Father's personal wine collection, after all, and I wouldn't want it to go to waste. I think it's a rare vintage."

"You *are* a naughty girl," Will teased. Disentangling himself from her limbs, he stood and wrapped the blanket around his waist. "Sir Reginald will be most displeased."

"Sir Reginald is a son of a bitch, and he can go to the devil for all I care." And take his Mrs. Gaylord with him, she added silently. "But right now, I think I would very much enjoy a picnic in bed."

"If a picnic in bed will make you happy, then that's what you'll have, Miss Wainscott," Will said with a mock bow, looking slightly ridiculous with his tousled hair and near nakedness. "After all, I aim to please."

Aisling only smiled, thinking just how well he *did* please her. Perhaps the picnic could wait a bit longer, after all.

6

SMILING HAPPILY TO HERSELF, AISLING GUIDED
her little motorcar down Bedlington's dusty main thoroughfare, the engine a noisy hum. She pulled up in front of the
haberdasher's shop and cut the engine, supposing this was as
good a place as any. She had a few errands to run—a ruse,
mostly, though she'd buy some hat trimmings and pick up a
pair of shoes she'd brought in last week to be reheeled. She'd
make her presence known in town, however briefly, and then
duck inside the Coopers' cottage at the top of the road.

Anyone who saw her in town would assume that, after her
errands, she'd stop in to take tea with Louisa Abbott, the shopkeeper's daughter, as she always did. Or that perhaps she'd take
a basket of fruit and some of Cook's muffins and breads to
old Mrs. Simmons or to the poor Barrett brood. Either way,
no one would find it odd to see her little Renault roadster
left outside the shops for a couple of hours, even if they
didn't see her out and about.

Reaching over the door, she secured the brake, then
removed her goggles and gloves and placed them inside the
drawer on the dash. How she loved her shiny red motorcar,
and what pride she took in mastering it! It had been Jack's

before he'd grown tired of it and decided he needed a larger, more powerful one, one with seating for four rather than two. Aisling had managed to convince her reluctant brother to let her have the car, if she learned to drive it. It hadn't taken her more than a couple afternoons to do so, and she'd been racing around the countryside ever since.

Of course, that had given the wagging tongues of Bedlington yet another reason to consider her "fast"—both literally and figuratively—but Aisling didn't care. Even now, she saw a pair of women come out of the draper's and shake their heads when they saw her sitting there on the tufted red leather seat, unpinning the crepe de chine veil from her tweed motoring hat.

Aisling raised one hand and waved, smiling broadly. "Mrs. Roberts, Mrs. Appleton," she called out gaily. "A lovely day, isn't it?"

"Indeed, Miss Wainscott," they replied in unison, then bent their heads together to whisper about her, no doubt.

Still smiling to herself, Aisling opened the door and stepped down to the road where she stood briefly, dusting off her Jaeger-lined cream serge coat and tightening the muffler about her throat, before she set off on her errands. Thankfully, the sky was clear today, a bright blue without a hint of clouds. The air was brisk, but not unpleasantly so. A perfect winter's day.

Not a quarter hour later, she stood in front of Celia Cooper's cottage, looking around furtively before hurrying forward to rap on the door. The door swung open, and without a word of welcome, Will hustled her inside, gathering her into his embrace.

"Do you think anyone saw you?" he asked, his breath warm against her neck.

Aisling shook her head. "I don't think so. Besides, if anyone saw me headed this way, they'd assume I was on my way to the Barretts'. They're only a few doors up the road, after all."

"Ah, yes. The angel of mercy, visiting the poor," he said, sounding vaguely sarcastic.

Aisling bristled at once, pulling away from him. "Don't say it like that, Will. What would you have me do, instead? Ignore them?"

"I was only teasing you, Ash. That's what Jack calls you, isn't it? 'Ash.' It somehow suits you, I think."

"Really? How so, if you don't mind my inquiring?"

He shrugged. "I don't mind at all. It just sounds…I don't know, somehow modern. Like you. A modern woman. I saw you drive up in your jaunty little motorcar, you know. Is this your motoring ensemble?" he asked, gesturing toward her garments.

"Indeed," she said, reaching up to unfasten her coat and remove her muffler. "Along with a veil, goggles and gloves. You should see me in it all—I'm such a fright! Though not half the fright I would be without such things to protect me from the dust."

"Here, let me take those," he offered, and Aisling handed over her things. "Though perhaps I shouldn't leave them down here, just in case."

"In case of what? Your mother's untimely return?" Aisling couldn't help but laugh. "Pray, what would you have me do in that case, sneak out through your window?"

"Just how nimble are you?" he asked, leading her toward the stairs.

"Nimble enough, I suppose. It sounds as if you've experience in such matters. I'm not certain I approve," she teased, looking around, taking in her surroundings. After all, she'd never been inside the Coopers' cottage before. Not once in all her life.

It was, first and foremost, clean and tidy. Homely, but decorated in what she'd call comfortable simplicity. The room they stood in boasted a built-in window seat and inglenook, a sofa and a pair of spindle chairs with embroidered cushions. In the room's far corner stood a small Christmas tree, waist high and simply decorated with red bows, a painted gold star on top.

The floors were maple, with colorful rag rugs scattered about. The hearth was simple brick, the mantel uncrowded, with only a carriage clock and a photograph of Will looking scholarly in his Cambridge robes decorating it, along with a seasonal drape of pine boughs and holly. The walls were stark white, unadorned with paper, but framed botanical drawings were placed at pleasing intervals, and Aisling stepped up to one, a drawing of a multifronded fern, for closer inspection.

"Did you draw this?" she asked, noting the fine detail. It looked so very real, almost as if it were a pressed specimen, preserved forever in its most perfect form. Beneath the drawing, the species was labeled in a neat, familiar hand.

"I drew them all," he answered with a shrug. "Specimens native to Bedlington. I've no idea why Mum likes them so much."

"Beautiful," she breathed. "I had no idea you were so gifted."

"Perhaps one day I'll draw you, if you'll allow it."

Aisling nodded. "I'd like that very much."

"With your hair down. I've never seen anything lovelier than you with your hair down," he added.

Aisling couldn't help but laugh. "Funny you say that, as my mother has been lamenting my hair since the day I was born. 'There's nothing more unfortunate than being born a blonde,' she always says. Between my fair hair and light eyes, I'm about as far from fashionable as they come."

"Fuck fashionable," he said sharply, then, "You must forgive my language. I sometimes forget—"

"What, that I'm a lady? Don't apologize, Will. I think that's why I like you so much—you say exactly what you think. I admire that."

"Can I get you something?" he asked, gesturing toward the kitchen behind them. "I'm capable enough with a teapot. I'm sure there are some cakes around, too, if I look hard enough."

"No, thank you." Aisling headed for the stairs. "May I go up?"

"Of course. Come, I'll finish showing you around. It's not much, I know, especially compared to Wainscott House."

"I think it's charming," she said, following him up the narrow stairs. "What is it they call it, 'cottage quaint'? Wainscott House just seems so cluttered in comparison." It was the truth. With its Elizabethan styling and dark wood trim, heavy furniture crowding every room and knickknacks on every available surface, Wainscott House often felt crowded and oppressive, despite its cavernous size.

"You realize this entire cottage would fit easily inside your drawing room alone? I used to worry I'd make a wrong turn and get lost there when I was a boy. Here, this is my mum's room." He opened a door to reveal a small, square bedroom with a narrow bed in its center, a tall maple dresser opposite it.

Aisling nodded her approval, then moved on. It somehow seemed wrong to step inside the woman's room in her absence.

Will paused at the next door, and Aisling peered inside. "This is where Mum does her sewing," he said, his voice filled with pride. A sewing machine sat on a stand beneath the window, and tables held bolts of fabric, piles of linen and pieces of clothing. Baskets lined a row of shelves on the wall, filled with ribbons, flowers and lace. In the room's far corner, a rack held various garments including what looked to be Aisling's mother's lilac watered-silk gown. The hem had ripped last week, she remembered. Of course she would have brought it to Mrs. Cooper for repair.

Her cheeks reddening slightly, Aisling followed Will out into the corridor. More than anything, she wished she hadn't seen her mother's gown. It only reminded her of their differing circumstances, something she did not wish to dwell on, not now.

Luckily, Will did not seem to notice her discomfiture. "And this is my bedchamber," he said, opening the opposite door and leading her inside a room that was twice as large as the other two.

"I know, it's ridiculous, isn't it?" He laid her coat and muffler across the back of a chair. "I don't even live here anymore, and still she insists on me having the largest room. As if I were royalty or something."

"Perhaps you are," she said wryly, hoping he would appreciate her humor. "Your father could be a prince, for all you know."

The iron bed was larger than Mrs. Cooper's, and finer, too. There was a saucer of half-drunk tea on the bedside table, a book lying open beside it. A well-worn trunk sat on the floor by the footboard, its contents spilling out rather haphazardly. In the corner, a closet stood ajar, a row of suits hanging inside. Beneath a pair of dormer windows was a rolltop desk, papers scattered across it. A tall stack of books sat on one edge, looking as if they might topple over at any minute.

"One could never accuse you of being neat, could they?" she teased, taking in the clutter, the lived-in feel that her own room back at Wainscott House lacked, despite the fact that she actually *lived* in it. Will was only a visitor here, she reminded herself.

"I won't let my mother come in to clean as if she's my housekeeper. Is it really so bad? Believe it or not, I tried to tidy up a bit, just in case you came by."

She sidled up to him, batting her lashes like a coquette would. "So sure I'd make it up to your bedroom, were you?"

"I'm nothing if not optimistic," he answered with a wicked smile. "I did allow my mum to change the bed linens, however. I shudder to think what she must suppose happened in my bed last night to result in such a request."

Aisling laughed, surprised at how comfortable she felt alone in a man's bedroom, discussing bed linens as easily as they'd discuss the weather. Feeling bold, she reached inside her skirt pocket and withdrew the folded pages she'd tucked inside earlier that day.

"Look what I've brought you," she said, unfolding the pages and smoothing them flat. "It's one of my favorite scenes."

"Indeed?" he asked, reaching for the pages. "One of your own personal fantasies, I hope."

"If I say it is, will you indulge it? No matter how wicked it might be?"

"Good God, Aisling, don't tease me that way. Just how wicked is it?" As he scanned the page he held in his hand, his cock made a visible bulge in his trousers.

Aisling longed to reach out and stroke it, to coax it. But she would wait, patiently, 'til he finished reading. She sat on the bed, testing its plumpness, running her fingers across the worn coverlet while Will read, standing by the window, his hair falling across his forehead.

At last he looked up at her, his pale eyes piercing hers. "You really wrote this?"

She nodded. "I really wrote it. Are you shocked?"

"In a good way. I just never imagined that women like

you…I mean, that a gently bred lady…" He trailed off, shaking his head.

"Say it, Will. That a gently bred lady would wish to be fucked like that? Why not?" she asked with a shrug, hoping she sounded more sure of herself than she felt.

Indeed, a niggling doubt crept into her head—what if it *was* unnatural? What if the very idea repulsed him? After all, her knowledge of sex came almost entirely from reading erotica, not from real-life experience. *I'm a fraud,* she thought miserably.

"I'm only wondering where you've learned such things, that's all," Will said at last, sounding slightly awed.

Aisling shrugged, forcing her voice to sound breezy and light. "I read. Besides, I grew up in the country. Around livestock," she added. "That doesn't leave much to the imagination."

"No, I suppose not. Come here," he said, laying the pages on his desk. Aisling rose on shaking legs and quickly closed the distance between them. He took her hands in his, raising both to his lips. "Have you any idea how badly I want you?" he asked, his gaze burning with an intensity that nearly stole away her breath. "All the time. I can't sleep, I can't eat. You've entirely taken over my mind, my heart, my soul. How can I go back to Cambridge after this? How can I leave you here? It's as if I've been bewitched by you."

Dear God, there it was again—the notion that they were both under some sort of spell, that what they were feeling wasn't real. That poem, that damnable poem and her wish…was it possible? "There's something I should tell you," she murmured, no longer able to keep quiet her fears. "I found a poem, you see. On the solstice. I made a wish," she continued hurriedly, now desperate to get it all out in the open. "I wished for the perfect man, one I knew didn't exist. And yet…and yet you did. That very night, at Wainscott House, it was as if my wish had been granted the moment I laid eyes on you."

His eyes narrowed, his brow furrowed in confusion. "Wait. What does this have to do with a poem?"

She pulled her hands from his grasp and rubbed her temple, aching now. "I don't know. It was almost like a chant. I found it, tucked inside a box, a very old box. I read it aloud, and then I wished for…well, for this. For what we have. It's almost like some sort of white magic."

"But that's ridiculous," he said, shaking his head. "Surely you don't believe that?"

She squeezed her eyes shut and took a deep breath, then opened her eyes once more, gazing up to see the hurt there, etched on Will's face. "One minute we were completely indifferent to one another. And then the next…well, how else can you explain it?"

He raked one hand through his hair. "I think it was always there, a spark of some sort. Perhaps it's why you hated me so. God knows I hated you, hated the way you looked at me, as if I were worthless. I think I always wanted you, deep down. And hated you for not wanting me."

Aisling reached one trembling hand to her temple, feeling suddenly light-headed. "Perhaps you're right. I…I just don't know. All I *do* know is that I can't help myself, can't stay away from you. It must be the magic."

"Damn you, Aisling. It's convenient timing, isn't it? I bring you here today, show you the home I grew up in, show you firsthand the differences between us, between our families, and suddenly you claim that what we're feeling isn't real? That it's some sort of magic, summoned by some goddamn poem you found? I'm supposed to believe that?"

"I…I don't know, Will. Truly, I don't. I'm so confused,

feeling things I've never before felt. And that's exactly what I wished for, don't you see? I'm not myself, not who I was last year, not even who I was last week."

"Who are you, then?" he challenged, his eyes stormy now. "Tell me, Aisling."

"I don't know!" she cried out, hating herself, hating the hurt she saw there on his face. And the worst part? Even now, all she could think of was the secret fantasy she'd written about in the story he'd just read, the rumpled pages still lying there on his desk.

She wanted him still—oh, how she wanted him! Despite it all, despite her fears, her confusion. He was angry, furious, even—and still she was going to let him take her, just as she'd imagined he would, just as she'd fantasized about all night long, anticipating this day.

Without another thought, she rushed into his arms, rising on tiptoe to press her lips against his, her hands finding his trousers' fastenings as she did so.

"Damn it, Aisling," he said against her open mouth, his body taut against hers, his fully aroused cock pressing into her belly. "What is it you want from me?"

"Shh," she whispered, then moved her mouth to his throat, her tongue lapping against his bounding pulse. "That fantasy, Will," she ordered. "Now."

7

FOR A MOMENT WILL THOUGHT TO PROTEST, to refuse to fuck her in her current state of mind. It would be the gentlemanly thing to do, after all—refusing her. But damn it, he was no gentleman, and he was tired of pretending he was. She'd come to *him,* after all, that erotic clipping in hand, claiming it was her own fantasy—and now she was practically begging him, stroking his cock while she tried to unfasten his trousers.

By God, he would indulge her. What else could he do? He was weak where Aisling was concerned—weak and needy. It was as if his mind had been taken over by his longing, his desire, as if it was utterly beyond his control.

But he would not be fooled by her claims of white magic—of some poem, some wish, that had brought them together. That was rubbish. Perhaps it was her way of justifying what they were doing, what she was doing with a man so far beneath her. But he didn't believe it, wouldn't believe it. He was a modern man, a man of science, for fuck's sake. He acted on his own accord, his own desires. And he wanted her. Damn, how he wanted her.

"Turn around," he growled, disentangling her hands from

the front of his trousers. Reaching around her waist, he half dragged, half carried her back toward the foot of the bed and deposited her there. A discarded necktie lay on the edge of the bed and he reached for it, snatching it up and quickly looping the soft folds around her wrists.

In seconds, he had her captive wrists pressed against the bedstead, her back toward him. He could hear her breathing grow faster, more ragged as he slipped the cloth through the iron bars and tied a knot, making sure that the bindings were neither too loose nor too tight.

"Are you certain, Aisling?" he asked, once the knot was secured. "I'll stop now, untie you this instant if you're not."

"I'm certain," she answered breathlessly. "I trust you, Will. With all my heart."

Trust. How could she trust him, when he could barely trust himself? When she couldn't even trust her own feelings? Will shook his head, refusing to think about it now. Instead, he grabbed at her skirts and petticoat, raising them, bunching them around her waist. He heard her gasp as he tugged down her drawers, relieved that she seemed to be wearing fewer layers of undergarments than she had the day before. Anticipating *this,* no doubt.

Her hands still restrained, she bent over the bed's low iron footboard, her back arched, her thighs parted invitingly. In seconds he managed to shove down his trousers and free his straining cock, pressing it against her backside as he bent to kiss her neck.

"Like this?" he asked, grinding his hips against her pale white buttocks. "This is what you've fantasized about?"

"Yes. Oh, yes." Her pulse leaped wildly against his lips as he breathed in her scent—violets, sweet and fragrant, a scent that would forevermore make him think of her.

"Bend over more, then," he whispered, nibbling at her earlobe. "Show me."

She did, arching farther. She was already wet for him, glistening with desire. "Good God, Ash," he groaned, taking a deep, steady breath. "You're so very beautiful." He didn't want to spend himself, not yet, but the sight of her like that—her cunny ready for the taking—nearly undid him. Urging himself to slow down, to savor every moment, he reached down, parting her, slipping one finger inside her tight sheath.

"You're so wet," he murmured against her ear. "So ready." He drew his finger out, rubbing her wetness across the tight nub of flesh at her entrance. "It's not magic, Ash. It's desire, don't you see?" Desire that coursed through his veins like fire, that stole away his breath. He'd never felt anything like it before, this possessiveness, this primal need for a woman. And not just any woman—for Aisling.

"Now, Will," she urged breathlessly.

Slowly, carefully, he probed her slick entrance with the tip of his cock, his hands gripping her shoulders, his lips buried in her neck.

With a small cry, Aisling rocked her hips back against him, taking him deep inside her in one single thrust. Knowing full well he wouldn't last long, he found her clit with his fingers and stroked it, hard and fast, making her moan, making her writhe against his hand as he drove into her, again and again.

In seconds her cries became louder, more insistent. God, how he wanted to please her, to satisfy her to the point that she'd never desire another. He wanted her—only her—forever. He dropped his mouth to her shoulder, kissing her through the layers of clothing, wishing he'd taken the time to undress her before he'd tied her to the bedstead.

One more thrust, one more stroke, and together they

climaxed, their bodies shuddering against one another, his heart hammering against her back. Could she feel it? Did she know that he was in love with her, entirely mad with it? *I'm a fool,* he told himself, trying to catch his breath, to slow his racing heart.

"My hands," Aisling murmured, turning her face so that his lips rested against her jaw.

"Of course," he said, hurrying to untie the necktie that bound her. In seconds, he freed her, wincing as she rubbed each wrist, her pale skin reddened where the fabric had abraded her.

He dragged up his trousers, fastening them as she pulled up her drawers and shoved down her skirts. Once she was done, he reached for one of her hands, cradling it in his own. "I should never have agreed to this," he murmured, bringing her hand to his lips and feathering kisses across her irritated skin. "I would not hurt you for the world."

She smiled up at him, her eyes aglow. "Of course you wouldn't, Will." He released her hand, and she reached up to stroke his cheek. "I think you could use a shave," she said, rubbing her palm back and forth across the stubble outlining his jaw. Her touch was so familiar, so intimate—like a long-time lover's.

Without saying a word, he captured her hand, laying his overtop her smaller one and holding it there, against his cheek, rubbing his face into her palm. For a moment they stood like that, silent but for the sound of their breathing, slow and easy. *Comfortable.*

Will swallowed a painful lump in his throat, suddenly over-whelmed with emotions that made his chest ache, his eyes burn. If only this moment could go on forever, this tender little tableau. But it couldn't. Of course it couldn't. "Can I get you something?" he said at last, his voice unnaturally gruff. "Some tea, perhaps?"

She nodded, reaching up to tidy her hair as she did so. "That would be lovely, actually. I'm quite parched."

"How do you take it?" he asked, amazed that he didn't know, despite their intimacy.

She smiled at him, a tiny dimple in her left cheek. "Two spoons of sugar and a dash of cream. Should I go down and help?"

"Of course not, you're my guest. Sit—" he gestured toward the chair in the corner "—and I'll be right up with it. I can manage, I swear," he added when he saw her look of surprise.

Aisling nodded, her legs feeling strangely weak as Will hurried out. She could hear his footsteps on the uncarpeted stairs, fading away, and she sighed heavily. So many emotions flickered across her consciousness, all jockeying for position. Her feelings were such a jumble that she couldn't make out a single one—except perhaps satisfaction. Yes, that was it. Will left her satisfied, entirely sated.

When she was with him, everything felt strangely right. For the first time in all her life, she felt truly alive. Animated. Fulfilled. She shook her head, feeling foolish. *I'm making too much of this.*

She turned toward the desk, thinking to straighten the stack of books and move them safely from the edge. Only she moved too quickly and her elbow caught the edge of the topmost volume, sending it flying to the ground where it lay, open. Stooping down, she retrieved it. As she did so, a folded page fell out, fluttering down to the floorboards where the book had lain only seconds before.

Sighing in exasperation, she bent down and retrieved the letter, noticing Will's name written in a decidedly feminine script at the top of the page. Curious, she unfolded it, smoothing it down with damp hands. It was a recent letter, dated a fortnight ago. Her eyes scanned down to the bottom of the page, seeking a signature. *Entirely yours, Helena,* it read.

Her stomach pitching, she hastily shoved the letter back inside the book. *I should not have looked,* she told herself. She'd invaded his privacy, and there was no excuse for it. Shame mixed with something else—something unsettling—made her cheeks flush hotly.

For a full minute she stood there, drumming her fingers on the desk, staring down at the edge of paper that stuck out from between the book's gilt-lined pages while she waited for Will to return. And then, as if of their own volition, her fingers moved closer, slid along the cover's edge, itching to snatch back the letter. The curiosity was positively eating her up inside. Who was Helena? Were they friends? Lovers?

Aisling looked toward the empty doorway, listening to the sounds of rattling dishes and footfalls below. She tapped one foot impatiently, unable to stanch her growing curiosity. The letter was recent, and Helena had signed her first name—a sure sign of intimacy.

Glancing furtively one last time at the doorway, she made up her mind even as guilt ate away at her conscience. She *had* to know—otherwise she'd go mad, supposing the worst, imagining that Helena meant more to him than she did. For all she knew, they were engaged. The teakettle downstairs whistled plaintively, and Aisling knew it was now or never.

Taking a deep breath, she reached for the edge of the letter and pulled it out, unfolding it as quickly as possible.

My dearest William,

I hope you will forgive this letter, but I could not let you leave for Dorset without having my say, as you left my flat so hurriedly last night. I did not mean to make you uncomfortable, surely you realize that? But after what we've shared, can you simply throw it all away so easily? So carelessly?

I should never have lied to you—I know that now. Still, it does not lessen what I feel for you. I want you, William. Back in my life. My bed.

Think on it, my sweet William. I will have your answer upon your return to Cambridge. Perhaps then we will have reason to celebrate the new year.

Entirely yours,

Helena

She had her answer: Helena had been his lover. Was perhaps *still* his lover. How would he answer her when he returned to Cambridge? Would he simply forget Aisling, forget *this*, and return to this woman's bed? That thought alone made bile rise in her throat, made her blood run cold even while her skin flushed hotly.

An uncomfortable knot had formed in Aisling's stomach, making her feel queer, almost queasy, making her chest ache and her breath come fast—far too fast. And then she heard it—footsteps, on the stairs, getting louder.

Moving quickly, she refolded the letter and stuffed it back inside the book it had fallen from, straightening the stack and moving it toward the center of the desk with clumsy, awkward hands.

She turned back to the doorway just as Will strode in smiling, a tray with two steaming cups of tea and a plate of biscuits in his hands. She could only stare at him as he set the tray on the bed, reached for one of the teacups, and held it out to her.

She took it with visibly trembling hands, feeling like a damn fool.

The smile on his face vanished at once. "Good God, Aisling, what's wrong?"

Dear Lord, was she that transparent? "Nothing at all," she said, cradling the steaming cup in both hands. "I...I'm perfectly fine."

"You're a terrible liar. You're white as a ghost, and positively trembling. I wasn't gone but ten minutes. What can possibly have happened in so short a time? You're not thinking about that poem again, are you? Having regrets?"

"I'm...no." She set the teacup down on the desk behind her, her gaze straying guiltily toward the book with the folded letter inside.

She had to know, had to have answers. Even if it meant exposing her guilt. "Who's Helena?" she asked, refusing to turn and meet his eyes.

"Helena? How did you..." His voice trailed off, and she heard him move closer, toward the desk. "The letter," he said matter-of-factly. "Of course."

Her cheeks burning with shame, she turned to face him. "I was trying to straighten the books, that's all. It fell out. I know I shouldn't have read it."

"No, you shouldn't have," he answered, sounding slightly amused now. "But since you did, I must tell you that she means nothing to me. Helena was...someone with whom to pass the time, nothing more. We had an understanding of sorts. No strings attached, as they say."

"What did she mean about lying to you?"

"She was married. Separated, but married. When I found out, I ended it. And that's all there is to it."

"Not from her point of view. She wants you back, Will. Back in her bed."

"There's no chance of that," he said tersely.

"So she was just…just a casual lover? Had you many of those?"

"I'm not a monk, Aisling," he snapped. "I never claimed to be one."

"And did she…did she please you? In bed?"

A flush climbed up his neck. "Why are you asking these questions? What does it matter—to you, to us?"

Because she could not stop thinking about it, that's why. Because she couldn't get the image out of her mind—Will, in bed with another woman, kissing her, loving her, touching Helena the way he'd touched her. She rubbed her eyes with her fists, wishing she could stamp out the images, banish them forever.

This was jealousy, she realized. Pure, unadulterated jealousy. And it hurt—oh, how it hurt. She knew it was ridiculous, knew that Will had every right to his past. She hadn't come to him a virgin, and she'd known full well that he was likely far more sexually experienced than she was. It was only natural, after all. And yet…there was something about reading that damn letter, about seeing the woman's hand. And the worst part? She called him *William*.

Her Will. *Hers.*

Hot tears filled her eyes, scalding her eyelids. Aisling spun back toward the desk just as they spilled over, pounding her fists on the blotter in frustration.

"Bloody hell, Aisling. Are you crying? About Helena?" His disbelief was evident in his voice. In seconds he was standing directly behind her, his chest pressed against her back, his arms wrapped protectively about her waist.

"I can't change my past," he murmured against her hair. "I don't know what to say, but please, *please* don't cry."

"I never cry," she blubbered foolishly. "Never. Not once, 'til these last few days. Not 'til you and I…" She trailed off, shaking her head. She swallowed hard, trying to rein in the humiliating tears. "It's all too much, these feelings. Too much at once. I…I can't bear it."

She twisted from his arms, still blinded by the tears that refused to stop falling. "I must go."

"Don't go, Aisling. Not like this. Not over Helena, for Christ's sake," he pleaded while she retrieved her coat and muffler.

"I must," she repeated, refusing to look at him.

"But I told you, she means nothing to me. Nothing. Not like you, Aisling. Damnation, I think I'm falling in—"

"Don't say it!" she interrupted, before it was too late, before he said the words he could never take back, forcing her to face them, to face her own feelings. "Please. I can't hear it, not right now. Don't you see? It's just too much, too overwhelming."

"No, I don't see. Not at all. I never took you for a coward," he said coldly, a muscle in his jaw flexing as he stared at her, piercing her with his vivid blue gaze.

"Oh, but I *am* a coward. The worst sort of coward. I'm so sorry, Will. Please forgive me." Without awaiting his reply, she fled from the room, hurrying down the stairs on legs that felt as if they might give out at any moment.

In seconds, she made her way out the front door, nearly bumping into a woman on the walk as she headed toward the shops in the distance, toward her little motorcar.

"Miss Wainscott?" a voice called out, but she dared not turn around.

Instead, she simply hurried on, shivering as her boots beat a quick staccato on the cobbled walk, the winter sun blindingly bright to her swollen eyes.

Will stood at the bottom of the stairs for several minutes, debating whether or not he should go after her. Before he'd made up his mind, his mother came in, a puzzled look on her face as she pulled off her gloves and rubbed her hands together.

"Wasn't that Miss Wainscott I just saw leaving here?" she asked with a scowl.

Good God, how to answer that? "What are you doing home so early?" he asked instead. "I thought you'd be at Mrs. Brandon's 'til well after teatime."

"I thought so, too. Turned out her sick housemaid made a remarkable recovery and she didn't particularly need my help, after all. And don't think I didn't notice that you ignored my question, Will Cooper. Was it or wasn't it Aisling Wainscott that nearly bowled me over on the walk just now?"

"It was," he hedged, casting about desperately for an explanation. "It seems that I…I left something at Wainscott House when I dined there earlier this week. My gloves," he finished lamely.

His mother's faded eyes narrowed as she shrugged out of her coat and hung it on the peg by the door. "So I'm to believe that you left your gloves, and Miss Wainscott delivered them personally? What kind of fool do you think I am?"

He sighed heavily, knowing he'd lost. His mother was far too sharp. "I don't think you're a fool at all, Mum. But that's all I'd like to say on the matter, if you don't mind."

"Oh, Will, darling. Please tell me you're not trifling with Aisling Wainscott. Not with the likes of her. Nothing good will come of it. Surely you must know that."

He held his ground. "As I said, I'd rather not discuss it."

She shook her head, her mouth drawn in a tight, angry line. "I thought you were smarter than that, Will. Smarter than me. Don't you see? People like that—like the Wainscotts—they use people like us. Use us, then cast us aside. Aren't I proof enough of that?"

"You've done well enough for yourself, Mum," was all he said in reply, his windpipe suddenly tight, as if he were strangling. How he hated to be reminded of the cocksucker who'd fathered him, who'd deceived his mother with false promises just to get his rocks off, and then abandoned her. He knew his mother had been the victim, had been cruelly used, and yet sometimes he couldn't help the niggling doubt that she should have fought harder for the man she loved, the father of her child. And how he hated himself for such treacherous thoughts!

"Oh, Will," his mother said on a sigh. "It's too late, isn't it? How could you be so stupid? So foolish?"

He looked toward the window, where the late-afternoon sun shone brightly through the glass. "If you don't mind, I think I'll go out for a bit."

"You're stubborn as a mule, aren't you? Always were. Fine, then. Go." She threw her hands in the air in frustration. "Learn the hard way, if you must. But don't say I didn't warn you. Mark my words, she'll use you, then toss you aside like yesterday's rubbish."

Judging by Aisling's hasty exit, perhaps she had already done just that. Clenching his hands into fists by his sides, Will took a deep, calming breath, then reached for his overcoat and gloves. "If you'll excuse me," he said, his voice deceptively calm and collected.

He had no idea where he was going, but he needed to get

out, to get some air. Clear his head. Only then could he consider what his next move would be, as far as Aisling was concerned.

The only thing he was certain of was that it wasn't over, not yet. At least, not from his point of view. And if she thought it was, well…

He would fight for his woman.

8

IT WAS CHRISTMAS EVE. THE CALENDAR ABOVE
Aisling's writing desk was insistent upon it, no matter how hard
she tried to ignore the holiday, to eschew the good cheer and
jollity she knew she was supposed to feel this time of year but
never did. And this year the melancholy was worse than ever.

She laid her head back on the chaise longue's tasseled pillow
and stared up at the ceiling, listening to the sounds of bustling
activity below. Her father had arrived home that very
morning, Jack the day before. The entire household was now
in a tizzy, preparing for the Wainscotts' annual Christmas Eve
open house.

At that very moment, Aisling's mother was downstairs with
the housekeeper, making certain that every little light on the
Christmas tree was twinkling brightly, that every red velvet bow
was straight, that the eggnog was perfect and the wassail just so.

In no time, their guests would begin to arrive. A buffet
supper would be served, followed by a pantomime, and then a
concert featuring traditional holiday music. The evening's festivities would conclude at the stroke of midnight when the musicians played "Silent Night." Each guest would light a taper and
form a processional through the house and out the front door,

where they'd all gather in the driveway and stare up at the night sky for a few moments before blowing out their candles, gathering their coats and heading back to their own homes.

These events had happened in precisely that order as far back as Aisling could remember. Everyone in Bedlington was invited, and for weeks afterward the entire village would discuss the food, the decor, the table linens—every little aspect of the evening dissected in minute detail. Never in her presence, of course. In fact, in the weeks following Christmas it generally seemed that all conversation ground to a halt whenever she entered a shop. But Louisa, the shopkeeper's daughter, always shared the gossip with her over tea, embellishing each tale to such grand proportions that Aisling couldn't help but laugh about it.

The clock downstairs chimed the hour and Aisling sighed, turning her head to glance over at the amethyst velvet gown hanging beside her bed, the matching velvet slippers sitting at the ready beneath it. The ensemble was new, specially bought in London for this occasion. Her mother had thought the neckline scandalous, and even more so the back, which dipped far lower than anything Aisling had ever worn before. But Madame Aubergine had insisted it was the height of fashion in Paris, and Lady Wainscott had reluctantly relented.

At the time, Aisling had adored the gown, thinking it entirely perfect. But now the very idea of putting it on and going downstairs to greet guests seemed unpalatable at best. Mostly, of course, because Will would be one of those guests.

What he must think of her!

Two full days had passed since she'd run out of his mother's cottage. She'd spent those days at home, refusing to go out lest she run into him. She'd claimed a stomach malady had incapacitated her, and kept almost entirely to her room. There, away from prying eyes, she'd spent a good portion of the time crying like some sort of silly, lovesick schoolgirl while she examined her situation from every possible angle.

When she'd first let Will make love to her, there in Jack's study, it had been an impulse, nothing more. She'd wanted him, and so she'd had him. She'd acted out of curiosity, a desire for experience beyond what she'd had with Thomas Esterbrooke. It had been as simple as that.

But in the following days, everything had somehow changed. *She* had changed. Feelings beyond lust and curiosity had crept into her consciousness, into her heart, awakening it, awakening her. Before, she'd been an observer of life. Now, she was living life. Experiencing it—painfully so.

If only she'd never found that blasted box, that damn poem! Now she would never know for certain if what they felt was real. If only she could find that mysterious woman in the cloak, the one she'd seen there in the circle of stones on the solstice. Perhaps she had left the box there; perhaps she knew something about the poem. But Aisling hadn't even seen her face—she'd only seen her hair, whipping about in the breeze. And then she'd disappeared, without even—

A sharp knock sounded on the door, startling her. "Aisling, dear? Are you dressed?"

"Not yet, Mother," she called out, rising from the chaise longue and reaching for her hairbrush, trying to appear as if she were at least making an effort to get ready.

Her mother opened the door and peered inside. "Good heavens, dear! Whatever are you waiting for? Our guests should begin to arrive within the hour. I'll send Clarice right in." Her gaze landed on the dress, and she shook her head. "I'm still not sure about that gown," she said, shaking her head. "It's…it's positively indecent."

"Oh, hush, Mother. I haven't anything else to wear."

"That scarlet-colored watered silk, perhaps? It still fits nicely."

Aisling sighed, fingering the velvet gown. "I wore the red silk last year. You know how everyone would talk if I wore it again."

"I suppose. Still, this one shows far too much of your back. People are bound to talk about *that*."

"Didn't Madame Aubergine say it was the height of fashion in Paris this year?"

Her mother rolled her eyes heavenward. "It's not as if the folks here in Bedlington know what's fashionable in Paris, dear. Oh, well. I suppose there's nothing to be done about it now. Just...just stand with your back to the wall as much as possible, won't you?"

"I'll try," Aisling answered, though she had no intention of doing so. If she had her way, she'd claim another bout of illness and retire as early as possible—before the pantomime began, if she could manage it.

"Well, hurry, then," her mother said. "You haven't much time, you know." She closed the door, and Aisling heard her call out loudly for Clarice.

Seconds later, the girl burst breathlessly into the room. "I'm so sorry, mum." With a scowl, she snatched the hairbrush from Aisling's hand. "Here, sit and let me dress your hair."

With a nod, Aisling sat at her dressing table, staring at her reflection while Clarice began to drag the bristles through her tousled hair.

"Oh, I almost forgot!" The brush clattered to the marble-topped table as Clarice dug inside her pocket and dragged out an envelope. "This came for you earlier this afternoon. Quite mysterious, as it appeared after the regular post had arrived."

Aisling took the envelope with shaking hands. There was nothing on it but her name, typed.

"Who do you think it's from?" Clarice murmured around a mouthful of pins, now gathering Aisling's pale hair up on her crown and securing it.

"I've no idea," she lied.

Will. It had to be from Will. Who else? She took a deep, fortifying breath, willing her racing heart to slow.

"Well, mum, aren't you going to open it and find out?"

Trying her best to look nonchalant, she laid the envelope down on the dressing table. "Not now. It's probably just from Louisa Abbott, with some last-minute gossip she felt the need to share before the party. I'll open it later."

"Perhaps it's from a secret admirer," Clarice said with a dreamy smile. "And perhaps whoever he is will be in attendance tonight. Here, put on some rouge. You're far too pale."

Aisling twisted off the cap and lightly dabbed a bit of the cream onto her cheekbones as Clarice wrapped her coiffure with an amethyst velvet ribbon, the same shade as her gown, and secured it with pins.

"There, mum. Just lovely! Now, let's get you dressed so you'll have time to read that letter before the guests arrive."

Will straightened his tie as he stepped into the crowded ballroom. Wainscott house was packed, people standing shoulder to shoulder as servants pushed their way through with silver trays filled with savory canapés and flutes of champagne. Long tables lined the far wall with silver chafing dishes, the delicious aromas wafting over the crowd. On the far table sat a decorated wassail bowl, delicate glass cups stacked in front of it.

Boughs of holly and fir were draped across every available surface, mistletoe hanging in each and every doorway. Wainscott House at Christmastime was definitely a sight to behold.

Somehow he'd missed their annual Christmas Eve party the past couple of years—he couldn't even remember why.

Had his mother been ill last year? Yes, that was it. And he'd spent the previous Christmas in Cambridge. His mother had taken the train up on Christmas Day and they'd spent the holiday touring the Botanic Garden's glasshouse—a private tour, as it was closed to the public—and then eaten dinner at the University Arms Hotel. Despite her protestations of it being far too fine, he'd made his mother stay the night there at the stately hotel, and he'd taken great pleasure in seeing that she had one of the finest rooms overlooking Parker's Piece.

This year, he would not have missed the Wainscotts' open house for the world. His mother had allowed Mr. Beeton to escort her there, leaving him free to search for Aisling among the festive, boisterous crowd. He only hoped she'd received his letter. He'd paid a boy from one of the shops in the village to hand deliver it, and he had no idea if the boy had actually done so, or simply pocketed the money and tossed the letter away.

Either way, he would see her tonight. See her, and speak with her. She could not go on avoiding him. In his letter, he'd asked her to meet him in the library once the pantomime began. They'd have at least a half hour, likely more. Long enough to say what he had to say to her.

He began to elbow his way through the crowd, determined to find her.

"Champagne, sir?"

With a nod, he took a delicate crystal flute and downed its entire contents with one jerk of his wrist. He set the empty flute back on the tray while the serving maid scowled at him, shaking her head in disapproval.

The champagne burned a path down to his stomach, warming him, giving him confidence.

"Cooper, old boy!" someone called out, and Will turned to see Jack Wainscott making his way toward him. "Aisling, come say hello to Will Cooper with me, and try and be jolly, won't you?" he bellowed, obviously already far into his cups.

"Glad you could make it," Jack said once he reached Will's side, clapping him on the back. "Have you had your supper yet?"

"No, I've only just…" Will trailed off as Aisling appeared at Jack's side. She looked positively stunning in a purple velvet gown, her narrow waist accentuated by a wide band of black, the skirt narrow at her hips and only flaring as it reached the floor, trailing out behind her. The deep U-shaped neckline was made modest only by crisscrossing bands of wispy black fabric, exposing a generous amount of skin. Indeed, the gentle swell of her breasts was bared to his hungry gaze.

"Scandalous, isn't it?" Jack asked, following the direction of Will's gaze. "Still, it *is* only Aisling, and let me warn you, she's as waspish as ever tonight. I suggest you take care where she's concerned."

Aisling's gaze met Will's in a heated battle, but she remained entirely mute.

"Miss Wainscott," Will said at last, bowing sharply. "You look lovely tonight."

"Thank you," she murmured, her face as blank as a statue's.

"Do me a favor, eh, Cooper? Keep an eye on her and make sure none of the village swains get any ideas, will you? Especially that Lucas James. Oh, come now, Ash," Jack added, seeing his sister's frown. "Cooper here doesn't bite. Do you, old boy?"

Will shrugged. "Not unless she wants me to."

Jack threw back his head and laughed heartily. "I vow, the pair of you! Do try and be civil, won't you? Ah, look. It's Mrs. Brandon with her niece. An heiress to a small fortune, they say. Best go inspect."

With one last clap on Will's back, Jack left them.

For what felt like a full minute, neither of them said a word. They simply stood, being jostled by the crowd as they stared at one another.

"You look breathtaking," he said at last, leaning toward her to be heard over the din of the crowd.

Her smile positively lit up her face. "Thank you. You look rather dashing yourself. I can't remember the last time I saw you in evening dress. It suits you."

"I'm glad you approve," he teased, bolstered by the direction of the conversation. Perhaps this boded well for later. "You received my letter?"

"Yes," was all she said in reply.

"And dare I hope that—"

"Aisling, darling!" Lady Wainscott appeared from nowhere, favoring Will with a bright smile. "Oh, good evening, Mr. Cooper. How nice to see you! Is your mother here?" Without awaiting his response, she turned her attention back to her daughter. "Dear, the Brandons just arrived with their niece, Miss Gilchrist. You must go greet them at once, and see that your brother doesn't make a fool of himself, won't you?"

"Of course, Mother. If…if you'll excuse me, Mr. Cooper," she said, allowing herself to be led away by the arm. Once she'd taken a half-dozen steps, she turned, glancing back over one shoulder, her unreadable gaze meeting his for a fraction of a second before she continued on her way.

Will tamped down his anger, wondering just how calculated Lady Wainscott's interruption had been. He hadn't long to think on it before Louisa Abbott plucked at his sleeve.

"Will! Thank goodness. Come, escort me to the supper table, won't you? I'm positively famished and I can barely make my way through this crush."

"Of course," he said, forcing himself to smile as he offered his arm. He liked Louisa Abbott—always had. They'd grown up in the village together, had been childhood playmates. She'd always been uncomplicated and refreshingly direct.

Why not her? he asked himself, admiring Louisa beside him—her willowy frame, her simple good looks. She was of the right age, after all. Smart. Attractive. But most important, she was part of his world. Whereas Aisling…

How much simpler everything would be if it were Louisa who made his blood sing, his heart race, who made his cock stiffen with just a single thought of her.

"It all looks delicious, doesn't it?" Louisa asked as they reached the buffet tables. "I vow, I didn't eat a single bite all day, saving up my appetite. You *are* going to join me, aren't you?" she asked, handing him a plate.

"Of course." He took the plate and began to fill it without really noticing what he was taking.

Minutes later, he followed her into the adjoining room and found seats at an empty round table laid with red and cream brocade linens, a silver candelabrum casting warm light that competed with the overhead electric chandeliers. "Shall I get you some wine?" he asked, setting down his plate beside Louisa's.

Louisa nodded as she took her seat. "That would be lovely. Hurry back, won't you? I hate sitting all alone."

He returned not five minutes later, surprised to see the table now entirely full of diners save his empty seat.

"There he is," Louisa called out. "Look, Aisling has joined us. See, I told you he wouldn't mind," she added.

He forced his face into a mask of ennui. "Of course not. Here—" he placed one wineglass down in front of Louisa before taking his seat between the two women "—I hope you like red."

"Yes, thank you. I was just telling Aisling that this is the largest crowd I remember seeing at Wainscott House on Christmas Eve. Oh, this roast beef is divine!"

Will stared straight ahead, twirling the stem of his wineglass between his fingers. How long must he remain there, between the two women? On his right, Louisa continued to chatter on brightly between bites, enthusiastically complimenting the food, the company, the decor. On his left, Aisling seemed to push her food about her plate, saying very little and eating even less. He was painfully aware of her there, her shoulder brushing against his every so often. He could smell her scent—violets, as always—could feel the heat of her, warming his skin.

Every time she leaned forward in her seat, he glimpsed the vast expanse of porcelain skin bared by the low-dipping back of her gown and nearly groaned aloud as his cock twitched in his dress trousers. Bloody hell, he was growing hard just sitting there beside her, desperate to touch her, to brush his fingertips down her bare back, toward her buttocks.

How he wanted to lift her to the table and hike up her skirts, to spread her legs and feast on her cunt, to flick his tongue across her clit 'til she cried out, arching off the table, clutching at the brocade table linens, her mouth an *O* of ecstasy.

"Good God, Will. Has the cat got your tongue? You look as if you're a million miles away!"

He blinked away the vision and turned toward Louisa. "I'm sorry. Just a bit distracted today, that's all." His napkin slid off his lap and he reached to catch it, his hand somehow colliding with Aisling's as he did so.

He heard her breath catch, though her face remained as unreadable as before. And then somehow her hand found his again beneath the table, her skin as hot, as flushed as his own.

As the conversation continued around them, their hands

met and retreated, fingers brushing flesh, capturing and re-leasing. He thought he'd go mad with it, this illicit touch. As he massaged the center of her palm with his thumb, it seemed as if they were the only two people in the room, despite the crowd, the merriment surrounding them.

"Cooper, old boy! There you are."

Aisling's hand slipped away as Jack appeared behind them. "Good, good, keeping an eye on my sister, I see. If you've finished your supper, come and join us for a smoke."

Will flexed his now-empty hand, wishing Jack would go away, that they'd all go away.

"It's all right, go on," Louisa said with a nod. "You're just sitting here like a dumb ox, anyway."

Which left him with no choice but to agree, damn it.

9

AISLING GLANCED BACK OVER HER SHOULDER, making sure no one was following her, and hurried toward the library. The pantomime had just begun—she could hear the sounds of laughter floating down the empty corridor from the ballroom.

It was time.

Her little velvet slippers tapped against the marble floor as she quickened her pace, determined to arrive without discovery. When she'd decided that she would meet Will at the requested time she could not say. Perhaps she'd always meant to, from the moment she'd read his letter, though she'd told herself then that she could not possibly do so—that being alone with him was dangerous, far too dangerous.

But sitting there beside him at supper, pretending they were no more than casual acquaintances had near enough killed her, and she knew she could not let him leave Wainscott House tonight without seeing him in private, without speaking her piece.

She had to make him see, make him understand. She had to say goodbye, even if it was the most painful thing she'd ever done. Because she couldn't go on like this, wanting him, loving him, knowing she could never truly have him. For how could she? There were so many reasons why it would never work.

Reaching the library at last, she took a deep, fortifying breath, then opened the door and stepped inside.

Will was standing at the far end of the room, gazing out the window, his hands shoved into his pockets. A light snow had begun to fall, pattering gently against the glass. Though he must have heard her entrance, he didn't move, didn't turn around. He just continued to stand there, staring at the night sky beyond the glass.

Aisling closed the door, turning the key in the lock. Moving slowly, silently, she took several steps toward him, wishing beyond measure that he would turn around, that he would speak. When she was no more than an arm's length away, she paused, reaching out one hand toward him, meaning to pluck at his sleeve. Instead, she dropped her hand back to her side, swallowing hard.

And then, like a statue come to life, he turned to face her. Dear God, but he was handsome in his black trousers and tuxedo coat, his boyish tumble of hair falling across his forehead as it always did.

As his penetrating gaze met hers, his mouth lifted into a smile. "I didn't expect you would come," he said at last.

"I had to come. Had to tell you…well, there's so much to say. But first I must apologize. I had no right to read your letter that day in your room, and even less to hold its contents against you. I should not have run out like I did. It was foolish of me. Foolish, and childish."

"You don't have to apologize to me, Ash," he said, shaking his head, though he made no move toward her, no effort to touch her, to take her in his arms.

How she wanted to be in those arms!

"Oh, but I do. My behavior these past few days has been nothing short of erratic, my mood swinging wildly from one extreme to the next. I cannot make head nor tail of it myself, so I can only imagine how puzzling it must be for you."

He shoved his hands more deeply into his pockets. "But you've always been a puzzle to me, Aisling. This week, last year, a decade ago. I've long since given up trying to figure you out. Besides, this thing between us…I think it took us both by surprise. You cannot apologize for that. You cannot apologize for being yourself."

She shook her head, wrapping her arms about herself, suddenly cold. "But don't you see? I'm not myself, not anymore. I was always so sure of who I was, of what I wanted from life. And now…" She trailed off, shaking her head. "Now I'm not sure of anything."

"I'm sure of what I want," he said softly, and Aisling's breath caught in her throat. "I want you, Aisling. Only you. Always."

Aisling squeezed her eyes shut, taking a deep, rattling breath. Her greatest desire, and her greatest fear—all in one tidy package. However would she bear it?

"I love you, Aisling." His fingers brushed her cheek, softly, gently. He had moved closer, so close that she could feel his warm breath against her neck.

Her eyes still closed, she reached blindly for him, pulling him closer, wanting to feel his lips upon hers. "I love you, too, Will," she choked out as he pressed his lips to her throat, just below her ear. "I do, and I'm so very frightened by it."

"Why?" he murmured against her skin. "I won't hurt you, Aisling. Ever." He trailed featherlight kisses up the column of her neck, back down toward her collarbone, raising goose-flesh on her skin.

"Because, don't you see? We'll always wonder, never be quite sure…" She shook her head, unable to say more, knowing he would think it utter nonsense.

Grasping her chin between his forefinger and his thumb, he forced her to meet his gaze. "Never quite sure of what? You must tell me, so I can give you every assurance imaginable."

She swallowed hard before speaking. "The poem, Will. My wish. There was a woman there in the circle of stones that day, a woman I've never seen before or since. She was there one minute, and then, just before I found the box, she simply disappeared into thin air. Like some sort of spirit."

He released her chin, shaking his head with a low chuckle. "I think you've been reading too much fiction, Aisling. Surely you know that's not possible."

"If you'd asked me a fortnight ago, I would have laughed with you and agreed. But…but I can't explain it, Will. You had to be there. It was just at the moment of the solstice, and it felt odd, almost magical. Even as I made my wish, I knew it was impossible, knew I was wishing for a man who did not exist. And then, there you were, that very night at supper. And you're everything I wished for, everything I hoped for."

"Isn't that enough, Aisling? What more do you want from me? I'm willing to give you everything, don't you see? Everything. I know I can't offer you much. Damn it, it sounds bloody ridiculous even suggesting it. You, growing up here—" he waved his hands toward the door "—and me, the bastard son of a washerwoman. That's it, isn't it? I'm asking far too much of you." He turned away from her, raking a hand through his hair.

"That's not it," she cried, clutching at his sleeve, pulling him back to her. "It's not. I swear to you it isn't."

"It isn't? Then pray, enlighten me. You say you love me, that—"

"I do love you. My heart…it's near to bursting with it. It's not as if one day I looked at you and said, 'Oh, dear me, I think I've fallen in love with Will Cooper, isn't that lovely.' No, it was so much more intense than that, almost violent. And don't you see, I've never before felt anything intensely, much less violently. Never, in all my years. But after reading the poem, and making the wish…" She shook her head. "It's like we're both under a spell. How can I ever be sure of my feelings? How can you?"

"Because I don't believe in spells, Aisling. I simply don't believe that you can read a poem, make a wish, and suddenly find yourself feeling things you weren't meant to feel. And the Aisling I've known all these years is a sensible girl who doesn't believe in such nonsense, either."

"I'm no longer that same girl," she said, shaking her head. "All I used to care about was my writing. I would lose myself in my stories for hours on end. And these past two days, I've tried." She took a deep breath. "God knows I've tried to write, to put my newfound experience to good use. I've sat for hours, pen in hand, staring at the blank page. But you know what? The words won't come. For the first time in years, the words simply won't come."

"Have you considered that you no longer have the need to write your fantasies? That you're living them now, instead? You should try another form of fiction—a novel, perhaps, or poetry. Don't you see, in Cambridge there are people like you, writers and poets. You could join a literary circle. Stay at home and write while I'm off at work. I could buy us a house, something modest but cozy." He looked so earnest, so eager, so damn adoring that it tore at Aisling's heart.

Tears welled in her eyes. "And what then, Will? How long 'til the doubts creep in? 'Til you begin to wonder if my feelings for you are real, 'til you turn to Helena for comfort? 'Til the spell wears off and we find ourselves shaking our heads in confusion, wondering just how we found ourselves in such a predicament?"

He grasped her shoulders, shaking them hard. "My feelings for you will never change, Aisling. Never. I promise you that."

"I want to believe that, truly I do. But if they do…don't you see? It'll be too late," she said, tears welling in her eyes. She was a coward, after all. Just as she feared. "If I were to go with you to Cambridge, to…to…" she stuttered.

"To marry me?" he supplied.

"Yes. If I did…my parents, they would never accept it. Society would never accept it."

"Since when have you cared what society thought? Damn it, Aisling, be truthful for once."

"I am being truthful," she said miserably. "But you must see what's at stake here."

He released her shoulders, nearly shoving her away. "You truly are a coward, then. Goddamn you, Aisling. You stand there, denying what we feel, denying what we have." He began to pace, his hands shoved back in his pockets now, his anger palpable.

A single tear traced a scalding hot path down Aisling's cheek. She couldn't move, couldn't speak. She'd been gone too long—surely the pantomime was over by now. Yes, she could hear the faint lilt of Christmas hymns coming from the far side of the house. Soon it would be midnight, and the guests would be lighting their tapers and heading outdoors.

She took a tentative step toward him, wanting to soothe him, to try once more to make him understand. But he turned on her, grabbing her by the shoulders and pulling her toward his chest.

"Damn you, deny *this,*" he said, his voice a low growl. His mouth slanted over hers, hot and demanding.

Aisling could not resist—she had no desire to. She opened her mouth against his, murmuring his name as her tongue sought entrance to his punishing mouth. Desire coursed through her, warming her skin, making her heart race as her tongue mingled with his, searching, exploring, tasting.

She felt him stiffen, felt him try to pull away. *No.* Her fingers tangled in his hair, drawing him closer, refusing to let his mouth leave hers. She wanted to lose herself in his kiss, wanted him to make her forget her doubts, forget everything but how exquisite it felt there in his strong, comforting arms.

Rising on tiptoe, she deepened the kiss, her fingers moving from his hair to his jawbone, cupping his face, holding on to him for dear life. He tasted of wine, of tobacco—entirely male, utterly intoxicating. Dear God, but she could kiss him like this forever; she could never get enough. *Never.*

She moaned softly when his hands moved down her shoulders, to her back, his fingertips grazing her bare skin, moving toward her backside. And then his hands were between their bodies, cupping her breasts, his fingertips massaging her peaked nipples through the layers of clothing.

The friction made her squirm, made her thighs dampen. Pleasure coiled in her belly, radiating down her limbs, making them weak.

With a low groan, he tore his mouth from hers, trailing hot, wet kisses down her throat, over her collarbone, his tongue finding the valley between her breasts. Lower still his mouth moved, his teeth nipping at her now-puckered nipples through the fabric of her gown. Aisling tipped her head back, holding Will's head to her breast, guiding it, whimpering quietly as he sucked and laved.

"Oh, Will," she said on a sigh. "I do love you. Truly, I do."

His face still pressed to her gown, Will fell to his knees, his arms still wrapped around her, clinging to her as if for dear life. Aisling stood there trembling, listening to the first faraway strains of "Silent Night" growing louder as voices joined in.

They were out of time. The guests would be departing soon. Her mother would come looking for her—for all she knew, she was looking for her now. She stared down at Will, still on his knees, the side of his face pressed against her skirts. He was fumbling in his waistcoat's pocket, reaching for something.

And then he released her, holding something up, something that glinted in the dimmed light, like a jewel, a gem. "Marry me, Aisling," he said, gazing up at her hopefully. "I know it isn't much, isn't nearly what you're worth."

All the breath left Aisling's lungs in a rush. There wasn't time—wasn't time to think it through properly, to think logically and reasonably. She turned her head, unable to look, unable to see his offering, knowing full well that, however simple, however modest it might be, it would be the most beautiful jewel she'd ever seen, the most desirable. "I…I can't, Will. Not now. But that does not mean—"

"Don't," he said, rising to his feet, shoving the ring back inside his pocket. A shadow had dropped over his eyes, dulling them, dimming them. "Don't say another word."

The voice of the carolers grew louder, more insistent. Tears filled Aisling's eyes, making her vision blurry. How she despised herself—her cowardice, her insecurity, her inability to trust her own feelings. And there was nothing—nothing at all—she could do about it.

Unless…unless she took a chance. Unless she changed her answer. Unless she took what Will was offering, something she wanted more than anything in all her life, something that would perhaps make her the happiest woman alive. If only she could believe it, if she could trust in it. If only she had faith.

"Wait," she said, reaching for Will's sleeve as he made to move past her. "It's just…I'm not certain, but perhaps—"

"No," he said firmly, removing her hand from his sleeve, shaking his head. He was smiling now, a sad, rueful smile. He leaned in, kissed her softly on the mouth, then stepped away, straightening his coat as he did so. "Thank you, but no. Happy Christmas, Aisling."

And then he left her there, feeling as if her heart had just been cleaved in two.

From out in the driveway, the sound of the carolers' voices rose in unison, then faded into nothingness.

Sleep in heavenly peace.

At that moment, Aisling knew she'd never again know peace. Not as long as she lived.

10

WILL SPRAWLED IN THE CHAIR IN THE CORNER of his room, one hand clutching a glass of whiskey, the other cupping his throbbing temple. His vision slightly blurred from the drink, he stared at the foot of his bed, trying his damnedest to erase the vision of Aisling there, her wrists tied to the iron bars.

If he inhaled deeply enough, he could almost recall her scent—the scent of violets mixed with desire. The memory of their coupling hung heavily in the air, almost a living, breathing thing. He took another swig of whiskey, hoping to drown out the memories—the feel of her skin, the heat of her cunt sheathing him. How would he ever get her out of his head? How would he cure himself of this hopeless infatuation, this ill-fated obsession?

Somehow he had to. She'd refused him—fucking refused him, and just minutes after telling him that she loved him. He threw back his head and laughed at the irony of it. She loved him, yes. But not enough to marry him, apparently. A sharp, piercing pain tore through his gut.

Well, he was done with her, then. He rose on unsteady legs, taking one last draft of his drink, then slamming the empty glass down on the desk. He wouldn't think of her. Wouldn't dream about her. And, most important, he wouldn't give her the chance to come running back to him with more excuses, more ridiculous nonsense about magic and spells forcing them to feel things that weren't real.

His feelings *were* real, and right now they were ripped to bloody shreds.

He reached for his trunk, throwing open the lid and gathering the stack of books from his desk, tossing them inside without care. Forget staying through the new year—Christmas had come and gone, and he was ready to go back to Cambridge, back where people respected him, where they didn't give a damn who his father was, or what his mother did to make her living.

He refused to sit around, twiddling his thumbs, waiting for Aisling to see the truth. She'd had her chance, damn it. There was nothing else to keep him in Bedlington. Only memories.

Just walking through the village brought them back, one by one, long-forgotten memories of days gone by. The huge oak at the edge of the village green, the one Aisling had climbed at Jack's dare and then gotten frightened, clutching the tree's trunk for dear life, refusing to come back down. He'd climbed up himself, pretending to be far braver than he was where heights were concerned, and led the trembling girl down by the hand. She couldn't have been more than six or seven at the time, her wheat-blond hair held back by a bow, her white dress ruffled and flounced.

And then there was the grassy field where they'd played cricket as children—he, Jack, Aisling, Louisa and the Brandon children. So many Sunday afternoons spent there. Aisling always got to choose her team first, and she always chose Will, claiming he was faster than the rest of them. Which was true, now that he thought about it.

And then there was the circle of standing stones near Wain-scott House where Aisling liked to sit and write, nibbling on her pen. How many times had he stopped and stood beneath a tree, secretly watching her, wondering just what kind of words she put to the page? He'd imagined her writing poetry, just because it seemed the kind of thing that a proper young lady like Aisling would do.

He vividly remembered the day that Jack went up to Eton, leaving her behind. It had seemed so unfair—she'd always been the smartest one, smarter than any of them. All her play-mates had been sent to school, even Louisa—everyone but Aisling, despite her intelligence, because young ladies of Aisling's station didn't get formally schooled, of course. They were taught to speak French, some German, perhaps. They studied literature and music, learned to sew and to paint. Useless things, all. Aisling had been groomed to be some gentleman's wife and nothing more, despite the fact that she was wickedly clever, that she was far better at sums than her brother was.

He shook his head, forcing away the memories, willing himself to stop thinking about her as he tossed his belongings haphazardly into his trunk. Tomorrow he would get on the morning train and go back to Cambridge, back to his life there.

And Aisling…she would stay in the past, damn it. Buried in memories, where she belonged, before he'd been stupid enough to think otherwise.

Damn it all, what he wouldn't give to take back those words he'd spoken so carelessly on Christmas Eve. He shook his head, glaring at the hateful little box that sat on his dresser holding the ring he'd gone all the way to Dorchester to purchase, so bloody confident that he'd be able to convince her to marry him.

He'd actually gotten down on his knees like a lovesick fool! No doubt she was having a laugh about it now. Crossing the room in three long strides, he took the box and threw it as hard as he could, not giving a damn where it landed. It didn't matter; it was rubbish now, as far as he was concerned.

His anger now spent, he collapsed back in the chair, cradling his head in his hands. A wave of humiliation washed over him as his vision blurred, his eyes suddenly damp.

Damn you, Aisling Wainscott. Yes, he would get on that train tomorrow, and he would never look back.

Aisling felt a hand on her shoulder, and turned to find Jack standing there behind her.

"Good God, Ash, what's the matter with you? You've been sitting here staring out the window for hours."

Aisling just shrugged in reply, turning back toward the window. The sky was gray and a heavy fog was rolling in, obscuring the trees in the distance, moving slowly toward the house in dark, curling wisps.

"Actually, you've been moping about since Christmas," he accused. "As if it isn't morose enough around here with Mother upstairs crying all day."

Because Father had left, returning to London—to Mrs. Gaylord, of course—the day after Christmas. The gifts had barely been put away, the fruitcakes and various other seasonal treats not yet entirely consumed. But that hadn't stopped Sir Reginald from fleeing back to his mistress with the barest of excuses, the bastard.

She glanced down at the new ruby-and-diamond bracelet she wore on her wrist, her father's gift, and a rather lavish one, at that. *I'll give it to Jack to sell in London,* she thought to herself, fingering the exquisite gems. It would fetch a fair sum, fattening her bank account.

"Aisling?" Jack sat down beside her on the settee and reached for her hand. "You must tell me what's wrong. I can't bear to see you like this."

"What do you mean, 'like this'?" she asked, refusing to look at him, to meet his gaze.

"Why, pale and drawn, your eyes red rimmed, as if you've been crying. You, crying! God only knows you've never been one for tears."

"My eyes are just...just irritated, that's all. I'm sure I'm coming down with something."

"I'm sure you're lying, Aisling. Come, now, it's me you're talking to. I know you as well as I know myself. There's no fooling me—surely you know that by now."

"I'd rather not talk about it, if you don't mind," she said sharply, pulling her hand from his grasp.

"Oh, no. You're not getting off that easily. You can't simply brush me aside like you do everyone else. I'll hound you 'til you break—you know that I will," he threatened, his voice light and teasing.

"Oh, bugger off, won't you?" Aisling snapped. In her heart she knew that Jack didn't deserve it, her ill temper. Yet she could not tell him the truth. It didn't matter that Will was Jack's friend, that he was as educated as Jack was. It was well and good for them to be friends, but for Will and Aisling to be lovers? No, Jack would never approve. Worse, he would be furious. There was no telling what he'd do, what he'd say. Besides, it didn't matter. They were done. There was nothing left to discuss.

"Aisling, please," Jack tried once more, his voice so tender that Aisling thought her heart might break. *Again.*

"I can't," she choked out. "I can't tell you what's happened, Jack. I wish I could, but I can't."

For a full minute, Jack simply started at her, not saying a word. And then realization lit his eyes. "It's a man, isn't it? You look heartsick. I hate to say it, but you look just like Mother does right now." He stood, an angry flush stealing up his neck. "Who's done this to you? Tell me, so that I can wring his bloody neck, the bastard."

Aisling inhaled sharply, refusing to give in to the blasted tears yet again. No, she was done crying. Done feeling sorry for herself. It was time to pull herself up by the bootstraps and get on with life, such as it was.

"It's done, Jack. Over. Besides, if anyone's neck should be wrung, it's my own."

He shook his head. "You may be stubborn, tenacious, even. Irritating at times, yes. But deserving of whatever is making you look so damn miserable? No, I don't believe it."

"Then I don't know what else to say, Jack."

"Whoever he is, he's not worth *this,* I can tell you that," he snapped.

"That's just it. He *is* worth it. And I'm the biggest bloody fool in all of England."

Jack paced a circuit back and forth, his hands thrust into his pockets. "I can't even imagine who. It isn't as if there have been any eligible men around here, not lately. The Dalton brothers, I suppose, but you barely glanced at either of them."

Aisling fiddled with the hem of her sleeve. "The Dalton brothers are a pair of boorish pigs."

Jack stopped his pacing and knelt beside her, the color drained from his face. "Dear God, Aisling, please tell me you haven't been dallying with Lucas James!"

"Good God, no!" she answered, taken aback. Lucas James

was the butcher's son, two years her junior, and as thick and dumb as an ox. "Just how desperate do you think I am?"

Jack raked a hand through his hair. "Well, it isn't as if there's been anyone else around these past few weeks. I mean, besides Will Cooper, of course."

Aisling willed her face to remain blank so as not to betray her. "And weren't you chastising me just last week about him, calling me a snob?"

Jack laughed uneasily. "I was, wasn't I?"

Aisling said nothing in reply, hoping that Jack would drop the subject and leave her in peace.

"Though mark my words, you could do far worse than Will Cooper, gentleman or no. Just don't tell Mother I said so. I mean, of course she wouldn't approve, not at first. I imagine she'd come around eventually, though. After all, Will's a good chap."

Jack rubbed his chin thoughtfully. "Now that I think about it, you two are as well suited as any two people I've ever met. You're so much alike, the pair of you. And truthfully, I've always thought that perhaps he secretly fancied you, though he'd never in a million years admit to it." Jack sighed loudly. "If only you weren't such a blasted snob. Ah, well. I suppose if you won't tell me..."

Aisling shook her head, trying her best to appear calm when beneath the surface she was anything but. He'd come too close to the truth—far too close.

"Will you at least promise me, then, that you'll stop moping around? Go write one of your scandalous stories or something. The editor at the *Boudoir* is positively begging for more of your work—I can't get it to him fast enough. If you can't be happy, at least make us some money while you're busy being miserable."

"You'd like that, wouldn't you?" she asked with a wry smile. "Money for nothing."

"I'd like for you to be happy, Ash," he said, all serious now.

She swallowed a lump in her throat, thinking just how much she loved her brother. "I know, Jack. Please…just give me time."

"Very well." He leaned down and kissed her on one cheek. "Carry on, then."

She just nodded, unable to say a single word in reply.

Several hours later, Aisling sat in bed, propped up with feather pillows behind her back, the heavy eiderdown quilt pulled up to her chin. The little wooden box with the poem inside sat there in her lap, though she resisted the urge to open it and examine the old parchment yet again. Instead, Jack's words were playing over and over again in her mind.

He'd thought Will had fancied her all along. Was it possible? Hadn't Will himself said something to the same effect? If only she could remember his exact words.

Something about a spark that had always been there, about wanting her, and hating her for not wanting him. But what if she *had* wanted him? What if she'd been angry—with him, with herself—all these years because she had realized they were perfectly suited, but assumed that she could never have him?

Hope flamed brightly in her breast. Perhaps these feelings they had for one another weren't so new, after all. Perhaps they'd been there, taking root, blossoming all these years, until they were both ready to recognize them, until Aisling was brave enough to defy her parents—because that's what it would require for her to cast her lot with Will. She knew it to be true, despite Jack's approval, his optimism.

Her mother was not nearly as liberal minded as her brother was, no doubt about that. The bastard son of a washerwoman would never be good enough for Lady Wainscott's daughter, no matter his education, no matter who his father might be. Perhaps Aisling could only recognize her feelings for Will once she was old enough, strong enough, to go against the opposition she was sure to face in the form of her mother.

And if that were true, then it had nothing to do with the poem, nothing to do with the wish she'd made on the solstice. Or perhaps the poem only made her realize her true feelings, made her subconsciously wish for someone exactly like Will, so that she could finally acknowledge that *he* was her winter's desire. Her summer's desire, her autumn's desire, her spring's desire.

He was her *every* desire.

Throwing back the bed linens, Aisling swung her legs over the side of the mattress and reached for her dressing gown, standing as she belted it tightly around her waist. She retrieved the little wooden box from the bed and placed it on her desk, beside her typewriter, and sat, reaching for a pen and piece of paper.

She would write Will a letter; she would tell him what was in her heart, what had always been in her heart. She would tell him that she'd been mistaken. And then she would beg him for another chance, another opportunity to prove herself worthy of his love, his ring. They could start over, lovers *and* friends this time.

First thing tomorrow morning, she would drive to the village and deliver the letter herself. She only hoped it wasn't too late.

11

AISLING SWALLOWED HARD BEFORE REACHING up to rap on the door. Clasping the letter in front of her, she took a step back and waited, listening as the sound of footsteps grew louder.

Please let it be Will, and not his mother.

The door swung open. "Miss Wainscott," Mrs. Cooper said, her brow furrowed as she stared down at her.

Aisling cleared her throat, her resolve wavering. "Good day, Mrs. Cooper. I…um, I do hope you're well."

Mrs. Cooper's eyes narrowed a fraction. "I'm very well, thank you. Have you come to fetch your mother's gown? I'm not quite done with it, I'm afraid."

"No. I came…that is to say…" She trailed off miserably. Now what? *The truth.* There was no other way. "I was hoping to have a word with Will."

She wiped her hands on her apron. "You've come to see Will?"

"Yes, I….ahem, you see, I need to speak with him. I know this is a bit irregular, but—"

"Well, miss, I'm afraid you're too late for that," she interrupted. "He's gone back to Cambridge, left this morning on the early train. Judging by your appearance here today, I suppose I have *you* to thank for his sudden departure."

"I'm sorry, Mrs. Cooper. I don't know what he's told you—"

"He's told me nothing," she snapped. "Not a single word of it, though I've got two eyes and ears. I know my own son, and I know when he's hurting. Hasn't he had a hard enough time of it, all these years, without you toying with him?"

Aisling didn't know what to say. She'd never felt so small, so ashamed as she did at that very moment. She'd driven him away—and not just from her, but from his mother, too. All because she'd been too afraid to listen to her own heart.

"I…I came here today to try and make it right," she stuttered, her cheeks burning uncomfortably under the woman's scrutinizing stare.

"Well, as I said, it's too late for that. Now, if you'll excuse me, I have work to do." She pulled the door shut with a *thump,* leaving Aisling standing there on the front step, her legs suddenly weak and wobbly.

She hadn't counted on this. He'd said he was staying 'til after the new year. As she'd lain in bed waiting for the sun to rise, she'd pictured several different scenarios in her mind, imagining exactly what she'd say to make things right. But this? Never. In each of her imagined scenarios, she'd had the chance to speak with him, to give him her letter.

Turning away from the door, she shoved the letter inside her coat pocket and began to walk through the thick fog, back toward her motorcar. What now? She hadn't any idea how to proceed, short of taking the train to Cambridge herself, and she was lucid enough to realize that she needed to think it through more carefully before she did something like that, showing up unannounced on his doorstep.

First of all, her mother would never allow it. Second, she had no idea where, precisely, he lived in Cambridge. *Perhaps Jack would agree to accompany me,* she thought as she reached her motorcar. But that would require telling him everything, confessing her sins, she realized.

No. She couldn't tell Jack, not yet. Damn Will for taking the coward's way out, for fleeing Bedlington the way he had! What was she to do now? Simply mail him her letter and sit patiently awaiting his reply? For all she knew, he might reconcile with this Helena woman before her letter even arrived.

With a huff, she opened the car's door and scooted inside.

A telegraph, perhaps? No, she could never say the things she needed to say in a telegraph. *It's hopeless,* she realized. Entirely so. She'd lost her chance, just as she feared.

Reaching into the compartment on the dash, she retrieved her veil and goggles, putting the silly-looking glasses on before pinning the veil to her hat and pulling it down around her face. Feeling almost numb, she went through the motions of starting the car, pushing the plunger on the dash, then hopping out to turn the crank. The engine roared to life, and she returned to her seat, gripping the wheel tightly as she forced herself to concentrate on the fog-obscured road.

I should have walked, she told herself as she guided the car off the village's main thoroughfare and onto the wider, tree-lined road that led to Wainscott House. The dense fog made it near enough impossible to see, even with headlamps lighting the way. It was just after noon, and it was already as dark as dusk. Somewhat eerie, she thought, tightening her grip on the wheel.

At least the fog had brought with it warmer air. It almost felt balmy compared to last week's frigid chill. Still, the dreary gray skies did nothing for her mood, nothing to—

"Damnation!" she cried out, slamming on the brake, the

force of the sudden stop slinging her so far forward that she nearly cracked her forehead on the wheel. A figure had appeared in the road directly in front of her, seeming to materialize out of thin air.

Aisling blinked several times, trying to focus her vision on the woman who stood there, not five feet in front of the car, wrapped in a black woolen cloak. Dark, curly hair peeked out from the hood's folds, the woman's face cast entirely in shadows.

"Pardon me," Aisling called out loudly over the engine's hum. "I'm so sorry, I didn't see you there. Can I offer you a ride?"

The woman shook her head, then lifted one arm and pointed toward the woods to her right.

Whatever did she mean by that? There was nothing over that way, no houses. Nothing but the circle of stones, off in the distance… Of course! It was the woman she'd seen on the solstice—she was strangely sure of it.

"I must speak with you," Aisling called out, her heart pounding in her breast. "Just let me cut the engine." She glanced down at the dash for a single second, then looked up again, gasping in surprise. The woman was gone. Vanished, just like that, in the blink of an eye.

All the breath left her lungs in a rush. No, it couldn't be. She reached over the door to pull the hand brake, then stood, looking in every direction, searching wildly for the woman through the thick curtain of fog.

"Miss?" she cried out. "Please, come back!"

Nothing. She'd simply disappeared. Good God, but she was losing her mind. Reaching back over the door, she released the brake and continued. She was overwrought, that was all. It was the fog, making her see things that weren't there. That had to be it.

A quarter hour later she reached Wainscott House, pulling

up into the driveway and cutting the engine. She unpinned her veil and hurried inside, listening carefully to see if anyone was about. The house was quiet as a tomb. Peering down the corridor, she saw a light shining from her brother's study. He must have heard her car motoring up the driveway, but mercifully he did not open the door and call out to her, so she walked up the wide staircase toward her room.

She knew what she had to do, and quickly, before anyone waylaid her. She would put an end to this nonsense—and now.

Not five minutes later she stepped out the back door, the little wooden box clutched in her hands. The poem was folded up inside, just as she'd found it. She moved silently across the park, past the swimming pond and off toward the copse of trees in the distance.

Ducking through the bare, spindly branches, she hurried on, easily finding her way despite the limited visibility. After all, her feet knew this path well. Finally, the stones came into view, wispy fog seeming to cling to them.

Taking a deep, fortifying breath, she continued to the center of the circle and placed the box at her feet. Kneeling beside it, she removed her gloves and opened the box's fastening, just as she'd done on the solstice. She took out the parchment and unfolded it with shaking hands, her anger mounting, gathering strength, burning like fire through her veins.

It had to be done. The poem had brought her to this—this deep despair, this dark melancholy. All because she'd allowed herself to believe in it, however briefly, however reluctantly.

But now...now she knew better.

"Take it back," she cried out, her voice echoing off the stones. "I don't want it. I don't believe in your magic. Do you hear me?"

With that, she ripped the old parchment into tiny little bits and tossed them into the air, watching as the torn pieces rained back down to the damp earth, littering the center of the circle around her.

And then she heaved a sigh, her shoulders sagging. Never again would she allow herself to feel those things—love and longing, passion and desire. She couldn't. Her heart felt as ripped to shreds as the poem, and nothing could put it back together again, no more than she could reassemble the scattered pieces of parchment.

Stooping down, she retrieved her gloves from the ground and shoved her hands inside them, flexing her fingers as she rose and turned to leave, to head home. But a figure standing there, off in the distance, stilled her feet. She couldn't see properly—the blasted fog made it impossible. But it looked like... Dear God, but it looked like Will!

No, I'm imagining it. She shook her head, hoping to clear it, to make the vision disappear. *Just like the woman in the road.*

But the figure didn't disappear. Instead, it started moving toward her, moving out of the fog, becoming less specterlike and more solid with each passing second. She could've sworn it was a man—a man wearing a dark coat and bowler hat. He stepped into the circle, entirely revealed now.

It *was* Will. She didn't know how or why—didn't care, really. All that mattered was that he was there, not a dozen feet away now. One hand rose to her throat as she swallowed hard, unable to speak, unable to move a single muscle, afraid he would disappear if she did so.

At last he stood directly before her, close enough to touch. His mouth lifted into a smile, his bright blue eyes the only spot of color in the otherwise bleak, gray surroundings.

"This isn't real," she murmured. "I'm imagining it. You can't be real. You went back to Cambridge on the morning train."

He nodded, removing his hat and holding it against one

hip. "I made it as far as London. Changed for Cambridge, and as I sat there waiting for the train to depart, they called another leaving for Dorset. The return train. Something told me I had to get on that train, had to come back to you. I couldn't do it, couldn't leave you."

"I'm so glad," she breathed. "So very glad, Will."

His gaze met hers, held it for a heartbeat's second before he turned away from her, looking around the circle as if he were seeing it for the first time. "I had a feeling I'd find you here."

"You were right," she said hurriedly, before he could silence her. "Entirely right, about everything. It wasn't the poem, wasn't the magic. I think whatever it is we're feeling was always there, just waiting for us to discover it. I should never have doubted it, doubted *you*. Will you ever forgive me?"

"There's nothing to forgive, Ash," he said with a shrug. "How many times must I say that to you?"

"I should have been more sure of my own heart, more sure of yours. But now…"

"Now, what?" he prodded. "Will you let me kiss you, make love to you and then change your mind again? Decide it *is* the magic, after all? Back and forth, all over again?"

"I won't," she answered, entirely sure of it. "Never again. I know I have no right to ask you to trust me, to believe me. I would not fault you if you didn't, if you turned around and left right now. But please, hear me out first. It's all I ask of you."

He nodded, looking exhausted, she realized, his face drawn, his eyes shadowed. "I'm listening, Aisling."

"You're my perfect match in every way, Will Cooper. My heart's desire, everything I've ever wanted in a man. All these years, I've resisted my mother's efforts, refused to have a season, refused to marry Thomas Esterbrooke, because I knew—deep in my heart—that I wasn't meant to be some fancy gentleman's wife, the mere possession of some man who would never consider me his equal, his partner. I think deep down I always knew I was meant to be yours—a botanist's wife, an artist's lover."

Will's mouth twitched, as if he was suppressing a smile. "Just so you know, I'll never be able to afford a country house, an estate like the one you grew up in. I don't go to London unless I have to, and I employ no servants. My life is simple, modest—nothing like yours and Jack's. I'm not certain it's fair to ask you to give up the things you're accustomed to, the privilege you were born to."

Aisling shook her head, desperate to make him see, to make him understand. "But without you, those things mean nothing to me, Will. I know it sounds trite, melodramatic, even. But it's the truth. I've never been more sure of anything in all my life."

"Your parents will never approve. They'll likely disown you, you know."

"That's their misfortune, then. Besides, Jack will be on our side."

He cocked one brow. "What makes you say that?"

"A conversation we had just yesterday. He doesn't know, was only speaking hypothetically. But he made his approval perfectly clear."

"You really think we can do this?" Will asked, dropping his hat to the ground and reaching for her hand.

"Well, just so *you* know, I won't be anything near an obedient wife, and I throw things when I get angry. I can't cook, so you'll have to do more than just get your own tea. Oh, and I don't care how fashionable it is to take a mistress. I'll require full fidelity, utter devotion—otherwise, I'll castrate you myself," she teased, her racing heart slowing at last.

"I have no doubt that you would," he said with a laugh. "Anything else I should be aware of?"

"I think that's about it. For now, at least. I'm sure I can come up with more later."

"So, it was Esterbrooke then, was it?" Will asked with a mischievous glint in his eyes. "Gad, I almost wish I didn't know that. Now every time I see the man, I'll be tempted to knock his bloody teeth down his throat."

She couldn't help but smile, strangely pleased by his show of jealousy. "Trust me, Will, he's no competition, none at all. When I compare…well, never mind that."

Will removed his gloves, shoving them into his pockets, and then he pulled her up against his chest, his lips just inches from hers. "So, what do we do now?"

"I can think of several things. Several naughty things, in fact."

"You *do* realize you're still wearing your driving goggles, don't you?" he asked, grinning down at her.

"Hell and damnation!" She reached up to her face, surprised to find that she *was* still wearing them. With a wince, she removed them, shoving them into her coat pocket. "How foolish I must have looked! Why on earth didn't you tell me before now?"

He shrugged, pulling her back against his chest, stroking the sides of her face with his callused thumbs. "You looked so charming, having your say while wearing them. You can't even imagine…threatening to cut off my bollocks while you glared at me, looking almost cross-eyed. It was adorable, really."

Slowly, his mouth moved toward hers, his eyes never leaving her face. Aisling thought she'd go mad, waiting for his kiss, wanting him, needing him. When their lips touched at last, she moaned, barely able to stand the very exquisiteness of it. Gently, tenderly, he captured her lower lip, suckled it, his hands sliding down her back, cupping her bottom as he drew her closer still.

Tipping her head back, she opened her mouth against his—inviting him, near enough begging him. He answered her silent plea, taking her mouth harder this time, tasting and retreating 'til Aisling flung her arms around his neck and refused to let him go, kissing him deeply, thoroughly, until they were both breathless.

"Have you any idea how badly I want you, Aisling?" he asked, his voice rough and ragged.

"Right here? In the circle of stones?" she teased, trying to catch her breath.

"Why not? I'm sure this place has seen such things before, back in ancient times. Some Druid ritual, perhaps." He dragged her toward the tallest of the stones, pressing her back against it, caging her in with both hands on either side of her head.

She ducked under his arms. "Yes, but afterward you'd probably be expected to sacrifice me." When he turned to face her, she leaned into him, pressing herself against his erection while she nipped at his neck.

"Do you have a problem with that?" he asked, smiling wickedly. "Me, sacrificing you to the gods?"

In reply, she moved her hand to his cock, grasping it tightly through his wool trousers.

"Yes? Well, then, we'll do it differently. Start a new tradition." He captured her around the waist and lifted her, pushing her back against the stone. Bending down, he reached under the hem of her coat, under her skirt and petticoat, trailing his hands up her limbs, to her hips, bunching her skirts up at her waist. "Are you cold?" he asked, reaching for the tapes that held up her drawers.

"Warm me," she answered with a shrug. Reaching for his

coat, she began to unbutton it, one by one. "Fuck me—right here, right now."

"Trying to shock me again, I see," he murmured, slipping a finger inside her wet sheath, making her gasp with pleasure. "And here I thought you were a proper young lady. A baronet's daughter."

"Didn't you know?" she said breathlessly as he began to stroke her. "I'm to be married to a botanist—a very wicked one. Now unfasten your trousers."

"Bossy, too," he said, pushing open the front of her coat, exposing her throat, pressing his lips against her lace collar, his breath warm and moist against her skin. "But I suppose one of us will have to be obedient."

She felt him fumble with his trousers and sighed with relief when she felt the tip of him pressing against her sex, searching for entrance. Raising one leg, she hitched it around his hip.

"This botanist," he said, his voice gruff. "Do you love him?"

"Oh!" she cried out as he thrust into her, pinning her against the stone. "Yes. Yes, I love him."

Again, he thrust into her—harder, more insistent this time. "Then he's the luckiest man alive." Faster, harder, he began to drive into her. Aisling met his every thrust, tilting her hips toward his, her breathing growing more ragged as the now-familiar coil of pleasure made her begin to tremble, made her limbs go weak, made her sex weep with desire.

With one last thrust, Will pushed her over the edge, her insides pulsating against the length of him as his hot seed pumped into her, warming her.

"Dear God, Aisling," he groaned, collapsing against her. "My love," he whispered. "My life."

Aisling's heart swelled, a quiet sob tore from her throat as tears burned behind her eyelids. Only this time they were happy tears, she realized. Good tears. Tears of joy. One slipped down her cheek, but Will's thumb wiped it away before it reached her chin.

"You," he said, his gaze meeting hers, their bodies still joined, "are the most exquisite creature I've ever known."

Return his head, upon my breast, burn bright of winter's desire. The words slipped into her mind, uninvited. A line from the poem, the one she'd just torn into a million little bits. And yet...it was fitting, wasn't it?

Thank you, she thought, *for returning him to me.* Whatever the cause, whatever the reason...it didn't matter. She had her winter's desire, and she was never letting him go.

Kissing her softly on the forehead, Will withdrew from her, reaching down to fasten his trousers. With gentle hands, he pulled up her drawers, retying the tapes before smoothing back down her skirts. "I do hope you're not freezing," he murmured against her temple.

"No," she said, finding her voice at last. "It's so warm today. Perfect, really, for such outdoor pursuits as this."

"Come with me, back to my mother's cottage. I've got something for you there. If I can find it again, that is. It would seem that I throw things when I'm angry, too." He retrieved his hat and tipped it back on his head, then held out his hand to her.

Aisling just nodded, linking her fingers with his.

"So, what do you think of our new tradition? Here in the circle, I mean?" he asked, smiling down at her with that lazy, cocky grin she loved so well.

She gave his hand a squeeze. "I think we should return here each year and repeat it. On the winter solstice, perhaps."

"Didn't it snow this year on the solstice?"

Aisling shrugged. "We'll just be quick about it, that's all."

Suddenly Will stopped and turned back toward the stones. "Wait, what about that box? The little wooden one with the strange symbol on it. You left it in the circle."

"Oh, I don't need it anymore," she said without glancing back. "Besides, I think it belongs there." She tugged on Will's hand, and with a nod he matched his step to hers.

A wind picked up as the lovers continued, their heads bent together in quiet conversation, their laughter echoing through the copse of trees. Back in the circle of stones, the little pieces of parchment lifted off the ground, swirling briefly around the circle like snow, and then scattered on the breeze, disappearing into the mist.

Hope reborn, come with the sun
dispel the chill of darkness
bright fire of dawn
reach to our hearts
burn bright of winter's desire.

SARAH McCARTY

He is everything her body craves...and everything her faith denies.

Tucker McCade has known violence his whole life: orphaned in a massacre, abused as a "half-breed" child, trained as a ruthless Texas Ranger, he's learned the hard way that might makes right. So even he is shocked when he falls for Sallie Mae Reynolds, a Quaker nurse.

National Bestselling Author

SARAH McCARTY

A HELL'S EIGHT EROTIC ADVENTURE

Tucker's Claim

Spice

Every night they spend together exploring new heights of ecstasy binds them ever closer, slowly erasing their differences...until the day Tucker's past comes calling, precipitating an explosive showdown between her faith, his promise and the need for revenge....

Tucker's Claim

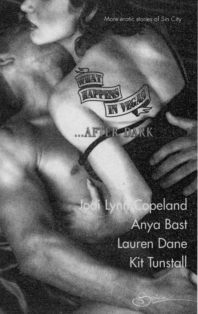